CW00553625

MIDNIGHT RUN

OLIVER A. KENTON

SKY RIVER
PRESS

For Mum and Dad, who never got to see.
And for Sophie, Ava, and Victoria, who did.

"There was a door to which I found no key: There was the veil through which I might not see."

The Rubaiyat of Omar Khayyám -

"Photons have mass? I didn't even know they were Catholic."

Woody Allen -

1

LEON ARONOFSKY

Leon Aronofsky jolted awake, twitching and confused in what seemed to him in that moment to be the centre of a huge but rapidly receding explosion. Although, as he hadn't really spent much time with explosions, living in northwest London, he couldn't be entirely sure. He struggled to make sense of the extraordinary crashing sound, and residual bilious sensation rippling through his body, as he surfaced messily from deep unconsciousness. Despite his best efforts to focus on what was happening, Leon's thoughts remained fuzzy and thick.

Was that even real, he wondered, with his head pounding, and eyes still firmly closed. Or just the tail end of an intensely vivid dream, infused with the noise of a heavy door abruptly slamming shut somewhere nearby? He circled around the plainly stupid idea a few times in the achy purple blackness of his mind. What did he know about heavy doors? His friend Tom Kennedy made a brief but not untypical mental appearance, and ridiculed him just for thinking it.

"Heavy like one of those big James Bond vaults, with the *giant, round, laser-proof door*?"

"Heavy like a fire door," Leon imagined himself responding.

"A fire door made out of plutonium?"

"Yes, Tom. A radioactive door. For when there's a—"

OK, not a door, he accepted. Something more immediate. A giant book, maybe. A set of giant, dusty encyclopaedias, falling off a high shelf. In a single box. That broke apart when it landed. Imaginary Tom raised an eyebrow. Who keeps encyclopaedias anymore? Or perhaps, he conceded, since this was an office party, it was a chair being hurled across a meeting room, and into a glass wall.

Or maybe—and Leon could feel himself shrink as the unwanted thought tumbled into view—just maybe, it was a bomb. I mean, sure, he considered, as make-believe Tom made a swift retreat, why not? Bombs produce exploding sensations. Everyone knows that. And there are so many bombs these days. Or threats of bombs. And chemical attacks and IEDs. Drones, suicide bombers, and so-called "dirty bombs" (plus all the sniggering schoolboys that went with them). And what about photobombs? It suddenly seemed like a credible, if slightly terrifying, possibility. Terrifying enough that he might even open his eyes to see if he was right. But the throbbing pain behind them made him hold off a little while longer.

And while, yes, he had to admit that most of the bombing action he'd ever heard of was usually in far-off countries, and of all that, the constant bomb-y media noise of it all—in advertising and civic spaces, on the news, in the papers, train stations, bus depots, and municipal monuments—along with the ringing in his ears and a crappy, bitter taste in his mouth, gave him pause.

Leon thought about all those public announcements on the Tube and mainline stations that he'd ignored over the years. The unattended or suspicious packages that he'd never looked for or reported on. Like the good civic-minded citizen he thought he was. Then he sighed.

Of course, despite all that, it still seemed very unlikely, he thought. No matter that the *Daily Mail* insists we're living in a ruined state, with terrorists lurking on every park bench, next to the feral, skunk-smoking children and elderly park racist, he'd never actually met a single person in his admittedly low-key, near-flung travels between North Finchley and Kilburn, or the West End, who'd ever seen or experienced a bomb up close. Or even, for that matter, reported on a dubious package that later had to be blown up a by a public servant.

But whatever had just happened to him, it had certainly felt real enough. A heavy, arresting, pummelling sensation to all the soft parts of his body but from the inside. And in that sense, it wasn't something he'd really experienced before.

If nothing else, the drubbing was certainly brutal and startling enough to wrench him from the depths of his formerly boozy stupor. But then, for just that same reason, could he be entirely certain this whole episode hadn't simply been an intoxicated delusion? Perhaps it was simply the result of too much drink, and whatever it was that Tom Kennedy had evidently spiked him with earlier that night.

Then, suddenly, Leon's mind pivoted backwards, past the prickly impressionistic images of earlier that night (him and Tom and—oh God, Izzy too—on the heaving, makeshift office dance floor anyone?), to when, as a teenager holidaying in Israel, he'd been awoken, terrified, by the sonic boom of a low-flying F-15 Air Force patrol. That was it, he decided firmly. That must be it. A sonic boom. But in the middle of London? It still didn't make any sense.

Of course, it really didn't help that his head was pounding so hard. Nor that his body felt so grotesquely stiff, dry-mouthed and, as he finally, slowly attempted to move his wretched limbs from the prone, crumpled position he realised he was in, slightly broken.

And what was the cold, flat surface pressed into his face? And that peculiar stink? A burnt *something*, fused with an odd-smelling floral perfume. A flowery, herby perfume, plus a special something extra, something fetid he couldn't really place. The subtle hiss, and trammelling of water in pipes. And then...wait. His eyes snapped open.

"Oh my God," he groaned aloud, as the grim realisation came to him all at once. "I'm in a toilet. I'm on the floor...of...a...toilet!?"

He lurched upwards, cracking his head on an unseen hand basin, and recoiled in a sickly combination of pain and disgust, his face pinched tight. And since, even with his eyes open, it was basically still pitch-dark, he began to mentally scan himself for signs of damp. Of wetness. Of—he could hardly bring himself to go there—of soiling. He reluctantly started grabbing and clutching at his clothes in search of additional clues. Gratefully, he seemed wetness-free, and let go of a long sigh.

How long had he been lying on a toilet floor, he wondered, with some dread. He tried to reconstruct a dim catalogue of events from the treacly montage of barely remembered chatty interactions, fruity banter, and shared conversations of the night before: a not untypical works-party experience, along with all the competitive project deconstructions (who had the worst project, with the most psychotic client), and peals of dissent, awkward humour, and recriminations that would surface along the way. The account guy, who just wanted to talk about revenue and forecasts. The vapers and the smokers, relegated to the side entrance, and fighting it out like a tuneless *West Side Story*, as the night wore on. All those monstrous, intoxicated dance moves by normally quiet and conservative colleagues who should not, ever, break out The Travolta. But do anyway.

And then, the inevitable but necessarily crude character assassination of Derek Tyler by Tom. Before, moments later, witnessing the equally predictable confessional from drunken Derek himself, as he draped himself over a reluctant co-worker, and delivered an uncharacteristic (and it has to be said, in his case, a deeply uncomfortable) display of lurching affection.

And then what? Leon's own staggering voyage from the dance floor to the front desk, to a fateful, green-faced goodbye with Izzy. He shuddered like a wet dog, as this memory of their awkward parting invaded his fragile mind. And then, finally, it would appear, his journey to the toilet and, he must presume, unconsciousness. Embarrassment followed by humiliation and ignominy. *Another great night out, Aronofsky,* he thought. *One for the books.*

Leon let that sit and fester for a while before trying to shrug off the poisonous self-recriminations and, finally, make a clumsy effort to move himself more properly into a seated position. He groped about in the enveloping blackness with one outstretched hand, looking for the wall, or a door to lean on. He was then able to focus on the weird, suffocating, humming noise he thought, until that moment, was just in his head.

What on earth is that? he wondered, as he moved his head gently from side to side to get a better fix on it. Everything sounded deeply muffled and far away, as if he was deep underwater, or on a rapidly descending plane.

He reached into a pocket for his phone and tapped the screen for some illumination but nothing happened. He pressed the side button. Still nothing. Then he pressed it again, repeatedly, as though somehow more urgent pressing would produce a different result. Nothing again. Not even the faintly useless prompt telling him he should charge the phone.

He felt confused. He was sure it had been fully charged earlier. Although of course, at this point, he couldn't be quite sure how long ago *earlier* actually was. He fumbled with power switch-volume combo for a hard reset, and finally the device woke up, shedding harsh but incredibly well-designed light into his porcelain cell.

Now that he could see a bit, he was immediately relieved to find, by virtue of the expensive tiling, posh taps, and more tasteful soap arrangements, that he'd at least managed to make it to the seventh floor—the client suites—before passing out. After all, if he was going to lie down and press his face into the floor of what was, essentially, a public toilet, then this was definitely the one to do it in.

OK, he decided, as he took in the truth of his vaguely smelly surroundings, *it's not the worst it could be: I haven't wet myself, and*

I'm not covered in vomit. Many would consider that a real achievement.

Perhaps, he considered, after sitting for a while, there was still a chance to rejoin the party. After all, he could simply slip quietly back into the room and pretend he'd been there the whole time, unobserved by anyone that would call him on it. Or feign that he'd just been outside singing "The Jet Song" with all the other ex-smokers.

Or possibly, more likely, depending on how deeply he'd actually embarrassed himself before sloping off here in a clumsy bid to escape—he wasn't sure what exactly—and falling unconscious, he should just slink furtively home. After all, he couldn't just sit here for the rest of whatever was left of the night. In an office toilet. Like a schmuck. He'd just have to chance it.

So, finally, in a faint bid to act decisively but without actually deciding anything, Leon peeled himself painfully off the tiled floor, unlocked the door, and gingerly shuffled out into the waiting pitch black gloom.

2

LINDEN SNARK

The crisp, early morning desert sun cut long, deep shadows across the red-brown earth and rock that ran for miles, in every direction, beside a long, narrow, unmade road. Tiny rodents scuffled by the roadside, among the scraggy dried-out brush and stones, carefully scrapbooking desiccated shoots for nest material, or specs of food. While, high above, a solitary buzzard circled in the distant brightening sky, steadily slipping in and out of view against blue mountains on the far horizon. And rangy lizards began their sluggish, creeping journey onto the bouldered foothills below, to bask inertly, and gaze unblinkingly into the wide, open space beyond, as tiny desert flowers stretched and bloomed around them.

All this remained unseen by the sleepless Linden Snark, Under Secretary for an obscure and generally undocumented subsection of the US Department of Defense. Snark listed grumpily in the backseat of his solitary, militarised SUV 'limousine', as it lurched and bounced its way over the cracked and puckered unmarked, unmade road.

He hated making this trip. Not simply the tedious, long hours of near silent cross-country travel, but all the dust and sterility, and the incessant whine and air-conditioned heat of his final destination.

He'd tried hard, early on at the start of this segue of his near fifty-year intelligence career, to enjoy it. Or if not actually enjoy it, then to at least 'get something' from the experience, as his second ex-wife had suggested at the time. He bought a popular guide-book to the state, and a couple of notable memoirs of the South-west. He figured if he was going to lay over here for weeks or even months at a time, then he may as well learn something about the place, beyond what he'd picked up from random episodes of Rockford, watching him getting beaten up at a truck stop, on his way to Vegas. Or, earlier still, the camp, sanitised, and theatrical Old West of The High Chaparral.

He even paid real money at some artsy White House fundraiser for a damn picture book by some famous photographer he'd never heard of. But it was all wasted on him. He couldn't do it. He wasn't made for it: an East Coast city boy, all the way through, with city-boy allergies and an inexplicable dread of an unstructured environment. Despite every effort, and the best part of a decade running the show, he still loathed pretty much everything about the desert.

Eventually, he simply chose to concede and accept the environmental challenges of his post as yet one more occupational hazard. Much as he had, in his professionally formative years, accepted the risk of being shot at in Vietnam, garrotted or maimed in Central America, or secretly jailed and tortured in the former USSR, without hope of reprieve or acknowledgment. But, hell, that didn't mean he had to like it.

Perhaps, more than all the piercing dry heat and dust, the desert fauna, and the vast, open ranges of empty, hot earth—all wasted, in his view—he simply hated the unrelenting lack of *civilisation*: no libraries, no theatres, no decent schools, world-class universities or useful industry, no art galleries, not even one decent, cultivated restaurant within 150 miles, or a quiet piano bar, with proper leather chairs, elegant women, and a discreet cigar lounge where he could have a real conversation.

The fact is, he just didn't see the value in hiding out here in the wilderness, so absurdly far from the world. For Christ's sake, he silently complained (and not for the first time), as the Humvee crowned a steep rise, revealing another forty miles of arid nothingness, snaking off into the quivering distance: if those damn Brits could build a facility right in the middle of their capital city, then why the hell couldn't we? Yes, yes, danger to the public, anonymity, oversight, all that crap. He got it. And yeah, sure, they'd had no choice, but even so—*even so*—there are limits.

But, regardless of all those reasons, none of it made the trip any more palatable. What really killed it for Snark, what he just couldn't see, at least not in a way anyone had ever been able to reasonably justify to him, other than the fact that this was what was decided in the fifties—the 1950s for crying out loud—was why in the hell he couldn't just fly here direct. It was a goddamn Air Force base, after all.

Finally, one limo, two planes, one armoured transport, and eight long hours after he started out from his Washington brownstone, Snark's vehicle turned into the final half mile run up to a simple, unmarked set of slatted iron gates connecting an otherwise anonymous wire-topped chain-link fence that ran off into the far distance on both sides. It was punctuated with dusty, sunbleached, peeling signs at regular intervals declaring, in assorted red-and-black Helvetica, that the land beyond was Private, Dangerous, and promised Prosecution, or worse, to anyone who saw fit to cross the boundary.

The gates spontaneously parted in anticipation of his arrival, revealing an additional red-and-white striped pole barrier, blocking the roadway ahead. A military policeman, clipboard in hand, stepped sharply out of an adjacent whitewashed concrete guardhouse, as the car made the final approach and crawled to quiet stop.

Snark observed absently as the MP unshackled a chain from the gate mechanism, and the car inched forward, moving up alongside the approaching soldier. The guard and the driver exchanged a few words through the open window, IDs were presented, and a name was checked off on the list. The policeman craned his neck, attempting to peer into the back, as the driver jabbered on, hoping to catch sight of today's rare VIP visitor. And Snark nodded involuntarily in his direction, despite being separated by a panel of semiopaque privacy glass.

The guard stepped back from the car and, signalling to his partner in the guardhouse, watched as the barrier rose slowly upward. Snark's driver revved the engine unnecessarily, and the Humvee lurched forward, gravel crunching beneath the wide-set tyres, leaving a frothy, dust-filled trail to fill the vacuum behind, as it gradually picked up speed and headed down the unmade track to the valley floor below.

Snark fished a cell phone from his crumpled suit jacket, as they rounded a bend in the road, and noted the main installation ahead; still a couple of miles away, and some five hundred feet down, it was partially embedded in a rocky promontory, almost invisible if you didn't already know it was there, beside the sprawling, flat desert basin below. He could just make out the barely used specialist runways shimmering on the very far side of the complex, next to a huddle of hangars and ancillary buildings. He grunted audibly in frustration and looked back at his handset, prodding the screen with his fat, wrinkled finger. It rang just twice, before a sharp, well-practised voice could be heard picking up.

"Yes, sir!?"

"Get me Carson," he bellowed, almost as soon as the call connected. "Tell her it's Snark."

3

HYPERION

Leon had long suspected there was more to the seventh floor than was generally acknowledged, or seemingly noticed, by his friends and colleagues in the office complex where he worked, as a planner, in the midsized, moderately successful, occasionally notable, digital media agency, Hyperion.

As the accepted home of the so-called *client suites*, the seventh floor was always quieter, more prestigiously furnished, more luminous (thanks to the extensive skylights in the roof) and less obviously, or continuously, populated than the rest of the building. It was also, by general agreement, blessed with much nicer toilets. This was a curious contradiction since, presumably by much less generalised agreement, it also served as the destination-of-choice for anyone in the sometimes alarming, but largely unspoken about, position of needing-to-take-a-crap-at-work. And who, under any circumstances but the most dire—a savage sudden-onset gastric attack, perhaps, or a severe hangover—couldn't possibly face the monstrous, unloved facilities provided on the other six floors of the building?

Certainly, this was the only place Leon would ever go. If he needed a dump, yes, but often as not, if he simply became overwhelmed by some capricious combination of exhaustion, depression, or just plain boredom through the course of the working day. Or, very occasionally, when he was sometimes caught in an overextended client meeting, and needed somewhere private and relatively clean to attempt a short, recuperative nap.

However, as he repeatedly and unsurprisingly discovered but rarely recalled in the moment of need, toilet cubicles make lousy cribs. There was just something criminal about the relative planes of the commode to the back-wall-enclosed cistern (these were *client* toilets after all. And they should never be made to confront an actual flushing mechanism) that made the whole operation much harder than it should be. And so simply closing the lid and rashly leaning back against the wall in an attempt to get some rest rarely, if ever, provided the much-hoped-for respite Leon desired.

Thus, his heavy-eyed plots would inevitably progress poorly: from a back-wall *slump*, to the tempting-but-just-out-of-reach-vanity-sink *lean*. When this, naturally, failed to satisfy, he would have no other choice but to attempt to prop his apparently sleep-enlarged, neckless and drooping head into his equally weak and enfeebled hands. It was a problem.

Eventually, he concluded that this lack of sleep viability was actually built-in to office toilets by design, presumably to address the globally recognised, and potentially dangerous, misuse of corporate hygiene facilities. So, finally, he would just give up, and default into doomscrolling on his phone for a while, before splashing his face with cold water and sloping back to his professional meeting-based obligations; along with the opportunity to ask important-sounding but generally meaningless questions.

It was during one such mini-escape, early on in his career at the agency, that Leon had first begun to notice something odd about the place. Not in a specific, fully conscious way exactly—after all, he was still so newly arrived at Hyperion that much about his working life there still seemed strange and subtly disquieting—but there was definitely something off-colour about the place he couldn't put his finger on.

In particular, there were certain individuals he'd occasionally find milling about on the seventh floor that just didn't seem to fit. Individuals that, for reasons he couldn't really articulate, simply didn't seem to chime with the more typical slack-jawed, skinny-jeaned, skateboarding, sushi-munching, flat-white, double-shot agency drones who slithered about the place. Nor, for that matter, could he connect them with the slew of eager, half-suited account managers, wannabe social media doyennes, or regular, everyday client-humans he was used to seeing, despite his almost fifteen years in the business.

Maybe it was their lack of even the most basic, polite interactions, though he couldn't be entirely sure, since rude or occasionally indifferent colleagues and clients were far from uncommon agency norms. Perhaps, instead, it was the specific manner of their indifference that struck an unseen chord, the small print, and minor ticks of their acute, preoccupied sobriety, rather than just fact of it.

Leon would experiment from time to time, to see if it was just something his new-kid-in-school brain was making up but found he was still unable to coax so much as a hint of a half-smile, a nod, or even something approaching a receptive look in response to his internationally recognised stranger greeting: *the raised eyebrows*. Politely offering a *good morning* or *afternoon*, rarely elicited anything beyond a taut-lipped, barely recognisable nod.

Perhaps, though, it was their palpable sense of absolute autonomy that he just couldn't figure out. After all, none of them worked at Hyperion as far as he could tell, and yet somehow, when Leon ran into them on his travels to and from the WC, or to an occasional meeting, he would often feel it was he, and not they, who was a guest in the building. It almost felt like he had picked an office block at random, pitched up wherever the lift took him, and simply decided to join in whatever work activity he found there.

Finally, it was simply the sheer volume of strangely unaccompanied and unrecognised visitors (unrecognised, that is, by pretty much anyone at Hyperion, as an extended campaign of subtle questioning had later confirmed), going in and out of the otherwise permanently unavailable Jupiter Room that gave him pause (yes, all the meeting rooms were named after planets. A novelty Leon had assumed, then, was tenuously related to the building's alleged former life as part of a NASA-sponsored research office that had later dwindled and fallen into disrepair, along with the Apollo program, during the 1970s. Plus, naturally, there were nine meeting rooms, so it was a good guess either way).

Of the nine existing meeting rooms, Jupiter was the one suite that nobody ever seemed able to book. And yet, whenever Leon would pass by, it was almost always empty, with projectors and conference phones that, in the event you tried to squat there for any significant period of time—whether casually for a private phone call, or officially with a paying customer—never seemed to work. And, even then, if you tried to linger, one of the random strangers from *head office*, or wherever they came from, in the stiff-looking suits would inevitably appear, and declare with an indignant sigh, "This room's booked. Sorry." Although they rarely seemed sorry.

The main door to the fifth floor, where the Strategy and Planning team generally resided, slammed shut, breaking in on Leon's idle recollection of his first few months at Hyperion.

Derek Tyler strutted in, as was his way of a morning, wearing his customarily tight middle-aged-man-in-Lycra outfit, which he wore because, as he liked to tell anyone who asked (and often even if they didn't) "I cycle into London." And would then wait to see if they asked him about the experience. If they didn't, and they usually wouldn't, he'd chuck them a bone anyway.

"You wouldn't believe the roads today. It was like the fucking killing fields out there."

That was usually enough, for everyone.

The overall arrangement of skintight shorts and sweaty, luminescent tops wasn't an especially compelling spectacle, but he obviously enjoyed it. Which, for Derek, was often the main reason for his doing anything. Not in any kind of joyful or life-affirming way but as an act of unfettered self-regard. A well-practised act that could usually be brought to bear on whatever else he was actually meant to be doing: generating or presenting work for his clients, conducting annual appraisals, even a random clear-down of the stationery cupboard, which he would often do in a state of loud, stress-inducing rage as he threw out dry or lidless Sharpies, and half-used Post-it pads into the bin.

Even when, occasionally, he would bring his children into work, whether for sudden lack of childcare at home, or for their apparent edification and enrichment, was never made clear (he was big on enrichment), it was almost always, somehow, about Derek. Naturally this didn't make him a lot of friends at the agency. Not that he'd have noticed.

The office had shower facilities, of course, which, strictly speaking, he should have used to wash and change before coming up to the floor to work but it seemed, as ever, he was just too focused on announcing his arrival.

"Morning, ladies," he crowed, inappropriately, as he click-clacked across the wooden floor in his cycle-shoes, towards his desk by the window. Only two or three people bothered to look up from their desks or made any kind of reciprocal noise or gesture. Plus Leon, who remained determinedly mute since, technically, he was already looking up when Derek arrived. The remaining twenty-odd co-workers continued to be engrossed, or at least pretended to be, in their various phone calls, laptop screens, newspapers, toast-making, or staring out the window routines.

"Stacey, I've been thinking," announced Derek, dramatically, as he attempted to untangle himself from his headphones and began emptying the contents of his expensively branded pro-biker backpack. "We all need new chairs. I need a new chair. These chairs provide unforgivable lumbar support. I need more. We need chairs that support us. We need chairs that enrich us, physically."

Stacey, Derek's unfathomable, and unfathomably patient, personal assistant, stared blankly at him from her workstation opposite. This wasn't the first time she had heard this pitch.

"We won't always be in our prime, Stacey," he continued, indifferent to the eighteen-plus years between them. "Even me. Even the disciplined!"

"Do you really want me to check again, Derek, or is this just you still working out?" she responded, flatly. "There's no magic facilities budget. You know this. And the LumbarStar-whatever it is, is still the award-winning chair you made us bulk-order last year."

"Yes, I want you to check again. Ask them. Go down to Facilities and speak to them personally. Explain there's now a better model, with more controls."

"What more could you want to do with it?"

"I want full control of my chair."

Having fully disgorged his pack of laptop, phone, notebook, and cables, Derek proceeded to head back to the main door, clutching a small towel.

"And I need to update the workshop timings for Blue Rinse on Thursday. I sent you a note. Can you arrange that for me, please," he broadcast openly, before buffeting past the just-arriving Tom Kennedy, without any acknowledgment (of course), and letting the heavy metal door slam shut behind him once again.

Tom, self-proclaimed "Art Director to the Stars and Apprentice Wizard" since he'd once, on a freelance film-related gig, got to design some stationery for Ian McKellen, and one of Leon's few actual friends, stopped just short of physically bumping up against the rapidly exiting Derek, and attempted to reseat the lid on his foaming take-out coffee.

Leon beckoned him over with a surreptitious tip of the head, although it was fully understood that chit-chatting to Leon was really the only reason Tom was up there in the first place.

"Leon Trotsky," announced Tom, mischievously, and not for the first time, as he arrived at Leon's desk. He licked the vestigial caffeinated froth from the back of his hand.

"Mr President," replied Leon, in kind.

"Where were you today? Wondered if you'd been *held up* again this morning," said Tom, wagging his fingers as air quotes around the words *held up*. "Or simply killed by former soviet agents on the underground. I couldn't decide." He mimed an exaggerated, twisting knife attack.

He was of course referring to their regular pre-work meets at the coffee shop around the corner. Most of the staff at Hyperion went there, often several times a day. Leon and Tom once tried to work out how much money the cafe must make, but it quickly became a painful exercise and they simply wrote down, "a lot."

"No, not killed. Not today."

"Good. I'm a busy person and have enough to do, without having to find time to mourn your death."

"Just the usual. Running late. Although to be completely honest, I've grown a little tired of that place and their burnt-milk lattes." Leon made a sour face, to emphasise his disgust. "I think if you're going to wear a T-shirt that says *Barista* on it, there should be actual rules in place. Otherwise, you're just a regular coffee-maker like the rest of us."

"I'm with you, man," said Tom. "I really only go there for the porridge anyway. How goes the work today?"

"Today, Mr Kennedy, I have something extraordinary for you. Amazing. Today, I will be preparing the final synthesis of our soon-to-be-famous Hyperion Synchronous Cat Arclight Tracker market analysis."

"The fabled SCAT. You still working on that?" said Tom, pulling up the empty chair next to Leon and plopping himself down, all legs and arms.

"Yes, I'm still working on that. Apparently, there's a significant consumer need to be met by using multi-billion-dollar satellites to track where your cat goes when it leaves the house."

Leon poked a small, furry desk-friend model of a Saturn V rocket with his pen. "It can't all just be to poop in your neighbour's garden."

"Good. Great. Sounds like a keeper. I can't wait to see someone else develop the creative for it," said Tom, flicking a paper clip across Leon's desk.

"Oh, I see. Someone else? That's going on the list, I'm afraid." Leon picked up his phone and pantomimed typing out a message to HR. "...reluctant to support. Deflection. Of. Responsibility."

Tom smiled, enjoying the well-worn gag.

"More importantly," demanded Tom, placing a finger purposefully upright onto the desk, "Will you be sticking around for the drinks this evening?"

"Drinks?" feigned Leon.

"Yes, drinks. Don't pretend. The all-hands meeting, followed by drinks to celebrate our big win at the Triple-Tech awards."

"Ohhh. Those drinks. I suppose we'll have to sit through one of Derek's here's-one-I-made-earlier routines but, yes, I'll come. Just for one though."

Tom leaned slowly back in his chair to consider Leon's answer.

"Why must you insist on always short-changing me with the 'I'm only coming for one' routine."

"How many should I come for? What's the basic currency I should be aiming for? Just so I know."

"What if you just left it open-ended? You never just have one drink, anyway, so why bother even setting a limit up front?"

"Good question. Maybe I like to surprise myself."

Tom popped back up and leaned in towards Leon. "And the real answer is..."

"I don't have an answer. That's the answer. I'm not twenty-four. I get overtired. I'm like an infant that way. I can't go out with the assumption I'm just going out to get smashed. I don't want to get smashed. I'm allergic to getting smashed. It's genetic."

"Genetic," repeated Tom, disdainfully.

"I've told you this before: Jews don't drink—we eat."

"What are you talking about? You get smashed pretty much every time we go out."

"Yeah, maybe so. But I've really had to put the work in."

"Just come along. We'll get the guys together and head out afterwards. Plus..." He looked around, conspiratorially. "You know who'll be in the building, on the same day we're having a works party? It's the perfect storm."

Leon raised an eyebrow, attempting to hide his inner enthusiasm, like he hadn't already thought about this. "Hmm. Izzy," he murmured.

"Yes, Izzy. Massage therapist to the stars."

"Does everything have to be 'to the stars' in your world?"

"It's a badge of honour."

"To you, maybe. I don't go in for all that celebrity validation. It's not a shortcut to measuring a person, you know. It's coincidence at best."

"That's because you don't know any celebrities."

"*You* don't know any." Leon raised a hand in protest, before Tom could respond. "No. Not even Gandalf."

"What if it was Leonard Nimoy? What if, say, Izzy had once given Spock a backrub at work? Then it would be—"

"Nimoy is different," interrupted Leon. "You can't just invoke Nimoy to win an argument with me."

"Why not? I thought that was the deal with you: that celebrity Jews carry more weight."

"Celebrity Jews? Really?"

"OK, sorry. Space Jews."

"Thank you. It's an important distinction. I mean, there's not many to go around, right? So they have to be used sparingly. It's written down somewhere."

"OK, fine. No celebrity endorsements. But look, either way, the sadly Nimoy-less universe has brought you Isabella Jones, and a legitimate boozy night out together. You've been talking about it for months. Invite her along. You can just be casual about the whole thing—she'll already be in the building."

"I can do casual. Casual is my thing," agreed Leon, boldly. Then thought about it some more. "Although, seriously. It is last-minute—she'll have plans. Who doesn't have plans last-minute?"

"Look, dude, just think about it," said Tom, standing up at last, cup in hand, his mission basically achieved. "That's all I ask."

"Yes. Fine. I'll think about. I will definitely think about it. Two drinks! Now get moving. I have consumer feline goodness to extract. The world needs more cat."

4

ISABELLA JONES

I sabella Morten Jones, who hated her middle name and, sometimes, even her 1980s-obsessed mother for giving it to her (in honour of former teenage pop idol, Morten Harket), gathered up the scattered post from her doormat. There were the usual wasted flyers for random pizza delivery she'd never order. An estate agent's card, promoting sales and local market expertise that, as a tenant of someone else's flat, she had no use for. And, as ever, a handful of confusingly pointless bin-cleaning businesses that, she was convinced, must surely spend more on advertising than they could ever hope to make washing people's evidently disgusting bins.

"Seriously?" she muttered, as she headed back into the kitchen to instantly recycle. "Who goes in for all that crap?"

And, oh, what's this? she mused, as she pulled away the last pizza flyer. A real, handwritten letter. Just like in olden days. She slid a finger under the lapel, and tore it crudely open, with a mix of pleasure for the format, and at least some contempt for the letter writer, since she already had a good idea who it was from. Izzy clenched her jaw and sighed, as she pulled the slim contents out.

Yes, as she suspected, another grovelling missive from Steve. Stephen Langard, formally of Langard Media Associates, a more or less failed social media marketing and copywriting service, of which Steve was the only Associate. Steve-o. Former boyfriend, former friend, and lover who, five months earlier, had belligerently given up his rights to all these honours.

Izzy had finally decided that as lovely, funny, and charming as he could often be, she didn't really enjoy being screamed at by a man who secretly loathed himself but remained unwilling to change, despite any (and many) self-proclaimed epiphanies.

Nor, she had decided, did that bitter-edged charm give him—an itinerant, self-aggrandised copywriter who rarely lowered himself to do any actual work—a licence to live off her indefinitely. After all, he was happy to shower in her hot water, watch her pay TV, eat her food and enjoy getting steaming drunk on her booze. But what seemed less appealing to him as time moved on, was paying for any of it or contributing to their life together in any meaningful way.

"...I know you're probably still angry," he went on, "but I needed to try to..."

No, she thought, *enough. Enough about what Steve needs.*

She'd had enough of his casually plaintive, "hey babe" texts, listened to the simpering please-call-me-back-when-you-get-a-minute voicemails, and winced at the embarrassing "self-deprecating" selfies, but no. On balance, Izzy was very done with having to wipe angry spittle off her face after what became a series of progressively incensed, drink-fuelled episodes that concluded, on their very last evening together, when he decided to inform her that she was both pointless *and* talentless. Only to then have her nice Habitat plates smashed when she disagreed and asked him if he was planning on getting a job anytime soon.

So that, she reminded herself, was that. He blew it. She didn't bother reading the rest of his Jane Austen note. He needed to live with the consequences of being a dick, and she needed some new dishes.

Izzy swigged down the dregs of her now-cold coffee, grabbed her bag and keys, and headed out the front door to work, screwing up the letter, as the door closed behind her, and tossing it in to her filthy, dirty, unwashed bin.

Work for Izzy meant, basically, two things; one was as a PhD student, an undertaking she genuinely enjoyed, perhaps even loved, inasmuch as a person can ever really be said to love their work. But, naturally, it didn't make her any money. While the other, just as naturally, was work of necessity. A modest money-generating but relatively thought and responsibility-free activity, as a *freelance corporate massage therapist*, with her own collapsible wheelie massage chair. A job that gave her flexibility around both her study, and her need to pay her bills.

After all, life as a post-graduate student of Cosmology, Neuro-robotics, and Computing was hardly a gold mine. And, despite some limited funding, it had cost her more in fees and loans than she could practically hope to make back in the near future. So, then, if this was not actual love, she was certainly under its spell: thrilled and fascinated by what it might make possible, once you got past all the hysterical noise around generative AI, predicative text, robot dogs, Terminators, automated financial advisors, and military drones.

Over time, the Cosmology part of it had drifted to more of a sideshow, and really only existed as a nod to her graduate studies of theoretical physics. For a variety of reasons, Izzy had become frustrated by the purely academic application of her gifts, and had begun to realise that, as compelling as the mysteries of the universe might be, she was just more interested in people. And, more specifically, in helping people. So when, by chance, she'd found herself at a symposium on artificial intelligence in the first months of her master's degree, the proverbial light went on, and she decided to simply translate her deftness and enthusiasm for complex mathematics into complex computer programming.

It didn't take her long after that to conclude that the medical applications of AI, and in her case, AI-enhanced robotic augmentation—mainly for people born disabled, or later damaged by accident or tragedy, rather than your actual cyborgs-from-the-future—was the way she wanted to make a difference. But, of course, staying in research, and away from an anonymous graduate post in a giant biotech, was an expensive pastime. Even with the occasional optimistic private bursary, or industry grant, she would still need actual cash for food and washing-up liquid and rent.

Finally, with so much of her life devoted to *mind*, Izzy had grudgingly come to realise that her increasingly softening body also needed attention. So, on top of her studies, she began a progressively physical regime of yoga, CrossFit, and the Israeli martial art, *Krav Maga*. This last choice was partly inspired by a not-so-fleeting crush on Jason Bourne (although *not* Matt Damon, as she was quick to point out), but mainly so she could guard against getting attacked on her way home late from campus, or in case she ever needed to defend herself with a phonebook and a ballpoint pen.

To her surprise, she quickly began to enjoy the simple mindfulness of structured physical discipline and focus. It gave her a way to switch off when she needed to. And then, eventually, an unexpected form of income when she began providing lunchtime *wellness classes,* which in turn led to her becoming a *travelling masseuse* for busy corporate types with bad postures and a good benefits package. A perk for them. A reasonably well-paid, part-time gig for her. Better, she figured, than the casual bar work she'd done previously. The hours were better for one thing. And while both choices risked the occasional cloying letch, at least the business customers tended not to be filthy drunk. At least in the office. And, if nothing else, they were generally subject to strict HR policies that were more effective at modifying their behaviour than the pot luck of closing time, and whatever value systems remained after five lagers and three rounds of Jägerbombs.

. . .

Izzy's phone began to chime just as she started down the stairs into the Tube station. She paused halfway down and pulled her phone out of her bag. It was her money-work booking agency.

"Hello? Gloria?" Gloria was her main agent.

"Isabella, Hi. It's Gloria." She always introduced herself. "How are you, darling?"

Izzy winced a little. She sometimes found Gloria a little theatrically over-familiar for a woman in her line of work. A little bit out of time or place somehow. Like she'd planned to be a very different kind of person at one time, but somehow ended up working in corporate therapy services for twenty-five years by mistake.

"Hi, Gloria. What can I do for you? I already have a booking for today. I'm just heading underground now."

"Ah yes. Very good. So glad to have caught you. Look, sorry to be a pain in the backside and all that. I realise it's last-minute. But unfortunately, I need to cancel your job this afternoon."

"Oh crap."

"Don't be like that, darling. It's nothing personal. Apparently, they have some event on this evening, and just need the space and the time back. It's just for today."

Izzy hovered on the station steps without saying anything, caught between coming and going.

"Everything OK, darling?" tried Gloria, after a moment, when Izzy didn't respond.

"No. Yes. Sorry," said Izzy, staring up to the street. "It's nothing. I just left all my kit there last night, that's all. My foldaway chair and stuff. I dropped it in on my way home, to save me hefting it back out again today."

"I'm sure they won't mind storing it for you," said Gloria, attempting to be conversational.

"Maybe not," replied Izzy, with a sigh. "But tomorrow's gig is in a completely different part of town. I'll have to go in today anyway, after school, and pick it all up."

"Oh, didn't I say, dear? Tomorrow's job is off as well. I think that one's for good."

5

CHOICES

Thirty minutes later, Izzy climbed her way up the escalator leading from the underground platform, through the snapping exit barrier, across the seething ticket hall and, finally, up the steel-capped steps and onto the sunlit streets of southeast London.

Where to first, she pondered. Pick up her wheelie chair from Hyperion and be done with it? They won't want it left there all day, surely. But neither did she want to have to drag it around with her like a dead body, and then have to find somewhere to store it everywhere she went.

Or should she be a good girl, and head over to the library to try to finish up the quantum reasoning research piece she'd started weeks ago? She didn't really want to do that either, and thought about just going straight to the lab to see if last night's code dump had improved the prototypes at all? Too soon, she decided. Duty pulled her towards the library, while her instinct for a nice bit of ready-made distraction felt equally powerful. Library, lab, or client? Work or... Screw it.

She turned right, and threaded her way through the meandering day-trippers, fashionistas, and foodies of Borough Market, towards the celebrated Hairy Mammoth Coffee Company which, in her opinion, was highly overrated. Not that it stopped her from going in anyway, and picking up a skinny latte, before heading off to the Hyperion offices on Southwark Bridge Road.

Derek strutted out of the lift and across the foyer as Izzy came through the sliding doors, pushing her sunglasses up into her thick, dark hair. He was bellowing extravagantly into his mobile phone but not so absorbed that he didn't notice her as she passed. He made an I'm-just-on-a-call motion with his hand and eyebrows, although she wasn't sure why. Perhaps he'd confused her with someone else.

She recognised him of course. A massage regular. A chatter upper. One of those who misunderstood the faux intimacy of this small perk, and weirdly used the session as part social, part confessional. But she couldn't remember his name. This wasn't unusual. She rarely remembered the names. Her sessions were generally so fleeting and irregular, and like today, could often be cancelled at the last minute, that she didn't see the point. But behaviours tended to stick in the mind. His was far from the worst, but generally, with one or two exceptions, she regarded anything more than polite compliance from her clients as an imposition. It was just work.

Lauren, the receptionist-come-assistant-studio-manager, looked up and smiled.

"Hi, Izzy. Nice to see you," she squeaked.

"Nice to see you."

"We weren't expecting you today."

"Yes, I know. I just—"

"I called your agency first thing." Lauren was not the best listener, nor, for that very reason, the best receptionist. "I spoke to Gloria. Told her to cancel today's session. Sorry," she continued, tipping her head to one side and crinkling her face, just so, as though she were delivering bad news to a small dog.

"Yes, Gloria phoned me already. She said you have a thing on."

"Yes!" beamed Lauren. "A party. We're celebrating. You should come!"

"I should?" replied Izzy, doubtfully. "Well, thanks. That's a lovely offer, but I—"

Derek leaned in suddenly, his phone still glued to his head.

"You should definitely come. It's a party. Everyone should come to parties," he said, before trying out another version of his can't-talk-now gesture and walking away.

Izzy and Lauren looked knowingly at each other, then turned to watch him depart.

"It will enrich you!" he roared, from across the hall, disappearing back into the open lift as the doors closed behind him.

Izzy wasn't sure if she wanted to be enriched. It wasn't really something she'd ever considered she was missing out on. She turned back to Lauren.

"I'll add your name to the list anyway," said Lauren, efficiently.

"Uhm...Lauren." Lauren looked up. "You know I don't actually work here, right?"

"Oh yes, that's fine. Guests are allowed. Not for everyone obviously. But Derek can invite people. You can be Derek's guest."

"Derek's *guest*? I don't really think—"

"It's just for the list," winked Lauren.

Izzy felt a little uncomfortable by this sudden turn of events. She wasn't typically against parties and, naturally, was as happy to drink free corporate booze as the next person, but did she really want to go to a company do, filled with, essentially, complete strangers? Sure, she'd been coming in twice a month for over a year now. And although she recognised many of the faces, knew a few of their names, and had even had some fun chats and the odd lunch with a couple of them, Derek—that was his name!—hardly came close to fitting into that narrow category of people.

Her mind briefly flitted to Tom Kennedy and... whatsisname. She'd had lunch with them a few months back and, much to her surprise, in that moment, realised she actually quite liked whatsisname, even if she couldn't remember what he was called. They always showed up as a pair. Tom and...nope. Nothing. Anyway, there was always a few like that, wherever she set up shop. And she decided then that she could probably tolerate an evening in their company without much effort. She made a mental note to casually find out the guy's name somehow, and then just decide later whether to actually go to the party. No one would notice either way.

"OK, great. Thanks, Lauren. Maybe it will be fun. Any entertainment laid on?"

"Entertainment!" she laughed, not really getting the question. "You are funny."

"Uhm. Yes, I suppose." It was time to cut to the chase. "So anyway, the actual reason I'm here is, I just wanted to see if I can leave my kit here for the rest of the day. I left it downstairs last night?"

"Your clothes?"

"No, not my *kit,* kit. My work chair. It folds up. On wheels? About so big?" Izzy raised her hand up to just below her chest.

"Oh, your *massage-y* chair."

"Yes, my massage chair. But, well, look... As I'm now not working later, I basically didn't want to wheel it around all day. Am I OK to leave it with you guys for now? I'll take it home tonight."

"After the party? You might need some help," giggled Lauren, and then added when Izzy seemed less moved by the suggestion, "Yes! 'Course it's fine. Leave it there all week if you like."

"Thanks so much, Lauren. You're a lifesaver."

Izzy turned, pulling her sunglasses back to her nose, and put her earbuds in. Then she sauntered back out of the sliding, clear glass doors, and into the street feeling in a strangely good mood.

Maybe it was the spring sunshine. Maybe it was drawing a hard line under Steve, or just being given her afternoon back, but despite Izzy's best intentions to jump into proper library work, she found herself veering away from her south London school buildings, and cutting back across Southwark Bridge Road towards the Thames, zigzagging her way into the small warren of backstreets that spill

out onto the river. With the busting late April sun in full force, the place was heaving with more than the usual volume of aimless, chattering tourists, muddled school groups, and random springtime drifters like herself.

She stopped close to the bank and gazed along the old river for a while, vaguely conscious of its insistent history. The looming proximity of the reconstructed Globe Theatre inevitably crashed into her thoughts, and all those passing by, but not in any meaningful way. Just a fleeting half daydream of the river in the *old days*. In the imagination. Filled with working boats of one sort or another. Of trade, and celebration, and all those ice fairs she'd heard so much about in school, rather than the sun-bleached plastic tourist clippers and occasional waste barges that cruised up and down it today. But mostly she thought about nothing at all, just letting the warm sun wash over her face, and faintly pondering the randomness of the universe, and her invitation from Hyperion.

She'd buried herself in work lately, she realised. Since all that Steve crap. But she was done with that now, surely. No more hiding away. No wounds to tend. Maybe she should just go for it. Carpe diem and all that.

The tide was out and she watched a few adventurous beachcombers on the far side picking through the muddy ruin of stones, and building waste, and God-knows-what slimy things that littered the tidal shore of the river.

Yes, why not, she thought. *It might be fun.* She turned and wandered slowly over towards the Tate, wondering if she had any clean things to wear.

. . .

As a result of all her faffing about, Izzy arrived much later to her facility than she originally planned. Ultimately, she had avoided the library altogether, and headed straight for the lab where Robson, one of the institute's more trusted techs, was hovering by the door tinkering with the coffeepot. He looked at her with mock disdain, admonishing her with a casual wave of the empty mug in his hand, that read: *Actually, you do have to be crazy to work here. It doesn't help.*

"Really, Jones?" barked Robson, glancing theatrically up at the clock. "But you expect me to be here each day, right?" he said, ambiguously.

"So sorry, Robbie. I got carried away doing some...off-site research."

"Sure you did," he said, smiling affectionately, and handing her an empty mug, with a gaudy flower pattern from 1974 along with deep concentric tea-stain rings inside to match. "Here. You can fix your own coffee."

"Yes, sir," she replied, slightly disappointed not to get the Mr Men mug she generally favoured, but wasn't about to complain. "Any biscuits left?"

"Not unless you brought any with you."

"I don't buy biscuits, you know that."

Robbie waved her comment away.

"So, how are our little friends today?" said Izzy, nodding towards the workbench on the far side of the room, where there were a number of robotic limbs on stands, and other less obvious devices, in various states of repair.

Each device looked like a jumble of unmatched parts, with assorted wires running into makeshift consoles that were attached to an array of monitors showing columns of numbers, graphs, and other diagnostic data.

"Not much action that I can see," said Robson, heading over to the workbench. "When I last checked in, your code was still compiling."

"Still!?" Izzy replied, surprised. She finished pouring milk into her coffee and joined him. "I left it running last night. It should really have finished by now. How are we ever going to get these prototypes working, I wonder?"

Robson reached down and picked up a prosthetic robot hand, adjusted the fingers into a point, and wagged it at Izzy. "*We* are not going to do anything. My job is to keep this lab running. Yours is to make the things inside it work."

"Yes, of course," Izzy said with a smile.

"Maybe you should just spend more time with them. They get lonely." He used the replica hand to wipe an imaginary tear away from his eye.

6

GREGORY QUINN

A glossy black electric saloon car, with dark tinted glass and a satellite antenna on the roof, crept along the narrow side street in the former Victorian London warehouse district where Hyperion was based. The tires scrunched noisily against the cobbled sidings running along the kerbside, as the car pulled in tightly, before coming to a near silent stop.

The door opened with a silky, expensive click, letting out a steel-tipped wooden cane that hits the ground with a neat clack, followed by its owner; Captain Gregory Theodore Quinn, USN, retired. A smart, fit-looking man—despite the cane—wearing a good suit and a pair of aviator sunglasses. He stepped awkwardly from the wide, handleless door and onto the kerb.

Quinn marched confidently through the full-height sliding glass doors, housed seamlessly in the centre of an immaculate, cubic, glass-walled ground floor of an otherwise tired-looking, old-world red-brick warehouse. A leather document case was tucked neatly under one arm, his cane—he walks with a barely perceptible limp—and small brown paper bag in the other.

A well-groomed, disciplined man, with a tight jaw and an apparent taste for expensive cologne, Quinn gave the impression of being someone who had been built from much cruder material, one carefully considered choice at a time. The overall effect was impressive enough, yet enigmatic, since, despite a naturally warm and engaging manner, he often seemed to be all business, and would often leave others looking forward to a more personal connection that never really came.

Quinn stopped sharply at the main reception and, placing his case, cap, and bag neatly on the chest-high stone ledge of the main desk, leant forward and deployed his Big American Smile.

"Good morning, ma'am. I'm here for the EMF meeting," he declared, firmly.

"Good morning to you," replied Lauren, enjoying the formality.

"Seventh floor," suggested Quinn, trying to be helpful.

"EMF meeting, seventh floor. Got it. Do you have a name?"

"Miles Benedict."

"Oh, you're here to see Miles," chuckled Lauren gently, and jotted it down on the pad beside her anyway. "I actually meant *your* name?"

"Tell him Quinn's here."

Miles Benedict was well used to controlled, administrative chaos. He considered it a bit of an occupational hazard and, as such, had made it one of his defining features. As Hyperion's Director of Accounts, Government and Heavy Industry contracts, he was, perhaps, the longest-tenured employee at the agency. No one really knew for sure, and he wasn't really telling.

He was rumoured to be one of the founders of the business from some twenty years earlier, but with no one else remaining from that period (the rest of the original leadership having quickly disappeared following the US-based Hypomatics acquisition in 2017, presumably to squander their massive payouts), it was difficult to be certain either way.

The unresolved question was why, if true, he hadn't simply joined his colleagues in complete financial liberty. Maybe it was gambling debts, drugs, or gigantic alimony payments, newer colleagues speculated. But with nothing ever confirmed or denied by Miles himself (a bit of a black hole for conversation at the best of times. Basically, the guy at the Christmas party you never wanted to get stuck with) speculation was all anyone had to go on.

Under other circumstances, he would have been managed out long ago, or likely paid off during a period of corporate "right-sizing." But for Hyperion, he'd become life insurance, providing a handful of steady, long-standing, high-paying government contracts that, to date, had somehow ensured the agency stayed firmly afloat during more hazardous economic times: from the 2008 financial crisis to the pandemic in 2020, and everything in between. Benedict had somehow seen them through it all, even as the rest of Hyperion's client base had become virtually decimated by such changing tides, and diverted their costly marketing, digital, and innovation budgets elsewhere.

No one really knew how he had done it. And in hard times, no one wanted to ask. But if they did, "Slow and steady wins the race!" was pretty much all they ever got from him in return.

Over the years it had given him a curious, untouchable quality, with a correspondingly free hand in how he ran and staffed his roster of typically off-site projects and campaigns. So, while people didn't particularly *want* to work on his projects, or hang out with him at the pub, the company didn't want to lose his seemingly impervious income.

If nothing else, certainly in the good times, that income would pay for the ridiculous studio entertainment budget, including an in-house bar, the foosball table, and the spring, summer, and winter parties. And no one much cared where the money for those came from either.

Benedict's phone began quietly vibrating, inching its way gently across the desk in front of him. The movement, more than the sound, caught his attention. He swiped the screen and plugged an earbud in.

"Benedict," he announced, firmly. It was Lauren.

"Hi Miles. I have a Mr—"

"Captain," interjected Quinn.

Lauren unconsciously raised an eyebrow. She didn't meet many captains.

"I have a *Captain* Quinn in reception for you."

"Excellent. Thank you, Lauren. Please have him meet me on seven."

Lauren replaced the handset of her desk phone and smiled at Quinn.

"He'll meet you on the seventh floor. Can I show you to the lift, *Captain* Quinn," she said, emphasising all the syllables, with due care.

Quinn returned her smile. "You mean the elevator over there, by the stairs?" he responded, teasingly, and gesturing with his head. Lauren made an innocent face. "Thank you, ma'am. I think I can find my way."

She gave him a guest security pass. Grabbing his document case, Quinn strode over to the lift, which opened the moment he arrived. He was just that kind of a man, thought Lauren, as she watched him casually from her perch behind the desk. He stepped in, turned, and pressed the button to seven. The doors closed. Lauren sighed and returned to scrolling through the celebrity gossip on her computer screen.

Benedict was waiting pensively, tight-lipped but blank-faced, in the lobby of the seventh floor as the lift arrived with a delicate chime. He swiftly adjusted himself as the doors parted, and Quinn stepped out.

"Captain," he said, as warmly as he could muster. "So good to see you again."

"Dr Benedict, sir."

"No doctors, here, please," he said, with a barely perceptible blink of discomfort. "Or sirs. You're in Blighty now. Call me Miles."

Benedict reached out, and the two shook hands.

"Can I fetch you something to drink, Captain? Water, perhaps? I imagine you must be a little dehydrated after your flight."

"I'm good, thank you," replied Quinn. "Although some coffee would be much appreciated."

The two men walked in tandem over to an elegant, expensive-looking, recessed kitchen area to one side of the hallway. The countertops and much of the floor space around were stacked with boxes of wine, glasses, and packs of beer. Benedict began opening cupboards at random, looking for cups.

"We're having a little do this evening," said Benedict, peering over his shoulder apologetically.

"So I can see," replied Quinn. "Anything I should be worried about?"

"Not unless free booze and a bunch of heavily intoxicated design professionals represent much of a threat to you. I imagine you've seen worse."

"Oh, I don't know about that. What is it they say?"

"Never work with children and animals—or designers." They both chuckled.

Benedict placed two small ceramic cups into the celebrity-endorsed coffee machine and started fiddling with the settings.

"Just steer clear of the toilets," continued Benedict, "and you should be OK."

"Noted."

Captain Quinn took a moment to look around, as Benedict finished jostling the sputtering coffee machine to get it to work. One wall of the kitchen featured a large picture window that faced onto a small inner courtyard below. A mishmash of red-and-white-brick buildings. Some late-Victorian mixed with mid-twentieth century modifications, pipework, and air-conditioning units. Presumably all part of a larger complex, he considered, of which this building was just one.

"These all yours?" he asked, thoughtlessly, gesturing at the window.

Benedict made a noise as he picked up the small cups.

"I wouldn't say mine, really. No," he deflected.

Quinn nodded.

"Of course. Heard anything from Carson or Stanhope yet?"

"Stanhope arrived earlier this afternoon. He could hardly contain himself."

"It's a big day for him."

"We'll see about that. Let's go in, shall we? The others will be waiting."

7

SPECIAL OPERATIONS

Snark's armoured limousine rolled down the garage ramp, clattering over the speed humps and into the dimly lit subterranean garage. There were similar vehicles sitting in neat orderly rows, along with a handful of regular civilian SUVs and the odd sedan. A shuttered carapace descended over the entranceway, as his car continued its way down another four levels, leaving the receding daylight behind.

The car turned left on the final down ramp, and headed all the way along to the far end of the parking level. A woman in an immaculately pressed uniform stood waiting by the kerbside in front of a bank of elevators. One of the elevators was already open. An armed military policeman, gaze fixed into the middle distance, stood stiffly to one side, between the elevator hub, and a small-windowed service door marked Strictly Emergency Use Only.

Snark immediately recognised the woman as Frances Carson, Head of Operations and, to all intents and purposes, his second. An XO in military terms, even if this wasn't strictly speaking a military facility. She basically ran the place for him when he was in Washington, or overseas. And often when he wasn't. As Snark had long come to recognise, she did a damn fine job doing it.

The car came to a smooth stop beside her. She stepped

forward and promptly opened the door for Snark, as he rolled out ungracefully, with a grunt and a creased shirt. His suit jacket was crumpled in one hand, a leather satchel clasped in the other.

Carson stepped back from the kerb and performed a crisp salute.

"Good morning, sir."

"And to you, Frankie. No need for you to come all the way up here. You know that."

"Yes, sir. I do. There's a lot in play. I thought I would brief you on the way back down."

He nodded to the driver, who was already out of the vehicle, pulling a battered cabin case from the trunk.

"Thanks for the ride, soldier," said Snark with a wink. "I owe you one."

"Sir," replied the driver, with a stiff salute. He then turned on his heel, headed back to the front of the car, stepped in, and closed the door behind him in a single action.

Snark and Carson watched him silently, as he drove back towards the exit ramp, then turned at the same moment, and reached for the case.

"I got it, OK?" said Snark. "Let's go."

The elevator lights dimmed intermittently as they descended the remaining eight levels, down to the operation rooms. The floor numbers ticked off on the display with a subtle chime as they passed.

"London states they're pretty much ready to go," began Carson. "We're running additional simulations now, as per plan. Syncing up the telemetry feeds."

"Pretty much? That sounds the same as *not ready* in my book."

"I agree. I told them the same when they called in. But you know how it is with Benedict's team. They're excitable."

"For a bunch of damn Brits, anyway. Am I right?"

"Indeed."

"Carson, this whole thing needs to be ironclad before we hit the button on it. You know that. I don't want a goddamn Three Mile Island on my hands again. Or worse."

"It will be, sir. We've seen to that."

"Good. Good. I know you have. What time are we looking at?"

"Zero hour is currently scheduled for 1900 hours, sir."

The elevator arrived at its destination. The doors split sharply. Snark marched out, with Carson half a step behind.

"1900? Damn strange scheduling, Frankie. What are we waiting for—dinner?"

"That's 0300 local time, sir. Chosen for MPUD: *Minimum Population Urban Density* risk. We have calculations that—"

"Got it. Everyone's at home in bed."

They turned a corner and pulled up at an office, with another MP on duty, along with another salute.

"At ease, soldier," commanded Snark. He had never been comfortable with military protocols, even when he was in the service. In an ostensibly civilian setting, he found it even harder to accommodate.

He reached in for the handle, but the MP was already ahead of him, briskly opening the door with his white-gloved hand and stepping aside. The frosted glass pane in the door was marked Director of Special Operations in plain gold-etched Helvetica.

They ploughed straight into Snark's office, and the door closed behind them. It was a large space, with a correspondingly large and well-used couch, a couple of armchairs, and an out-of-place ornate coffee table—complete with a well-stocked drinks tray and glasses—stretched across one side.

An equally outsized and highly polished antique wooden desk sat squarely in front of the back wall, which was mostly comprised of floor-to-ceiling glass, facing onto basketball court-sized operations room, with banks of workstations, an immense multifaceted video screen visible on the far wall, and people with headsets milling about busily in between. It easily gave Kennedy's Mission Control a run for its money, and for many of the same reasons.

Snark's own desk was an orderly affair. An in tray and three phones, next to a pen station and a single large-format computer monitor. On the remaining wall was a washroom door, two tall file cabinets, and another oversized video panel, facing the couch.

The panel appeared to mirror the main screen from the hall outside, displaying several rotating video feeds from different sources; people at workstations, in various locations, some close-up views of a number of unusual-looking machine parts and, in the centre, a wide view of a large hangar space of some kind. In the middle of the hangar was a tall, wide, bulky steel box, about the size of three or four shipping containers. It had an opaque glass window on one side, and on the other, a large door with an equally large handwheel mechanism. It was like a high-security jail cell.

Running down the side of the screen was a string of fluctu-ating data, a scrolling list of near indecipherable telemetry and visual codes. Plus, of course, the obligatory timestamps from different geographies: Los Angeles, New York, London, Hong Kong, and Sydney.

Snark hung his jacket on a coat stand by the door, threw his satchel onto the couch, and then joined it. He leant back with a sigh, legs outstretched, rubbing his eyes and kicking off his shoes.

"My God. These shoes will actually kill me," he said, waving a hand. "Pull up a chair, Carson. So, Jordan Milk—what's the latest?"

Carson slid into one of the armchairs, picked up a remote from the table, and pointed it at the wall monitors. The wall display re-formed into a single presentation, showing a large grainy image of Jordan Milk: dot.com billionaire to global tech-nology innovator, ad hoc philanthropist, acclaimed business entrepreneur, and, of course, founder and CEO of MilkBar, the global social media network and a highly diversified Silicon Valley tech corporation, not to mention his ever-growing stable of smaller private tech, aerospace, and investment-based ventures.

The shot of him was at some outdoorsy event, midconversation with another person, who was silhouetted in the foreground. A string of data flowed down the right-hand side of the screen.

Snark leant forward and popped open a large bottle of water with one hand, while pulling two glasses towards him with the other.

"Too early for a scotch?" he asked, with a little grin. Carson raised an eyebrow. "I'm kidding, for crying out loud. So, what have you got?"

"As you know, sir, we've been actively tracking Milk for some time now and, for the most part, his public activities are close to what you'd expect," began Carson.

Headlines and images compiled on-screen as Carson spoke: Milk in various settings from public, business, and technology events, to a handful of celebrity, social, and promotional venues, in different cities and countries around the world. Many pictures were from the press, while others were evidently taken covertly.

"He's been at all the right places, with all the right people; the German car expo last fall, with his new hydrogen car, followed by COP23. In January, it was CES and Sundance, February was the annual MilkBar Developer Shake-Shack, and in April, the IOPs Nanotech and Gravitational Waves event. It's Vegas Tech Summit this month, and in June, Apple's WWDC, where he's rumoured to be making a personal appearance. July it's StartUp 24, and another round of White House national arts and science fundraisers—he's attended two already this year. And that's without all the usual hospital tours, special-needs appeals— including his own educational trust—Marvel event premiers, and a Taylor Swift promotional jaunt down in Sydney—"

"It's frankly astounding he has any time to run a goddamn business."

"Two notable absences in his schedule...based on comms we were able to intercept from his offices. Official word is that he was taking time out at his Alaskan retreat."

"Alaskan retreat! These guys kill me. Do we buy it?"

"We checked, of course. Everyone played nice. His private

plane logged flight plans with the FAA, even made the actual trip to Alaska and back, as per schedule. The plane was met by a limo, which we tracked to his prime location. All good. Except we can't be certain he was actually on the plane. Someone was definitely picked up, yes. But no eyes on the ground."

"Plus, he has more than one plane, right?"

"Right. He has three company-owned jets at his disposal, notwithstanding the experimental electric HTOL vehicles built out of his facility near Barstow, which—if rumours are to be believed—he apparently borrows from time to time without warning, or any paperwork we can trace. The other two jets appeared to remain in their registered hangars. One based in NYC. The other in Phoenix."

"And that's all you got?"

"Yes and no. As I say, sir, official word is he's in Alaska the whole time. But we also picked up a rogue locality spike in the comms chatter...could be an anomaly as servers switched from one orbital cell location to another. We sometimes see that in satellite-based internet, such as private planes...or he really was in California."

Snark stared up at the screen. Of course he was in California. He had to be.

"We need to lock this down, Frankie. We need to do it today. This afternoon. Now. We have—what—eight hours till we pull the trigger on this thing? If Milk gets out in front of the great experiment, that's seven decades of work down the toilet."

"Nine years, sir. Technically speaking."

"OK, nine years. I'll give you that. But that's after waiting around for sixty years with our dicks in our hands, for someone to figure all this shit out. Pardon my French. But that's still nine years too many to throw away on this joker. Billionaire or not. Where is he now?"

"He's on a press junket, in London. Meeting with the BBC, we believe. For an in-depth—"

"Of course he is," grouched Snark, dismissively.

Carson clicked the remote and continued the briefing.

"More troubling, though, is that we've also seen significant, and highly irregular activity at one of his private start-ups in the valley—Particulonica."

"Oh?"

"Our data began to indicate an unusual spate of hires, to start with. Then mobile comms and data infrastructure tripled. Followed by construction crews in and out the past ten months, and a substantial, rapid expansion of the facility, if local planning applications are anything to go by."

"OK, so another Milk business is a runaway success. Whoop-de-do."

"Indeed, sir. No surprises. And we would have chalked it up the same way, except for one thing."

She clicked the remote. The screen switched to a satellite view of Milk's facility, overlaid with what looked like a heat map. A small, single area to the right was bleached out. The onscreen graph indicated a corresponding spike of high-intensity activity.

"Which is?"

"Six days ago, this site started drawing increasing amounts of power off the grid at unprecedented levels."

"For such a small tech business?"

"For any business. Power consumption was off the charts. Power company had to put in emergency measures to stop it browning out the whole valley. Then it abruptly stopped."

"Stopped?"

"Stopped. Went completely dark, electrically speaking, as of forty-eight hours ago."

"For Christ's sake, Carson. Why the hell am I only hearing about this now? We need to swamp that place. Get in there and shut it down now!"

"Already did, sir. Teams went in six hours ago, while you were still in transit. The preliminary reports came in only a short while ago."

"And!?"

"And nothing. The site was dead. Completely empty. The facility was closed up like new, and already up for lease. We checked out the California business register. Milk, or Milk's lawyers anyway, officially closed the company eighteen hours ago. Filed for closure with the state. Set up residual benefits for a small number of actual employees—everyone else contacted in—but all of whom are either administrative only, with little to no understanding of the business, or subject to an ironclad NDA. And I mean Supreme Court-proof ironclad. They even put on a fire sale to get rid of all the office furniture which, by the way, was immediately acquired in one hit by another company. The whole nine yards. We're still looking into—"

"Don't tell me. Milk bought his own lunch."

"Looks that way. We anticipate the usual string of shell corporations, but we're north of 80 percent certain Milk is just relocating the facility. We're still digging.

"In any case, our teams broke into the site, and cleared the entire building, including a couple of basement areas and a single, apparently huge, sub-basement containing the scattered remains of some kind of technical installation."

"What kind of installation?"

"Pure speculation at this point: anything from a large data farm to a buckyball machine for all we know, but most likely something far more specialised and industrial if the leftover concrete infrastructure is anything to go by. Otherwise, the entire place is complete empty."

"Christ Almighty."

"We think he's readying a new operation, sir."

"Oh, you think?" Snark got up from his seat and marched over to his desk, grabbed one of his phones, and began punching out a number "Or we just missed the main event. Like a bunch of goddamn amateurs. Get everyone in here."

"Sir—"

"Now," he barked.

8

JORDAN MILK

Alexandra Loam, former *BBC Newsnight slugger* and present-day eponymous host and showrunner for one of the broadcaster's prime current affairs programmes, *Loam On Point*, flipped through the running order of the day's show, from the comfort of her customised, leather makeup chair. She insisted on leather as she was supposedly allergic to synthetic fibres, and refused to risk an attack of hives, or worse, before stepping out live into her self-proclaimed television crucible (she was once overheard to have told the *BBC's* Head of Current Affairs that "They burnt witches in search of the truth. We must do no less for the hypocrisy, duplicity, and utterly shallow self-absorption of our times!" right before demanding that they name the show after her).

"Where the hell is Linda?" barked Loam, as Saira, Linda's stand-in, gently dabbed and prodded at her mottled brow.

"She's on maternity leave, Alex," Saira patiently replied. "She left three weeks ago."

"Babies again. Why doesn't anyone tell me anything around here?"

"We had a leaving party for her," said Saira, pausing briefly to look directly at Loam in the large mirror they shared. "You gave her a cake."

Loam immediately returned to her notes.

"Of course I did. That woman has kept this media-busting face pristine for over fifteen years."

Saira remained unmoved by this declaration, and returned to smoothing out the complexion of Loam's media-busting face. As a prime time television makeup artist, she had heard it all.

"What's your name again—Sarah?" Loam asked, without looking up.

"Saira."

"Sarah?"

"No, Alex." This wasn't the first time she'd had this conversation either. "It's Saira. *S-a-i-r-a*. It's spelt *and* pronounced quite differently."

Loam continued scribbling small, spidery notations in the margin of her script. "Hrmph. Sounds the same to me, to be quite honest with you."

"Well, then I can't help you, I'm afraid," replied Saira, just as the floor manager stuck his head into the room.

"Ten minutes, Alex," he said.

"Got it," responded Loam automatically, looking up at Saira in the mirror. "Are we done?"

Saira smiled benignly and carefully tugged the protective tissues away from Loam's sharp blouse-collar before stepping back. "We are now."

Loam stood up from the chair and appraised herself in the mirror, curtly adjusting her head left and right, then craning it back to get a better view of her leathery neck.

"Perfect," she announced, bushing down her crisp shirt, and yanking the open knot of her brightly coloured vogue tie to a suitably jaunty angle.

Saira began to tidy her station, reuniting lids to pots and tubes of various balms, ordering things into neat rows, popping brushes back into her rollup case.

Loam spun about and headed straight out of the room, grabbing her tailored jacket from a hanger by the door as she passed. "Thank you, Sarah," she bellowed from the hallway and, slinging the jacket over her shoulder, marched off without missing a step.

Loam strode purposefully down the corridor, past various production offices, and out into a large open-plan space, perhaps half-full of people staring intently at their monitors, making notes, or yammering into their phones. Everyone else, she knew, would be on the studio floor by now, gearing up for the show. A few of the staff looked up, briefly, as she passed through, and Loam responded with a stiff nod, before taking a sharp left at the far end, and heading through the final windowed walkway towards the studio complex.

The corridor overlooked a large car park immediately below, spreading out to the borders of the ruddy parkland next door. In the distance, she observed a flock of birds taking flight from behind a knotted hedgerow and ascending in near perfect formation. *Just as it should be,* Loam thought.

Up ahead, she could see a cluster of production staff milling about energetically, headphones on, clipboards and smartphones in hand, to ensure they were primed, and in constant touch with the AV gallery, should their master, the producer, issue a command. A young production staffer broke away from the pack, and approached Loam directly with Loam's bespoke earpiece and radio mike in hand, ready for fitting.

This brought Loam to a halt just outside the green room, which she found immensely irritating. She didn't like to be randomly observed by her guests. As a rule, she would typically provide only a brief, cursory greeting to her inevitably famous guests, and usually only upon their arrival (her PA was tasked with ensuring Loam could always be stumbled upon doing something *producery*, and important-looking, as guests were escorted into the building). After that, she had decided a long time ago, they were on their own. Regardless of celebrity, influence, or wealth, she liked to maintain what she saw as a vital separation of church and state.

Today was no exception. Despite any grudging admiration she may secretly harbour, Loam held firm, and consciously avoided glancing into the room, refusing any kind of foretaste or gesture in the direction of the day's principal guest, Jordan Milk. *We'll see each other soon enough,* she thought, with some satisfaction. *And on my terms.*

The assistant fumbled and fussed as she attempted to separate out the cables and small boxes in her hands, looking and feeling a little embarrassed. Loam maintained her gaze into the distance, impatiently waiting for the task to finish.

"I, uhm, I have—" murmured the assistant, unsure of the protocol, and hesitating to place the small clip-mike on Loam's tie.

"Just clip it on," demanded Loam, briskly. "I don't bite."

Milk, meanwhile, looked up from his oversized phone and observed Loam through gaps in the slatted design etched onto the glass wall. She was receiving her finishing touches, and conspicuously ignoring her guests at the same time. It amused Milk to watch this microdrama unfurl. And, as he leaned back casually into the plump guest couch and took a sip of his apple-kuzu macrobiotic smoothie, he found he was neither surprised nor particularly bothered by it. *Some people just need a lot of theatre,* he thought. Particularly the ones who would be most horrified at the suggestion. Loam was textbook.

His gaze switched to Annie, his personal aide and, generally less-talked-about, bodyguard, to see what she made of Loam's little performance. But Annie was too busy typing things into her iPad to notice. Probably doing something for him, he realised, but even so, did she have to be so damn focused all the time? He immediately regretted the thought, as he was reminded of her generally unwavering commitment to him. He made a mental note to give her some extra time off while they were in London. Bodyguard or not, she didn't really need to babysit him 24/7.

Despite being a man of exceptional wealth, and increasingly significant influence, he never really felt he needed a bodyguard —after all, he was hardly George Clooney. Or even Arik Runyon, for that matter. God forbid. But neither was he completely without unwanted attention.

After twenty years of being seen as the so-called "founding genius" of MilkBar, a social-media iconoclast, industrialist, and digital doyen of Silicon Valley, Milk understood there were certain commercial, industrial, and, increasingly, celebrity obligations that seemed to come with the territory. Less tolerable, however, was the slavish, unasked-for devotion of strangers, overeager hangers-on, and, yes, even the occasional threats, real or not, that also seemed to trail after him. He had therefore come to feel that if he was going to drag an entourage of any sort around with him, they may as well be useful in a tight spot.

For many of the same reasons, Milk had long since become accustomed to the idea that people simply reacted weirdly around him. Or, at least, reacted to perceptions of him, his smarts, his absurd wealth, and his dubious celebrity status. And celebrated interviewers were not immune, it would seem, even if they were more accustomed to masking the effects.

He understood the reaction but only up to a point. After all, he was, at least in his own mind, just a nerd. A simple geek. A once-pasty teenager who had stayed home more than he should have, immersed in comic books and science fiction novels and who basically loved technology. But that was all such a long time ago. And he'd been very, very lucky since. He knew that much.

His love of ideas and possibilities had paid off enormously in ways he could never have imagined or predicted. And people wanted to be part of that success, to build on it, learn from it, enjoy it and even, inevitably, steal from it.

He thought of his most recent public litigation with Runyon's mob, as they once again tried to railroad a giant bucket of government money in their favour, based off the IP that Arik Runyon had pretty much ripped off wholesale from one of Milk's own technology spin-offs. Standard practise for that guy, reflected Milk. Why put the effort in when you can just buy or steal your way ahead? He'd always been that way, as far as Milk could tell, spending his father's money like candy, to strong-arm his way into whatever business took his fancy. He wouldn't be surprised if Runyon had lawsuits trailing all the way back to kindergarten.

For Milk himself, he didn't care so much about the money. It had never been a goal, or a weapon to use against others once he had it. For him, the only interesting thing about money was the freedom it provided to pursue his own ideas, and an increasingly ambitious agenda. But, of course, other people did care. Some of them just couldn't get past it.

Sure, Milk enjoyed a few of the trappings that came with it; a great place to live, good food, easy travel. He wasn't a monk. But he never wanted to be defined by it. To Milk, that was all just *stuff*. And he'd seen it distort too many friends and colleagues over the years to misunderstand the real cost that immense wealth brought with it. Whether it was his own, very singular fortune, or that of his friends (which in more than a few cases, he'd helped them to make). For some, it had just been too much. Sheer abundance, combined with a waning focus had destroyed them.

This had been a stark lesson when, early on, Beth Feynman, one of his best friends and early collaborators from college, rapidly descended into drug addiction and chaos after the sale of their first modest company, selling customised graphics cards to the booming PC gaming market. When, ten months later, Beth had been found dead in her apartment, Milk decided it was time to double down and use his newfound wealth to create his own purpose—and help others with theirs.

He registered MilkBar the very next day—named for an in-joke between him and his dead friend about sharing a milkshake

—without any real idea of what he was going to do with it. Then, on a passing whim, he spent the next five years turning it into one of the largest social and digital media platforms in the world.

Over time he had come to understand how this unique mixture of bleeding-edge technology, design, and business success, combined with an absolutely ridiculous and ever-increasing wealth, created an insane perception barrier between who he was—or thought he was, anyway—and who people imagined, wanted, even needed, him to be. Beyond any kind of lifestyle considerations, he quickly realised it gave him an incredible amount of freedom. And he took it.

Milk's phone began to chime. His fellow guests—an up-and-coming British TV actor, hot off a hugely popular police procedural (Milk had no idea who or what, but they'd chatted affably enough when he arrived and gleaned that he was portraying a "...bent copper with a disabled daughter, and a nasty drug habit") and a journalist from *The Times*, with a new political assassination to sell—both unconsciously paused from their previously polite exchange to watch him answer it. Perhaps they thought they would catch a glimpse of what the billionaire had next in store for the world.

"Milk," he barked, unceremoniously.

Annie looked up from her typing. She immediately noted the spike in his tone. It obviously wasn't a random check-in from his girlfriend. Milk nodded almost imperceptibly at her. And, in turn, her eyes flicked briefly across the room, to deliver her own magic stare and send the other guests' curiosity into retreat.

Milk stood up slowly, then wandered over to the window.

"Yes," he could be heard saying. "I'm doing the BBC thing now. It doesn't matter. Tell me."

His immaculate but casually dressed frame filled the window in silhouette, cutting a broad, graciously poised model-like shape against the shimmering spring light. It was no secret that he worked out, but the truth about his age-unfeasible full head of thick, elegantly silvering hair? If he'd had any work done, nobody was spilling the beans. Both the actor and journalist had fallen back into their own phone-based activity but were clearly still earwigging for clues. Milk didn't provide any.

"What time?" demanded Milk, loudly. He reflexively glanced at his wristwatch. "Did they find anything? Good. Make sure of it. Keep Annie in the loop. But I want to know immediately if anything shifts from plan."

Milk closed the call, then thumbed his way through a number of on-screen tasks, as Annie appeared at his side. He mumbled some instructions. She muttered in reply, nodding patiently, as the door to the green room suddenly swung wide open. Everyone immediately stopped and turned their attention to see what was happening. It was Theresa, Loam's assistant.

"Hi, everyone," she said, enthusiastically, although it was clear from her gaze and body language that her remarks were focused almost exclusively in Milk's direction. "I hope you've all been suitably taken care of. As you can see"—she gestured towards the wall-mounted screen monitoring the live feed from the studio—"Alex is just about to kick off the show. Barring any disruption, schedule remains locked. Joel, you'll be up in five minutes. Sybil, fifteen. Mr Milk, we'll see you at the top of the hour. I will come by to collect you personally."

"That's great. Thank you so much, Theresa," responded Milk, in his more typical mellifluous Californian tone. He had an uncanny gift for remembering everyone's names. "But that's really not necessary. I'm happy to work with your production team in the usual way. And please, call me Jordan."

He let his heartbreaking smile off the lead, and Theresa visibly reacted to the onslaught of surefooted American handsomeness, before instantly checking herself.

"Wonderful. Of course, *Jordan*. My pleasure," she purred, then turned and left the room in much the same way she had entered.

"OK, five minutes everyone!" she could be heard bellowing, in her backstage, ass-kicking voice, as she walked away. "Five minutes!"

The green room door glided to a soft *clump* behind her.

9

DAYDREAM BELIEVING

Leon stared out of the long rectangular window that ran along one complete side of the meeting room, cutting precisely into the distressed brickwork like an insanely oversized letterbox.

Derek was up at the front of the room, gyrating his arms in a studied *wax on, wax off* motion, presenting some industry research about the impact of *social media-based narratives* on the consumption of a bird-branded cosmetic moisturising product. As was often the case, he was sashaying back and forth to some unheard rhythm of his own, in an attempt to generate an impression of purpose. At the table, various members of the client party nodded their heads, as though to signify some agreement with whatever Derek was banging on about. A couple of them even took notes.

Outside, on the far side of the road, an array of different kinds of buildings, from different periods of the past century, could be seen elegantly framed against the steel-edged window. The most dominant of these were the upper floors of a midrange corporate hotel chain, and evidently a more recent addition to London's living museum of architecture. Perhaps only ten or fifteen years old, at least by Leon's relatively made-up assessment. If nothing else, it was more contemporary and, in its apparent modern cheapness, uglier than any of the reconfigured Edwardian ware-houses on either side. Or, for that matter, the one he was sitting in. But then again, he thought, can any of it really be considered authentic when, like the proverbial broom, much of the area was bombed and then rebuilt after the war?

It often struck Leon as surprising how many of the hotel rooms were fully exposed to scrutiny, with little to no obvious measures taken to protect the privacy of their occupants. Each faintly tinted window a proscenium into the ever-changing lives beyond. The top three floors even had notional Juliet balconies, although these were at best symbolic since, like so many modern air-conditioned structures, the windows themselves looked firmly unopenable.

Whenever Leon found himself in this meeting room (Mercury, for anyone keeping track), with this particular view, it wouldn't take him very long to begin peering voyeuristically across the street, in search of some vague glimpse of the forbidden. What-ever that was, he wasn't exactly sure. Just a nagging urge that he should look. For some ill-defined Hitchcockian moment, perhaps. Two strangers arguing bitterly over a mistaken identity, just before one of them seizes an ornament and takes it too far. Or maybe a Bond-like encounter, where the super spy observes a nefarious deal going down, moments before somebody gets blown away by an unseen sniper, propelling Bond into action. Or a naked person. It often just came down to that: the remote, implausible prospect that he might see a naked woman. After all, what else would people be doing in a hotel room in the middle of the day? But, of course, he had never really seen anything.

A handful of times he had glimpsed the maid service, making some adjustment behind the glass, or looming briefly into view during a feverish hoovering moment. Just twice in his three years at Hyperion had he seen a real, bona fide guest at the window. One was talking on her phone and idly resting a hand flat against the glass, while remaining disappointingly fully clothed. The other, a man, also dressed, appeared to just stare blankly out into the street, right before using the interior reflection to adjust his tie. It was hardly *Rear Window*.

A client suddenly began talking vigorously in response to an on-screen Venn diagram that described a make-believe ratio between story-based advertising and value-driven communications, dragging Leon's attention back into the room.

He leaned in, trying to pick up the thread of what was being discussed and see if there was an opportunity to speak up. To say something. To make at least one contribution to the session, and by doing so, go some way to justifying his professional existence. But his mind soon began to wander off again, as Derek sprang back to life, and it rapidly became clear this would just be one of those mutually assuring exchanges of industry girth, between the two most senior people in the room. Even if he'd been able to muster some rare interest in the day's topic, experience had taught Leon that this type of verbal trade had little to do with the meeting itself, and was generally best left to the grown-ups.

Instead, his attention drifted back towards the large, abstracted astronomy-based images and decals that adorned various parts of the room. On the end wall, opposite the projection screen, was an elegant arrangement of nine small black-framed photographs featuring, Leon knew, from numerous prior examinations, the gradual approach to the planet Mercury; a smudgy white dot at one end and, at the other, a geo-orbital view of cracked rocks and craters that he assumed to be the surface of the planet.

Behind these frames, on the wall itself, was a hugely exaggerated, highly stylised single-colour graphical representation of the solar system, with Mercury's position in highlight, supported by a spidery network of lines, each pointing to a random number of technical facts and statistics, for anyone who cared to look. All the meeting rooms were like this, with each eponymous planet receiving a similar visual treatment. And throughout Leon's tenure at Hyperion, particularly in those early weeks and months on the job, he had cared a great deal to look.

It was during that nascent period, when he was still very much absorbed with the idea that the agency held some as yet undiscussed purpose, that he had taken the time to catalogue the images and facts presented in each room, and cross-reference them with more official sources of information. Just in case. And as absurd as he realised this was, fact-checking was something he felt he could actually do. Best-case, he thought at the time, he could just shut up thinking about it. It didn't particularly help.

Yes, there were some odd factual anomalies that he tried hard to attribute to something grander but in reality, it was nothing more than he would have reasonably expected from lazy research or, more likely, a rushed design and print job. But despite that, his doubts lingered.

When he'd first noticed these curiosities, during those first months, he had immediately told his ex-wife, Alice. She wasn't his ex-wife then but it's possible this, among several other competing issues, may have been what his counsellor would later come to refer to as a "contributing factor" to her subsequent change of marital status. That and her affair with their former mutual friend, Sarah.

Leon would later claim in these sessions that he always liked —still liked—Sarah, and that if he was ever going to pick a gay lover for his wife then she would definitely be the one. Female, smart, fit, independent, mostly nonsmoking, employed, own car, into music, food, animals and country walks (not necessarily in that order). Enjoys travelling, and other women, especially the married ones. GSOH.

But since he didn't get to pick, didn't even know there was any picking to be done, he found the whole experience of finding Alice with another woman both a bit of a shock, and so much less exciting than many years of largely male conversations had led him to expect. He fleetingly considered the grounds for a complaint, although was unable to decide exactly who in any real sense was in charge of socially reinforced Sapphic fantasies.

They tried to work it out for a while; an awkward weekend

away, making some overambitious plans for their home, dressing up (too ridiculous for either of them, it turned out. And too hot. All that cheap polyester just made them horribly sweaty, in a nasty red-faced type of way. Although Leon did wonder, later on, whether they should possibly have gone to somewhere more specialised than just going for whatever costume deals they could find on Amazon), art galleries, movies, date nights. Everything Alice's many books suggested, and some things they didn't. Towards the end of their attempt to reconcile, Alice eventually suggested, perhaps more out of a final, desperate courtesy than anything else, that perhaps they come to an *arrangement* that included her still seeing Sarah in some way but more openly. Leon actually gave it some thought. On balance, though, he felt that if he was really going to have a wife then probably best it was one that preferred men in general, and him in particular.

"You know, I think there's something really odd going on at work," he had said, returning home late one evening during his first trimester at the agency.

"You always think there's something odd going on, sweetheart. Especially at work," Alice replied, lifting her head absently from the paperwork spread out loosely on the small kitchen table-for-two.

"Not true!" he blurted, defensively. "OK, yes, true. But this is different."

"Is it? Is it really? You've barely been there—what, three? Four months? You're still settling in. Getting into the rhythm of the place."

"OK, maybe. Maybe it's that too. But, listen, that meeting room on the seventh floor I told you about. The one that never works."

"Aren't they all on seventh floor?"

"Yes. Yes, all the meeting rooms are on the seventh floor. All the main ones."

"And named after planets. You told me this already," Alice responded, reaching for her glass of wine, and sitting back in her chair.

Leon was starting to become impatient. Was Alice deliberately trying to annoy him with her seemingly incessant recollection of detail, he wondered, or just accidentally? Or was this just her way of demonstrating how one person should listen to another person? Properly, that is. She had a tendency to do this—to try things out on him without any kind of warning. She read far too many self-improvement books and magazine articles, in his view. She would leave them in the bathroom, to be read by who, he was never entirely sure. It unsettled him, and he would remove them over a period of weeks, swapping them for design magazines that he'd nick from work. Only for the pile to be randomly refreshed when he went out or took a nap.

It seemed to Leon that Alice had always been in search of a better, different way of being herself than the—he thought—perfectly lovely self she'd cultivated relatively unaided in the first twenty-eight years of her life. As a result, he eventually became suspicious of her giving him secret lessons in How to Be a Better Person.

"I did," he said. "That's correct. The whole solar system."

"Including—"

"Yes! Including everything," he snapped. "But listen, today I started cataloguing the photographs, and the infographics in all of the—"

"You did what!?"

Leon started fishing about in his work backpack. "I started cataloguing photographs and—"

"Leon."

"Infographics in all of the meeting rooms, as well as the large ones framed in the foyer, by the lifts." Out came a sheaf of papers and his laptop. "Take a look at—"

"Leon."

"My initial findings." Leon started laying out his scraps of paper and spidery diagrams onto the coffee table in front of them.

"Leon!"

He looked up. Derek was staring at him expectantly, joined by the three clients, who all turned to look at him. While his colleague, Kara, stood patiently by the whiteboard, pen in hand, poised to capture Leon's thoughts, even as he struggled to find them. The clock ticked. A mouse raced along the base of the far wall.

"Uhm. Yes, Derek?" croaked Leon, finally.

It wasn't very long after that conversation with Alice that he broadly lost his passion for these anomalies, and instead became preoccupied with divorcing his newly gay wife, in some kind of amicable, pain-resistant way, and refocussing on work.

Derek joined Kara by the hungry, empty whiteboard.

"I thought perhaps you could take Bashir and Nadine through your *customer journey assessment* for the new Just Take a Bath Alliance strategy. The Journey to Cleanliness, you might say," he said, aping one of his oft-noted heroes, Dr Kellogg. Everyone chuckled shabbily. Except for Leon who, even if he were not scrambling to find his bearings, typically found Derek's near-constant wordplays to be something of an endurance test.

Leon glanced at the screen in search of help. But all he found there was a colourful research slide of the statistical outcomes for the top ten global bath manufacturers, over the previous twelve months. Some brands were up. Others were down. Two led the pack because of one significant differentiator, exemplified by a natty little cartoon graphic in the legend—their extreme focus on customers' bathing needs.

"Yes, thank you, Derek," said Leon, regaining a little of his fake composure. "I would be happy to. If we could just move to the next slide?"

Leon moved towards the front of the room hoping for the best, as Derek stepped back. The screen transitioned to a photographic montage of Post-it notes on a wall, with notes and arrows, and a person facilitating an off-screen audience, titled: Moving Beyond the Bath-Washing Experience.

. . .

Meanwhile, on the western edge of town, in a BBC television studio, Jordan Milk reclined comfortably in his chair, and took a casual sip from a tall, iced-filled water glass, as a VT playback on developments in artificial intelligence in the media wrapped, and Alexandra Loam gathered herself back to camera.

"Thank you, Sheena Reynolds," began Loam, acknowledging the video presenter, as though she was right across the room. "Clearly the debate about who's really got the smarts isn't going anywhere, anytime soon. If you ask me, it's still humans one, robots zero. Unless, of course, you're Garry Kasparov," she declared with a wink, referring to the former world chess champion.

"As ever, if you have been personally affected by any the issues discussed, don't forget to leave your comment below, as they say; you can email us at Loam On Point, send us a Tweet—are we still calling it that?—on X, or even give us a quick *shake* on MilkBar. Hashtag *loam-on-point*. Who knows, we might even read some of them," chuckled Loam darkly, before shuffling her papers and turning back to camera two for her close-up.

"And speaking of reading everyone's messages; it gives me enormous pleasure to introduce today's hotspot guest. Digital guru, business visionary, space innovator, SETI sponsor, and billionaire global media darling, the Milkshake man himself: Jordan Milk!

"Whatever your views may be on the man *Time* magazine recently named, 'Business Rear of the Year'—for the second time —you can be sure his busy algorithms have already anticipated, analysed, filed, and classified them, before folding them neatly back into the evolving space-time continuum of his global digital platform, *MilkBar*!"

Loam pivoted back towards her guest, as the camera cut to a wide two-shot.

"So, Jordan. AI? Data farming? Robots and space rockets? SETI? What's really going on here? Are you just ET trying to phone home, or is it simply all about the money?"

They both chuckled, even though this wasn't the first time Milk had heard this joke.

"Well, Alex, I think it's fair to say that nothing's ever *just* about the money."

"Easy for a billionaire to say, perhaps. But what if we asked the many, many low-paid factory workers you employ across the world?" snapped Loam, with a sudden ferocity. A lizard smile spread like oil across her face. Internally she high-fived herself. Loam, one—Milk, zero.

"Whether I'm really an alien? They would be the first to tell you, I would think," countered Milk, with a warm, disarming smile. Smooth as butter.

"Seriously, though, Jordan Milk," continued Loam, sharpening her knife. "You are among the wealthiest people on the planet. You indulge your interests, and your considerable finances on a multitude of—some would say—fantasy projects, while the majority of your workforce is living on nothing better than subsistence pay."

"Let me stop you there, if I may, Alex," responded Milk, unrattled by Loam's classic honey trap. "You may want to examine the facts a little more closely. Yes, the tech industry—despite the promise and improvements it brings for many of us—has been an environmental and socio-economic disaster for some parts of the world. And although we're far from the centre of that story, I'm still not happy about that legacy, or our indirect association with it."

"Indirect, Jordan? Really?"

"OK, nobody in technology is winning awards right now for their retail and manufacturing...social impact. But let me assure you that MilkBar takes every reasonable step—and then some— to specifically enrich and support the lives and ambitions of its employees across the—"

"Forgive me," interrupted Loam, smugly, once again. "But aren't you just singing from the usual corporate social responsibly hymn sheet?"

"If I can finish...?" Milk shifted forward in his seat, adopting a more intimate, animated manner. "MilkBar takes every step to enrich and support the lives and ambitions of its employees across the *world*—that doesn't just mean toeing the line on the CSR agenda.

"First, let me make it perfectly clear: we don't go anywhere we're not invited. We don't set up shop anywhere on Earth without, first, an extensive consultation with the communities we are planning to work with. Basically, if they don't want us—if we're not invited to the party—we don't come. Second, perhaps more significantly, we exceed minimum wage by on average more than 30 percent in every market we're in. In many cases the percentage is much higher."

Loam now leaned forward herself but in a pointed, interrogative position.

"Some might say that's just tossing money around for show. For political grease. For tax breaks, and a seat at the global business table. What about real sustainability for these communities you claim to serve? What do you say about the impact of automation, AI, and the resulting attrition of talent, the huge volumes of staff turnover we see in those sectors?"

"I say great. You know, I actually don't want people to work in my factories their whole lives, or to fracture and monopolise local employment opportunities. We're not supposed to be creating Victorian mass production 2.0 here.

"That's why we maintain a commitment to provide free access to long-term education and upskilling for every employee after they've been with us for six months or more.

"And you know what? If they want to take that education, and use it to move on or help make other changes in their lives to benefit their families and the communities they live in, I say more power to them. Good luck!

"The reality is, Alex, that many of them choose to stay. Our attrition rate is some 47 percent lower than industry averages, particularly for those regions with a high manufacturing base. And it's improving all the time.

"You know, for all of us at MilkBar, if we're not creating a better future for everyone, then it's not really a better future for anyone."

Of course, much of Milk's reputation in this area—on paper anyway—was public record. And Loam knew this. She'd done her homework. But she wanted to see just how much of it was plain old marketing whitewash and, more importantly, how much he personally knew about what was going on down in the weeds of his giga-corporation. She was grudgingly impressed, she had to admit. For a so-called billionaire playboy, he seemed unusually connected to the facts. And while part of that was just his shtick, it was clear Loam wouldn't get to trip him on this one. There's no upside, she had confirmed, in trying to prove his company's well-documented social agenda was a sham. She needed to get personal. Time to throw little mud around.

"So, let's talk about Bryson Hawke, for a moment."

"Bryson Hawke," responded Milk, with a slight twitch of the head so subtle that if Loam didn't know any better, she'd swear he was actually caught by surprise. "I can just see the hashtag explosion as we speak. What's on your mind, Alex?"

"We've received evidence that Hawke is consulting directly with one of your business interests—"

"Evidence? Last I checked, employing someone is not a crime, nor so far as I know is Mr Hawke a criminal."

"So, you admit he's on your payroll?"

"Evidence. Admit... Your line of questioning has taken a curious turn, Alex. I don't *admit* anything. I have a number of diverse businesses, in addition to MilkBar, yes. All of which, for the most part, maintain complete autonomy in how they run and who they hire. Contrary to what you may have read on *X*, I'm not a *complete* control freak." He smiled generously. "What I will say is we advocate for— that is, I advocate for—creativity, collaboration, and unconventional thinking wherever possible. Most especially in my business interests, as you put it. And while I don't know Bryson Hawke personally, his reputation for the, shall we say, unconventional is well documented."

"To put it mildly," interjected Loam, scornfully. "A man who maintains that he once worked at Groom Lake—a classified US military complex often referred to as Area 51—on alien technology? A man who has been publicly discredited by the same US government, no less, and by several of the notable education establishments he claims to have received medical and scientific training from.

"A so-called cult media personality, who has managed to operate on the fringes of the scientific community for decades, peddling unsubstantiated tinpot theories on everything from government-sponsored UFO programmes, to allegedly undiscovered elements that threaten to both free humanity and undermine the economic world order at the same time. What do you say to that?"

"I say he sounds like a man in need of a steady job," chuckled Milk, warmly.

This was echoed by laughter from his fellow guests, and others in the studio. Even Loam was hard-pressed to hide her amusement completely.

"If what you say is true, Alex, then I'm glad we could help him out."

Despite her mild enjoyment of their sparring, Loam remained frustrated that Milk had kept her so decisively at arm's length. He knew how to play the game better than she had anticipated, and his reputation was well deserved. But chatter from the production gallery urged her to move on—their time together was almost up. One last pitch, then.

"Your private space programme, Jordan. And these plans for Mars that you keep posting about. Some might say that these are just pipe dreams. Science fiction stories that, if nothing else, bleed huge resources away from your more philanthropic enterprises— such as those we've touched upon already today."

"An interesting deviation, Alex," responded Milk, without hesitation, or any sign of discomfort in the sudden changing tides. "But let me take your question at face value anyway," he continued, with a lavish grin.

"Plainly speaking, commercial space tech is a boom industry. In addition to AI, data, biotech applications—"

"Also, all part of your menagerie," added Loam.

"It's this century's gold rush. And yes, also some of my... hobbies, let's say. But, you know, it's all related. You can't just fly up to space on those giant throw-away missiles anymore. Huge up front investment, yes. Gigantic. But unlike fifty years ago, there are a lot of paying customers already lining up around the block, just waiting to jump in. And a global community, hammered by recession, social division, and growing isolationism. A community that's forgotten how we—"

"So, it is all about the money, then?" hacked Loam, attempting to make a dent in his soapbox. This really wasn't going the direction she had planned. "How much does any one person really need, Jordan?"

"Nice try," he responded. "But let's be realistic here. The world does not turn on good intentions alone. We can't all go back to being farmers, and doing the flower dance on the weekends— even if anyone really wanted that. The fact is, whoever moves the dial on this not only stands to do well commercially but, more importantly, I think, has the opportunity—I would even say the *responsibility*—to elevate the bar for everyone else.

"Look, I'm an optimist at heart. Money in this case is just a means to an end, and I'm only interested in doing this if it creates meaningful change and opportunity for everyone—otherwise why do it at all? All the profit, after running costs, will get reinvested for the same reason. I won't personally be taking a dime."

"I hope your investors and shareholders feel the same way you do," said Loam, in a last-ditch attempt to sour the Kool-Aid.

"Sharing is the principle that MilkBar was founded on, Alex," responded Milk, ignoring her attempt at corporate call to arms.

"And, ultimately, sharing is the only way we move society forward —the only way we have ever moved forward. That doesn't mean everyone will get a free car, and a golden ticket to space, or even that everyone will want one—at least not in the next thirty years. But just like the aviation, telco, and digital industries we have today, it does mean a new way of thinking about how we live and connect, our global society, and what it takes to build a future that everyone—*everyone*—on the planet can benefit from."

10

SPILT MILK

"As of right now," declared Linden Snark, "Jordan Milk represents the single greatest threat to this country since the Bay of Pigs." He'd been barking at his audience for ten minutes straight, and the hyperbole was just beginning to peak. "Now listen up, beautiful people—"

Snark stood in front of his huge desk, shirt sleeves rolled up, pen in one hand, the other in his pocket. Behind him, in the mission space beyond the glass wall, technicians could be seen zipping around like worker bees, switching between different consoles, calibrating settings on their workstations or gathering in small groups to presumably review their tasks. A couple of military folks, caps held tight under their arms, could be seen exiting an elevator on the far side of the deck and striding purposefully across the wide floor.

The rest of Snark's office was filled with henchmen. And henchwomen, of course (no one could say he didn't run a diverse organisation. Secret or not, this was still a government entity). Plus an eclectic mix of department heads and key personnel, including analysts, hackers, field agents, tech specialists, data scientists, operational planners, finance specialists, translators, and basic but exceptionally trained *muscle*.

Many of them were barely old enough to really get what he meant by the Bay of Pigs, but no one was about to let on. They simply looked on impassively or nodded sagaciously into the middle distance, waiting for the tirade to end and the orders to begin. But the mood remained restless and intense. Nobody liked being called into Snark's office, much less being on the receiving end of one his infamous *beautiful people* briefings. He rarely called them, but when he did it usually guaranteed that the stakes were higher than anyone would admit, and nobody would be getting much sleep for the next twenty-four hours. Sometimes people died.

"You've all seen the briefing notes," he said, looking directly at Carson.

"Everyone's received the latest intel packs, sir," she confirmed, nodding curtly.

"Developments?"

"Nothing as yet."

Snark returned his attention to the room. "And you all know what's happening today. In approximately"—he looked at his watch—"eight hours from now, this nation stands to take the single biggest technological leap since we pretended to send men to the moon."

An audible, if confused, murmur crossed the room.

"The moon, sir?" inquired Carson, tentatively.

"Just a bit of levity, Carson. So, you can all calm the fuck down, while we figure out what exactly Jordan Milk is up to."

He liked to mix things up a bit, to ensure no one could ever be completely certain how to take him. And therefore were required, in his view, to pay extra attention to everything he said, just in case they missed something vital and got screwed for it later. It happened.

There were a few smiles, some of them forced. Some just confused. The noise settled down.

"Latest intelligence," continued Snark, "suggests Milk has been building an extensive counter operation of some kind. It's not clear what, exactly, except that he's been sucking the power grid dry the length and breadth of California. And, if our data analysis is correct, whatever he's doing appears to have an uncanny parallel with the timing of Project Helios. That can't just be a simple coincidence.

"Impossible, I hear you say. And normally I'd be the first to agree. But it's worse than that. Not only does he appear to know something our own president does *not* know, he has somehow had the foresight, time, and obviously the resources to do something about it. So, either we are the single worst intelligence operation in the history of the planet, or it's a goddamn miracle and we should all be getting down on our knees and praying."

On Snark's large, wall-mounted monitor, images, graphics and data scrolled past, building a fluid collage of events, activities, and timelines.

"However, since I don't believe in miracles," he went on, "or coincidences, I'm willing to bet real money someone—possibly even someone in this room—has been spoon-feeding him this little enterprise of ours. And I can promise you, if that's true, we'll find out. And whoever it is will wish to God they hadn't been born."

Snark paused briefly to see if anyone squirmed.

"Anyone care to step forward now and save us some time? It could cut you some slack when it comes to handing out the locked-up-for-treason gifts. Just like dogs, they ain't only for Christmas."

He struggled to believe that the leak could have come from this group, but he paused again anyway. In his experience, it never hurt to sweat the room. He'd been lucky before.

"No? Great. Then this is where you all get to keep your jobs, your families, and your country safe," he continued, through a thin-lipped smile. "I want to know who betrayed us, how long it's been going on, what've they shared and—most important—to whom. You have seven hours and"—he checked his watch again —"forty-two minutes. We need to get out in front of whatever

Milk is planning and stop him. I want updates every thirty minutes until one of you finds out what. Now get to work."

The meeting broke up, and everyone piled out of the room with urgency and purpose. Carson lingered as the last of the group headed out the door.

"Should we just bring him in?" she asked, cautiously.

"Milk? Oh, he'd just love that, wouldn't he?" responded Snark caustically.

"It doesn't have to be one of our teams, of course. We can always tool up one of the civilian agencies for us. You know it wouldn't be the first time. Given everything else we have on tonight, it might speed things up."

"Maybe so, Frankie, maybe so. But my gut tells me that's exactly what he expects to happen. He'll be prepared. You know it. I know it. He's nobody if not a man who prepares. Let's just try not to give him everything he wants all at once, eh? A man who lives like he does..."

"Understood, sir," said Carson, plainly, as she reached for the door. "I'll stay on point with the assets. See what we can turn up."

"Thank you, Frankie. I know you will. And alert Benedict lickety-split, will you? I need to get on the horn for a White House committee briefing. And not his team. Just him. At this point, I don't think we can trust anyone outside of the core group."

"Yes, sir."

Snark returned to his desk and began making a call, as Carson left the room, letting the door close quietly behind her.

In London, Jordan Milk was back at his Park Lane hotel suite, stretched out on a long couch. He was reviewing the rough cut of his interview with Loam on a laptop, before it aired later that evening. It was part of his deal. He had no editorial powers exactly but, given his reach, he always insisted on first sight of any official media coverage or no interview. So, while Milk couldn't demand any changes per se, his incredibly expensive but equally skilful legal team had a way of ensuring that his *suggestions* landed in just the right way.

Despite this arrangement, teaser clips had already begun showing up on the rolling news channels and the social media counterparts, including MilkBar. It was to be expected. And, in this case, he was mostly fine with how it had turned out. Pleased, at least, with his performance, insomuch as he had managed to blunt the bulk of Loam's sharpest knives, such as they were. Pre-emptive damage limitation, as Annie called it.

Although, he had to admit he was a little surprised they'd found out he'd been consulting with Bryson Hawke. Or perhaps he was only annoyed that they'd found out so quickly, even though he knew better. *After all,* he reflected, *we live at a time where everyone knows everything.* Something, as one of the so-called captains of Silicon Valley, he felt partly, and uncomfortably, culpable for. But then again, even if that were not the case, Hawke was hardly the most discreet man on the planet.

"You know, Bryson, I warned you this would happen," said Milk, across the room to Bryson Hawke who, at that moment, was making himself lavishly at home from a table of delicious-looking hand-crafted pastries, perfectly-cut miniature sandwiches, fruits and an oak platter, laden with a wafer-thin charcuterie selection. "I just didn't expect it to be quite so soon."

Hawke looked up, and made a brief if impenetrable sound of acknowledgement, his mouth clearly full, even as he reached for another cream-filled delicacy.

"This will mean a fresh round of scrutiny for you, of course. Aside from your usual government bloodhounds, you can expect the media will be back knocking at your door again, and looking through your trash. I can help keep a lid on the worst of it but—"

"Hey, man," said Hawke, clearing his throat, and attempting to swallow the remains of a raspberry *mille feuille*. "I get it. What rolls around, comes around."

Milk wasn't really sure what Hawke meant by this glib missive but let it go, as he watched him sink into a huge, well-upholstered armchair that made him look like a little boy.

Recovering from the sheer effort of sitting down, Hawke began to lick his fingers clean, like a lethargic cat. Whether or not he had really absorbed Milk's caution remained unclear. Nevertheless, he reached over to pick up a full wine glass from a tall lamp table next to him, and saluted Milk with it.

"Dude, I just can't get enough of this place," said Hawke, obliviously picking at a tooth with the pinkie of his left hand. "Do you got any more of that cookie dough?"

11

HULK'S TEETH

Tom slouched on one of the guest couches in reception. He'd clocked off early in anticipation of the evening's events but had overestimated timings, and other people's enthusiasm—particularly Leon's. Or, he figured, Leon's meeting was just running late, as usual. Any meeting hosted by Derek tended to overrun. There was just something about the man's incessant self-indulgence that could not, apparently, be contained in standard thirty- or sixty-minute blocks of time.

But, in any case, Tom found himself faffing around without much to do, and leafed through a couple of the latest industry publications, so beautifully fanned out across the small wooden coffee table, to pass the time. He was dimly aware he might be upsetting some kind of subtle feng shui that Lauren had, no doubt, infused into the arrangement but had already caught up with the latest *shakes* on his MilkBar app, and was feeling bored.

Eventually Leon arrived, exiting the lift along with Derek, Kara, and the clients from Just Take a Bath. Tom watched them walk to the door and go through the motions of a professional farewell; lots of nodding, robust hand-shaking and, what looked like a well-timed humorous remark from Leon, if the polite laughter was anything to go by. Then they were gone.

Derek did a little celebratory pirouette once they were out of sight, almost knocking over Izzy who was just walking into the building. She gave him a wide berth, nodding at Leon who, along with Kara, was reluctantly receiving a high five. Then, seeing Tom, she headed over to where he was sitting.

Leon joined them a few moments later, apologising for the wait and for Derek, just as the hum and thump of music erupted from a couple of floors above,.

"Oh, I've seen worse," said Izzy, smiling, but mainly because she'd just remembered Leon's name. "Shall we head up?"

By the time they made it onto the second floor, where the party was being staged, ABBA had begun to stream frothily from Lauren's laptop to the poorly mounted wall speakers in each corner of the large room and, as the clock rounded on six thirty, the room was finally starting to fill up.

Hyperion's seasonal events were considered by many to be something of an occasion, and even though it was a little early in the calendar, this evening's summer party was to be no exception.

As such, Lauren had put a lot of effort into moving worktables, sofas, chairs, and novelty lighting into place. She'd organised drinks and caterers into the break-out meeting space at the back of the room and, of course, had been sure to demarcate the obligatory makeshift dance floor so that everyone would have the opportunity to embarrass themselves later in the evening.

Now that people were finally arriving, she busied herself, circling the room, attending to all the finishing touches, and pointing new arrivals towards the booze table.

As usual, everyone quickly began to self-organise into different sized groups and clusters around the room, driven by vague combinations of personal and professional affinities, or in some cases just by accident. After all, idly nursing a drink alone, in the wrong place, at the wrong moment, could mean being casually pinned down by the office bin Laden, or worse, one of the finance managers, who would gladly interrogate you over the billing complexities of whatever project you were working on.

By the time Leon, Tom, and Izzy had their drinks and found a corner to hide in, the rest of the crowd was deep in animated conversation. A few scattered souls stood apart in more solitary modes, placing themselves at great social risk by poking at their phones, but mostly everyone was starting to get into it when Nigel and his leadership team arrived.

Nigel Freon, eight-year veteran of Hyperion, former Director of Accounts (where he'd been known as "Big Nige," due in part to his stature but also to his correspondingly large appetite for client hospitality), now risen to partner and CEO of the UK office, ambled his way through the scattered but growing thickets of employees, to the front of the room. He had a thick glass tumbler of brown liquor raised in one hand, and a radio mike hanging limply from the other. Ahead of him was a large wall-mounted screen, already set up for *Nigel's Quarterly Update*, and other compelling company stats he had to share.

Miles, Derek, Mina, Shelly, and others from his team began to gather loosely around him in anticipation, and variously nodded, glanced, or flatly ignored him, as he approached the screen.

From the back of the room, Leon, Tom, and Izzy absently observed Nigel moving through the growing crowd with the kind of feline ease that belied what you'd expect from a man of his size. As a person, Leon had always found him hard to pin down. He would come across quite personable and warm in presentation mode, but up close he veered towards impatient and short-tempered, and easily distracted. He would often zone out if you weren't a client or weren't able to hold his commercial attention sufficiently.

Leon often wondered how it was that superficially meritless people like him were able to ascended the heights of *work mountain* so easily, or if they only got there by cutting others loose on the way up. It was a mystery. After all, he found it hard to imagine that Nigel's counterparts in Madrid, NYC, and LA, or any of the other so-called global officers, would get the same lack of engagement from him. According to office legend, Nigel had sometimes been known to just wander away whistling—with no kind of apology or explanation—in the middle of what had, until that moment, been an actual conversation.

Nigel turned to Mina and smiled.

"Shall we do this?" he said.

"I would," replied Mina, nodding to the room with a faint smile, then handing him the clicker. "This earnest attention can only last so long. The slides are all loaded up."

"Thanks, Min," he replied, with a wink.

She hated it when he abbreviated her already tiny name, and turned away to take a perch on a table edge nearby. Nigel gestured to Lauren to lower the music, then rotated back towards the room.

"OK, my friends..." he bellowed, as the music dwindled, but to little effect.

Miles looked over to Nigel and mimed using microphone action for him. Nigel smiled back, like a munificent lizard, and swapped his drink for the radio mike, as if he was way ahead of him, and already had the situation completely in hand.

Tom leaned into Leon and whispered, "Is Miles really suggesting Nigel perform a blow job!?"

"Doesn't really seem like the time for it," replied Leon. "These guys need to get a grip."

They both chuckled, and clinked their beer bottles together, causing Izzy to look up from her phone.

"What's that?" she asked, wondering what she'd missed that was so funny.

Leon felt a blush coming on at forgetting to behave himself in front of her, while Tom, equally embarrassed, let his mouth just waver uselessly in search of an answer. Fortunately, they were both saved by the sharp spike of audio feedback ripping through the speakers as Nigel switched the mike on. The room fell quiet.

"OK, then!" began Nigel, extravagantly. "Alright! That's

certainly one way of doing it," he continued, wagging the mike at the crowd like a mystic doll.

"So, welcome everybody. Welcome to what should be a great night for us. I'm really excited to get everyone together like this. It's not just an early summer party, but a celebration—of us, and of what we can achieve when we all work together. I'm proud of that.

"I can tell you something else—we're not even six months in, and already it's been a stellar year for us, with new clients, new projects, and new people coming to join our Hyperion family. On the people front alone, we've grown by—what—almost 30 percent since March?"

It wasn't 30 percent, but Nigel never worried himself with that level of detail for a meeting like this. He knew no one would ever check or call him on it publicly.

"And that, my friends, is not an easy thing to do."

He cast a benevolent gaze over the room, raised his glass, and clicked the clicker, changing the people-focused slide to yet more impressive stats that he could make claims about.

"And that's all down to you guys. You've all been working incredibly hard, and the I think the numbers speak for themselves—"

"I'm not hearing anything," ventured Leon, quietly.

"Those damn numbers," mumbled Tom. "You gotta love them."

"Oh definitely," responded Leon. "I can't get enough, to be honest. I carry dice around with me, just so I can get some numbers action whenever I need a hit."

Izzy perked up. She knew they were kidding around but, as someone who spent much of her working life programming complex machine code, she actually did love numbers.

"I actually do love numbers," she whispered. "I spend a lot of time with them."

"Really?" replied Tom. "As a, uhm, what do you call it? As a massager, I would have thought that—"

Izzy immediately began to boil at this admittedly not uncommon perception of her, and was about to cut him off when Leon jumped in.

"She's a frickin' scientist, you idiot," said Leon, jumping in. "Of course she loves numbers."

Izzy was surprised but quietly pleased at Leon's unexpected intervention, while Tom froze at this revelation, and the embarrassment that came with it.

"It's true," she said, cooling off at the sight of Tom's crushing discomfort, and that his remark was innocently meant. "I *love* them. Speaking strictly as a *massager*, that is," she grinned disarmingly.

"Oh man. I'm so sorry," said Tom, sheepishly. "I just—"

"Don't worry about it," said Izzy, with a wave. "You guys only see me in massaging mode once a month. It happens."

At the front of the room, Nigel was playing a corporate video, with fast intercutting scenes between people doing work, or discussing things in different settings, people thinking about stuff on their commutes, and sending emails from their phones, Post-it notes being scribbled on, and then moved about on a wall—interspersed with the usual time-lapse photography of cars at night, so that they all blurred into lines of superfast light streams. All of this was accompanied by pounding electro music—which Nigel clearly favoured, if his head-bobbing rictus grin was anything to go by—and a dramatic narration explaining how collaboration, Post-it notes, and fast-moving lines of light was about building connections and, the narrator went on to insist, the only way to help businesses transform.

Izzy turned to Leon. "What are you transforming businesses into exactly?"

"Nobody's allowed to say," he replied, with mock seriousness.

"Because it's...not a real thing?"

"Oh, it's real enough," said Leon. "It's like the Hulk but with much less rage, and more focus on people, optimisation, and revenue."

"The Hulk?"

"Yes. The Incredible Hulk. When puny Bruce Banner transforms into the Hulk—"

"Oh, like in the movie. And that terribly sad TV show."

"Technically," added Tom, softly. "Its primary source is the comic book."

"Yes!" said Leon, ignoring Tom's geeky clarification. "Super sad Bill Bixby, always on his own."

Tom began quietly *dah dah-dah-dah-ing* the mournful piano tune from the super sad TV show about the Incredible Hulk, where the doleful, misnamed David Banner, ends up on his own at the end of every episode.

"But the movie version," said Izzy. "The one with all the comic-book cuts? I loved all that."

Leon was secretly thrilled by this revelation. He loved that movie too.

"The ending is totally screwed up, though," insisted Tom. "You have to admit it. It's like the film ends, and then there's a whole other ending bolted on, with his dad as the, the uh—"

"*Absorbalon,*" suggested Leon.

Tom looked unconvinced. "Dude, I don't think the—"

"I do admit it," admitted Izzy, brushing the *Absorbalon* aside. "I agree the ending is completely bizarre, but I kind of liked it. It's a great movie."

As if Leon needed any further convincing of how much he liked Isabella Jones, this admission more or less sealed things for him. Almost nobody admitted to liking that movie.

"So anyway, why the Hulk?" she continued, nodding towards the screen

Tom nudged Izzy. "Shh. Here comes his bit."

On-screen, Leon could be seen in a group shot of a meeting, standing in front of another screen, moving his arms around in an explanatory way, then indicating a diagram, as if he was really landing a point.

"Hey, it's you!" said Izzy, as the voice-over rambled on.

"It is me," agreed Leon, quietly pleased that this all seemed to be timing out so well. "So, the thing with this was—"

"Do you think," interrupted Tom. "That when Banner changes into the Hulk, and then back again, that all his scars and ailments, all of his defects get healed?"

Leon sighed, slightly annoyed at the interruption but still enjoying the question. Even if it wasn't the first time he had heard it.

"This is about his fillings again, right?" said Leon.

Izzy remained blank-faced at the clarification, so Leon contorted the side of his mouth, and pointed at his teeth.

"Oh, those kinds of fillings," she said.

"Yes, of course it's about his fillings," confirmed Tom.

"But I thought we already cleared this one up," asserted Leon.

"We only thought we did. But as Izzy is an actual scientist, I'm following the scientific method," declared Tom, with an impish grin. "All good theories must be peer-reviewed, right?"

"Technically, Tom is correct," said Izzy, happy to join in on whatever this was. "You can't just mark your own homework. You need an expert review."

"Izzy seems like an expert to me," agreed Tom, waving a thumb in her direction. "See what she thinks."

"OK," began Leon, a little reluctantly. "What if Bruce Banner has a couple of fillings, say. Or a crown..."

"Bruce Banner?" Izzy knew who he was, of course, but couldn't resist shining them on.

"*Dr* Bruce Banner. The Hulk."

"Oh him, right. The sad guy."

"Yes. Him. The sad guy. So, let's say, when he changes into the Hulk, and everything scales up, what happens to his fillings?"

Izzy allowed herself to be engrossed by this question but said nothing.

"Basically, if his teeth cavities also grow to a correspondingly larger size, then presumably all his fixed, non-gamma-ray-infused dental work will just fall out. Every time."

"No wonder he's so angry," said Izzy.

They all laughed. Then, before Tom could say any more (as he clearly wanted to), Big Nige jumped back onto the mike, loudly enough that all discussion of the Hulk's teeth was immediately halted.

"This is amazing stuff, guys!" roared Nigel, extravagantly, meaning the video.

The screen bleached to white and was replaced with a large Hyperion logo, and the words, *Fast Forward 2030* appeared. In actual italics. Along with some go-faster stripes.

"Really. Such great stuff. This is just one of the many fantastic ways we're redefining our go-to-market strategy over the next five years. I don't know about you, but I love it! And, more importantly, our clients will love it too."

Once all the speech-making, client wins, revenue targets, and team news was dispensed with, the party had quickly got into full swing. Everyone had filled out the main space and even moved beyond it; some had spilled into the lobby by the lift, with others venturing down the stairwell, or even farther out into the street for a smoke or a vape. The lights were down, the finger food had been consumed, the drink was flowing thickly, and the music streamed loudly from the bad speakers above. But nobody seemed to mind that much, and inevitably it even forced some people to inflict dancing on each other, including Nigel, which, Leon felt, was quite some manner of cruelty to behold.

It was during one such incident where Tom and Leon, trading observations of Nigel's contortions for sociological purposes, while trying to resist various overtures from Lauren to join her, Izzy, and a few of the gang in a dance-off, that Tom decided Leon needed a little boost. He gave Leon a sharp poke in the ribs with his elbow.

"I've been observing you, my friend," he shouted, over the din.

"Oh, have you? And what conclusions have you drawn?"

"Well, I can see you are a man tempted to go out there and try out some of your moves."

"Your observations are in need of serious refinement. I don't have any moves, as you well know."

"Maybe not any you're willing to admit to in this limited setting. But I can see your foot's been tapping for some time now. And your fingers are thrumming on the neck of that beer you've been nursing, while your muse, it seems, remains unbothered by such conventions and, unlike you, appears to be enjoying herself. You and I both know where this is leading. Why not save some time, open up a bit, and show Izzy what you've got?"

Leon choked on the swig he was taking from his almost empty bottle of beer.

"You're joking, right?" he replied, stylishly wiping his mouth with the back of his hand.

"I am not joking."

"Showing her what I've got, as you put it, is exactly why I am *not* opening up."

They looked over to Lauren, Izzy, and a handful of other, mostly female, colleagues moving and shaking in the middle of the throng. Izzy looked back at just that same moment, and beckoned them, once again, to join in. Only to be completely obscured a second later by Nigel, Shelly, and Derek barrelling past, clumsily scooping people up in a horrible approximation of a conga.

"Oh man," hissed Leon. "Just look at that. What a mess."

"I think what you need," declared Tom, "is a boost." He then leaned in close to Leon and reduced his voice to a decidedly unsubtle stage whisper.

"I got us a little something extra from the bar," he said. Then leaned backwards and somehow magically produced a small tray containing six shots of translucent liquor.

"What's this?"

"Medicine for the rhythmically averse."

"Don't call it medicine!" barked Leon. "I've seen the kinds of things you put in your body, and there's nothing remotely medicinal about it."

"Two for you, me, and Izzy. This is the good stuff!" he declared, with a wink.

"Good for who, exactly?" replied Leon, suspiciously, but picked up two of the shots anyway.

Tom followed suit, and set the tray back down on the side.

"Here's to crime!"

They clinked glasses. Then threw them back, in quick succession, wincing hard at the harsh liquor, before slamming the glasses back on to the tray, upside down.

"What the hell was that? It was disgusting… Both times."

"Just a little livener. A drop of something special. A boost."

Leon performed a brief self-assessment, and soon felt a distinct if subtle, gleeful energy competing with the beer for his attention. He then peered at Tom, who managed to look incredibly sheepish for someone also so obviously pleased with themselves. Had he put something in the drink, wondered Leon, a little irked by the idea.

"I'm still not bloody dancing, you idiot!" insisted Leon.

But before Tom had time to formulate a response, the now-extended conga line of people pretending to enjoy themselves suddenly surged passed, and several arms belonging to Izzy and Lauren reached out to snatch the boys from their hiding place.

Leon feigned a protest, even as he fell in line ahead of Izzy. The shouts went up. Lauren was screaming into Tom's ear, which he appeared to enjoy. Izzy was grinning mischievously at the back of Leon's head, while he felt caught between the delight of her intervention, and the fear that he was mere moments from certain humiliation.

Nigel, however, unbothered by any kind of existential challenges, was still firmly up at the front of the line, whooping loudly, and waving his arms left and right—along with a large cowboy hat he had somehow acquired. And off they all went. Cha-cha-cha.

12

HOME TIME

Much later that evening, when the Nigel-led excitement had finally subsided into more generalised drinking, dancing, and talking shop, Leon, Izzy, and Tom, and a few others retreated once again to the back of the room to natter, chill out, and take stock.

Izzy looked around the room, and then at her phone: 10:54 p.m. She was surprised to still be there this late but also that, for a works party, it was still kind of heaving. This place really had something going on, she thought. Clearly everyone was enjoying themselves and, she had to admit, it had been a much better evening than she'd been expecting. She could probably have done without Derek's weird self-absorbed come-on after the conga incident, but Leon and Tom had been good company. Silly and interesting in equal measure. She could see herself seeing them again, if they asked. Or if Leon asked. Tom was on a spectrum all his own, but she could definitely see Leon again, if he'd get off the fence, and say what he clearly wanted to say. But that would clearly have to wait for another day. For now, she decided, it was time to go.

"OK, boys," she announced, finally. "It's been a fun evening, but I think it's time for me to make a move."

Leon, who had been chatting to Tom, paused midsentence, and adopted the mildly perplexed look of someone reaching for something to say but not finding it.

"It's official going home time then, is it?" asked Tom, after a moment.

"Are you suggesting," said Leon. "That there's an actual, official going home time? Who would decide this kind of thing?"

"I think the EU used to have a policy on it," suggested Izzy, joining in. "But obviously since Brexit, we're free to go home whenever we like."

"Ah," said Leon. "The gift of democracy."

"Ah indeed," replied Izzy, reaching down into her bag and rummaging around, clearly in search of something.

"I suspect it falls to the Home Office now," added Tom. "It's a domestic issue, and clearly their domain."

Izzy continued decanting her bag, pulling odd items out onto the table next to them, including an apple, a well-thumbed copy of *An Eternal Golden Braid,* and a cracked lipstick, while Leon and Tom pretended not to look.

"I see," responded Leon. "So, you think that home time is still a political issue. Do they also set official policy on bedtime and bathtime? Perhaps we've finally uncovered what they meant by 'taking back control'—that I can leave, go to bed, or have a bath whenever I like."

Tom laughed in approval.

"Oh crap," said Izzy, with a sigh.

"What's up?" asked Leon.

"I left my keys in with all my massage kit."

"But you have all your stuff with you here, right?"

"I do. I did. I was going to leave it until tomorrow. Lauren parked it somewhere for me."

"Behind reception?"

"Downstairs somewhere."

"Oh, I know where she'll have put it. We have a couple of old neglected meeting rooms, storage rooms now, that we keep downstairs. She'll have stuck it there, out of the way. I'll take you."

Izzy smiled and hoisted her bag onto her shoulder.

"Perfect. Tom, it's been an experience. Don't forget to submit your papers for peer review."

"Uhn?"

"On exposure to gamma radiation?"

They all laughed. Tom raised his bottle of beer. She leaned over and pecked him on the cheek.

"Good luck with the massager business!" he said, cheekily.

Leon and Izzy made their way down the stairs, past a feuding couple, and into the building's main foyer, where they found Lauren stockpiling small boxes behind the reception desk and chatting with her friend Jade-from-Accounts. A muted television was hung on the wall behind them, playing a late-night news programme. Jordan Milk was on again and, according to the subtitles, was discussing commercial space flight.

"Well, hey, you two," said Lauren, lasciviously, as she turned from her pile of boxes, and saw them heading over.

Leon could feel heat rising at her transparent implication. Jade twisted awkwardly to see who Lauren was talking to, but as she was partway through refilling her wine glass, mainly succeeded in spilling half of it onto the floor.

"Whoops!" squealed Jade, clearly smashed. "Don't worry, *everones*. I got it."

She held herself loosely like a drunk puppet, whacking the wine bottle down on the counter (only to have it saved from tipping over by a rapidly lurching Lauren), and scattering a pot of pens onto the floor to join the wine. Then she pitched forward, and uselessly attempted to mop up the pool of wine using the single tissue she was already clutching.

"Jade, it's fine. Stop! I'll get it," cried Lauren, as she scuttled around from behind her desk.

Jade did stop by abruptly snatching for the countertop, and threading her way hand-over-hand towards the seating area.

"Yesss, I agree," she slurred, making an equally sudden bow-legged break for the seats.

Leon scooted across to grab her arm and help her to safety, despite beginning to feel similarly soaked himself. That "special" drink Tom had given him, whatever it was, either wasn't working as planned, or was going into serious overdrive. He was finding it increasingly hard to tell the difference but was determined not to let on in front of Izzy.

"Oh, Leon," mumbled Jade, with a sigh, as he guided her gently backwards into a seat. "We must get some wines together."

"We will, Jade," said Leon, kindly. "First, a nice sit-down. Then we'll all get some wines."

Izzy stood off to one side, not quite sure where to look, prompting Leon to refocus his attention. He handed both a cushion, and the responsibility for Jade's wilting head, over to Lauren.

"Thanks, Leon," said Lauren, taking the cushion and propping Jade's head up. "I think maybe she's had a few too many."

"You think, maybe?" replied Leon, warmly, but worrying about his own rising addled confusion. Did she have one of Tom's drinks too?

"Bollocks!" blurted Jade, jerking her head up. Her eyes remained firmly closed, and a moment later, she sank deep into the plump sofa for a rest.

"Izzy needs to get her stuff, Lauren," said Leon, attempting to move things on. "Is it downstairs, in the storeroom?"

Lauren laughed, without any obvious reason.

"The storeroom! You are funny. Yes, of course, I can show you. Give me one second," she said, turning back to complete her box-moving and stacking tasks first.

Leon and Izzy exchanged glances, while the vivid hum and bustle of colleagues chatting in the stairwell, or those stealing outside for a vape or a smoke, rumbled around them, to the tune of muted 1990s house music thumping from above. In the distance, a boat horn moaned deeply from somewhere downriver.

"So," began Leon, attempting to seize the moment, even as a frothing nausea began to make itself felt somewhere he didn't want to think about. He realised it was risky timing, but he also wasn't sure he'd get another chance like this again.

He stuck his arm out, partly to steady himself against the wall but mainly in an attempt to appear nonchalant. Unfortunately, he missed. And then proceeded to fumble awkwardly with a number of alternative standing positions, before giving up and switching his attention to tidying up the fallen pens, in an effort to seem purposeful.

"So, yes," said Izzy, pretending not to notice.

"Well, I guess you're all set, then."

"Looks that way," she replied, with a sweet but curious smile, wondering if the colour rapidly draining away from his face was just bad lighting, or something worse.

Then, suddenly, Leon went from mild nausea to feeling horrendously sick. Despite a valiant attempt at pushing these sensations aside for Izzy's benefit, he knew he couldn't hold it back much longer. His head begun roiling feverishly—at least on the inside—and his vision started to blur. And it started to seem very likely that this would end badly for everyone: whether it was Tom's spiked drink, or Leon's basic, absolute terror of actually asking for Izzy's phone number, something definitely wanted out of his body. And it didn't want to wait.

He began to panic, pleading silently for it to stop, while at the same time attempting to appear very cool, present, and focused on what Izzy was saying. But instead of coming across as cool, he simply became incomprehensible, like a mumbling infant wino.

"Leon, are you—" began Izzy, realising it was definitely something worse.

"Shall we go, then?" said Lauren, briskly, oblivious to Leon's changing fortunes. She gestured towards the stairs leading down into the basement, while Leon endeavoured to suppress a heaving belch. He turned away, hoping they would just leave without him.

"You go ahead," he said, biliously, waving them on. "I'll...I'll be fine."

At that same moment, the lift arrived with a happy-sounding ding, and let a bunch of people out. Leon impulsively staggered off towards it, before Izzy or Lauren could respond. He knew he had to get as far away from Izzy as he possibly could. And while the lift might be a seriously risky choice, it was a faster escape than the stairs, with much less danger of falling on his face in front of other people. And under no circumstances, he knew with complete certainty, could he allow himself to become Izzy's "the guy who threw up on me at a party" story.

Izzy instinctively reached out a hand in his direction, as several partygoers fell into the lobby from outside, and obscured her view of his departure. Lauren maintained her perky grin, apparently still unaware of any change in circumstances, and gently tugged on Izzy's arm in the direction of the stairs. Jade shifted on her seat, letting out a loud stream of unintelligible, possibly word-like sounds.

Leon only just made it to the lift without throwing up. He turned, and hit a number of floor buttons at random, while trying to prop himself up, weakly, with one outstretched arm. He attempted to mask his desperation for the doors to close with a heroic, if slightly crooked, all-fine-here smile. Then some of the smoking crowd piled in after him. *They'll regret that choice*, he thought.

"Shall I wait for you here?" shouted Izzy, across the lobby.

But the doors closed anyway.

Izzy turned back to Lauren, a little unsure of her responsibility in this situation. Should she help Leon herself or just tell the others? Maybe she should go back in and find Tom. After all, she thought, these people work with him every day, whereas...or, maybe, she should just wait a bit, and see how the universe unfolded. That was her new thing.

"Do you think we should do something...?" she asked Lauren, tentatively, nodding at the closed lift.

"Nah," replied Lauren. "He'll be fine. I promise you. Let's go get your stuff."

13

COOKIE DOUGH

Bryson Hawke had fallen asleep in the sumptuously oversized chair in Milk's hotel suite. Milk was actually OK with this, for now, as he had enough on his mind without having to stage-manage Hawke's more unique appetites. Nor engineer a discreet exit from the building, given his propensity to go walkabout in foreign cities.

"Does he really have to stay in here, with us?" complained Annie, as Hawke let out another ripping snore.

She and Milk stood beside a large, ornate table, serving as a makeshift workspace. It was covered in various papers, laptops, discarded cups, plates, and glasses. In the centre was a large platter with the remains of some half-eaten sandwiches, miniature pastries, and a scattering of wilting fruit. They were joined by several others of Milk's employ, variously seated at the table or standing around nearby.

"He's generally better off where we can see him, I find. I've arranged a room to drop him in for when we're done here. Unless you want to risk waking him now?" replied Milk with a grin.

Annie glanced over at the slumbering former scientist, purported government whistle-blower (flatly denied, and officially discredited, by any government agency you care to ask, of course), and general all-round media punching bag, when any marginal science topics pop up.

"Are you kidding me?" she replied. "What—and listen to him droning on about the glory days of the Grateful Dead again, and how they were the '*vanguard of a government-sponsored incursion into public consciousness?*'" she continued, dropping partway into a hippie-infused impersonation of Hawke.

"Yeah, I didn't think so," responded Milk, impishly.

"You know, Jordan," injected Tony Phelps, a tall, thin, and conservatively well-dressed late-middle-aged lawyer, standing by the large plate-glass window overlooking Park Lane. A coffee cup and saucer was perched elegantly in his hand. "I still don't know why you keep him around. Dogs are much less trouble, if you need a pet that badly."

Milk smiled and sat down on the wide arm of an enormous sofa.

"Let me worry about that, Tony," he said, taking a moment to release his fatigue by stretching his arms high above his head. Annie cut him a sharp glance. "We have a couple of projects where his input has proved to be quite useful."

"But the cost, Jordan," replied Phelps. "I've said it before—he draws a lot of the wrong kind of attention. You have to consider the shareholders—"

"No, Tony. *You* have to consider the shareholders. That's what I pay you for. He has a highly singular experience and a unique perspective, and that's what I pay *him* for."

"Oh, really?" responded Phelps, moving back to the table and refilling his cup. "Conspiracy theories and secret military bases? UFOs!" he continued, spitting each letter in turn. "And so-called element 115, is it? Honestly, is that really what we're going in for now? We're funding a serious commercial space program here, Jordan. We're literally about to sign a crucial contract with NASA, and you think having this, this *crackpot,* on our books—"

Milk continued to look faintly amused. Annie stepped in between them.

"Guys, much as I'm sure we all enjoy a nice verbal scuffle, time is pushing on. Jordan, you and I still have quite a bit to get through this evening."

"Thank you, Annie," declared Milk, leaping artfully off his perch with more agility than you would expect, and moving back towards the table to grab another sandwich. "You're absolutely right. And Tony—you're right too. I get it. We're a global business. We have shareholders. We have people who want to make more money this year than they did last year, in a flatline economy. Including my mother. Who doesn't? We have a scrappy social media platform that's changed the world, the best electric cars, and some of the greatest tech and patented clean energy production on the planet. And we have our little space program. That's a lot, right? I understand why it freaks you out. Hawke won't be a problem, I promise you. It's just him and me, and a few ideas I've been kicking around. Everyone's gotta have a hobby, right?"

Annie shot him another do-you-think-you-could-just-shut-up look. Then, Jennifer Pierce, another sharp-suited business maven, who had spent much of the evening engrossed in her laptop tabulating data from one source to another, finally seemed to note the exchange.

"Exciting!" she squeaked, mentally casting an imaginary press release, and adding up the value of her share options again. "Anything you're ready to share, Jordan?"

"Oh, Jen. No, not yet. But I promise you'll be at least the eighth person to know." His watch made a sharp alert sound, and he looked down at his wrist to dismiss the notification. "Now look, guys, it's been a long day. You and Tony have been amazing, as always. But as Annie has kindly reminded me, there is more for me to cross off my list today, and the night is not getting any younger."

Pierce and Phelps briefly exchanged confused looks—they hadn't even got to the main part of their meeting, and Milk was already drawing a line under it. It wasn't entirely out of the ordinary for Milk to switch things up at the last minute but, even so, this left turn was hard to fathom since he had expressly flown them out to London the night before so they could cover off their business-critical agenda.

"Sir, if I may," began Phelps.

"Tony, you may not."

"But, the contracts...?"

"It's all good, my friend. I know I asked you to come out here at short notice, and I love that you did. But I'm afraid something's come up today that needs my attention more than you do. Let's postpone until Monday. And in the meantime? Take some time off. Be a tourist. Enjoy London for the weekend—on me. Annie, please see that the hotel extends everyone's stay. And give them an upgrade while you're at it."

"Yes, sir," responded Annie. "Already taken care of."

"There, you see? No problem too small. Now if—"

"Jordan," insisted Phelps, on the verge of a more definitive protest, before noticing how Pierce, and their respective aides were already hurrying to gather up their things. He thought better of it and, after a brief pause, simply said, "Thank you. That would be...delightful."

Milk smiled benignly. Annie was already up from her seat and moving towards the door, which she opened wide as a clear invitation for them to leave.

"Everything's been arranged," she said, with a practical, thin-lipped smile, much less benevolent than their mutual employer. "I'll be in touch about Monday."

The four executives scurried past her with varying nods and arrangements of eyebrows, still trying to wedge documents into their assortment of flapping, half-open bags and cases.

The large wooden door swung gracefully shut behind them. Or would have but for the luxury soft-close mechanism, which appeared calibrated to set the world record for the slowest possible crossing of the last two inches. Milk and Annie, in anticipation of the privacy it would afford them, became transfixed by the unfolding drama of door vs. frame. The door finally closed with an almost imperceptible if satisfying click. Hawke's eyes then snapped open, accompanied by a confused bark.

"What the hell, man!?" he yelled, at no one in particular, his legs jerking out in front of him.

"Bryson. Welcome back," said Milk, instantly refocusing. He gestured to the table where Annie was already unfolding what looked like a military-spec laptop, with an oversized hardened shell casing. "Come see what we've got."

"Gotta do God's work first, my friend," responded Hawke, climbing his way out of the chair with an unconscious groan, and hobbling off down the hall to the bathroom.

Annie gave Milk another admonishing look, which he ignored, then continued setting up the computer, synching it with a large but unfeasibly paper-thin monitor that she'd placed at the centre of the table.

A few moments later the flush sounded—Hawke apparently hadn't bothered closing the bathroom door—followed by the clamour of him washing his hands and face, and hacking something up from his deepest recesses. And then he was back in the room, drying his face on a crisp white hand towel, which he duly draped over the back of the armchair he had been sitting in.

Milk and Annie looked at him unenthusiastically.

"Sorry, man," he declared, sheepishly, acknowledging the less-than-thrilled faces of his two companions. "I spend a lot of time on my own." He held his hands up—guilty-as-charged.

"It's fine," said Milk, after a moment, and dismissed Hawke's apology with an absent wave of his hand. He switched his gaze back to the makeshift workstation.

Annie typed out an access code to unlock the software, and the main screen sprang to life. Several panels of different sizes and content opened in a flurry, then arranged themselves around the screen. One window pinned itself to the right edge, as lines of characters began tumbling down it, then, with a short beep, stopped just as suddenly. A cursor blinked patiently on the last line.

Annie typed in another series of letters and numbers at the waiting prompt. New strings of code began compiling, as the other windows filled with a jumble of images, raw data, and schematics of large, complex machinery. Hawke circled around to take a closer look.

"Dude..." he began, slowly. "Is that what I think it is?"

His voice seemed to subtly shed its standard hippie trappings, and took on a surprisingly precise and focused tone instead. He pushed forward to look more closely at the screen, as Annie stepped back, by way of an invitation for him to take control.

Hawke leant in and started rapidly tapping out familiar commands on the keyboard, forcing the virtual desktop to start reorganising itself. The onscreen layout gave way to a large three-dimensional image of what appeared to be two enormous tubular steel loops, conjoined at the centre, like a great big figure eight lying on its back. An additional pipe came into the space from somewhere beyond the back wall, and fused with what would be the top of the eight, while a matching configuration emerged from the bottom edge, before continuing its journey off frame.

The whole cylindrical contraption was intersected along its length, at regular intervals, with an arrangement of complex, boxy mechanisms wrapped with an arrangement of much smaller pipes, metal grills, and still smaller components that made the whole unit come off like a twisted futuristic metallic bird's nest.

Thick power cables emerged from each intersecting unit, then ran clockwise around the interior of the loops, forming an increasingly larger bundle as it met with each counterpart in turn, before converging at the centre where the two doughnuts met. This intersection was itself straddled by a much larger nest-like apparatus, with additional components, wires, and convoluted pipework that extended vertically in both directions.

Hawke used the trackpad to manipulate the image in various directions and magnifications, seemingly looking for something, then let his hand slip away, leaving the dynamic image to circle slowly around the artefact.

"This render is fantastic. You're really going to build the accelerator?" He seemed thrilled.

Milk smiled.

"Nope."

Hawke looked up at Annie, then back to Milk, momentarily confused. But it was clear from their expressions they were sharing something left unsaid.

"*Built*," declared Milk, finally, with some satisfaction.

Hawke's eyes immediately grew to twice the size.

"Wait. You *built* the *magnevox accelerator*?"

"I did."

"To my updated specifications?"

"I did."

"Oh my God, Jordan. I never, I couldn't, I... Jesus, it must have cost—"

"It did," said Annie.

"There's plenty more where that came from," reassured Milk. "The question you should really be asking is what did we do with it?"

Hawke clutched the top of his head, as though his excitement would cause it to pop off.

"Man! Tell me already!"

Milk grinned, and flicked a small object in Hawke's direction. He instinctively caught it in one hand. When he opened his fingers to look at it, he saw a semi-translucent dark grey sphere, not much bigger than a child's marble. The object looked almost like obsidian but with a metallic quality that seemed to infuse every aspect of it. He picked it up between finger and thumb to look at it closely in the light. Even though it was far from transparent, light still made it through somehow, and if anything appeared brighter than the original source.

It was much heavier than it looked, and felt extremely smooth to the touch, despite having a subtle, almost imperceptible texture at the same time, as if the surface was covered in minute indentations, like a miniature golf ball. It also felt surprisingly cold, almost painfully so, as though it was draining all the heat from his fingers.

Hawke's eyes had become intense as he examined the object, switching rapidly between excitement, terror, and curiosity as he turned it in his fingers.

"So, what do you think?" asked Milk.

Hawke shifted his focus to look directly at Milk and began to laugh.

"What do I think? I think it's the end of the fucking world."

Oblivious that the end of the fucking world had just been announced, Izzy and Lauren made their way across the foyer to a glass-panelled stairwell, opposite the main stairs, and running parallel to the front of the office building. A single staircase led them down into a poorly lit lower ground floor, with Lauren's absurd heels clacking noisily on the metallic treads as they descended.

Izzy had never been down here before. Despite the dim lighting, she was surprised to see it was virtually a complete floor, laid out with tables, benches, and workstations that mirrored the arrangements she'd observed on several of the floors above. However, she could also see by the sheer volume of junk—old computer monitors, cables, storage boxes, stacks of CDs, piles of printed catalogues, scrap paper, and building fitments heaped all over the desks—that it wasn't really used for anything. It was like the office's dirty little secret. And peppered down one side of the room, and along the back wall, sandwiched between banks of unused lockers, were a number of semi-opaque glass-walled rooms. Possibly former offices but, from what Izzy could make out, these were also choking with office bric-a-brac, file cabinets, pedestals, upturned desks, and more than a few old and broken swivel chairs.

"So, what happens down here?" asked Izzy. "Is this where office furniture comes to die?"

Lauren whinnied humorously at her remark.

"You're so right! I think IT used to be down here, before they moved it all. Before my time really." Her phone began to ring, visibly clawing away at her attention. "Now we mainly use it for keeping stationery, printer cartridges, odds, and sods. Stuff like that."

"Like a storeroom?"

"Yes!" she laughed again, not really connecting the dots, but finally giving in to her insistent phone. "Sorry, I really need to get this."

She wagged the handset at Izzy, and nodded in the direction of the nearest glass booth, as she raised the phone to her ear.

"Your stuff's in there," she said. "You can't miss it. Hi, baby—"

Izzy looked over, as Lauren wandered away chattering to baby, to see an open booth with a tall, thin box leaning diagonally against the doorjamb.

"The one with the open door?" she called out after Lauren.

"That's the one!"

"Should I just—"

"Go for it!" said Lauren, already halfway up the stairs, and disappearing from view.

Izzy wasn't sure if that last remark was directed at her, or her caller, but either way figured by implication that she was free to root around in this derelict space. It actually surprised her how deathly quiet the floor had become. Not a peep could be heard leaking from upstairs, and even Lauren's squawks and giggles had evaporated once she was out of sight. It must be well insulated, she decided, as she made her through the maze of junk to where her stuff was stored.

She poked her head into the open room and looked around. Much as Lauren had suggested: piles of boxes, half of them opened, filled with printer paper, ink, Post-it notes, marker pens, some large sacks of what looked like shredded paper for recycling, and at the back of the room, an old table covered in dusty old desk lamps and phones. But where was her wheelie chair?

"Oh crap," she said aloud. "I bet she put it somewhere else."

Izzy stepped into the neglected office space to get a better look at things. And, as she did so, her foot snagged the base of the tall box leaning against the door. It instantly slipped from its perch, and slid quietly backwards into the main room, making Izzy jump as it thumped hard to the floor in the otherwise silent workspace.

"Jesus!" she called out.

As she turned around to see what had happened, she finally glimpsed her wheelie chair leant up against the wall and partially tucked in behind the glass door.

"Why on earth would she hide it behind a door?" grumbled Izzy.

She gripped the door, and heaved it aside, so she could get access to her belongings. The folded chair had a pop-up handle on the top like a carry-on suitcase, and as she reached for it and adjusted the height, the office door closed beside her with a barely perceptible click. She froze. Something went off in her brain. The open door. The tall box wedged up against the frame.

"No!"

The box falling.

"No, no, no..."

The door closing shut.

She turned to grab the door handle, and pulled it down. It immediately jammed, with an audible metallic crunch. She yanked it again. Another crunch. Then she tried rattling it up and down but nothing happened.

"Oh my God!"

She tried it again. But it was really jammed now and wouldn't budge in any direction. Then she yanked on the door itself, trying to pull the whole thing back and forth but it barely moved in the frame. The whole thing was locked up tight as a drum.

"I cannot believe this shit!" she shouted, and belligerently thumped the door with the palm of her hand.

She peered out into the room through a narrow clear glass channel running vertically down one side of the door, in case

Lauren had made a reappearance. She hadn't. Izzy closed her eyes tight and let out a long, angry sigh.

"OK, Isabella Jones. It's just a broken door lock. You programme robots. You can do this. Take a breath."

She looked up. Took a breath. Then started hammering on the door with her fists and screaming for help.

Meanwhile five floors, and counting, above Izzy's hammering fists, Leon leaned as deeply into the corner of the world's slowest lift as he could possibly get. He felt smothered by the extreme proximity of so many people in such a ridiculously small space as he tried to fight the cloying nausea, and the terror he might actually vomit on them at any minute. He pressed his face against the cool metal sides and attempted to control his breathing. In what seemed like an infinitely slow ascent of the building, he tried to consider the pros and cons of what would happen if he really couldn't hold it together. How bad would it really be, he wondered? Could he live without seeing any of these friends and colleagues ever again? But who the fuck were all these people anyway, thought Leon, curtly succumbing to the unhappy drunkard's refrain.

The lift came to an abrupt stop and the doors slid open, flooding the compartment with a sonic rush of people and music, as everyone pushed and shoved to get out of it.

"Leon, are you coming?" someone said.

Leon couldn't say who, exactly, as his eyes remained firmly closed, and he was disgustingly drunk. He tried to wave them off, as he retched quietly (he hoped), and slid down the wall into a hunched position, with his head over knees. He breathed heavily. Just another minute, he prayed to himself. Less than a minute. Just hold on. His right arm darted up and started stabbing clumsily at the control panel in search of the close button. The doors closed anyway. And Leon's world went dark as the lift resumed its painful crawl towards the seventh floor.

14

CHEERS

"I'm so glad you like it," said Milk, at last.

"Like it!?" replied Hawke with a yelp. "You've changed history. You've changed everything, man. You've made a stable form of element 1-fricking-15! I *love* it. But if they find out about it—"

"*They*," said Annie, reaching over and abruptly extracting it from Hawke's fingers. "Won't be finding out anything."

"Hey!" said Hawke. "I wasn't done."

"You're done," replied Annie, placing the small orb into what looked like an oversized glasses case made of reinforced industrial plastic.

Were there other items in there? Other samples? Hawke couldn't tell, although the case seemed much larger than it needed to be for just one little marble.

"What else you got in there, Pandora?" said Hawke, with a leering smile.

Annie ignored him and folded the item away into a much larger protective hard case.

"Bryson," interjected Milk, diffusing Annie with a sharp look. "I wanted you to see this firsthand. The work we have done together these past years has been an incredible step forward, which we couldn't have made without your input. And the potential, as you have so colourfully put it, will have implications the world over."

"*Implications*!? Are you fucking kidding me? If you've been able to keep this off-grid for now, well done, man. I mean it. But this? Assuming it really works, you're talking about killing a four-trillion-dollar oil and gas business overnight. They'll fight you for it. Even you don't have that much money to spread around. And that's just for starters. Free energy, off the scale—just think of what we can do with it. Cars, transportation, agriculture, telecommunications, quantum computing, healthcare and medicine, education, heavy industry, and space travel, man. We finally get to go to space—for free!"

"I'd hardly call it free," began Annie, attempting to cool his enthusiasm. "Do you have any idea—"

"Let the man speak," cautioned Milk, warmly.

"You're missing my point," continued Hawke. "This will touch every single part of the global economy. Our own fricking economy, man... You think Uncle Sam's just gonna sit by and give you a cookie for this? Those military-industrial cats get one sniff of it, my friend, and they will be all over you like ants at a picnic: pulling you and your marbles apart, atom by atom. What do you think they've been doing to me for the past thirty years? And all I did was *talk* about this stuff on a local news channel."

"Assuming it works?" said Milk.

"Assuming. Yes. It works, though, right? It has to work."

Annie and Milk exchanged looks.

"Well, the data's limited at this point," said Annie, cautiously.

"Limited? Dude. This isn't the senior prom. Why is everyone being so shy? That little bead alone could probably power this whole hotel – indefinitely. And the ten next-door. Why aren't we popping the champagne?"

"We only just made this, like, three days ago, Bryson," said Milk, in an unusually awkward way.

"And?"

"And it cost two billion dollars an ounce to make," added Annie.

"*And*?"

"And, Bryson, there's really only one way we can test it properly. Yes, all early indications suggest that, set up right, it will generate more power than you put in—"

"Yes! Now that's what I'm talking about."

"But you know it was made for another purpose."

Hawke erupted with laughter again.

"The craft? The goddamn craft!? I thought you were just bull-shitting me, like everyone else. To keep me sweet."

"I don't need to keep you sweet, Bryson. I pay you a lot of money."

"A little too much, if you ask me, boss," said Annie, playfully. Milk hated being called boss, especially by her.

"Hey," said Hawke.

"Well, I'm not asking you, Annie. But I always appreciate the vote of confidence."

"Pleasure," she said, snapping closed the latches on the hard case. She then heaved it off the table and placed it on the floor by the window.

"And let's say I even believe you," resumed Hawke. "You think you can just waltz out there to some top-secret military cave, in the middle of the Nevada desert, knock on the door, and ask if you can play with their toys?"

"I don't need to," said Milk.

"Why—because you're Jordan Milk? Billionaire playboy and best friend of the president? Look, I love you, man. You know I do. God knows, you got me out of a real good jam. And I know what you're capable of—I mean, Jesus, you just invented fire two-point-zero—but even you, the great Jordan Milk, they will shoot on sight if you so much as step one foot over their boundary line without permission. Which they won't give you, by the way. Ever. Even at two billion dollars an ounce."

"I think I preferred it when he just snored his way through our meetings," sighed Annie, returning to the group with three flutes of cold champagne.

"I don't need to," said Milk, taking a glass from Annie, and offering the other to Hawke. "Because I have one of my own."

Hawke's mouth dropped open.

Milk raised his glass. "Cheers!"

15

3:00 A.M

Leon finally staggered clumsily out of the toilet and into the impenetrable blackness ahead, using his phone to light the way. He groped along the short passage like a hungover Boris Karloff, arms waving about and hands flapping, as the harsh LED light strobed against the walls of the confined space.

He stopped sharply at the partition door that would bring him back out to the main floor lobby and grabbed feverishly at the handle. He heaved the door back, anticipating the embrace of normality, and the luminous overhead lighting that came with it. But there wasn't any.

No strip lights. No streetlight drifting in through the shuttered windows. No service lights seeping up from the stairwell. No discreet murmur from the AC, or subtle fridge-whine emanating from beneath the counter of the adjacent kitchenette. Just an all-consuming, intoxicating, and virtually soundless gloom. Like the pressure deafness you get on a plane or a deep-running under-ground train. But instead of those engine sounds, there was just a persistent, faraway, and distinctly unmusical thrumming sound that Leon realised had been whirring away since he first came to.

His phone light dimmed suddenly, then went out altogether.

He tried the power switch. It momentarily woke the main display, but the LED backlight remained dead. *Shit.* He raised his hand and waved it in front of his face, trying hard to ignore the not-so-quiet panic scratching away in his animal brain. He thought, briefly, about how this could now become his, "so, I once woke up in an office toilet..." story, and imagined himself recounting it to friends on a good night out. But it didn't help much.

This is nothing, he silently explained to himself. *The building's probably on a timer. Or the DJ plugged in something he shouldn't have. That's it. Just a blown fuse. His speakers were—*

Leon froze. He tilted his head and strained to listen carefully to what he now began to realise was not the vague, distant sound of music being played four floors below. And the nagging sense of dread creeping around his feet abruptly swelled.

Where was the DJ? What happened to the music? Even four floors up, he should be able to hear *something* coming up the stairwell. The whirr and thump of dance music. The mumbling rhythm of people at a party. But there wasn't anything. No music, no distant rhubarb of conversation, no ripple of arguments being made and lost, or heave of people enjoying themselves. No barks of outrage, and delight, or laughter spiking out from the darkness. Just silence, and that distant indefinable machine-like thrum, slowly rising and falling, on repeat. Did the party finish already? He finally considered. Why didn't anyone tell him?

"What the hell is that noise?" he said, aloud. The muffled, underwater sound of his own voice surprised him as it broke into the dark. And then the smell hit him. A pungent, acrid aroma, like burnt flesh, against the thin, chilled air. Even in the barely discernible light of his phone, he realised he could see his breath fog.

He decided, finally, to call Tom. He wanted to know why his self-appointed *wingman* had apparently just let him wander off to this solitary fate. No signal. He waved the phone around hopefully, only then noticing the time was blinking 03:14.

"It's the middle of the fucking night!?" he barked.

Leon tried doing the sums in his head. The last thing he could actually remember. It was hard to think. Nine? Ten? It must have been around then when he and Tom were outside arguing about movie Hulk vs. the TV Incredible Hulk. For the second time. Or was that earlier in the evening? Ten at the most. Izzy went to leave at around eleven... Then he cringed as the ghastly vision of his green-faced parting with Izzy came back around. Him getting sick, just as she was leaving. *Great timing, you idiot.*

"So, I've been out for—what—five fricking hours!?" he muttered, incredulously.

His grisly stomach tried for another retch, and his already bone-dry mouth dried out some more. The sudden reality shift hit him all at once: that he'd apparently gone missing *and* been abandoned, as he lay face down on a piss-and-God-knows-what-infused floor, for over five drunken hours. And not so much as one missed call or a text? The catalogue of events, including, he must assume, his ungallant ditching of Izzy—what did he even say to her? He just couldn't remember and his complete disorientation at waking up in an office toilet, in the middle of the night, sent him reeling.

He lurched in the direction of the kitchenette, guided by the insipid light of his phone, and reached for one of the thick glass tumblers stacked up next to the sink. He cracked the tap wide open, instantly overfilling the glass, and downing it in one uncontrolled hit, as water piled up over the edge of the glass and down his chin. He didn't care. He needed it so badly, immediately, desperately. He refilled, and drank again, barely pausing to breathe as he gulped the water down. The nausea began to subside, his breathing to slow.

Leon took a step back, his now cold, wet shirt making its presence felt, as he finally began to calm down. He took a moment just to breathe. In and out. In. And out. And to consider his situation more thoughtfully.

He reached over the sink and poked a finger through the slatted wooden blinds to see what was going on outside. His gaze travelled over the rear-facing courtyard and adjoining buildings. Everything was where it should be, but also conspicuously pitch black—not a single light in any window—and starkly silhouetted against the sodium orange radiation of the unseen city lights in the distance.

So, definitely a power-cut of some kind, thought Leon. *And affecting just our buildings, it seems. Stupid DJ must really have screwed something up. He won't get booked again.*

Leon rotated the blind mechanism to let in more of the pathetic ambient glow coming from two streets away. It helped a little. He was finally able to take a look around. Coffee machine. Sugar tin. Tea box. Small stack of espresso cups. Dishcloth and washing-up bottle behind the sink. Neglected, sad-looking spider plant by the window.

And, turning around, the toilet door he'd just come out of. A weathered leather couch out in the middle of the hall, between all the meeting rooms. Fake weathered, obviously. Just one of many so-called strategic decor choices made by Derek, that he would loudly and often regard as "...the authentic mud of human experience."

The meeting rooms, with glass walls, all shuttered tight, and doors closed, along with repeating trios of small, square-frame photographs of "found objects" on the panels between each room. Everything as it should be.

"Right," Leon declared, to himself, as he pushed away from the kitchen counter, and headed towards the lift. His strength was finally starting to return. "You fell asleep in the toilet, like a total idiot. Party's over. Time to go home."

But then he stopped just as suddenly.

Something caught his eye in the gloom. Hard to be sure in the weak light, but it looked to him like one of the meeting room doors was open. Outwards. The wrong way. Hanging. Like something had prised it open. And if he wasn't just imagining things in the half dark, there was something else wrong with the doorway itself. The shape of it was all... Leon changed course, and gingerly made his way over to the far end of the hall, to see what was what.

Maybe there was some kind of accident during the evening, he thought. Then he noticed something underfoot, as he walked across the distressed wooden floor. Something gritty, like coarse sand, which intensified, and got scratchier, and more fragmented as he inched his way forward.

As he approached the room, his eyes continued to adjust to the dim light, and he began to see with increasingly uncomfortable certainty, the busted, gaping hole of what had once been a rectangular, steel-framed door.

What was left of it was twisted and overwhelmingly forced outwards, as though some giant, oversized animal had tried to stampede its way through the narrow, human-sized gap. The door itself hung in two pieces, dangling outwards by the thin mechanical arm of the fire-safety hinge.

The frames of the walls on either side of the doorway were similarly distorted, their formerly large glass panes shattered, and all hurled out in the same direction. He realised that was what he'd been walking on. Not sand but powdered glass.

The overall effect, now that Leon was up close, appeared as though something enormous had rolled at great speed towards the wall, and only just been stopped by it. At great cost to the wall. Except, there was no object. And seemingly no remains of one, that he could tell. Just the blown-out, bulbous shell of what had once been an ordinary office meeting room.

Leon gently prodded the hanging door with one finger. It moved easily against his touch, without any resistance, and began swaying gently back and forth. He immediately yanked his hand back, as though it was burnt. But the metal wasn't hot, he realised. It was freezing. He instinctively looked down at his finger. It looked stained by something. He couldn't make out what, but it felt smooth and gritty, as he smooshed whatever it was between finger and thumb.

The swinging door pieces suddenly sagged in front of him

and, with the groaning sound of metal under stress, abruptly crashed and clattered to floor completely, pulling part of the ceiling down along with it.

Leon jumped back just in time, as the debris landed at his feet. The noise subsided, and a swell of dust billowed up around him, making him cough and gag against the agitated awful smell and taste of burnt matter.

"What the fuck is going on here?" he growled insistently, finding it hard to comprehend what the fuck was going on. "Was there an actual explosion here?"

He probed the pile of wreckage gingerly with his foot, but nothing else happened. He performed the same test on the buckled door frame with the same results. Totally busted out but apparently stable. Assuming his scientific foot-prod test meant anything at all. Leon decided to tentatively venture through, and stepped into what was left of the former meeting room.

Inside, everything was scattered across the floor like rocks and stones and trees after a heavy flood. The large wooden meeting table was on its side, its back broken, and had been pushed hard into one corner. A bunch of soft-meshed plastic-frame chairs could be seen hemmed in behind it, like a waddle of penguins. Others were strewn about the remainder of the open space, also on their sides or backs. Some were in pieces, along with what was left of the all the conference equipment and stationery. The wall-mounted screen was shattered, as though pressed inward by the palm of some giant unseen hand.

Leon moved farther in, not quite able to grasp the situation. Someone either went completely nuts in here and trashed the place, he thought, or there really had to have been some kind of blast. Despite the poor light, there's no way this could be the work of a disgruntled colleague, however drunk and furious.

The scene was so dismal and extreme, even to Leon's untrained eye, that he now understood clearly: that was no sonic boom he'd felt upon his rude awakening in the toilet. It had to have been a real-life fricking explosion. But here? In the office where he worked, developing ad campaigns for sanitary products, for crying out loud? What the hell would cause an explosion like this—a new kind of weaponised tampon?

He walked over to the main window. It was also shattered, along with the wrecked blinds hanging in front of it. He pulled them down so he could look out into the street below. Aside from the lack of streetlights, everything looked pretty normal for three in the morning. A couple of passing cars, some pedestrians walking by in conversation. A solitary figure by the night bus stand, outside the hotel opposite. The hotel itself still seemed to have some lighting. Maybe they were on a different grid, he thought. Or maybe it always looked that way in the middle of the night.

Leon decided then, that whatever the hell this was, he didn't really want to be any part of it and turned to leave. But, as he started back across the room, he finally noticed another gaping door-shaped hole in the far wall.

With the subtle increase of city light bleeding in through the main windows, he could now make out the space where, previously, a large metal utility door had been. Leon had always assumed it was just a vestige of the building's former warehouse life – there were a lot of authentic "original features" left throughout the building repurposed for ornamentation, or possibly he suddenly hoped as a fire door. He'd never really given it any proper attention. Perfect, he thought. This should get me out of here, without having to faff about through the main entrance. Assuming the way down isn't blocked.

As he got closer, he could see from the jagged brickwork that the door mountings and large iron hinges had literally been ripped out of the wall. So where was the door? he wondered, just as his foot bit painfully into something incredibly hard and immovable on the floor, tripping him up. Leon flew forward, arms out, onto the ground. The clattering metallic sound, as he crashed into the buckled carcass of the former warehouse safety door, was almost as shocking as the fall itself.

Leon called out in agony, as the pain sheared across his ankle, and his humiliation gland kicked in all at once. It's always embarrassing to fall over as an adult, even when you're alone. Everyone knows that. And, in this case, the feeling of shock and pain was particularly intense, before it began to subside, and leave him with just a dull, generalised combination of pain and mortification to deal with.

Finally, Leon rolled off the misshapen door, which rocked crunchily with his shift in weight, and he paused to gently rubbed his aching shin and ankle bones.

"Well, I guess that's where the door is," he groaned, dismally.

He then took another look around the shambolic room, before picking himself up.

"Come on, Leon," he said, to encourage himself, as he stepped carefully over the metal panel. "You need to get out of here before something worse happens."

He made straight for the busted doorway, assuming it would lead him up and out onto the rooftop, where he'd be able to take a fire escape back down to the street, and then home.

16

GUT PUNCH

Izzy had given up intermittently hammering on the door and shouting for attention. Once she'd had a chance to calm down, she decided to give in to her fate, based on an agreement she made with herself that this was, *at worst*, just a temporary predicament. She figured that either Leon (assuming he'd survived his whiteout), Lauren or, worst-case, a random stranger, would show up sooner or later and set her free. With over a hundred people partying upstairs how long could it really be before someone appeared in search of something they'd left behind, or a discreet place to snog?

In the meantime, she attempted to make herself comfortable among the boxes and disused office clutter, and simply wait it out. She had a bottle of water in her bag, and a leftover granola bar she'd accidentally been carrying around for week. She'd be OK.

After dragging a few squishy cardboard boxes around, and arranging her coat just so, she was able to construct a suitable makeshift perch that afforded her some relative comfort. Then she lay back and waited for the universe to unfold. Inevitably, given the incessant, muted rhythms of the dance music upstairs, the warm, stuffy air of her cell, and plain old-fashioned boredom, she drifted off to sleep.

. . .

A booming, crashing noise lashed out around Izzy as she snapped awake to the sound of cracking, splitting masonry and rubble. Her eyes opened just in time to see the back wall of the small office space fragment and tumble apart. She instinctively flipped over and scrambled on all fours into the corner by the door, covering her head with her hands to try to block out the horrendous noise as, overhead, the lights buzzed and flickered before going out altogether.

The whole floor dropped momentarily into total darkness, while Izzy waited, terrified, in her downturned foetal position, eyes clenched tightly closed, for the room to fall on her. It didn't.

And yet, the almost unfathomable sounds of things breaking, crashing, and falling, of tumbling brickwork, of metalwork under strain, continued to whirl around her in a haze of echoes. Whether real or imagined, she couldn't be sure, until, finally, the clamour subsided into a dusty silence.

"OhMiGod, OhMiGod, OhMiGod..." pleaded Izzy, quietly, into her tiny corner of the room, as the quietness finally descended over her like a blanket. "What in the hell just happened!?"

Starting with just one eye open, she slowly began to unfurl, lifting her head, and then carefully turning her body back around to see what in the hell had just happened.

A solitary strip light above her partially restarted, buzzing erratically, leaving the dim light to flicker randomly on and off, as Izzy turned around. Finally, she repositioned herself with knees pulled up, and her back against the glass wall, now cracked in various places but still holding firm. What had earlier felt like a prison now offered her some strange comfort and protection.

Feeling that most of the action, whatever it had been, was over, Izzy pulled her phone out to see if she could learn what had happened or call for help. Although she suddenly felt a little unsure about who exactly she should really call—the police? Steve? (No chance). Her mum? What would she even say?

Hi, Mum! Just calling to let you know I'm trapped in a basement in London after the building collapsed. Or something. But I'm fine. Yes, I've eaten. How's the dog?

She also flatly refused to entertain the notion of some desperate, final phone call scenario, despite what it was she'd just experienced. But it didn't matter anyway. The handset was dead.

"Such bullshit," she sighed.

She then repeatedly thumbed the power switch to try to coax it back to life. When it finally booted up, she waited again for what seemed an eternity, as the device searched for a signal. There wasn't any. No 5G. No Gs at all. No Wi-Fi. And barely any battery, it seemed. Nothing.

She slid the phone back into her pocket, and falteringly pulled herself up into a standing position, to try the door once again. It was still locked tight, despite the apparent end-of-the-world issues affecting everything else.

"Right, Jones. Looks like you're on your own," she said, intentionally loudly, to stifle her quiet but growing panic.

She turned back to face the room, unconsciously brushing herself down. Much of it looked as it had before, aside from all the masonry dust, fallen ceiling tiles, and crumbling brick wall. Oh, and the smell. The weird smell. The smell she was only just beginning to notice. Harsh and sour. Like wood smoke after rain.

Despite the unsteady lighting, she was quickly able to locate her bag and jacket slumped on the floor, pretty much where she'd left them. The back wall, however, was something else. No longer even much of a wall. More like the cavernous maw of some giant shark, frozen midlunge. All broken, jagged teeth and menace. But also, she realised, like a way out.

"Alright," she said gratefully, grabbing her things. "I don't need to be asked twice."

Izzy carefully plotted her way through the maze of junk, then over the jumble of bricks and plaster that were slumped in a heap beside the long, ragged hole in the wall. She had no idea what this all meant, and she didn't want to know. In typical Izzy fashion, she would focus on what needed to be done now, and think about the big stuff later. Getting out of this crappy, dangerous room, for one thing, and then the presumably equally harmful building above it. It was the only thing that mattered right now.

Izzy stepped cautiously over the crumbling threshold and into the murky space beyond. She wasn't sure what she was expecting to find on the other side of the wall but a gloomy, damp, highly engineered concrete corridor wasn't it.

She paused to try to get her bearings and, as her eyes adjusted, realised the corridor was itself dimly illuminated by a series of thick utilitarian glass-shelled lights, like those she would some-times see on old underground stations. Utilitarian lights connected by utilitarian metal pipes. They at least seemed to still be working, she thought, positively.

Looking right, she could see they ran on for some distance towards...she couldn't really tell. More dark, broken places, she supposed. She could see from the intermittent, flickering light bleeding into the passageway up ahead that her egress had begun as a long series of smaller cracks and fissures that grew larger as they went along, before opening out into the literally full-blown hole beside her.

To her left must be the street, she thought. Assuming her sense of direction was holding up. And, therefore, it must surely be the best possible option for escape. Although, given the utterly weird shit that had just happened, who really knew? There were no markers or any helpful signage that she could see. Or, for that matter, any indication for whom this passageway had been constructed. But by then she had already begun moving off in that direction.

Almost immediately it seemed that the hallway came to an end. No sooner had she taken twenty steps into the dark, than she arrived at the bottom of a narrow, concrete stairway. She peered upwards but didn't get much from the experience as the stairs promptly turned a corner just one flight up. Then she tried leaning into the centre of the stairwell, to see if she could get a sense of just how far up they went. It didn't help much either. Even if it were not for the incredibly tight series of switchbacks, there was, as far as she could tell, very little in the way of stair lighting. God forbid someone should bring their elderly mother down here in the middle of February, she thought. Wherever down here actually was. But the one thing it definitely didn't seem to be was a direct way out onto the street.

She decided to climb a couple of flights anyway, just to check. Then scrambled up several more, taking her way above street level in her estimation. But still there were no exit doors to be found. No signs. No windows, vents, or any external features that she could see. Just the same slick, concrete walls, and the small, dim utility lights on every other floor.

Her options didn't seem very promising. Should she keep going up a random, anonymous staircase, to who knows where? Or head back down the long, blank, unidentifiable corridor to God-knows-what?

Just then, she heard a noise. A shuffle. A footstep. Several footsteps. She froze. It sounded like it might be coming from below, but she couldn't be sure. Who would be coming up the stairs, from where, and for what purpose?

Her heart started to race. She tried to contain her breathing, as she carefully backed her way into the corner of the narrow landing. Then the noise came again, but it was above her, she now realised, and instantly she turned to face it, straight into the looming shape of a shadowy figure coming down the steps towards her, with one arm raised. Were they attacking? Why were they attacking? She couldn't tell. She didn't think. She reacted. One swift blocking move with her left arm, as she stepped up, and a hard, Krav Maga knuckle punch to the gut. Her would-be assailant let out a strained bark, and folded in two, before tumbling down the last couple of steps, and falling faceup into the dim light. It was Leon.

"Leon?" she cried out, not quite believing that A. it was him and B. that she'd just taken him down so brutally.

But it was Leon, now with his knees up, clutching his stomach, and rocking on his back like a groaning, upturned beetle.

17

HELIOS

I zzy immediately knelt down beside him, slightly confused by his appearance but attempting to provide some kind of guilt-infused palliative care all the same.

"Oh my God, Leon, I'm so sorry."

"Me...too," gasped Leon. "That's. The last. Time..." he paused to catch a breath, "...I play hide. And seek. On the stairs."

He let out a long slow sigh-groan, and his body began to relax, now that he could accept he wasn't going to be maimed or killed by a stranger. As much as this had been a rude shock, he could think of plenty worse people to have punch him to the ground on a creepy hidden stairway. In fact, despite the utter weirdness of the situation, and the dreadful abdominal pain, he had to admit this had suddenly become an unexpectedly much better turn of events than he'd been expecting.

He made an extra effort to get himself upright, as he suspected the foetal position wasn't really a good look for him. Then they each, in their own way, manoeuvred themselves into seated positions at the top of the lower stairway.

"What the hell are you doing, creeping up on people like that!?" complained Izzy, as they settled in.

"What am I doing?" responded Leon, a little surprised by the sudden U-turn from nurse to accuser. "What the hell are you doing hiding on the stairs and attacking people!?"

"I thought you were going to hit me."

"Why on earth would I hit you!?" he replied, confused. Even without a shocking hangover, Leon suspected this still wouldn't make any sense.

"Well, obviously I didn't know it was you," she said, emphatically, but also, secretly, relieved that it turned out to be him.

"Who did you think it was?"

"I have no idea," she said. "A man looms out of the dark at me with his arm raised, ready to strike. What else should I think?"

"A man looms out of the dark? It was just me, walking down the stairs. I don't think there was any looming."

"Yes, you. There was looming. You definitely loomed."

"OK, I'll agree to a small amount of looming. But ready to strike? You stepped out of nowhere. I was just trying to stop you running into me."

"Oh, shut up," she said, playfully punching him on the arm.

"Enough with the hitting!"

Leon raised his hands in a mock surrender and they exchanged a smile in the half-light.

"Look. I thought I was on my own down here. Wherever here is. You took me by surprise is all."

"I will definitely try to rein it in next time."

"I'm sorry for hurting you. Although, I have to say, it was one of my best moves," she responded, with just a tiny bit of barely hidden glee. She'd never actually been able to do it for real before. Ronit, her Krav teacher, will be so pleased, she thought.

"I believe you. I get the distinct feeling you've been waiting to do that for some time."

"Well..." she began, sheepishly.

"It's OK. I'll live, I think. Frankly, it's not the worst thing that's happened to me tonight."

"Oh?"

"Don't suppose you've got any water in that bag of yours, do you?" he said, feeling immediately that he'd just said too much.

"Of course. Sorry. I should have offered."

She rummaged around in her bag, then handed him a bottle. He nodded and took a big swig.

"Thank you," he began, really savouring the hydration. "You know, just between you and me," he took another glug of water. "I may be just a tiny bit hungover."

"Hmm," she mumbled, as he handed back the water bottle. "I can't say I'm surprised. The last time I saw you..."

His toes mechanically curled in his shoes.

"Yes, sorry for suddenly bailing out on you. I was feeling a little bit...green."

Izzy laughed. "Oh, you were green alright. I think you'd have given Bruce Banner a run for his money." Leon laughed too, recalling their earlier conversation. "Tom will have to add you to his report."

"That bad, eh?" He winced.

"I've seen worse."

A distant police siren suddenly peeled out from somewhere in the city, bringing them back into the moment. They both looked around as though an answer to the siren was about to present itself, and stood up, ready to move.

"So, what are you doing here, man?" said Leon, suddenly serious, and gesturing towards the stairs. "I mean, it's three o'clock in the morning. The party's over. And I think..." he hesitated to admit what he knew; he didn't want to freak her out. "I think something...bad has happened here."

"Oh my God, yes! Tell me about it! I was going to ask you the same thing. Did you hear the explosion?"

"So, it was definitely an explosion?"

"What else could it be?"

"I dunno. I thought maybe a plane. A sonic boom."

"A sonic... Look, I don't know about you, but I nearly had a room drop on top of me. I'd like to get out of here. I presume we can just go back the way you came, right?"

"Uhm."

More sirens. But closer this time.

"I was thinking we head down," he continued.

"Down? Do you know where down goes?" she demanded.

"I didn't even know these stairs existed until ten minutes ago, so no. But I do know we can't get out the way I came. There's only one door, right at the top, but the power's down up there, and the whole floor is sealed off, as far as I can tell. No lift. Door to the main stairs was locked."

"Yes, same. I ended up climbing out of a hole in the wall."

"A what?"

"A hole. In the wall."

"Man," declared Leon, shaking his head, not quite sure what a hole in the wall might signify. "This is nuts. Well, we can't stay here, obviously. Let's head down. It must lead out somewhere, eventually."

They turned together and, without any more discussion, started down the stairs.

"I want to know what the hell just happened," shouted Snark. The mission room was half in chaos as technicians scrambled to adjust, punishing their workstations and communications networks with streams of remote commands. "Carson, get London on the horn. I want to speak to Benedict right now."

"Already working on it, sir," replied Carson. "No one's responding."

"Whaddyah mean no one's responding?" he yelled. "These goddamn jokers. Where the hell is Quinn? Why hasn't he checked in? What did we send him there for?"

Carson, typing hastily at a nearby console, looked up at two henchmen on the periphery of their cluster. She nodded at them and gestured a sharp get-going motion with her thumb. They immediately got going and headed off towards the exit.

"No one's been able to reach Quinn, either, sir. All mission comms are down."

"Jeezus. Is this Milk? Has it been confirmed? Do we even know where he is?"

"Unclear, sir."

Snark turned sharply and marched towards a briefing room on the far side of the mission area. "Situation team, with me," he bellowed.

A number of scattered personnel from across the room stopped what they were doing and gravitated in Snark's direction. He buttonholed a small group from Tactical Ops as he crossed the floor. They were dressed in black combat fatigues (what else) and huddled around a large multifaceted workstation. A couple of them were debating something on-screen. Another was muttering urgently into an old-fashioned wired-in phone. The last two looked up expectantly as he approached. Snark rewarded their expectations with a sharp, two-fingered point.

"You and you," he said, as he passed by. "Join the party."

The two men immediately peeled away from their assembly and fell in step behind him.

Carson finally swivelled away from her terminal, closing it off with a rapid, well-practised keystroke, and scooted gracefully over to join the tail end of the group as they entered the briefing room. The door closed behind her.

Snark flicked a control on the desk as she took her seat beside him. A dynamic arrangement of data and images flicked onto the large wall screen at the end of the room. On the lower half of the screen a series of eight CCTV feeds could be seen. All but two were filled with a combination of static and heavy digital interference that made it impossible to make anything out. Of the two remining scratchy feeds, one looked down an anonymous, poorly lit and empty service corridor; the other was a high-elevation view of a wet city street at night. London. If the passing double-decker bus was anything to go by. The frame was partially occluded by the angled silhouettes of nearby buildings on either side. Possibly it was mounted in an alleyway of some kind. After a short time, the two feeds took their turn switching over to white noise and then, maybe thirty seconds later, switched back again. One after the other. Like clockwork. Presumably all the camera feeds were on rotation, thought Carson idly, even though she pretty much knew the answer.

"Project Helios is dead," announced Snark. "Or, best-case, severely compromised. We have to assume from this point on that not only are billions of dollars and decades of research at risk, but if we don't get out in front of this—and I mean by the time we leave this room—then the whole goddamn operation may be about to blow wide open. There won't be any crashed weather balloons big enough to save our asses this time, and we'll all be answering questions on CNN before bed."

A murmur went around the room. Everyone looked at Snark then, briefly, at each other. Possibly wondering which one of them would get to be interviewed on CNN.

"If we're not all in jail by the end of the week," continued Snark. "I fully expect to spend the remainder of what will quickly become an inglorious career stuck in congressional oversight committee hearings until I retire or die. Whichever comes first. Right now, it's an even bet. I want all options on the table."

Mariko Lane, a quasi-political appointee and class A bureaucrat from the top line of her exquisitely tailored, blue pinstripe suit down to the tips of her highly polished matching navy-blue shoes, took the opportunity to dive right in. She pointed her pen pointedly at Snark.

"Look, I don't want to be the one to say it but somebody has to. We discussed this possibility almost six months ago. We rushed in. I warned you this would happen, and that we needed better safeguards," she said, plainly, then leaned back in her chair. Job done.

"Oh, yes? That's so helpful, Mariko. Thank you. Next time I need that kind of input, I'll just invite my mom to these sessions."

"I'm serious, Linden," added Lane. "Something needed to be done months ago."

Morris, a staunch Snark supporter who, when she wasn't fawning over his every word, imagined herself as some kind of peacemaker, leaned forward benignly.

"We need options, Mariko. Not recriminations. I think what Linden's trying to say here is that there's a—"

"I know very well what he's trying to say, Morris. I don't need a translator. And what I'm *actually saying* is it's been just seven months since we cracked the source code and finally unlocked this...this thing. Just seven tiny little months. After hammering away at it for seventy years."

"Your point being?" said Snark. "We all know the history."

"My point being, we researched the shit out of this for decades. Slow painstaking, methodical research. We spent the past fifteen years dismantling the source code alone, once that cell phone network schism opened up the frequencies. We analysed every single digit backward and forward. We still don't know where—or what—the hell it's broadcasting.

"We ran multiple simulations, from multiple facilities, and orchestrated field actions globally at yet more huge expense and then—suddenly—the lights go on, and it's like Dad's tossed you the keys to his Porsche with a wink and told you to be home by ten. I just don't understand the rush."

"We prepared everything with extreme care and attention," confirmed Morris, uselessly.

"I don't really believe it," stated Lane. "I just don't see how the data, or the expense, frankly, has ever supported a full-scale run at this time. Despite all the fantasy military and technological bene-fits your team constantly crows about, Linden. I told you six months ago. I told you last month. And I'm telling you again now. I'm sorry," said Lane, standing up, as though to leave, "I have no option but to escalate this."

Snark was unable to suppress an eye-roll. The others looked on furtively, worried that they might get drawn in.

"To whom, exactly, Mariko?" intervened Carson. "Really. Just so I can help facilitate. Should we contact HR again?" she said, mockingly.

This wasn't the first time these kinds of threats had been made by Lane, although with all the standing up from her chair and gathering of things, she did seem much more serious this time around. Perhaps she felt her opportunity to sweep in and push out the old guard—in this case, Snark—was finally here.

"I don't consider this amusing, commander."

"Nor do I," she replied. "But this isn't a simulation or a keynote at one of your manufactured symposiums. We have an actual, honest-to-God Texas-sized security breach to take care of. Let's try to limit the grandstanding to just the weekends, shall we?"

Lane opened her mouth to respond, but Carson cut her off.

"Please sit back down, Mariko, or we can just have you escorted from the room—and into custody."

Lane raised an eyebrow involuntarily, as though this idea had never occurred to her before. She sat back in her chair.

"Thank you, Carson," began Snark. "Given the circumstances, my recommendation is—"

"Sir, if I may?" interrupted Steven Macintyre, Tactical Operations team leader. His arms were stretched in front of him, holding rigidly on to his comms tablet.

"Yes, Mac, you may."

"The way I see it, sovereignty aside, we have no choice but to act decisively, and send in our own surgical team. The Brits don't have the resources or infrastructure we need. I suggest—"

"It's not the 1950s anymore, Steven," cut in Carson. "We have a Starbucks on every corner—even in Britain. I think we'll be OK."

"Let the man finish, Frankie."

"No, of course, ma'am," yielded Macintyre. "I wasn't suggesting the British weren't *capable* of containing the site. But the middle of London? It's going to get messy pretty darn quickly.

Before anything else happens, I suggest we mobilize one of our own units, and send them in to recover the data. My men here can be ready in—"

"No shit," interrupted Snark, as he glanced at Carson, hardly believing his ears. "Do you guys need time to go home and pack? Say goodbye to the missus?" he continued, with mocking concern. "We're six thousand miles away, for Christ's sake. I want that site locked down now. I need our data found, and the Helios device recovered. I want it done now. Not later. Not after top-secret coffee and donuts. Now."

Macintyre bristled visibly under Snark's disdainful response.

"Sir, I merely meant to suggest... What I thought... My thinking was that we could deploy one of the Cardinals. They're ready. The tests indicate... What I'm saying, sir, is we could be onsite within the hour."

"Oh my God, Mac. You want us to clean up one mess...by flying you over in a fricking suborbital spaceplane no one's ever seen, based on undocumented technology and—what—land it in the middle of London Bridge? CNN will just love that—once they've finished investigating the giant hole in the ground."

Carson leaned over and briefly muttered something in Snark's ear. He nodded in return.

"Sorry, Mac, I need you right here, coordinating security. We don't have time for you to spin up your new stealth toy. Which, just for avoidance of any doubt, is still 100 percent classified. International situation alert or not."

"It's just I—"

"Mac, I get it. But let's be clear, there's going to be one hellava scramble in London town in the next fifteen minutes, if it hasn't already begun. And our teams need to get there first—before the yokels start swarming the place and asking stupid questions. Carson, our local assets are primed, right?"

"Yes, sir. Already on standby."

"Fine. Let's do it. Debate club is over. Initiate the Berlin Protocol."

18

DISTORTION

Leon and Izzy arrived at the bottom of the staircase and continued briskly past the makeshift exit of Izzy's former cell. Leon glanced at the partially collapsed wall with some surprise.

"That hole?" he yelled, as they scurried on.

"Yep. I'll tell you about it when we get out of here."

He had to admire her optimism.

They followed the narrowing fissures and cracks running along the remainder of the dim corridor until, after a while they seemed to peter out. Perhaps the walls were stronger, the farther in they went, considered Leon. In any case, the deeper they went into the complex, the more uncertain they began to feel, and their pace started to slow.

Finally, they reached a junction, intersected by a double doorway, and paused. The two metal doors were of similar design to the one Leon had fallen over in the meeting room above. But unlike their upstairs counterpart, these appeared to have been smashed open from the inside, rather than ripped off their hinges. They seemed buckled and distorted by the experience and were pressed hard against the walls on either side. Pressed *into* the walls, it looked like to Izzy.

"This doesn't seem right," she said, pointing at the door to their left. "It's like the door's actually been pushed into the wall. Like it's made of clay, or something. What kind of an explosion would do this but not destroy everything at the same time?"

Leon shrugged. "It's my first explosion."

He then casually grabbed the handle and gave it a tug, expecting to reveal a nice door-shaped hole in the wall, like Wile E. Coyote. But it didn't move.

"I saw something similar upstairs, if that makes any difference. Whatever it was, it travelled a long way."

He yanked it again, harder this time, but still the door remained rigidly fixed to the spot. A two-handed pull didn't help either. Leon and Izzy looked at each other, slightly puzzled by this unexpected turn. Then Izzy added her weight to the effort, and they both attempted to wrench the door back from the wall. But still, nothing.

They leaned closer to get a better look.

"It's as if..." began Leon, curiously running a finger down the line where the wall and the door met.

"...the door is actually part of the wall," said Izzy, finishing his sentence, as she followed his finger with her own. "Like a film set."

"Or an ornamental broken door," he suggested, raising an eyebrow. "Maybe it's a themed tunnel, and they were going for a certain look."

"What, like 'bomb chic?'"

"Well, it's better than the alternative," he replied absently, examining the palms of his hands. "Have you noticed the dust on everything? I don't even know if it is dust. It's like a very fine powder. It's all over the floor and the walls. Slightly damp, I think. It was the same upstairs too."

He showed her his hands. There were faint smears of what looked like greyish-brownish powder where he'd touched the door handle.

"I hadn't specifically, but now you mention it. I can feel it under my shoes. Like the floor is kind of gritty.

"Exactly. Is that from the blast?" he said, as they stepped back from the door.

Izzy gently smirked and raised her shoulders. "My first explosion too."

Leon smiled in return. Fair point.

"Maybe they just never clean down here," he said, poking his head through the open doorway. There was a single step down into another corridor running left and right on the other side. Then he looked back at Izzy.

"What about the humming? You can hear that humming sound, right?"

"Oh God, yes. You can hear that?" she said, excitedly. "I thought it was just my ears. After the room blew up. Which way?"

"Right?" suggested Leon, and they resumed walking. "I thought the same. Well, actually, I thought it might be the world's worst hangover at first, but yes. I've been hearing it since I woke up. A sort of droning hum."

"Rising and falling. And..." Izzy paused and cocked her head to try to get a better fix on the sound. "Is that water too? It sounds like rain."

"You think it's rain?" said Leon, straining to hear what she described. "It sounds much louder now. We must be heading in the right direction."

"Depend what you mean by right. Do you think going to the source is a good idea?"

"I think it's the only idea. We can't get out the way we came. And whatever's making that noise, it must be somewhere accessible. A generator room or something."

"Which is good why?"

"I don't really know. But this can't be the only way in and out. It doesn't make any sense. Maybe there are people there. Maybe they can help."

"And if there aren't any?"

Leon looked at her blankly, not really sure if she really expected an answer.

They let the implication hang there for a moment, then they walked on in silence towards the hum, and the growing sound of rain.

Aside from a couple of sharp turns, the corridor continued for some distance without much change. Same dim lights, fluttering off and on at random intervals. Same damp, pungent air, filled with the odour of burnt hair. Same gritty feeling underfoot. But the noise continued to draw them onwards. They passed a series of closed doors. Closed, but also badly deformed and, on closer inspection, sealed cleanly into their frames, like the ones they had already come through.

The indeterminate throbbing persisted, becoming noticeably more present as they made their way along the passageway. Not louder exactly but cleaner, more physical, more foreground than background. Like a picture coming into focus. Obviously, some kind of machinery must still be operating down here, thought Leon, but nothing he could put a name to, like a car or a motorbike, or a lawnmower. Closer in rhythm to the large temporary air-conditioning units that get wheeled out to shops and hairdressers in the summer but more refined. The difference between a pub beer glass, and the posh wine glasses his mum gets out on a Friday night.

Then, up ahead, another set of double doors. One smashed into the wall like the first set, its partner half on the ground, ripped from its top hinges and half on the floor, like a broken wing. Beyond the doorframe, the space appeared to open out considerably, the faulty lighting providing fleeting glimpses into a much larger space as they approached. From the little Leon could make out, it looked like total chaos: blocks of furniture strewn awkwardly across the floor, or tipped clean over, stacking up in places like a train crash. Izzy grabbed his arm.

"Leon, stop. Look at this."

He stopped and looked, as Izzy crouched down beside the fallen door.

"This just isn't right," she said, warily.

"What is it?"

"It's buried in the floor, Leon. This door is half in the ground."

He looked again more closely. She was right. The door really was buried, as though it had simply slipped effortlessly into wet concrete, only to have it set perfectly, instantly, around it. And, like the door they had examined in the hallway, it was impossible to tell where one surface ended and the other begun.

"Man," said Leon. "This is too... The last one could have been a design choice. Maybe. But this is something else. Nobody would—"

"See if we can pull it loose."

"Really?" said Leon, not entirely convinced it would help.

"Just give it a try. Please? I need to know."

They both grabbed a section of the partially submerged door and heaved. Totally solid. Not a peep of movement. Leon gave it a firm push with his foot, just to be sure. Nothing. Like pushing against a wall. They looked at each other, then into the tumbledown space beyond the doorway.

"I don't like this," said Izzy. "There must another way out. Let's go back."

Leon felt a surge of discomfort. While it was hard to disagree with her, he instinctively felt this was the right way to go. He had no real idea why. Just a generalised sense that this was what they should do. Or perhaps a not-so-generalised sense that, with Izzy staring at him plaintively, he just wanted to be the kind of person who would know, for a fact, that this was what they should do. Then he realised that Izzy was apparently expecting some kind of response.

"Yes," he said, finally.

"Yes?"

"Yes, I agree with you. I don't like this either. The smell. There's dust everywhere. The furniture's a mess. Nobody cleans up," he said, with a slightly more domestic response than he had been expecting when he opened his mouth. But fortunately, Izzy smiled.

"OK, you're right," she said.

He was right!? He didn't know how he got to be right, but he wasn't about to argue.

"What choices have we got?" she continued. "Whatever happened here... Whatever this means..." She gingerly kicked the frozen door with her foot. "It's already happened."

Leon hadn't really been focusing on things happening, he realised. Or whether there might be more things to come. An hour ago, he was asleep in a toilet. Now it was all cryptic choices.

"Maybe," he said. "Maybe it's just the start of something worse. Listen to that noise. The water. Are we under the Thames now? I don't really want to be drowned under the Thames, to be honest. Drowned in a flooded room, under the—"

"You feeling OK, buddy?" said Izzy, disarmingly, and halting Leon from spinning out.

Don't be a dick, he thought. *Now isn't the time to unravel. There's no way Izzy wants to be stuck underground, in the middle of the night, with someone who unravels.*

"Yes, sorry," he replied, at last. "I have tendency to ramble when I'm trapped in a secret underground bunker."

"Oh? I thought this was your first time."

"First time for the blowing up part of the tour. Shall we see if we can get out anywhere?"

Izzy nodded briskly, and they cautiously moved on, through the open doors, and out into the larger room beyond.

19

WAX MUSEUM

Three miles away, in a concealed underground section of a partially derelict industrial unit next to Battersea Park, Rav Manchego was on the end of a scrambled, hard-line call receiving his orders.

Despite the locker-room banter, his team were already preparing their mission packs with an orderly, highly choreographed precision. The kind of synchronised efficiency that can only be achieved through years of working together in tight-knit, high-stakes operations. Each man laying out his equipment, in turn, onto the steel-topped workbench, and pulling items down from a secure station behind them: primary weapons prepped and loaded, sidearm and tasers secure, backup ammo in place. Gas-powered rappelling gun primed. Frag, smoke, stun, and chaff grenades arranged in strict rotation. C4 packs and thermite gel checked. Watches synced and radio channels set. Maps. Compass. Knife. This was not a drill: they were ready to move out.

"Yes, ma'am," barked Manchego, into his handset. "Vehicles have been on standby since 02:30. Sentinels have reported in. Condition 5—building is in complete comms blackout. Confirm —building is in blackout."

He turned back to face his team, satisfied to see his men

making final checks, securing toggles, and battening cords into place.

"Ops team is at running speed, ma'am. Just give the word."

The men, half an ear on their leader's conversation, instinctively responded to these words by pulling on their packs and securing their weapons at the ready. Eleven men in formation, awaiting final orders.

"Affirmative, ma'am. Thank you," declared Manchego.

He slammed the phone down onto its cradle and looked his team hard in the eye, assessing each of them man by man. They all knew from bitter experience the consequences of poor mission formation. But he let them wait anyway, in silence, like hungry dogs.

"I need not remind you," he began, at last. "We're on civilian time here and do not—I repeat—do not have local operational kill authority. That means no collateral damage. No direct contact with domestic security or provocation—I'm looking at you, Sims —should they arrive. Unless you have explicit confirmation of a hostile combatant, no fire. Even if fired upon."

"Sir, what about all the, uh, research personnel?" asked Sims. "Should there be any onsite?"

"So-called *research personnel*, as always, fall under general order number one. No one is to be left behind. Understood?"

The men firmly nodded their understanding of the euphemism.

"We have one mission. Get in, secure the *asset*, light a torch, get out. We are ghosts. Don't fuck it up."

The room erupted with a unified, "Yes sir!"

"Get to your vehicles."

The men broke up and jog-marched out of the room and along a short corridor, before fanning out across a small but functional array of low-ceilinged parking bays. These were all occupied by identical, black-windowed SUVs. They climbed in without any pause, four at a time, doors slamming, engines kicking into gear, and tires squealing as each car lurched sharply onto the exit ramp.

Above ground, a steel shutter completed its ascent into the roofline of a faux industrial frontage, built into the Victorian railway arches alongside a closed-down car mechanic on one side, and a dilapidated print works on the other. The three vehicles jumped out onto the street, one after the other, then sped away down a barely accessible access road, kicking discarded boxes out of the way, and throwing loose litter into the air as they zipped through.

Leon and Izzy stepped carefully through a field of scattered desks and chairs, and wrecked utility shelving containing an array of equally damaged computer equipment. Stacks of barely recognisable electronics, jammed into fallen metal racks, like components from some super specialised hi-fi system. Parts of it reminded Izzy of the huge AI labs and data farms she'd seen once on an exchange visit to MIT, but for Leon it was like something out of a bad sci-fi movie.

"You know," began Izzy. "I feel like I've seen a setup like this before."

"You mean this isn't the only destroyed underground computer lab there is?"

"No, not destroyed. Not even underground. A lot of this equipment—it's hard to be certain in this light—is really ultra-high-end machine learning stuff."

"What does ultra-high-end mean?"

"It means every one of these racks, or what's left of them, is probably worth a couple of million dollars."

"There's a lot of racks in here."

"Tell me about it. Just keeping this kit cool enough must be costing someone a small fortune. But what's it doing down here? What did you say your company did again?"

"Advertising. Search. Web and mobile stuff. We don't even

have the latest laptops, never mind machine learning. Although I have to say, we talk about that shit, All. The. Time."

"I'm just not seeing it. The running costs alone... It's Silicon Valley money. But if you were going to build one of these places, you'd never stick it down in an old basement."

"I didn't even know there *was* a basement."

Above them, something creaked and shifted, like old metal in a storm. You could feel a change in the air. Much of the ceiling structure was already busted apart and hanging down like jungle vines. Light fittings, tiles, and cables, intersected by long struts and thick beams, cutting into the room at different angles, like fallen trees. Leon began to wonder what was holding it all up, and if it was even safe to be down here at all.

"This whole place looks like it could collapse at any minute," said Izzy, echoing his thoughts.

"It really does," replied Leon, scrambling for something reassuring to say but not really finding anything. "Maybe it's done with the collapsing. Maybe that noise is just...settling."

"Settling?"

Leon shrugged. "Maybe we should just push on. Forwards or backwards, the risk of a crushing death seem pretty square odds at this point."

"You're fun," said Izzy.

"I try."

They continued to edge their way into the cavernous space ahead. The half-light wasn't helping but even so it was hard to get their heads around just how large this space was. The room was huge. An open working space of some kind, if the assemblies of busted workstations, office debris, and ruined hi-tech junk was anything to go by.

On the distant far wall, they could just make out an array of massive screens. All broken, of course, aside from one that still flickered on and off with static. In front of them were banks of what looked like fixed terminals, each with an assortment of built-in screens and knots of controls. It was hard to be sure in the gloom but, to Leon, it looked a lot like Kennedy Space Center, with the main lights turned off.

Nearby, more loose arrangements of desks, side pedestals of drawers, and wall partitions had been scattered in multiple directions. Upturned. On their sides. Drawers open. Some half buried in the ground, like the doors they'd seen on the way in, or weirdly merged into each other, in awkward combinations, along with a range of smashed and misshapen monitors, keyboards, and stacks of papers that seemed to be everywhere. Clusters of busted, broken chairs huddled together in little groups. The sound of water came on more clearly, drizzling and streaming into a space somewhere close by. The humming. The sound of people groaning.

"Wait," said Leon.

"What?"

"Is that someone calling out?"

They strained to listen more carefully. In among the din of machine noise and water, there was a distinctly human sound. Groaning? Calling out? It was hard to be sure, but whoever it was, whatever they were trying to communicate, it wasn't a happy message.

"It's coming from over that way, I think," said Leon, pointing towards the back-right corner of the hall. "Behind that stack of... whatever they are."

Izzy leaned out to try to get a better look, but the view was obscured by a confluence of half-sunk lockers, upturned office furniture, and more ceiling clutter.

"Do you think people are hurt back there?" she said, hesitantly.

"We should probably take a look."

They moved slowly to the right, edging their way along the melded clutter of stacked-up furniture until they reached an opening they could get through without having to climb over things. They squeezed through the gap, hoping to find—at worst —a bunch of highly irritated people who, presumably, had been employed to work down here, at their weird, secret underground jobs. But what they found instead was something they could never have begun to imagine.

Izzy let out an involuntary yelp, unable to really grasp what she was seeing

"Jesus Christ," barked Leon, struggling with a surge of nausea.

In front of them were perhaps twenty or thirty people, spread out across the back half of the room. Or what had once been people. Instead, the whole place looked like a wax museum after a fire. The handful of people who remained recognisable were almost incomprehensibly blended with other objects; with scattered furniture, and equipment they had been working at, the seats they had been sitting in, with the floor, with the room itself. With other people.

Leon and Izzy were transfixed by the gruesome horror of it all. Most seemed mercifully dead, to Leon's admittedly untrained eye, or at best, unconscious. A few writhed gently, dead-eyed, like some hideous living Francis Bacon painting, despite being merged with their consoles, or enmeshed in their chairs, or both. Some were partway sunk into the floor or the wall. While others, in small groups of twos and threes—it wasn't exactly clear—were fused together in unthinkable combinations, like a perverse human sculpture. It was as though everything in this space had spontaneously liquefied and then instantly set.

Leon and Izzy turned to each other in a moment of genuine shock and fear, sure only of each other, while the world as they knew it was suddenly up-for-grabs. Izzy instinctively reached for Leon's hand, needing something real to hold on to. Leon reached right back.

A moment later, something suddenly shifted in the ceiling above their heads. A sharp clattering, like marbles falling through a maze, and the distorted wrenching of metal under pressure, instantly jerked them back from their sickened trance.

Leon impulsively yanked Izzy deeper into the sea of disfigurement just as the ceiling broke open, unleashing a cacophony of pipes, twisted metalwork, wires, and dirt into the room, followed by a river of water that hammered down from the open wound above and into the space around them. They dived screaming onto the ground, and scrambled under a large, partially sunken table for protection, as the whole room took on an eerily *Titanic* feeling.

They held on tightly to each other as the water surged and frothed around them, terrified it would never stop. But it did, draining away almost as quickly as it had arrived. While, in the background, the persistent machine-like humming sound that had been following them around distinctly shifted gear and volume.

Finally, they dared to open their eyes and release their iron grip on one another. They were OK. They had survived. And, after taking a moment to breathe, they looked back into the room.

Right in front of them, almost at eye level, partly immersed into the floor at a slightly jaunty angle, despite the circumstances, was an incredibly wet Miles Benedict.

"Hello, Leon," he said.

20

BERLIN PROTOCOL

Outside it had started to rain. Not heavily but steadily, in a fine continuous early summer mist. Three black four-by-fours—the "Berlin" team—pulled a hard fast left from a near-empty Southwark Street, and into a narrow side road that ran behind the mixed commercial and domestic building complex that housed Hyperion's offices.

The cars kept a tight formation even as they glided sharply to a halt, one by one, roughly halfway down the road. They sat there for several minutes, engines running, as Rav Manchego, in the lead vehicle, pored over last-minute details of the building. He circled two areas of the blueprint on his in-car display and aster-isked a third.

"OK, all units, listen up," he said, adjusting the tactical mike wired into to his helmet's combined mini-cam and heads-up-display. "We have the special packet directives. You know what we're looking for, and what we may be facing. What we don't have is time.

"This site could go code zero at any minute, so we are in and we are out. You know the drill. We've done this a hundred times—backwards *and* forwards."

He tapped two icons on his display and hit send.

"I've updated the schematics on your HUDs. Ingress points have been revised, based on latest intel. Gamma squad you're on A, Delta on B. Miller, you will need to shut down the access grid as soon as you are through that gate. We can't do it from here. And we don't have time to wait for home delivery."

"Yes, sir!" came the instant acknowledgment over the radio.

"Alphas, you're with me. Everyone, on my mark: three, two, one—"

The doors on all three vehicles broke open simultaneously. Each group poured out in formation, and assembled into their units by the kerb, yanking their visors down as they arrived.

Manchego immediately took point and, using a raised, flat palm, indicated the three ingress areas of the darkened building complex ahead. The teams split off.

Manchego's unit moved swiftly to a nearby rusted iron gate embedded in the thick Victorian wall running parallel with the road. He made short work of the old lock, and they moved through the gate in single file, followed immediately by Gamma squad. Delta unit headed left, and disappeared round the next corner.

Once past the gate, Gamma pushed right, through a dense undergrowth, while Alpha headed straight on, taking an old, crumbling path towards a small cluster of buildings some 150 feet ahead.

They quickly arrived at an old, sealed-off service entrance that looked like it hadn't been touched in sixty years. Without speaking, one of the men instantly stepped forward and tacked on four sets of small plastic charges. The group then stepped several feet back, and hunched over, with their backs turned, as the micro explosives went off to reveal the entrance.

Just inside the doorframe was a short flight of brick stairs leading down into a large workshop space. There were two long benches down the middle of the room, covered with a collection of old boxes and a few scattered tools. It had clearly been a building maintenance workshop at one time. Everything was covered in thick layer of dust. And, other than the door they'd just come through, it also appeared to be completely closed off to all additional access points; no other doors or windows, not even a visible air vent that Manchego could see, despite his night vision-enhanced display. The effect was like a frozen moment of time. Almost as if one day, thirty years before, someone had just locked the door and then forgotten to come back.

"We been given a bad intel, boss?" squawked Pike, the ordnance specialist who had taken out the doors. "It's dead in here."

"Just keep looking," commanded Manchego, and signalled for the squad to proceed.

Additional worktops ran along the length of each side of the room, supported by a mix of shelves and cupboards. And as the team moved farther in, Manchego was finally able to make out what looked like a large bricked-up doorway in the middle of the back wall.

"This is the place," he muttered, and again, signalled his team to proceed.

They immediately surrounded the workbenches in the centre of the room, threw off the stranded junk into the corner, and moved the benches out of the way, stacking one on top of the other. This revealed an uneven floor, made up of a patchwork of wooden boards and planks, as if it had been repaired badly many times.

Pike stepped forward and laid a thick, braided cable into a large square over the floor. He took the ends and wired them into a small black plastic cube as Manchego and the rest of the team stepped behind the stacked benches at the end of the room. Pike quickly followed suit.

"Miller?" rasped Manchego, quietly into his throat mike.

Static on the airwaves.

"Miller. Report."

"Grid will be down momentarily, sir," replied Miller, finally.

Delta team had just broken through site access B, deep inside the main complex's machine room. Miller was crouched inside a narrow, caged compartment at the back of the hall, busily reconfiguring a densely packed industrial electronics unit in the dark. The whole thing looked like a monster circuit breaker but with several hundred micro sockets, all cross-wired in series.

The only light came from a small device on the floor by Miller's feet, with a long thin wire that was alligator-clipped into the primary row of sockets. Its tiny yellow screen whirred with digits spinning too quickly to see, like a Vegas slot machine on acid. One by one the digits came to a stop, each with a different number, and a series of five small red lights across the top of the device began to flick from red to green.

"Miller...?" came Manchego's impatient voice over the radio.

The last digit came to a halt. The row of lights flashed briefly, then all went green, followed by a sharp electronic *beep*.

Miller glanced up to see his comrades waiting, poised for action, next to a large, visibly misshapen, double-wide steel door. It bulged in the middle like a giant fist had tried to punch through it from the other side. He looked back at the device and pressed a small black lever on one side. There was an audible click, followed by a short wrenching metal sound coming from behind the steel door. Then came a hard mechanical pop of a large mechanism falling into place. A solitary red emergency light came on above the circuit breaker. No more fanfare. No mess.

"It's done sir," radioed Miller, plainly.

"Copy that," confirmed Manchego, looking to his ordnance officer on the far side of the room. He nodded briefly. "Do it."

Pike pressed an unseen switch of his own, and the cable square on the floor lit up like a white-hot firecracker, instantly resetting everyone's night vision, and scorching a deep furrow into the wooden floor. The smell of cordite, burnt wood, and metal was intense.

Two men moved forward, displacing Pike from his post, and prised open the large makeshift panel. They tossed it into the corner along with the rest of the junk. In the recess below was a rusted iron grate, hinged on one side and padlocked on the other. This too was quickly disposed of, revealing a flat grey steel hatch with a wheel-valve in the centre. On initial inspection, it appeared frozen, possibly welded closed.

"Pike?" suggested Manchego.

"We have it, sir," responded the nearest man.

"Quickly. It's yes or no."

The two soldiers pulled two short-arm crowbars from their packs, inserted them into opposing gaps in the wheel, and heaved. The wheel shifted slightly on its axis.

"And again," said the first soldier, as they repositioned the bars. "One, two, three…"

They pushed again, leaning their whole-body weight into it. There was a dreadful metal-on-metal squeal, and the wheel lock was freed. They pulled open the steel hatch with another sharp grind of metal, revealing a dark pit below. Manchego stepped forward and, using the torch mounted atop his Sig Sauer semiautomatic, aimed straight down into the hole.

A brief visual sweep revealed nothing but a narrow welded service ladder leading up a couple of meters from the floor below. Manchego lowered himself from the edge of the hatch and then dropped down into the dark. The rest of the unit quickly followed.

Once below, they could see a long corridor ahead, dimly lit with a string of flickering service lights. Much like the ladder, the metal walls appeared largely misshapen and cracked in places, as though something large and heavy had barged its way along, pounding from side to side as it went.

"Gamma, Delta. Report," ordered Manchego quietly, signalling his own team to halt.

A moment of static, followed by a clicking sound.

"Delta team in position," responded Bosko, the Delta team lead. "Ready on your mark, sir."

"Delta confirmed," said Manchego. "Gamma? Gamma team, report."

More static.

"Gamma team, report."

The static continued. Something was wrong. They all knew it.

Manchego looked back at his men. They patiently waited on his word to proceed. Poised for the kill, like hungry dogs, he thought. Waiting for scraps.

21

COMPLETE BULLSHIT

"Holy fucking shit, Miles," yelled Leon, jerking backwards in a mixture of surprise, horror and protest.

Miles attempted an unkempt smile. Clearly in pain but trying to hide it. "Nice to see you too," he said, polite as ever.

"Nice to see me!? What the hell's going on here, Miles? What are you even doing here in the..." Leon wrestled with how best to express the awful picture he was seeing. "In the ah...the uhm... the..."

"The ground, Leon," winced Miles, helpfully. "I'm in the ground."

"Yes, in the bloody ground. How is...? I mean, are you...?" It seemed such a bleakly redundant enquiry, but he just couldn't stop himself from speaking.

"Well, let's just say I've been better and leave it there. More to the point—what are you doing here, Leon? And who's your friend?"

"Isabella," announced Izzy, holding out a hand, without really thinking it through. "Isabella Jones."

They both glanced at her floating hand; then she awkwardly withdrew it. Miles attempted a disarming smile, despite his obvious pain and that his landlocked arms made it impossible for him to reciprocate in the way fifty-eight years of social programming compelled him to. Both his arms were partially sunk into the ground, along with the lower half his body, leaving three fingers and a thumb on his right hand to poke awkwardly out of the ground. That was pretty much it for handshakes.

"Oh, I'm so sorry," said Izzy, regretfully.

Benedict attempted, at least in his mind, to wave the comment away. But in the absence of any actual waving ability, a small shrug of his right shoulder and a couple of wagging fingers had to do all the work.

"Nice to meet you, Isabella Jones."

Leon, struggling more generally with finding himself in a room of half-buried, mostly dead human beings, ploughed on with the stubbornly awkward formalities.

"Izzy, this is Miles Benedict, Director of Accounts at Hyper... wait a minute. Director of Accounts? Government contracts? This place, whatever it is..."

Leon looked wildly around the room for something, anything, that would provide an official clue as to its purpose. Past the grotesque human tableau, to the oversized wall of screens, the busted workstations and, now that he was paying attention, what looked like a giant round bank vault door in the far wall. Complete with the oversized ship's wheel at the centre (this too was partially buckled and fused into its own frame at the base, leaving an uneven gap at the top, with a sliver of yellow-blue light leaking through it). And alongside that, to the right, a window. A big old thick glass window (that looked into what?), with the same yellow-green-blue light strobing gently behind it and the insistent humming machine noise that Leon now realised he'd been hearing since he first woke up. All at once it became impossible to ignore the fact that the throbbing sound, the eerie glowing light, the hideous dead people, and the unaccountable shock of Miles's presence here were all connected.

"...you're not down here by accident."

"I'm not," agreed Benedict, practically.

"So, your job at Hyperion...everything I know about you is, basically...complete bullshit!?"

"Well, it's not *complete* bullshit," Benedict remarked, with a faint smile.

A clattering sound erupted from somewhere nearby. Something falling or breaking, or both. But somehow with more intention than before. Leon followed Miles's eyes up to the ruined ceiling, expecting another downpour of building crap.

"What's in there, behind that door?" asked Leon, indicating the giant vault.

"Look, we don't have much time," said Miles, bluntly.

"Seriously, Miles? You can't just brush this off. What the hell is going on down here? What is this place? What happened to all these... What happened to *you*?"

"Should we call someone?" asked Izzy, feeling a little helpless. "Is there a phone that works? You obviously need help."

"So many questions," responded Miles. "I really wish I had time to answer them for you—"

"It's not like anyone's going anywhere," suggested Leon, with a wave of his hand.

"Leon!" said Izzy, punching him in the shoulder.

"I'm sorry. I don't mean. It's just that..."

"It's fine," insisted Miles. "Everybody needs to calm down. People will be here very soon, Leon, and I need you to do something for me."

"Thank God," declared Leon, with great relief. "We can finally get out of here."

"They're not coming to help, Leon. They're..." Miles hesitated. Whether in pain or uncertainty it was hard to say, and Izzy shot Leon a we-should-do-something look. "They're coming to kill everyone."

"To what!?"

"To kill everyone they find here. Including me, you, and your lady friend. And then they're going to set fire to the place—if the machine doesn't do it for them first," said Miles, bobbing his head in the direction of the vault.

As if on cue, the machine suddenly began to pulse in a new way. Its light and sound slowly increasing in volume and intensity, and syncing into some urgent, exotic rhythm of its own.

"Jeeezus, Miles," said Leon.

Miles's face reacted to a powerful spasm of pain, then briefly recovered.

"Look," he gasped. "I get it's a shock. And I'd love to explain everything but, right now, I really need your help and, unless you literally want to end up in the ground"—his eyes flicked around to his less fortunate colleagues—"dead, or buried like me, you need to get the hell out of here in the next five minutes."

What remained of the room's half-trashed lighting suddenly went out completely. Aside from the yellow-green light emanating from the vault window, the room plunged into a pitch-black gloom. The sound of electronic relays could be heard clicking into place nearby, as a series of dark red emergency lights scattered across the room came on.

Miles, Leon, and Izzy all looked round sharply as, somewhere close by, came the sound of people shouting—although not close enough to make out what was being said—followed by an exchange of gunfire. Erratic bursts. More shouting. Then the sound of collapsing masonry.

"Gamma team, I say again: report," demanded Manchego, severely. This would be his last call. "All teams on standby. Gamma is no response."

The static continued to hum and crackle then suddenly broke apart in a spike of harsh noise that quickly deformed into a mix of indecipherable shouting, followed by gunfire.

"Kraus, report. Where are you?" insisted Manchego. "What the hell's going on down there!?"

The connection continued to crackle and spark. Someone was talking but it wasn't clear who. The words were cutting in and out.

"Boss...someone else...another team...waiting for...knew we... They fired on us... But wait... 'thing's wrong. The machine... happened down he...Oh my God...fused with... They're melded with...floor. Everyone's dead! ...'od another wave. Retreat. Retr... Team down... Oh my God, I'm sink...I'm sinking into the..."

The connection cut off. A series of clicks. Then nothing. Silence. Manchego looked again at his team. Nobody stirred.

"Delta team, did you get any of that? Are you seeing anything?"

"Nothing like that, sir. Just the noise. Just the electrical sound. It's getting pretty loud. And then...wait. There's—"

"What?"

An eruption of weapons fire cut sharply into comms. More shouting. Another burst of fire. Then static, followed by silence.

"Alpha team," said Manchego, addressing his own unit. "The mission is compromised. But operational priority must be maintained. Looks like it's down to us."

He looked left and right as each man, in turn, nodded their commitment. He raised his right hand and signalled with two fingers that they move off in a two-column formation. The unit split, then moved silently, at speed, down the deformed corridor ahead.

They soon hit a hard left turn, followed by another steel bulkhead twenty feet in front of them, the remains of a tall valve-gate door appearing to hang like a drunk from one side of the twisted frame. The door had obviously been completely breached by a pressure wave of some kind. And what was left of the misshapen door was partly submerged into the wall behind it. They paused, and Pike stepped forward to examine the ruin more closely, running a finger down a length of metal where it met the wall. It was completely solid, with no visible seam between either surface.

"It's like a single unit, sir," he said.

"What kind of explosives are we looking at?" demanded Manchego.

"In this environment? With zero scorch marks, or without destroying everything else? No kind of explosives, sir. Nothing that could do this, short of a hydrogen device. But as I say—"

"OK, unless it's about to go off again, we can let the boffins worry about it. Document it for her ladyship, then join up the rear ASAP," ordered Manchego.

"Yes, sir," acknowledged Pike.

He crouched by the door mechanism, pulled a shoe-sized cloth-bound bundle from his pack and rolled it open to revealing an array of specialist metal tools. The rest of the unit had already moved on.

Beyond the distorted bulkhead was a long run of rippled passageways, almost all of them deformed and misshapen in different ways. And yet, still no sign of fire or heat damage. Whatever tsunami-like force had pushed its way along this route had to have been almost pure kinetic energy. Manchego had never seen anything like it, and he liked to think he had seen a lot.

They kept moving forward. The deeper they went into the complex, the louder and more physical the pulsating machine hum became, to the point of becoming operationally distracting. It felt like being pulled deep underwater as a wave crashes overhead. But nobody wanted to be the first to say so. They had a mission to complete and, in their line of work, the difference between failure and simply dying on the job was allowing doubt into the room. An unforgivable option among Manchego's ranks. For Alpha team, success was the only choice available.

Then, suddenly, a sharp, singular, metallic noise sounded some way off in the darkness ahead. Despite the thickening air and the relentless hum, there no mistaking the echo of a weapon being loaded. Manchego signalled the group to halt with a closed fist.

He looked back at his unit, nodding his respect to each man in turn, and they to him. Not everybody comes back from a gunfight.

Manchego took a tentative, silent step forward. And then another. Alpha team primed their weapons. He raised his flat palm and signalled go. Then, without another word to be said, they pushed on quietly into the world-ending darkness ahead.

22

KEYS

Izzy looked back at Miles, and shuffled closer to him, trying not to freak out about what they'd just heard.

"OK, just tell us—what do you need?" she said, urgently, not quite able to grasp Miles's horrifically unfixable situation. "I don't get the sense we can simply...pull you out of there."

"You can't, unfortunately. Forget about it. No one can do anything. What I need"—his face folded in pain as he let out a cracked, sharp breath—"What I need is much more...practical."

"Something to drink?" asked Izzy, pulling the water bottle from her bag.

"Not unless you have any scotch," he replied, only half joking.

"Just water, I'm afraid."

"Leon, there's a key in my pocket," said Miles, wagging his head towards the upturned console next to where they were lying or, in Miles's case, submerged. "I need you to grab it for me."

"A key?" Leon looked blankly at Miles. What kind of key could he be talking about? "Oh, you mean like the key to get out of here?"

"No. Not to get out of here—"

"I think he means a data key, right?" speculated Izzy, reflecting on all the tech around them.

"The key to my house. It's in my jacket on the back of that chair." He gestured again, more urgently.

"Wait—what? Your house keys? How is that going to help?"

"Leon," chided Izzy.

"It's not going to help anyone right now, Leon," insisted Miles. "But those people coming here to kill everyone? It's not just for fun. They want this"—he moved his head in a circular motion to mean everything in the room—"and they want what I know, all the information I have saved, to make it work."

"You still haven't even told us what *this* is, Miles," said Leon, mimicking Miles in an exaggerated head sweep. "I don't even know what you're asking. You want me to feed your cat and water your plants after you're—"

"You're just going to have to trust me. We don't really have time to argue. But, please, help me with this and I promise you'll get your answers."

Somewhere close by—perhaps just behind a far wall or a door —there was another rapid exchange of gunfire and shouting. Between the sheer size of the cavernous room and the eccentric heart-stopping hum of the as-yet-unnamed machine, it was hard to get a proper fix on where it was coming from. Only that it was closer than before. Too close.

"Sounds like you're not going to get much of a head start," continued Miles. "Take the key from my jacket, go to my house, and retrieve the files I've stored there before anyone else does."

"What kind of files are you talking about?" asked, Leon. "You mean like on a computer?"

"Kind of."

"Kind of?"

"You're a smart kid, Leon. You'll figure it out."

Another solitary shot rang out, followed almost immediately by a forceful metal-on-metal grinding sound. It moved in and out of intensity, as though something or someone was drilling. It seemed to be radiating from the far end of the room, not from the machine vault itself but somewhere disturbingly close to it.

"Look, I know you're in a tight spot and everything—" blurted Leon, crassly, and involuntarily shook his head as his words fell out of his mouth.

Izzy, equally unimpressed, shot him a seriously-what-is-wrong-with-you look.

"Sorry. I'm sorry," he continued. "I don't mean...but *kind of*? That's not super helpful."

The drilling continued to whine, seemingly in competition with the hidden machine.

"Leon, I'm trying to be brief here," said Miles.

"Look, even if we manage to do this," said Izzy. "And that's a big if, at this point—what are we supposed to do with these...files? Send them to the papers? Take them to the police?"

"God, no. Don't do that. Find a man called"—a surge of pain interrupted him, causing him to swallow his words.

Leon tried to pull him back. "Find a man called...?"

"...You must have met him," Miles continued, after a moment, and wheezed hard. "He was in the office earlier today. American. Walks with a... He will help you."

Leon had no idea who he meant.

"OK. Sure, Miles," agreed Leon, mainly to reassure a dying man. He looked up plaintively at Izzy, as he reluctantly began to accept the inevitability of this request. "But how do we—"

Suddenly, without warning, a large three-metre section of wall to the right of the machine vault blew wide open. Almost simultaneously a group of armed men emerged through the still smoking breach and fanned out into the space in front. Leon and Izzy turned sharply, half ready to bolt. Fortunately, their presence was obscured by the chaotic wall of desks and chairs and destroyed equipment, which gave them pause.

Leon and Izzy looked back to Miles, trapped in the floor. Then, from the opposite side of the vault, something rammed heavily into the back of a set of double doors. They shook with the force of the impact but didn't open until, a moment later, they too blew apart and another group of black-uniformed men hammered through. An immediate exchange of gunfire broke out across the cluttered space, with each group taking up positions behind stacks of fallen furniture and equipment.

The deafening sounds of weapons fire, bullets slamming into metal and masonry and men's voices seemed to explode in every direction. Whoever these people were, it was clear they weren't planning on making friends.

Despite himself, Leon had an inexplicable urge to see what was happening and strained his neck to see if he could get a glimpse of the action through a gap in the wall of debris behind them. Just as he did so, the machine vault let out an enormous, blinding pulse of white light, coupled with an incredibly deep and resonant vibration, like some ancient call to arms. Something must have hit it. The gunfire ceased, and for second there was total muffled silence, like after a snowfall. Then the machine humming started back up again with renewed and quickly rising intensity.

"Time's up," coughed Miles intensely, over the din. "It's not safe. Find the American. He'll know what to do. You have to leave."

The clamour grew louder still. Corresponding waves of vibrations started moving around the room, juddering everything in their path. Light fittings, tiles, and cables started falling from what remained of the ceiling. The piles of upturned desks and chairs and workstations started to come apart, with items tumbling and smashing to the ground. The huddled raft of chairs opened up and trembling their way across the floor. There were cries of pain and panic. Whether from the soldiers or other survivors, like Miles, buried in the ground, it wasn't clear. It really was time to leave. Izzy grabbed Leon's arm and pulled, as he turned back to Miles.

"What do we... where... We must be able to do something for you, Miles," screamed Leon, feeling a little desperate, as building matter began falling on and around them.

"You can take my bloody keys and get the hell out of here is what you can do," demanded Miles, "West Hampstead. Acol Road. Big red door. You can't miss it."

Izzy looked around feverishly for a way out that didn't include people who wanted to shoot them, or a giant machine that seemed on the verge of exploding.

"Isabella!" roared Miles. She snapped back to him. He bobbed his head towards the back of the room. "Service door to the left. Long corridor, then up a set of stairs. There's a door at the top." He began to cough again. "Code is...5...671...2."

"567..." Leon began.

"56712," barked Izzy. "Got it."

"It'll bring you out by Marks and Spencer on Southwark Street," wheezed Miles.

"Marks and Spencer!? Jesus, Miles. We're not buying sandwiches."

"Try to focus, Leon," responded Benedict, kindly. His body twitched and a grimace of anguish crossed his face, "We're all about to die."

Leon and Izzy looked at Miles, painfully discomforted by the knowledge he was a man about to meet his end (and possibly them along with him). That this was someone vital they would never see again.

The noise of the machine jumped up to eleven. The vibrations started fusing into a single, humming note. It was impossible to hear anything else. What was left of the roof began to rain down hard, making it difficult to see clearly.

Miles nodded almost imperceptibly.

"Run," he implored softly, closing his eyes.

Leon and Izzy scrambled up from under the table, grabbed Miles's jacket, and sprinted for the door at the back of the room as if their lives depended on it. They actually did.

.   .   .

Leon and Izzy stared silently at their reflections in the plate-glass windows of Marks and Spencer, breathing hard, dimly aware of all the summer dresses, underwear, and meal-deal offers vying for their attention. The world still looked normal. On the outside.

That they were standing there at all, caked in dust and sweat and God-knows-what kind of human particles, still didn't seem entirely real. The sheer noise and pressure had been almost incomprehensible as they'd busted their way through the narrow service door. Even running at full tilt, they barely made it across the threshold at the end of the corridor ahead of the red-blue fireball that had erupted in the room behind them as they left it.

The pressure wave alone had thrown them to the ground just as they burst through the already deformed double doors at the end of the passageway, and they scrambled quickly to push them closed, literally a second before the firestorm hit. They could feel the fire roil and heave behind the doors, like a giant wave, before retreating a moment later, and taking all the air with it.

Their ears popped with the sharp change of pressure, while the doors began to creak and shift and crack behind them, wrenched by unseen forces. The same subtle but potent pulling sensation then began to latch on to Leon and Izzy, like a tidal undertow, dragging them back to the machine, or what was left of it.

They clambered awkwardly to their feet, pushing hard against the force, as their clothes snapped tight, and fought them as if they were running underwater. Izzy's backpack then began to pull away on its own, yanking her back towards the splintering doors. She glanced at Leon, who grabbed her hand as the straps stretched across her shoulders, and they pushed forward together, one step at a time. The pieces of dead and flickering strip lights above their heads began peeling away and other debris flew past them until, finally, they reached the end of the passageway and the narrow stairs virtually on their hands and knees, so strong was the pull of gravity.

They reached out and just managed to grab hold of the stair rail as the two doors that had been their protector, only moments before, snapped away from their frame, and were sucked into the dark void filled with broken men, women, and machinery in the service of something they could not quite imagine.

Leon and Izzy's silent vigil was abruptly cut short by the noisy arrival of a convoy of assorted emergency vehicles, all converging on the intersection up ahead. They turned to follow the sirens, and saw that the intersection of Southwark Street and Southwark Bridge Road was being rapidly sealed off. More flashing cars and trucks began to arrive from other directions, while, above, two helicopters hovered into view from the east, and began circling the area, low enough that the searchlights hurt their eyes as they passed overhead.

"Oh man," said Leon. "Just look at this place."

"I guess we didn't make it all up, then. What happens now? Are we supposed to just go back home and sleep it off like a bad hangover? This will be all over the news by morning."

"Will it? You think what we just escaped from... What Miles just told us—"

"Miles didn't really tell us anything."

"He didn't have to. The guy was submerged up to his chest in a concrete floor. In the floor, Izzy! So were half the people down there. The rest were dead or worse. You think that's going to be on *BBC Breakfast* tomorrow between Carol's weather report and the sports update? And then there's this..." Leon was holding up Miles's house keys.

"I take your point."

"But reported or not, it seems I have a dying man's request to take care of. God knows why. And then how long will it be before he's identified down there, and someone else starts snooping around his place in search of answers? Can't say I fancy that conversation very much."

"You don't have to do it on your own, Leon."

Leon hesitated. The thought of fulfilling Miles's request, what-ever it turned out to be, was more than a little bit terrifying. So, of course, he didn't want to do it on his own...but it was hardly what he'd had in mind for a first date either.

"You don't need to say it. You didn't even know Miles until thirty minutes ago."

"Oh, but he was your best friend, right? I must have missed that bit."

"You shouldn't even have been there, Izzy," insisted Leon. "You should be back home, sleeping. Trying to forget about the guy who almost threw up on you."

He ventured a clumsy smile.

"Neither of us should have been there, Leon."

"True."

"And anyway," continued Izzy, before she could stop the words coming out. "Maybe I like people who thr—"

Leon's smile switched to a frown, as Izzy's collapsed into a cringe.

"Maybe you what!?"

"Uhm. That didn't come out well."

"Well, I didn't want to say," said Leon, suddenly feeling more hopeful about everything.

Another truck thundered past, larger this time. More armoured-people-carrier than fire service, Leon registered, despite the blue flashing lights.

It pulled up at the rear of the growing cordon and a cascade of men and women—it was hard to be sure which, as they were all wearing some kind of hazmat suits—piled out of the back doors as they were flung open. They were quickly joined by four men from the cab, each sporting combat gear and an assault rifle.

"But look," continued Izzy, apparently unaware of what was unfolding behind her. "Whether we were meant to be there or not, we barely got out with our lives. We were just part of some-thing that obviously wasn't meant to happen. And that we weren't meant to see. But we did see it, Leon. We saw what happened to those people. It almost happened to us. So, if we can help—"

"Help get ourselves killed too, you mean," said Leon, nodding towards the escalation of militarised human activity happening up ahead.

Izzy turned to look, just as one of the armed personnel lowered what turned out to be a pair of binoculars aimed right at them.

"I think we should probably get out of here," said Leon.

From somewhere deep below them came the muffled clamour of falling masonry and the wrench of steelwork. A series of cracks began to rip their way down the middle of the road next to them. The lab disaster, whatever it had been, clearly hadn't ended with their escape onto the street. A lot of shouting began to rise from the crowded intersection, along with the angry diesel noise of heavy machinery being moved into place.

The man with the binoculars was joined by two comrades, arriving from either side, and the three of them began talking and pointing in Leon and Izzy's direction. Then, after a moment, the uniformed trio started walking purposefully towards them.

"Come on," said Izzy, grabbing Leon's hand as she turned and started to walk in the opposite direction. "We're just a young couple on our way home from a night out, OK? Nothing to see here."

Leon didn't need to be asked twice, and quickly fell in step, briefly wishing this wasn't just a cover story they were making up on the fly. It didn't take them long to reach the Pret a Manger on the next corner, by the intersection of a pedestrian walkway that led past a short run of bars and restaurants, before opening out at the end, towards the looming half silhouette of Tate Modern.

"Down here," instructed Leon, pulling Izzy to the right just as the soldiers, still some distance behind them, broke into a jog.

Leon and Izzy didn't initially notice this change of pace but certainly weren't immune to the shouting that abruptly broke out as they had turned into the side street.

"Oi. You two! Stop!"

As soon as they rounded the corner, Leon and Izzy bolted like dogs on a racetrack. They tore down the alleyway, straight past a closing bar clearing down for the night. There were three large plastic containers on the pavement, filled with empty beer and wine bottles and a fourth being wrestled out of the door by a tired-looking barman, still wearing a white half apron that had seen better days. Leon instinctively heaved at the two closest bins as they passed and managed to yank them over, spilling glass bottles all over the ground, which dutifully rolled in every direction.

The barman swore loudly at them, but they didn't stop running, and cutting straight across Sumner Street at the end of the alley, and towards the Tate, narrowly missed by a speeding Black Cab as it rumbled passed.

The noise of the rolling glass immediately focused the attention of the three soldiers as they arrived at the end of the long walkway, and they switched their stride into a sprint.

Leon and Izzy skewed off to the right, partially obscured by the cab, towards a scrappy, dense array of bushes and stubby trees that ran alongside of the gallery. Leon looked up, startled by the tangled shape of buildings sharply silhouetted against a huge smoky orange plume of what he presumed was the remains of his offices. It weirdly reminded him of a Monet's sunset river painting of London. Or maybe it was just the towering cathedral of art next to him, exerting an uncanny influence.

"Over here," barked Izzy in a harsh whisper, pointing to the bushes on their left.

Leon looked over at the dark mix of greenery and young trees bordering the gallery and saw a small break in the hedgerow just as Izzy made a sharp beeline towards it and dived in. He quickly followed and they both rolled to a stop just ahead of the main footpath. They hastily crawled farther in on their hands and knees and turned awkwardly about in the spiky undergrowth so they could get a better view of the street they had just run across.

The three soldiers came to a sharp halt as they reached the opposite kerb, while a trickle of liquor bottles still skittered and rolled about their feet. They began to scan the options left and right for, presumably, the most likely escape route. Leon clenched his eyes briefly, and muttered a silent prayer: *not here, not here, not here.*

"Why are they even chasing us?" whispered Izzy, abruptly. "It's not a crime to be outside at four in the morning. Maybe we shouldn't have run."

Leon looked blankly at her.

"Maybe they just want to return something we dropped," said Leon, blithely. Izzy didn't seem very happy with this response and turned back to look at the men.

"It just makes us look super guilty, is all I'm saying."

From their narrow vantage point, Leon and Izzy could see the soldiers talking agitatedly to each other. The one who seemed to be in charge pointed left, and then upwards, towards the new twisted wing of the Tate extension, as he presumably handed out instructions. He then spoke into a radio pinned to his lapel before turning around and returning the way they had come. The remaining two soldiers gave each other a limp fistbump, then split off left and right at a walking pace. The barman reappeared a moment later, with a helper in tow, and chased after the last few stray bottles as if they were wild birds on the loose.

"Just when you thought this thing couldn't get any weirder," suggested Leon.

"So how long do you suppose we have to hide out in the bushes? I'm getting a damp bum."

"They might be trying to lure us out. Let's give it a while longer and see if any of them come back. Even if they're really after us for...who the hell knows what reason, surely they have bigger problems to deal with. There's a giant burning hole in the ground on the next street. They certainly didn't send all those people just to pick us up."

They looked at each other uneasily in the dappled sodium

streetlight that cut in through the foliage. Neither of them really wanted to consider the alternative.

So, they waited. With increasingly damp bums. For the right moment to make a break for the Tube, if it was even running. Listening to the sound of yet more sirens, and the now more or less stationary helicopters hovering above the rooftops nearby, licked by the blooming red-and-orange light below.

23

PAYPHONE

S ix thousand miles away and two hundred feet under the desert floor, Snark, Carson, and a retinue of Snark's minions and technicians stood transfixed by the video and data feeds spooling out across the giant multiscreen, at the front of the basketball court-sized control room.

"What the hell just happened!?" roared Snark. "Do we even have any actual assets onsite or is this yet one more billion-dollar bullshit experiment gone wrong? Why the hell is Quinn still MIA? All I'm seeing is Her Majesty's finest swarming all over our dinner party."

"It seems that Manchego's teams have been cut off, en route, sir," said Carson, attempting to soothe the situation.

"You call a block-sized sixty-foot imploding fireball getting *cut off*?"

"I just meant—"

"I know what you meant, Frankie. Helios is fucked. What's plan B? I want a plan B, C, and D in my office in fifteen minutes. Whatever happens—and I don't care what it takes—we have to get ahold of what's left of the device, or the next best thing—the raw data—before either the Brits, Milk, or Ronald Goddamn McDonald and whoever the hell else is wandering around down there can get their sticky little hands on it. Or do I have to spell it all out for you again?"

"No, sir!" responded Carson, sharply.

Snark threw his half-full foam coffee cup at a nearby console and stormed off towards the rear stairs and his office, ignoring the mess as the cup exploded on impact. Carson nodded to Macintyre and his team, and the six of them moved off to a side conference room.

"And clean that shit up," shouted Snark at no one in particular, as he ascended the stairway.

The rest of the room immediately returned to intense activity.

As Carson entered the conference room, she indicated to Macintyre with a brief look that he should lock the door behind him. She went around the table and took a seat across from Macintyre and his men, who remained standing to one side of the door, steepling her hands on the table in front of her.

"OK," she began. "The experiment is down. Gone. Lost for good, probably. Not entirely unexpected, maybe, given our limited understanding of the technology but, even so, it seems we should have been better prepared."

Macintyre went to speak, "Ma'am—"

"We'll have plenty of time for finger pointing later, Mac. Right now, let's review what we do have, and make some choices."

Carson pressed a switch on a small, embedded console in the surface of the table. The feed from the main room flipped onto the monitor at the end of the room. On the top right was a clock, counting off the seconds and minutes since the device had gone off. 16 minutes: 38 seconds. 39. 40. 41...

"All live machine data is dead. Same, we have to assume, for any personnel we had on site—including Manchego and the rest of our recovery teams."

Carson's phone rang. She glanced directly at Macintyre, then snatched it up off the table.

"Yes?"

"Carson, thank God."

It was Quinn. He was breathing hard, and the line was shot through with noise.

"I thought…" he continued. "I thought the entire operation might have been compromised."

"What the hell are you talking about?" demanded Carson, letting the lack of military protocol pass, for now. "Where have you been? Snark is tearing the walls up as we speak."

Macintyre's group exchanged looks with one another. Developments.

"I bet he is," panted Quinn. "Listen. I haven't got much time. Everything went down, ma'am. And I mean everything. The whole site is on fire. It's like a giant burning jellyfish right now. Power, comms—even the water supply is shot, judging by the first responders. And my division handset by the way? Totally fried, unless all you need is a crappy torch. Which is why it took so long to—"

"Wait, the handset? We built those things to stand up to a first strike. Where are you calling me from?"

This comment sharpened Macintyre's attention, but Carson raised her hand to hold him off.

"Sure we did," said Quinn, caustically. "We'll just have to return them to Amazon when I get back. I'm at a payphone in a subway station, for Christ's sake. They only just came back up. The phones. It's totally unsecure, and there's a line of terrified people forming behind me."

"OK, Greg. I get it. Then let's be quick. What have you got for me?"

"Look, it's not much at this point but what I do know is this is not—I repeat *not*—an experiment gone wrong. I was there. Everything ran like clockwork. The initialization data? It works, Frankie. It was working. The device lit up. It was beautiful. The results were tracking. Benedict had begun the activation sequence and then—boom. This was sabotage. Plain and simple."

The line behind him was getting restless. There were only three working phones and ten times as many people waiting.

Minor pushing and shoving had already started to break out across the overcrowded station concourse. And somewhere behind, Quinn could hear pleas and cries and the sound of hysterical tears, despite the crackly announcements coming over the public address system, asking for calm.

"Then how did you get out?" probed Carson, getting suspicious. What's the likelihood Quinn would be the only survivor? she wondered.

"I really don't have time to explain," he replied uneasily. The natives were beginning to turn their attention to him. Somebody started shouting.

"Come on, Yankee boy!" yelled a man, a few rows back.

"Greg, you either explain or I'm cutting you off and out of the program right now. Intel or no. You can find your own way back home and get yourself a dog." With seven decades of work on fire, she wasn't about to take any chances.

Quinn sighed and tried miming an apologetic I'll-literally-be-one-more-minute gesture at the gnarly mob behind him.

"Look, there was an explosive device. I saw it. Literally a second before it blew. I didn't have time to react. It took out all of the actuation servers."

"The what, now?"

"The actuation serv...the computers that control all the physical mechanisms in the experiment, surface controls, robotic arms and regulators, the vault doors. The safety valve basically. Somebody killed it. And everything that happened after that... It wasn't Helios. At least not to start. Somebody wanted this meltdown to happen, which means—"

"Right," said Carson, dubiously. "And you just happened to see it? And just happened to be the only one who made it out alive?"

"Jesus, Carson. What do you want me to tell you? That I put it there and I'm turning myself in?"

"It might help."

The shouting man stepped out of the line and approached Quinn directly, grabbing him from behind. He didn't want to be friends. Quinn reacted with swift precision, grabbing the man's hand and instantly turning it back on itself so its owner was forced to twist around with a sharp yelp. Quinn immediately followed through, wrapping himself around the man's neck and pulling his arm up and back into a half nelson in one swift motion.

"I'm. On. The. Phone," said Quinn, as plainly as he could. The rest of the queue all shuffled backwards, while the man, unable to move from Quinn's iron grip, shook and growled unhappily.

"Greg," yelled Carson. "What's going on?"

"I'm at a fricking payphone. What did you expect?"

"I'm still waiting."

"It wasn't just me. There were four of us, OK? At least in my section. Me and three technicians. I was at a workstation at the back, right next to the server stacks. I was watching the screen data and looked up to see what was happening in the vault when I saw it. Maybe thirty feet away. Hidden between the top of the cabinets and an air vent."

Carson grabbed a Sharpie with her free hand, pulled the lid off with her teeth, and scribbled a note on a pad on the table as they talked. She batted it across the table to Macintyre who looked at it, nodded, then signalled to his men who all turned and left the room together.

The man Quinn was holding finally stopped squirming, and he loosened his grip a little.

"Are you done being an asshole?" whispered Quinn, sharply. The man grunted and nodded reluctantly. Quinn released him. The man pulled away sharply at the same time and tried to cover his humiliation with a swagger and a grimy look as he walked away.

"And?" came Carson's crackly voice.

"And I only had enough time to register what I was seeing when it went off," continued Quinn. "The ceiling came down. We were thrown back. One of the guys was killed outright. The rest of us were saved by him and what was left of his terminal. Then the device started humming."

"What do you mean humming?

"Man, I don't know what else to call it. It was a sound like nothing you've ever heard. Whatever was about to happen, it didn't take a genius to realize it wasn't going to be good. I kicked the other two awake and the three of us scrambled out over the wreckage. The place was in chaos. Full of dust and smoke. You couldn't see more than two feet ahead, but you could hear shouting from the front. Over the alarm system. And the rising noise of the machine. Shouting or screaming. It was hard to tell which. Miles was barking orders—"

"Benedict is still alive?" interrupted Carson, finally sitting down in her chair.

"God, I don't know. He was. He probably isn't now. I couldn't see him and he sounded in pain. We made it to a set of emergency stairs and out onto the street just as the thing went off.

"One of the guys I was with must have got caught in the shock wave because he never made it out. The other one was terrified and pretty much made a run for it before I could do anything— straight into an oncoming vehicle."

"Is he dead?"

"It wasn't pretty. If he isn't, it won't be long. I only had enough time to check him over and grab his lab ID before the police started taking over the scene and moved me away."

"The police? But this only just happened. How could they know?"

"I thought the same thing. I circled the perimeter looking for... I don't know what I was looking for. But the streets were filling up with emergency vehicles and locking down the area before I could do anything useful."

"Jesus, Greg. You know what this means, right?"

"Yes, ma'am."

"Somebody expected this to happen. They planned for it."

"Yes, ma'am. Someone with access to a Level 5 restricted site. That's damn near impossible."

"Until today, I would have agreed with you. Things change. I'll talk to Snark."

"He's going to love this."

"Leave that to me. Do you still have access to Benedict's place?"

"Yes, but—"

"Look, right now, we have to assume everyone, and anyone is in on this—including Benedict. Hell, I've half a mind to bring you in right now."

"Wait, you're—"

"I'll send out an additional cleanup team to scour the site. In the meantime, learn what you can, then get yourself over to Benedict's house and see what you can find out there. And don't call me again unless you have solid intel, or you're actually dead."

"Yes, ma'am."

Quinn replaced the receiver, then moved off sharply towards the station exit, ignoring the now much longer line of people and the dull, familiar hip pain that walking without a stick would inevitably make much worse.

24

WATERLOO SUNRISE

West Hampstead was still empty at this hour. Just the oddball early risers. A couple of runners, competing with themselves, an insomniac dog walker, and the now-artisan organic milk provider delivering to the local middle-class hand-wringers. One lonesome gent, hood up, hands in pockets and clearly worse for the night before, staggering back to who-knows-where. There were a few cars on the road. Almost as if the world was still the same as it ever was.

Leon and Izzy headed up the stairs and out of the Tube station, passing a couple of early-start commuters going in the other direction. Leon popped his arm out to halt Izzy's progress just as they reached the pavement boundary and pulled her sharply to one side of the exit.

"Call me paranoid," he said, craning his neck out into the street for a better view of who, if anyone, might be waiting for them. Izzy followed suit, attempting to peer in the opposite direction.

It didn't seem to their untrained eye that anyone was lurking with intent. Just the random hoodie on the other side of the road, struggling to keep one foot in front of the other and already some distance away. They nodded at each other, turned left out of the station entrance, and headed purposefully along West End Lane towards where Benedict had, until last night, lived.

It had taken them longer than anticipated to get north of the river. Partly it was the extended hiding out in the bushes, waiting longer than they probably needed to for what felt like a safe moment to make their move. But then, since their idea of what a safe moment actually felt like had largely been rewritten by the evening's events, it didn't seem that they should be rushing anywhere.

In any case, they had eventually crawled out from their hiding place and scuttled quickly back over the small green, past the Tate extension, to make their way carefully towards the Thames: their unspoken thought being that Southwark Street was already off-limits and the riverbank, though likely deserted at five thirty in the morning and harder to hide on, would for that same reason make it easier to spot anyone who might be out looking for them. Either option was chancy but, absolute worst-case, Leon suggested, they could always jump into the river if they needed to. Izzy was less keen on that idea.

"Nobody wants to jump into the river, Leon," she said, as they shuffled past the Hopton Street houses and up an alleyway towards Blackfriars main line station and the river walk.

"Maybe not. But they won't want to go in either, right?"

"And that's what stops people with guns, is it? They're not cats."

Leon winced. Did he have to keep being a dick?

"OK, fine, it's just an option. It's got to be better than getting caught in a dead-end street. Besides, I'm willing to bet they are better at running on land than we are."

"Speak for yourself, soldier," responded Izzy, with a smile. "Let's just keep moving."

The riverside entrance to Blackfriars station was closed, as expected, so they scooted under the bridge, past the OXO Tower and wove around much of the Southbank arts complex, before deciding they were far enough along to head back inland and zigzag their way towards Waterloo station. Southwark station had been a closer option, but they had decided that the much larger former international terminal at Waterloo provided better and more public scope for running away and hiding, if they needed to.

They had planned to head straight into the Underground and then down to the Jubilee line but, perhaps unsurprisingly, the York Road access was closed off completely. The police had set up cordons around the main station entrance, so they could check people in and out.

Leon and Izzy hovered by the Italian restaurant on the corner of Sutton Walk, opposite the station. Even from this distance they could see a small unordered queue of confused travellers had started to form up ahead, like a human dam. Leon started reading the menu in the window.

"What the hell are you doing?" demanded Izzy.

"I'm looking at the menu."

"I can see you're looking at the menu!"

"I'm trying to appear inconspicuous. Look at this," he said, pointing.

"I don't much fancy Italian at five o'clock in the morning," she replied, ignoring him, and scanning the crowd for what she imagined might be hostiles.

However, remaining inconspicuous turned out to be easier than they first imagined. Despite the hour, the area was surprisingly busy with people traffic, either starting or ending their days. And presumably made all the worse by being held up, or at least slowed up, by the police intervention.

Izzy turned back and looked directly at Leon.

"What?" said Leon, raising his arms defensively. "It's supposed to be nice..."

"Why don't you just stare at your phone and wander around like everyone else here?"

Leon turned around and saw that it was true. People were scattered across the intersection, standing on their own or in small unaffiliated groups looking intensely at their phones. Even those trickling their way up to the station appeared transfixed by their devices.

"Either everyone has ordered the same Uber, or the news is out," Leon decided.

Izzy looked taken by surprise, as if it hadn't yet occurred to her. She took her phone out of her pocket and started fiddling with it.

"What does it say?"

"It seems to have died."

"Mine did the same. Try restarting." Leon fished his out of his pocket. "Although I thought the connection was fried by the—" He raised his handset up to see a small stack of notifications from his news app. "Ah. It's back."

"What does it—"

"Huge Gas Explosion in London Bridge," read Leon aloud from a news story. "'A large gas explosion rocked the London Bridge area at approximately 0300 this morning, waking many local residents and inflicting what appears to be significant property damage on the Southwark Bridge Road. Emergency services have been in attendance, including what appears to be a number of additional military support vehicles.'"

Leon paused and looked openly at Izzy.

"A fricking gas explosion!?" she said. "You have got to be kidding me."

"I'm just reading what it says. What did you expect them to say —Secret People-Melting Technology Experiment Goes Wrong in the Middle of London?"

More sirens could be heard in the distance.

"I know. I know. It's just that you'd think they could come up with something better than that."

"They?"

"What else does it say?"

"That's pretty much it." Leon looked back at the article. "... Emergency services. Military support, yada yada...OK. Here we go," he continued. "'Despite the high security presence, this is not believed to be a terrorist-related incident at this time. Priority has been given to putting out the fires, controlling the damage, and moving local residents to safety. Although some individuals appear to remain unaccounted for, only minor injuries have been reported so far. Despite the apparent size of the incident, Charles Bracknell, the city's chief emergency service coordinator, would only confirm, when pressed, that "...there have been no registered casualties. We would consider this a one in a million stroke of luck." But they would continue to comb the site carefully once it is secured..."'"

"Secured!? One in a million? Jeezus—just wait until they find all those half-buried guys in the basement."

Leon lowered his phone and slowly looked around as though reassessing the world for the first time. He turned back to Izzy, who was now unconsciously holding on to his sleeve.

"They're not going find any buried guys in the basement, are they?" she said, softly.

"I don't think they are, no," replied Leon, reluctantly, unsure how best to comfort Izzy, or even if should.

Leon and Izzy exchanged a look. In that moment they both felt that the world, as they knew it, had paused. Frozen in time, like a still frame from a movie. And the people around them, just supporting artists in someone else's story. For the first time since escaping from the "gas explosion," and whoever it was that had been chasing them, they felt alone and scared. And entangled in something so much bigger than a narrow brush with death. Too big.

Until that second, they'd been running on adrenalin and purpose. But it was someone else's purpose. A dying man's request. They'd just been content to get out of there in one piece. But now? Should they really continue? They didn't even really know each other. But they were also the only ones who knew what had really happened. What would they find when they got to Benedict's place? Who would be waiting for them?

Leon finally reached for Izzy's hand but was interrupted by a pungent homeless man who lurched into view, pushing an old supermarket trolley filled with an assortment of unrecognisable things. He stopped right in front of them and broke into a loud coughing fit as he went to speak, snapping them out of their shared reverie.

"Mornin'," declared the man, finally, before hacking up a noxious brew and spitting it out onto the pavement. "Nice one," he said, to himself, with some apparent semblance of pride.

Leon immediately felt the urge to move on and put his hand gently against Izzy's back in what he hoped was a universal let's-get-going gesture. But the homeless man noticed this and raised his left hand in a friendly gesture. He was old. Or at least he looked old through the tangled mess of hair and matted beard. Who could really say for sure?

"Sorry about that, mate. Really. Soz. I knows you're here wiv' your girl—"

"She's not my—"

"It's OK, lad. None of my beeswax, is it? You got any change? I wanna bit of breakfast and I'm struggling at the minute," he said, holding out a hand darkened with grime and hard living. There were a few blackened coins in the centre of his palm.

Just at that moment, Leon noticed two soldier-like men over the shoulder of the vagrant, marching towards them from the far end of York Road. The same two people, he suddenly realised, who had shouted them into a bush only an hour before. OK, he couldn't be 100 percent sure it was the same two men, but there was something about the fatigues they were wearing. Something about the way they were scanning the area with such serious intent. And the gun that one of them appeared to be holding.

Pretty brash, he thought, given all the police presence. Brash or perhaps simply there with permission. Whatever or whoever they were looking for, Leon didn't think they should wait around to find out if he was right or not. He elbowed Izzy and nodded towards the soldiers. Her eyes immediately widened. She recognised them too.

"We have to move," said, Leon, quietly. Izzy bobbed her head subtly in agreement.

But the homeless man and his cart was in their way, and was continuing his hard sell on breakfast money, making it difficult for them to slip away quietly. Leon reached in his pocket and pulled out a crumpled twenty. The drifter's eyes lit up.

"Oh, tha's beautiful." The world of contactless payments was starting to put homeless people out of business, so this was way more than a treat. Not just breakfast today! "What can I—"

"Listen," said Leon, before handing over the note.

"I'm all ears, geezer."

"See those two guys." Leon nodded again in the direction of the soldiers, who were still some ways off but not showing any indication of slowing down. It wasn't that Leon imagined for one second that he and Izzy were on some kind of wanted list, but he couldn't take the chance. The homeless man turned his head to look.

"Who, them two? Her Majesty's o-press-orrs?" punctuated the man, starkly, in response. He clearly had some private axe to grind.

"Yes, them."

"What about them?"

Izzy looked at Leon, imploringly, with zero idea what he was doing. Just give him the money, and let's go, she seemed to be saying.

"They're friends of ours," said Leon.

"Wot of it?"

"So, they...we were with them a little while ago. At a place. And it's payday for them, right? They're loaded. Look at them, all shiny and brash."

"What was you doing wiv 'em?"

"What were...?" repeated Leon, not really prepared for the question. "We were at a party."

"Yes," interjected Izzy, who was starting to catch on. "A fancy-dress party."

"Oh luverly," said that man. "I used to love them. Until I got. Until... But wot are you two dressed as?"

"Sailors," blurted Leon, knowing full-well they looked nothing like sailors, but unable to stop himself from speaking.

"Civvies," corrected Izzy. "He meant civilians. It was a Soldiers and Civvies party!"

Now it was Leon's turn to look at Izzy with incredulity. She held out her hands. It was clear by the homeless man's furrowed expression that this didn't really work for him either, and all he really wanted was the money and to get away from these two idiots.

"What about them?" he said, finally.

"OK," said Leon, placing the twenty-pound note squarely into the man's still open palm. "I'm just saying, those two, they're loaded and really committed to helping London's...homeless. They can't wait to give it away. When they find out that Steve gave you this..."

The soldiers hadn't noticed them yet—if indeed they were even looking—but had passed the closed York Road Tube entrance now and were closing in fast. Any closer, and Leon and Izzy would have to make a sharp exit drawing exactly the attention they had hoped to avoid.

"You're Steve?"

"I'm Steve."

"He's Steve," said Izzy joining in, with a broad grin. "Steve and Stefanie." She pointed artfully at herself.

"Steve and Stefanie," parroted the man, clearly confused by all this extra information when, in most circumstances, he was used to being thoroughly ignored.

"Yes, when they find out their buddies Steve and Stefanie gave you this, they'll double it!"

"They love doubling things," continued Izzy. "Uhm...that's why they go everywhere as a pair."

"Gotcha," said the homeless man, at last. Although he really didn't. "So, I tell 'em that Steve and Stefanie gave me this." He waved the twenty giddily. "And they give me more?"

"Yes!" said Leon and Izzy at the same time.

"But only if you surprise them right now," insisted Leon. "We'll wait right here. We can't wait to see the looks on their faces!"

"Oh, this is bonus night, alright. Janice is gonna love it!" crowed the homeless gent. He immediately set off with his trolley to intercept the two soldier boys.

Leon and Izzy lingered just long enough to watch the man snare the squaddies in some kind of discussion. Presumably involving breakfast. And Janice, whoever she was. Their frustration was immediately apparent but, presumably, the scope of their mission didn't include shooting a random homeless man in a very public setting.

In any case, Leon and Izzy didn't stick around to find out and quickly fell in step behind a small group of passing workmen, wearing Hi-Viz jackets, before making a swift beeline over the pedestrian crossing and heading up to join the messy queue entering the station.

This immediately presented another potential barrier, as the police seemed to be engaging everyone who entered or exited the rail terminal. Although it wasn't clear, even as they drew close, what they might be looking for.

"Do you think we should be more prepared?" murmured Izzy quietly, as they shuffled their way forward.

"For what? Unless you have any bombs hidden on—"

Izzy punched him in the arm.

"Ow! What's that for?"

"Be serious for one minute. What if they ask us where we've been?"

Leon looked back, briefly, to confirm that the old man was still keeping the soldiers fully distracted. It seemed he may have started to lose his audience, as one of them had pulled away and was gesturing firmly for his comrade to follow. But his friend was struggling to negotiate his way past the trolley. All good.

"What if they do?" said Leon, turning back. "We haven't actually done anything wrong. You know that right?"

"I know. I just think, we probably don't want to advertise to anyone that we've been anywhere near the, uhm, gas explosion," replied Izzy, making air quotes with her fingers.

"Totally. You go for it. I'll follow your lead."

They arrived at the front of the queue a moment later and were met with a couple of dour but efficient policemen, standing behind a wide fold-up table that had seen better days. The surface was grubby and scuffed, with the sticky remains of old plastic tape. Clearly this had all been rolled out at a moment's notice. One officer was just finishing with a woman ahead of them, taking a cursory poke through her bag. The other turned directly to Leon and Izzy.

"Morning," he said, cheerfully, without changing his expression to match.

"Everything OK, Officer?" asked Izzy, looking towards the station.

"No problem. Just a quick bag check. Standard after a security incident."

"We don't have any bags."

"What about the one on your back?" asked the second officer.

"Oh, yes, sorry. Forgot I was wearing it."

Izzy slipped the bag from her shoulders and laid it out on the table.

"Open it please, madam," he said, and Izzy obliged, shuffling it and herself across towards the second policeman and unzipping the main compartment. The police constable began to look through half-heartedly.

"You said there been an incident?" ventured Izzy.

"No, madam, I didn't. You seen the news this morning?" he said, without looking up.

"The gas thing?" suggested Leon.

The officer looked up from Izzy's bag at this comment, then smiled flatly, with his mouth but not his eyes.

"Nothing to worry about, sir," said the officer, pushing Izzy's bag back towards her.

"I thought the news said it was just an accident," added Izzy. "Why is that a—"

"As I say, madam," interrupted the copper, firmly. "*Nothing* to worry about. Go right ahead." He stretched his arm out towards the main door by way of encouragement to move on.

Izzy pulled her bag from the table and they both paused, as if anticipating a little extra interrogation for their trouble.

"Something I can do for you?" said the policeman, when it seemed they weren't moving on.

Leon went to speak, but Izzy beat him to it.

"Come on, sweetheart," she said theatrically, grabbing his hand and leading him up the steps to the main concourse. "We'll miss our train."

"We're going to meet her mother!" announced Leon, as he was dragged away, half mouthing the words like a drunk trying to be extra quiet. The policemen watched them go. One of them put their thumbs up.

Leon and Izzy trotted up the steps to the tall, ornate stone arch that housed the main doors, then scooted into the station itself, where a corresponding set of bobbies were positioned just inside of the doors, talking to a queue of exiting passengers. They headed diagonally across the concourse towards the escalators leading down into the London Underground, and Izzy let go of Leon's hand just as abruptly as she'd taken it.

"What did you say that for?" she said.

"Say what?" asked Leon, a little confused.

"Tell them we're going to see my mother."

"I was following your lead. I thought it would help. Nothing to do with gas explosions—that was the brief!"

"That was *not* my lead. They even didn't ask where we were going."

"I thought they might like us more if we seemed like extra helpful citizens and volunteered something."

"OK, great. Well, let's add that to the list. Rule number one: don't tell people we've been near the fake gas explosion. Two: don't try to impress the police that we're extra helpful people. We don't need them to like us, Leon. We need them to forget us."

"You're very good at this. Are you sure this is your first time escaping from a secret underground bunker and being chased by dangerous men?"

"Well, I did go to Ibiza on holiday once."

"Oh?" said Leon, with a knowing look, and his eyebrows raised.

"Don't ask," she said.

"Is that rule number three?"

They both laughed and headed down the escalator towards the Jubilee line and Miles Benedict's West Hampstead home.

25

NUMARK WAS HERE

Quinn made his way up the steps leading out of London Bridge Underground station and back onto Southwark Street, past an uneven procession of confused and frustrated people heading in the opposite direction. It wasn't clear why any of them were going there, as the Tube would not restart for several hours, and aside from some oversubscribed antique payphones, it didn't have a lot else to offer at this time of night. In times of emergency or confusion, it seems, people will do anything to get out of the house and join a queue.

Once clear of the station, Quinn cut away from the main road and threaded indirectly back towards the incident. He made his way along the edge of Borough Market, then wove through the low-level housing estate behind it to Gatehouse Square, where an arched doorway at one end of a long, late-Georgian brick wall opened onto Southwark Bridge Road. Though he had been mainly hoping to avoid the emergency response mashup that was assembling itself on the main intersection farther down the road, he also hoped this route might enable him to slip into the site relatively unseen. He was partially right. About the mashup. A lone policeman was stationed by the open doorway and it was clear, as Quinn stepped over the threshold, that cordons had already been set up in every direction. By the complete absence of bridge traffic to his right, he had to assume it was being diverted at the other end. Meanwhile, it appeared that Sumner Street, directly opposite, was being set up as a secondary operations post.

"Can I help you, sir?" asked the constable, as Quinn emerged through the archway. "This area is currently off-limits to the public."

"Thank you, Officer. I understand. Although, technically, I'm not really the public," replied Quinn, fishing some ID out of his inside pocket.

The police officer scrutinised Quinn's credentials, making a show of looking between him and the photograph on his card.

"Gary Numark, is it?" he asked.

"That's right, Officer. Gary Numark. You can call me Gary."

"I won't be doing that, sir. I will have to call this in, though. Not sure your money's any good here," he said, referring to Quinn's US credentials.

"Completely understood."

The policeman turned his back momentarily, instinctively looking towards the main command post, to radio in his ID check. Just as he did this, Quinn grabbed him tightly round the neck with his right arm and squeezed tightly, while looping his left arm in the opposite direction and hooking his hand around the back. In one swift motion Quinn was able to disable the surprised policeman. He quickly dragged him back though the open archway, and behind the high wall where they couldn't be seen from the main road. Although, fortunately, all eyes in the area were on the collapsed, smoking inferno farther down the street. The policeman struggled and heaved under Quinn's tightening grip, but rapidly his strength and effort faded as the blood to his brain diminished and he finally fell unconscious.

"There we go, my friend," muttered Quinn as the man's body went abruptly and completely limp. "It's all good. Time for a little nap."

He carefully manoeuvred the slumbering policeman down a

couple of steps and into the corner where the wall met the next set of buildings. In front was a row of parked cars that would make for a suitable cover. Of course, this was easier said than done as the man was now just a hundred-eighty-pound, five-foot-eleven-inch dead weight, with no easy-grip handles. But then this wasn't Quinn's first time lugging an unconscious police officer out of sight. In a last heave, he pulled the man back towards the wall, his feet dragging on the ground, and laid him down carefully behind a large black SUV. From his inside pocket Quinn removed a small zip wallet and pulled out what looked like a roll of nicotine patches. He tore one off, peeled the backing off, and popped it onto the policeman's neck, just as the man started to stir.

"Easy now. That should keep you nice and sleepy," he said. The officer murmured briefly and incoherently, though his eyes remained closed. "And with nothing worse than a nasty hangover to show for it."

Quinn hesitated, but a moment later the man had clearly slipped into a much deeper sleep. He took care to silence the officer's radio, before removing his hat and the public-friendly Hi-Viz jacket with Police printed on the back. Underneath was a sturdy black tactical vest, which he also unclipped and took for himself. The vest was adjustable, fortunately, but the jacket wasn't and remained a little oversized for Quinn's slightly smaller frame. He would just have to live with that and hope nobody paid him too much attention.

From the main road came the sound of large industrial equipment being manoeuvred into place and generators being put to work. The fire service, he assumed, starting to tackle the blaze head-on. Time to get moving, he decided, before they compromise the site any further. Either way, he wouldn't have long.

He stood up, pulled the police cap down over his head, and made his way back out onto Southwark Bridge Road, where several fire engines and support vehicles had indeed positioned themselves tactically beside the unstable ruins of what, until an hour ago, had been an ordinary row of warehouse-style office buildings. The churning heat was palpable even from this distance.

Attempting to go in the front was pointless, Quinn surmised, if not physically impossible due to clear explosive fire damage to the surface buildings. He wondered fleetingly whether any of the emergency services had been briefed by anyone on the extensive underground facilities. Or even if there was someone on site with that knowledge to brief them. But they would know soon enough. And, no doubt, there was a well-oiled WWII bunker cover story in a file cabinet somewhere that would soon be put to use.

Right now, he had to try to gain access to the central core to see if he could save—and then delete—whatever he could from the experimental data. He knew there'd be special recovery teams in play, but he couldn't afford to let them get their hands on it first. They were just too damn leaky, and too easily skewed by large sums of money. It's not for nothing that they're called mercenaries, he reminded himself. But then again, Manchego was different. Everyone knew that. For him every job was a personal point of honour. And if there was only one person still operating down there—assuming the blast hadn't just vaporised everyone outright —it would be him.

Quinn cut sharply across the main road, and past the makeshift operations unit being set up on Sumner Street. Fortunately, everyone was too busy with their own orders to pay him much attention. Just as he hoped, he looked enough like he belonged to the human apparatus that, aside from a couple of nods, no one even blinked as he passed them by. He continued purposefully down Sumner until he hit the first intersection where a couple of bobbies, dressed just like him, were posted on each corner. He nodded tightly at the nearest policeman as he approached.

"How many times are they going to walk the bloody perimeter, mate?" grunted the man, almost inaudibly.

"I said the same thing," replied Quinn, adopting a passable faux London accent. "I'll bring you lot a brew on my next turn."

"Nice one," he said. The policeman on the opposite corner just nodded, then looked away.

Quinn turned a sharp left and carried on down Great Guilford Street. Sure enough, it wasn't long before he caught sight of the three neatly parked Ops vehicles about halfway down. He doubted anyone would be coming back to retrieve those anytime soon and made a mental note to have someone on Carson's crew arrange pickup.

From here it was easy enough for Quinn to pick up on Manchego's trail. The man was nothing if not efficient. Why park three blocks away when you can leave your car right in the middle of a future crime scene? I guess they were in a hurry, he reflected, forgivingly. The rusty gate looked superficially untouched, although signs of a professionally forced entrance were easy to read if you knew where to look. He tickled open the timeworn mechanism with the end of a steel pen he pulled from his inside pocket, slipped through the gate, and silently made his way through the overgrown path on the other side. It didn't take him long to arrive at the old service entrance in the rear of the burning complex which, for now, appeared relatively unaffected by the blast. He paused all the same to assess it properly. It was clear most of the structural damage and incendiary action was on the Southwark Bridge Road side of the compound, but the sound of burning, stressed masonry and failing steelwork remained uncomfortably close. As did the rippling waves of heat from the fire and the acrid taste of dark smoke. It reminded him of burnt hair. And skin. While small particles of ash and charred paper seemed to drift in the air around him, like a dirty snowfall.

Quinn pressed on through the fractured service door. It was clear from the scorch marks and debris that this was the way that Manchego's team had come, and it didn't take him long to pick up the rest of the trail.

He lowered himself through the open hatch in the middle of the floor, and slid down into the corridor below, using the rails of the misshapen steel ladder. With no residual power the space below was in almost absolute darkness, save for the trickle of weak light leaking in from the hatch above. Quinn flicked on a small penlight and made his way down the passageway, towards the primary operations room.

It wasn't an easy journey. Aside from the difficulty of navigating through a poorly lit environment that was clearly damaged and likely unsafe, the metallic smell of burnt human beings had increased considerably. He tried to put that thought to one side as he wove his way carefully in the dark. The penlight was useful but its focus was narrow, and in a relatively confined space it often only illuminated obstacles the second before Quinn hit them.

He passed through the unseen, warped remains of the large airlock door, but not before clipping himself on the outer spokes of the flywheel. He paused to see what he'd hit, using the penlight to trace off the form of the large door, noticing how it was bent out of shape and partially fused into the wall of the corridor. This didn't surprise him. He'd seen this kind of damage before—molecular liquefaction, they called it—a known risk produced by several other experimental sites across the world. But between the exterior damage aboveground and the level of integrated molecular distortion he was seeing here, this fallout was on another order of magnitude. He also knew what the effect could do to people, and shuddered as he began to think for the first time since he arrived that the ones he could smell—the burnt flesh—might be the lucky ones.

He moved on. Then, only a few meters ahead, as if in answer to his fears, he literally stumbled over the remains of a man, half sunk into ground. He steadied himself against the wall then turned the penlight back onto the corpse, tracing the contours of the man's body where it met with the floor until he reached the top. The back of his head was partially submerged to the neck, leaving the face to stare blankly at the ceiling, bleached out by the harsh light and frozen in place like a grotesque Halloween mask.

Quinn recognised the man as one of Manchego's regulars: Simeon Pike, a specialist of some kind, although of what, he couldn't remember, or when he had last seen him. He knelt down to close Pike's eyes with his open palm, when he noticed that he had also been shot in the head.

"Whoa," said Quinn, quietly. "This I did not expect."

He flashed his penlight off into the darkness either side, as if to defend himself from a similar fate, but of course no one was there. It just didn't make any sense. Who would have done that, and why? Was it a mercy killing? After all, if Pike had already succumbed to molecular liquefaction, it might even be considered a kindness. But if the liquefaction had already taken place, then how did the shooter escape its effects? Someone else had been here.

Quinn grabbed Pike's night vision lenses, which came back to life after a quick reset, and killed his torch. The vision tech had clearly suffered some damage, probably from the blast, which limited his field of view but was still better than the penlight's narrow band. And had the advantage that, unlike the penlight, it wouldn't give his presence away, if any shooters were still lurking.

He took the added precaution of lifting Pike's sidearm before cautiously resuming his journey inward. He threaded his way down a series of corridors, all visibly affected by the earlier blast and, in a strange way, hard to take in. Combined with the compromised night vision, it felt to Quinn like he'd entered a corrupted fairground hall of mirrors, where parallel lines ceased to exist. It induced in him a subtle nausea and he seriously considered returning to the penlight when as turned the last corner and everything quickly turned into a house of horrors.

Even as an experienced operative who had already seen too much of the world's abominations in his travels, Quinn was halted in his tracks. The sub-operations area was like walking into an insane slaughterhouse rendered in molten wax. There were clusters of dead bodies, although you could hardly call them that. The remnants of bodies, of what used to be people, were clumped together in unnatural formations, or spread out like lumpen mounds of clay. There were almost no other word for it. Of course,

Quinn had read all the reports of what could happen, and even seen much of the documented evidence but never in person. And none of it quite prepared him for the grim, nightmarish reality he was now faced with.

It had never been his way to question his orders before. He had always known and accepted the risks of this line of work but, for Quinn, the potential rewards had always felt worth it. And not out of some kind of simple-minded patriotism but for something larger and, he knew only too well, idealistic. It was the greater good of the human project that drove his commitment to the cause. But for the first time, that commitment was wavering and he laughed aloud at his own naivety.

"Jesus, Manchego," he muttered. "You poor dumb bastards. Walking into this..." but he couldn't finish his thought. He heard a noise some distance away. He knew it could simply be the building structure shifting and heaving under the stress of the fire damage raging above—God knows it was hot and smoky enough down here—but there was something about it he didn't like. Too specific. Too metallic. Too... the noise came again, closer this time. He thought about Pike and his instincts took over. Despite his repulsion, he moved in closer to the nearest pile of human sculpture and found what he hoped he wouldn't see: headshots in every skull. Precise, execution-style wounds, intended to bypass the merely injured and ensure there was a clean kill.

He checked the two other groups, as well as four additional solitary bodies he found spread out much deeper into the room, which clinched it for him; these were clearly enemy combatants based partly on appearance but also, none of them suffered from the signature headshot.

Stepping back, it was clear they had all been in a gunfight but before the shock wave came through. Which meant the molecular liquefaction was all post-mortem—just like Pike. Manchego's team weren't victims of the explosion but of an assassination. Somebody had been sent to end them. To make sure they couldn't complete their mission or report on it. But who would do that, and why?

Another sound rang out. A scraping of metal against metal somewhere much closer but still beyond the burning smoky haze that obscured much of the hangar-sized lab space. Quinn quickly documented the scene using a live capture feature on the night lenses for later analysis. Then looked up just in time to see a man in body armour emerging through the smoke ahead. It was clear from his bearing that he hadn't yet clocked Quinn. Quinn raised his weapon and fired. A single headshot. Like for like. The man went down.

Quinn immediately turned and ran back in the direction he had come from before the sound of his shot drew others. He didn't get what he came for—nobody would. The data core would be totally compromised along with everything else down there. But he got what needed: proof that this whole catastrophe was no accident. Somebody had wanted this to happen.

He'd keep that to himself for now, he decided, as he climbed back into the old exterior service room. For now, he had to get to Benedict's place before anyone else.

26

BENEDICT'S PLACE

Following a slightly delayed train service, and a faux stealthy exit from West Hampstead Tube, Leon and Izzy headed down a more or less deserted West End Lane at six fifteen in the morning. Past a jumble of handsome late Victorian period properties, mansion flats, and the occasional 1960s carbuncle, until they reached the intersection with Acol Road, where they stopped and perched on a nearby wall.

They were tired. It had been a long, troubling night and despite a brief, fitful head-drooping nap on the Tube, it was all starting to catch up. They'd barely exchanged a word since leaving West Hampstead station. But on the plus side, the sun was just beginning to come up and, with that, some small sense of calm and relief finally descended on Leon for the first time since he had woken up in the company toilet. And while he struggled to consider this a date, exactly, he had to admit that—aside from almost dying—he'd had plenty of worse nights out with women.

"OK, genius," said Izzy, at last, taking a long swig from her water bottle and offering it to Leon. "Are we really going to do this?"

Leon took the bottle and gave it a wiggle. It seemed to him like there was nothing left, and he couldn't help feeling a bit peeved that she'd passed it to him. He made a childish show of looking at it, then pouring the last two drips into his mouth. "That hit the spot."

"Oh, I'm so sorry. I wasn't... We could go and buy—"

"Don't worry about it," he said, with his best impression of a smile. "Let's just go to Miles's house. We've made it this far. Even if nothing else comes of it, he can owe me a bloody drink of water."

They stood up. Izzy put her empty bottle back into her knapsack, and Leon rubbed his face, trying to push the sleep out of it.

They ambled down Acol Road, past yet more interesting and presumably expensive houses until, after a few minutes, they saw one up ahead with a large red front door—as promised—at the top of a short run of steps. A Victorian townhouse, in pretty good condition as far as Leon could tell from this distance. Miles had done all right for himself, he thought. All those government gigs and, then, ah. He remembered.

"He probably paid for that with all his danger money," he said, signalling with his hand for them to slow as they approached.

"How much money *is* danger money, do you think?" whispered Izzy.

"Who can say? Enough to buy a posh Victorian house, by the looks of it."

"Do you think it comes as job perk?"

"Like health insurance? I wonder if it says it on his pay slip—tax, national insurance, pension, danger money..."

Izzy smiled at him. *This one's funny,* she thought.

"Let's take this slowly," he continued. "There might be someone there already."

"Who's going to be there—his wife and kids?"

"I don't know! I don't know if he had any."

"His mum?"

"His mum? So, you think he sent us on this little mission of his so that we, two complete strangers, could go to his house—where he still lives with his mum at fifty, or whatever he was—at six in the morning to wake her up and tell her he's dead?"

"Sorry! It was dark. He was fused with the floor."

"I was thinking more like an assassin."

"Shh. I think someone is there."

They scuttled across the road to get closer, and peered in through the sparse foliage of the thin, spidery hedge separating Miles's house from the rest of the street. They could just make out what looked like the top half of an elderly lady poking up above a half basement recess at the side of the stairs that ran up to the main entrance of the house. She appeared to be locking a door. Izzy jabbed Leon in the ribs.

"See?" she whispered.

"See what? How do you know she's not just an old lady killer sent to guard the place?"

The old lady, killer or not, finished locking her door, climbed the few steps up from the basement and walked to a paved area just to the side of the house, where an absurdly small grey-brown Italian car was waiting for her. She put a couple of bags into the tiny boot, and then climbed into the car and started the engine.

"Turn away," said Leon. "Don't let her see us. Pretend we're looking at your phone."

"What if she's just a distraction so the sniper can get us?"

Leon shot her an unhappy look. *I'm trying here.*

The car backed very slowly out of the makeshift drive, reversed-turned towards them and then, with a brief crunch of the gears, drove away in the opposite direction. They watched the car go, then looked at each other. It was now or never.

They crept carefully past the already open gate and up the moss-stained old steps to the large front door. They both strained to get a look in through the main front window but there wasn't much to see. Just some half-open shutter blinds and behind that a dimly lit room of some kind. Living room? Lounge? Dining room? It could have been anything.

Izzy shrugged and fumbled in her bag for Miles's keys, while Leon maintained a watch on the street for anything vaguely threatening. She found the keys, selected what looked like the most front door-ish option, and stuck it into the lock. It slid in easily with a barely perceptible but satisfying *snick*. With a brief glance over her shoulder at Leon, Izzy turned the key, pushed open the heavy, ornate Victorian door, and walked into the house.

Inside it felt cool. Not in a Shoreditch expensive coffee kind of way but chill and a little damp, as old Victorian brick houses can sometimes get when no one's been home for a while. The hallway was sparsely but elegantly decorated, with classic black-and-white Victorian floor tile leading neatly away from the front door through the rest of the ground floor and, to their left, a neatly carpeted stairway, complete with a finely polished dark wooden banister. Leon carefully pushed the door closed behind them and thumbed the deadlock switch into place.

"Do you think that will help with burglars?" whispered Izzy

"I think it will help stop anyone just barging in on us," he whispered back. "Or slow them down, at least."

"Fair point. Do you think we should...call out? See if anyone's home?"

"Let's just assume that Benedict knew what he was doing, and that whatever he had in mind didn't include freaking out his family. Assuming he has any."

Izzy nodded and stepped quietly forward to examine a couple of nearby pictures, nestled on an occasional table by the wall.

"Doesn't look like family stuff to me," she said, offering a frame to Leon.

He declined. "Let's just find his office and get out of here before anyone else comes looking."

Izzy put the picture back carefully and moved quietly up to the end of the hallway, peering into an open lounge room on the right as she passed.

"I'll look upstairs, then, shall I?" declared Leon, wavering as she headed off without him.

"Why don't you look upstairs?" responded Izzy, as she slipped into the kitchen at the rear.

He was two-thirds of the way up the stairs when he heard Izzy scream, and came stumbling back down again. He zipped through the hallway and into kitchen before coming to an abrupt halt.

What he found there was Izzy, standing rigidly by the garden door, with her back turned and one hand griping the fridge handle on her left.

"What!?" he said, panting slightly. "What is it? What's happened?"

She turned to look at him, darkly.

"Mouse guts," she announced slowly, with a pained look on her face.

"Mouse what?"

"*Guttss*," she hammered back at him. "*Mouse. Guts.*"

"Oh, Jesus, Izzy, I thought something had actually—" began Leon, stepping to one side and peering round her to discover a bloody, eviscerated mouse spread out over the floor adjacent to a closed cat-flap in the back door. "Ewww!" he reacted, a little repulsed, and instinctively stepped back. "That's disgusting!"

It was disgusting. The mouse was in several pieces, with its oily, discoloured giblets spread out extravagantly across the floor.

"I know," said Izzy, closing her eyes. "I *trod* in some." She was wearing open-toed flats.

"Oh dear," responded Leon. "Do you think you can still walk?"

"This is serious!"

"You mean, after the night we just—"

"Yes, Leon," she interrupted, jabbing at him with a finger. "Even after all that. I. Don't. Like. Mice. Especially dead ones."

"OK. Alright. I get it," he conceded, softly.

"It's looking at me, Leon. With its little dead eye. It's blaming me."

"I know," he said, taking her hand. "Let's get you away from this terrible carnage."

Leon led Izzy gently over to the kitchen table and sat her

down, a little surprised by this sudden turn of events. Considering how robustly she'd appeared to handle the insane calamity of the previous night, he couldn't have anticipated that a mere mouse would cause her to unravel so completely. But, on the other hand, he was also a little relieved to find that she was basically human after all. And, if he was being honest with himself, that it wasn't him instead, losing his shizzle over this admittedly grotesque crime scene. *I mean,* he thought, *what if the place had been overrun with slugs?* He shuddered just to think about it.

"I'll get you some water," he said, finally, and walked over to the cupboards by the sink and began fishing about, looking for glasses.

He found some and took two out, then ran the tap until he was sure it was nice and cold. He filled them and carried them back to the table, giving one directly to Izzy and putting the other on the opposite side for himself.

"Thank you," she said, taking a large swig and noticeably relaxing.

Before joining her at the table, Leon returned to his search around the kitchen, opening and closing cupboards at random before finally finding what he was looking for in a small utility room at the back of the room, right next to the murdered rodent. He came back out a moment later with a dustpan and brush, and waved them in a playfully victorious manner.

"We'll get this cleaned up. It won't take a moment," he said, proceeding to bend down and, kind of reluctantly, gather up the gory remains into the plastic tray.

"Sorry, Leon," said Izzy, rather mournfully. "Not exactly my best moment."

She wasn't best pleased with coming off like a helpless idiot. It was just a dead mouse, she thought, reproachfully. What was she thinking?

"Don't worry about it," replied Leon, waving it off. "After what we've seen tonight? I'm sure it's just your brain letting off a bit of steam. A delayed reaction. I could probably do with a good scream myself."

"Well, you'd think so," she said, half getting up from the chair. "But mice are a...uh. Here, let me help you."

"I've got it," answered Leon, standing up and looking about. "Where do you think—inside, or outside?"

"Definitely outside. Who knows the next time anyone's going to be in here?"

"Good point."

Leon turned towards the garden door, pulled back the bolt at the top, then unlocked it using a key that was already in the lock. He turned the handle and yanked open the unwilling door, which was partially swollen into the doorframe. And then he screamed.

Standing on the step, waving a steel crowbar, was Captain Gregory Quinn.

"Hi there," he said.

27

ONES AND ZEROS

Izzy jumped up, muffling a squeal of her own, as Leon knee-jerked back from the open door, dropping bits of mouse back onto the floor. The American activated his Big American Smile.

"Not exactly what I had in mind for breakfast, buddy," he said, glancing down, and stepping up and into the room "Although I've eaten worse."

Izzy instinctively shifted closer to Leon. Another joker to deal with. But an American joker. Could this be Miles's man? Leon was considering the same thing, but given the events of the night before, neither of them were in a rush to find out.

"Can we...help you?" demanded Izzy.

"Well, I guess that kinda depends," replied Quinn.

"On what?" enquired Leon.

"On what you're doing here, in my friend's house."

Quinn lingered in the doorway, his hands spread apart in an open gesture. Or at least as open as hands could be when one of them was gripping an iron bar.

"Aren't you going to invite me in?" he said.

Leon and Izzy exchanged looks. Invite him in? Is this guy

crazy, or could he be...? At which point Quinn saved them all the heartache and just stepped into the kitchen anyway, closing the door behind him and turning the lock, all in one fluid motion.

"Let me save you both the heartache," continued Quinn, popping the key into his shirt pocket and handing Leon the crowbar. "Would you mind?"

Leon, a little taken aback by this request, simply took it wordlessly from his hand and moved to the side. He looked back at Izzy, who was giving him serious WTF-eyes, while Quinn made his way over to the kettle and filled it from the tap. He proceeded to pull mugs out from a nearby cupboard and laid them out on the counter.

"Let's have a drink, shall we. Unless you've had breakfast already?"

He didn't really seem to expect an answer. Nor did he get one.

"I thought not," he continued. "Coffee? Tea? I'll make coffee. You look like you could use some."

He opened another cupboard and pulled out a French press and a bag of coffee grounds that had been neatly folded closed at the top. It seemed like he had been here before, thought Leon. So, either this really was Miles's contact or he was just lucky when it came to kitchenware. He looked at Izzy who appeared to be thinking the same thing. How could they be sure, he wondered.

Quinn finished pouring out three mugs of coffee, then turned back to his steadfastly unenthusiastic audience with a smile.

"Sit down, already," he implored. "It's just a cup of coffee."

Leon and Izzy sheepishly took a seat at the table as Quinn deposited a mug in front of each of them.

"I don't know about you guys, but I've had a hellava night."

Leon's mug had a picture of two yellow cartoon ducks, leaning towards each other as though about to kiss, while Izzy's was much plainer; a blue brushstroke splashed across white.

"Milk?"

"No thanks," said Izzy emphatically, just as Leon went to

speak. He would have quite liked some milk, but Quinn took her as speaking for both of them and sat himself down at the table. "But some answers would be nice."

"Answers? OK, let's start over," began Quinn. "I can see you're both a little freaked out, and to be perfectly honest with you, I wasn't expecting anyone to be here either. I'm Greg."

Leon and Izzy looked at him, blankly. Leon wondered if Greg was going to kill them. Izzy decided to just go with it.

"I'm Isabella. Jones. Isabella Jones."

Leon wasn't expecting her to be quite so forthright, but now that she'd just come out with it, Quinn turned to look at him expectantly.

"Leon," said Leon, gruffly, reluctantly.

"There we go. Isabella Jones and Leon. That wasn't so hard, was it? Now we can be—"

"Look, Greg," interrupted Izzy, suddenly. "While I appreciate all this nicey-nice coffee morning chit-chat—and pardon my French here—but who the fuck are you?"

She had to know. Either this was the person they had been told to find, or they had ended the worst possible night by running into a random psycho.

"She's all business, eh, Leon?" responded Quinn with a wink.

"Yes, Greg," spat Izzy, indignantly. "I'm all business when it comes to complete strangers pushing their way into a house where they clearly don't belong and threatening—"

"Whoa! Now, hold on just a minute, lady. No one's threatening anyone. And unless I'm way off the map here, I don't think either one of you are exactly paying houseguests."

"What about the crowbar?"

"What about it? I gave it to your boyfriend here."

"He did give it to me," admitted Leon, agreeably, feeling the urge to join in. Especially now that he'd been described as Izzy's boyfriend. He lifted it slightly off the chair next to him where he'd hooked it over the back, as though to prove it.

"He's not my boyfriend," replied Izzy. "And you still haven't answered my question."

Leon tried not to let any hint of disappointment leak out of his face.

"OK, fine. You want to take it down that route. We'll take it down that route," said Quinn, fumbling around inside his coat pocket briefly and fishing out a leather wallet, which he then flapped open for them both to see. "I'm Gregory Quinn. Captain, United States Navy."

This really could be Benedict's man, thought Leon. He pulled at the wallet for a closer inspection and Quinn let him have it.

"It says here you're retired," declared Leon, still feeling conflicted.

"Yes, I am retired. Retired from flying planes, that is. Retired as an active ranking officer in the American military. But I'm not retired from the US government, where I maintain a uhm... consulting position for various agencies, and where—until last night, anyway—I worked with people like your colleague, Miles Benedict."

"Wait," said Leon, allowing himself to relax a little at this revelation. "So, you knew Miles?"

"Yes, Leon. I knew Miles pretty well. And the fact you slid all the way out to past tense without a pause tells me just what I suspected when I found you lovebirds lurking in his kitchen: that you know something about what happened to him. And, since there's no sign you broke into his house, that he sent you here."

Quinn let that hang there for a moment, while Leon and Izzy recalibrated what they thought they knew. Again. After a moment, Izzy went to say something, but Leon beat her to it.

"You said colleague."

"I did."

"But how do you—"

"How do I know you were colleagues? Let's just say it's one of my jobs to know. As I suspect you are beginning to figure out for yourselves, Miles was involved in, let's say, an unusual line of work."

"You're talking about that, that whatever it was that blew up last night?" suggested Izzy.

"Yes, Isabella Jones."

"Izzy."

"Yes, Izzy. That and quite a bit more. My job was to help him."

"Help him do what, exactly?" asked Leon.

"Security."

"Great job," Leon replied, raising his cup in a toast, and relaxed enough to take a swig of his bitter, milkless coffee.

Quinn winced imperceptibly at the implication.

"So, what are you doing here, then?" said Izzy. "More security?"

"In a manner of speaking."

"Great," declared Leon. "Perhaps we should call the fire brigade in now, and save them some time."

Izzy kicked him under the table. She didn't see it was helpful to antagonise Quinn at this point, friend of Miles Benedict, retired captain, or not.

"Sorry about him," she said, as her waning fear finally shifted to genuine curiosity.

"Hey," responded Leon, not really sure if he was annoyed or pleased by her intervention.

"No, I understand completely," appeased Quinn. "I'd feel just the same. But look, we don't have a lot of time. I'm not here to burn the place down, I can promise you that. I just need to find something, and my guess is you are here to do the same. Maybe we can help each other out?"

"Help each other how?" asked Leon, finally softening to the idea that they had indeed connected with the right person. "We don't even really know what's going on. Miles just told us to come his house and retrieve some kind of files."

"Files? Did he tell you what was on them?"

"All he told us," added Izzy, firmly, "is that someone—*the*

American—that's you, we're now assuming, would know what to do with them."

Quinn nodded slowly.

"Do you?"

"Do I know what to do with them? Yes, I might. But first, we need to find them. And we need to do it quickly. Unless you already have?"

Leon shook his head.

"We only got as far as the dead mouse before you showed up."

He noticed Izzy's eyes briefly flicker with embarrassment and regretted bringing it back up, imagining that this remark may come back to haunt him in some way. But her composure quickly returned and they all stood up at some unspoken cue.

"I imagine he must have an office or a study somewhere," said Izzy, absently smoothing down the front of her top with one hand. "That seems like a good place to start."

"It does," agreed, Quinn. "Why don't you two take a look around, and I'll keep watch down here, in case we get any unexpected visitors."

They shuffled out from their chairs and wordlessly headed back into the main part of the house. Quinn made his way to the front lounge and took up position to one side of the large bay windows, where he could get a clear view of the road outside. Leon and Izzy, trying not to think about what he might have meant by visitors, headed up the stairs in search of the files.

The upper landing held no real surprises. One large master bedroom, elegant in a classic sort of way but practically furnished, with little in the way of any adornments. The bed was made but there was a half glass of water on the nightstand, and a stack of books next to a scrappy lined pad with some vaguely indecipherable notes etched on the top page. It also contained a coffee ring, where the pad had presumably been used as a makeshift coaster.

"Nothing here," said Izzy, after a brief look around.

Next door was another bedroom. This one had a single bed it in, with a sparse selection of books, toys, and games visible on the shelves. There was also a dated-looking football poster above the bed, although Leon had no way of knowing from when. Izzy went to the window and peered out through a gap in the curtains, which were already closed. Leon moved on.

He passed the bathroom, and at the rear of the house found an incredibly overstuffed office-come-spare bedroom. The sort of room where tidiness comes to die.

There were books and papers and stacks of files on every conceivable surface, including the bed itself, which was barely visible under the clutter. Any walls not clad in overfilled book-shelves were concealed by notes pinned on top of notes and pictures, on what looked like a background of yet more notes and papers.

To Leon's right, opposite the rear window, was taped a large, wall-sized star map of some kind, or at least that's what it looked like to him. Constellations of stars, with tiny printed words and numbers next to each cluster, like satnav coordinates. A few of the groups were smothered in Post-it notes, with spidery writing and doodles on them, along with an arrangement of small photographs that were spread unevenly across the entire tableau. Some of them looked like they'd been cut from newspapers or magazines, while others looked like original prints.

He stepped farther into the room and turned around to get a better look at the collage. And as he did so, it became clear there was also web of cotton or string pinned at various focal points, and intersections, in a pattern or arrangement that was not in any way obvious to Leon. Whatever it signified, it would take more than the fifteen minutes he expected to be here to decipher. Or maybe there was no meaning, he thought briefly, and Miles was just a total nutter.

"Izzy," he called out. "I think I've found something."

The fresh morning light streamed in clearly through the sash windows from a cloudless sky. From this vantage point, Leon could see the greyed-out London skyline silhouetted above the rooftops of other houses at the far end of the garden. A small reminder that despite all the chaos he had stumbled into, there was still some sense of order in the world.

Izzy came through the door and, as she did so, Leon noticed that several of the cotton threads spidering their way across the wall met—or possibly started at (it was unclear from which direction you were supposed to read it)—at a fixed point, in the middle of an array of A4 sheets of paper that had been crudely pasted together to the right-hand edge of the larger map. Presumably these sheets were intended to form a whole of some kind, but had been patched together so poorly that it didn't quite work. It was the sort of thing that typically bothered Leon, and he resisted the urge to rearrange them so they lined up properly.

"What's all this?" asked Izzy, joining him in the middle of the room.

Leon shrugged.

"I really have no idea," he said. And they stared at it together in silence for a short while.

The clumsy office paper montage appeared to show a diagram of swoops and curves and shaded areas, set against an organised grid of narrow columns, like in an atlas of the world. In fact, the whole thing reminded Leon of the giant world maps that NASA used on those movies about the moon landings. The ones where they tracked orbits of rockets in those wavy lines. But, in this case, it looked like a gridded map of the world with all the countries removed.

Behind the pin, where all the threads met, was another scrap of paper that looked like it had been scrunched up at one point and then, later, rescued and carefully smoothed out again. It too was covered in small annotations but in this case written in Biro. In the centre was what appeared to be a series of digits, over-written in multiple stokes and circled excessively in some urgent swirl.

"You know what," said Izzy, at last. "I think that's binary code."

"Binary?"

"Yes, binary. Ones and zeros. Off and on. Mathematics. Computer code."

Izzy stepped up to the wall to get a better look at it.

"You really know this stuff," said Leon, feeling both comforted and impressed by her apparent grasp of the situation. But also a little dismayed by his complete lack of it.

"I do," she replied, leaning closer in. Using her finger, she traced the path from one of the blocks of annotations on the main map back to the salvaged scrap of paper, where the lines all met. "And if I'm not mistaken..." she trailed off.

Leon watched her for a while, expecting her to finish the sentence. But she soon appeared lost in thought, and didn't say anything more.

Suddenly, there was a noise from downstairs. Quinn.

"Did you find anything?" he shouted up.

"We might have," shouted Izzy back.

Leon stepped closer and tried to see what she was seeing.

"We have?" he said, as Quinn suddenly appeared at the door.

"What have you got?"

Izzy stepped back and made a casual sweep with one hand.

"Astro navigational coordinates. Intersectional trajectories. Relativistic time intervals and structured, celestial mechanics. And, if I'm not mistaken, a phone number for the local Indian takeaway. Starting to ring any bells, Greg?"

"Uhm."

For the first time since he arrived, Quinn appeared hesitant. Unsure, even, whether he should say anything at all. Either he wasn't expecting to find this here, thought Izzy, or he wasn't expecting whoever found it to understand what any of it might be.

"Yes, *uhm*, Greg," she snapped, snatching the older scrap of paper from the centre of the web and waving it at him. "This seems like some pretty serious space physics shit, for a guy who worked at an ad agency in what"—she looked fleetingly at Leon for an answer—"accounts?"

"Accounts," confirmed Leon, with a nod. "Government accounts," he added, with extra emphasis on the word *government*, in a thin attempt to suggest that he too possessed some special insights about what was going on here. Although he really didn't.

Despite this being all very intriguing, he couldn't help starting to feel a little intimidated by how effortlessly Izzy had somehow appraised and understood what they had found, while he had only got as far as thinking about Tom Hanks in *Apollo 13*. *This girl must really know her space physics shit,* he thought.

"That's a really great question, Izzy," countered Quinn, now moving to the centre of the room himself to take in the full experience of Miles's makeshift cosmological plan. He let out an involuntary long whistle as the size and substance of it all hit him in the face. "Miles Benedict, you canny old bastard," he declared quietly, clearly impressed, before turning back to Izzy.

"And you understand everything you just said to me?"

"Some of it, yes. Most of it. I mean I'd need time to work through it and see what the data is actually saying, but broadly, yes. I do."

"Amazing," responded Quinn. "What is it you said you did again?"

"I didn't."

"Yes, that's right. We'll have to get into that. And what about you, Leon? There must be some reason why Miles sent you both here."

Leon suppressed his irritation at the implied slight and looked at Izzy. How much should they really let on, he wondered. Quinn might be upset that Benedict was dead. He might be upset with *them*. She didn't let on either way.

"I think," began Leon, his gaze evasively sidling back to the wall, "that it probably had more to do with…availability, than any actual choice on his part. He was a little, ah…preoccupied at the time."

"Was he? Was he, indeed?" Quinn nodded, seeming to finally connect the dots, and come to a decision. He perched himself on the end of the bedframe. "OK," he declared, raising his hands in an open gesture. "Enough dancing. We have to—"

"Wait," interrupted Leon, suddenly, moving back to the wall, where the paper in Izzy's hand had been. "There's something else."

He reached up and peeled away a short, thin strip of decorator's tape. Stuck to the back of it was a tiny memory card, its brassy connector pins catching the light as he turned it in his fingers.

"You think this is what we came for?" said Leon.

"I think, Leon," began Quinn, stepping forward and seeming to reach for the card, "You're not just a pretty fa—"

"Whoa, hold on there," said Leon, taking a step back, and lowering his hand. His irritation was no longer suppressed. "I'm not just going to hand this over, like it's Christmas."

"Leon—"

"No, I don't think so. You know, yesterday was a normal day. I got up. I went to work. I made fun of my boss. In a regular office, in the middle of London. Just like everybody else. Then we had a party and—I admit it—I had a bit too much to drink and fell asleep in the toilet. Glamourous, I know. But none of that explains why when I woke up in the middle of the night, everything I thought I knew about the world had gone to shit."

"Leon, I—" tried Quinn again.

"No, I'm not done. I woke up to find that the place I work at was apparently a front for some kind of, I don't even know what. There were people there, Greg, dead. Dead! Dead and dying people, some of them deformed or melted into each other. Or what would you say," he looked across at Izzy.

"Fused," she said.

"Fused, right," he continued. He couldn't stop now even if he wanted to. "Fused people, Greg. Hidden in some wacky and apparently super-secret underground building, just sitting there in the middle of London. With regular people going to work on one side and buying Marks and Spencer sandwiches on the other.

"And in the middle of this, this bunker, is total chaos, and broken, twisted people and some massive unrecognisable machine throbbing away—apparently, I now realise, on its way to blowing everything up. And just when me and my friend here think we've seen enough, we stumble across Miles Benedict—my work colleague, Miles Benedict—buried up to his middle in the floor. Not even buried. Immersed. Like he's in water. And he tells us we have to come here and get something important. Something so important that a minute after he says this people start shooting guns. Guns, Greg. Guns, in the middle of London. That may be a fact of life where you come from, but here we don't generally shoot each other.

"And we just manage to get away from the people with guns when the whole place goes up in a giant fireball and suddenly there are more people with guns chasing us down the street. In regular old London town, where on the news the whole thing is being written off as 'a gas leak' and we now have to be searched before they'll let us into a bloody Tube station.

"And now, here we all are, three hours later, whooping about some *Star Trek* shit on the wall. So, no, Greg. I am not just going to give this to you. I'm tired. I'm horribly hungover and I'm freaked out. And no one's getting anything until I get some more coffee—with milk—and you tell us what the hell is going on here."

Quinn looked to Izzy in search a possible ally. He didn't get one.

"What he said," responded Izzy, bluntly, relieved that it was all out in the open but also quietly impressed by Leon's sudden grip on events. She observed the resolute expression resting on his pretty face. Quinn was right about that much, she thought.

"OK, buddy. I hear you," relented Quinn. "It's been a tough night for all of us. Let's do it." He offered his hand towards the door.

.   .   .

They sat back down at the kitchen table, resuming the same seats, although not before Leon had reached into the fridge to grab the milk. He placed it ceremoniously next to the half-full coffeepot. It was still warm to the touch and, having checked it with the back of his hand, Quinn lifted it partway off the table and looked directly at Leon.

"Please," said Leon, grudgingly.

Quinn then turned to Izzy who simply nodded. He filled their cups, making a point of adding milk to Leon's, and slid them gently across the table. Leon drank down half the cup before letting out a big sigh.

"I thought you were supposed to be down here, anyway," he began. "Keeping an eye on things for us?"

Quinn glanced at his watch, and pressed a switch on the side that made a brief but audible clicking tone.

"I was. I did," he replied. "I'd already dropped some micro proximity sensors outside, on my way in. I'll know if anyone approaches."

"Ohhh, he dropped some micro proximity sensors, Izzy. We can relax now."

"Leon," said Izzy, resting her hand lightly on his arm. "You made your point already."

Quinn didn't react either way and simply took a swig of his own coffee, cold from earlier.

"September 1944. Europe was a year away from any kind of peace. London was still under siege. The so-called Blitz campaign had ended three years before but, even so, the bombs kept falling. Not like 1940, 1941 obviously but, still, they came—just as random, just as unexpected, just as deadly. Deadlier, in fact, as the war progressed, and the Nazis started getting their rocket act together. The V-1 started showing up. Then, just as quick, the V-2." Quinn paused to check they were keeping up.

"The world's first long-range guided missile," added Izzy.

"Yes, exactly. The V-2. Everyone knows about those, right? We teach it in schools. Hell, Von Braun sent Americans to the moon using the same technology."

"Well, technically, the Saturn V was—" began Izzy.

Quinn stopped her with a pointed do-you-want-to-hear-this-or-not look. She stopped.

He continued, "Right, yes, Brainiac. But you get my point. Everyone knows about that stuff. It's public record. It's history."

Now Leon wanted to interrupt and ask what this had to do with anything, but Quinn saw this coming and headed him off.

"I'm coming to it," he said, holding up one hand. "Now, what isn't so publicly well known is that the V-2s weren't the only things flying around at that time. First, you have to understand that the Nazis were experimenting with all kinds of shit. Anything and everything they could get their nasty little hands on to gain an advantage over the Allies. Nuclear fusion. Particle emissions. Antimatter. Anti-gravity. Even teleportation, if you can believe that. You name it, they had boffins and, in their minds, a bunch of disposable European slaves in a cave somewhere working on it.

"And every now and then one of their experiments would fall out of the sky and get picked up by our boys, which was then hidden away in one of our own caves. Slave-free, of course."

"And London Bridge was one your caves?" suggested Leon.

"Not quite. Most of what they sent over was a bunch of science fair crap. Hats off, I suppose, for trying, but no cigar. And it was nothing we weren't investigating ourselves, since we're being so honest, and failing at just as badly.

"But then, in September 1944, something else happened. Even after eighty years, and a bunch of other *incidents* in the decades since, we barely understand most of it."

Izzy picked up the coffeepot and drained what was left equally into everyone's mugs, making sure to drop a splash of milk into Leon's. He smiled. She smiled back.

"But that night, at the end of a long, hot summer, those goddamn Nazis must have been having a fire sale because it seemed like they were sending everything they had over to

London, with barrages cropping up all over, like fireworks. Except by now, you see, Britain was prepared. It wasn't 1940. They had anti-tank, anti-aircraft, ballistic—you name it—sites set up all over the capital. And it seems that whatever the Nazis were up to that night, it had caught someone's attention."

"You mean the RAF," offered Leon.

"No! Yes, but no. Not them. More like the RSF, you might say," responded Quinn, strangely playful, now that he was into his stride, and placing an unusual emphasis on the *S*.

"Royal...*Sea* Force? You know, I don't think—"

"No, Leon. Not Sea."

"Wait," said Izzy, as she began to connect Benedict's spare bedroom collage to what Quinn was saying. "You're talking about spaceships? Come on."

"Space*ship*, in fact. Singular. Your actual bona fide flying saucer," Quinn confirmed, with a gauche display of his trademark grin.

"In 1944? But it would be three more years before anyone even uttered those words."

"Officially, yes."

"Jesus Christ, Greg," exploded Leon, feeling suddenly incensed by this revelation. "This is the story you're going with? We ask you for the truth and you try to fob us off like we're a couple of first-year potheads. I know what we saw down there in that lab didn't make any kind of sense, but a flying saucer? In London? Nobody sees flying saucers in London, much less keeps one in a secret underground lab." Leon used his fingers to place quote marks around the end of his sentence.

"And yet..." shrugged Quinn.

"Thanks for the history lesson, man, but I'm tired and this smells like just more bullshit than I take right now." Leon went to stand. "Come on, Izzy, we don't need this."

"No, Leon, wait," said Izzy, soothingly. "That stuff upstairs? The maps? All those equations? For a space hobbyist it's wayyy off-the-grid. But if what he's saying is even half true and you started taking seriously the idea of plotting hyperbolic motion across—"

"Hyper what?" said Leon, sitting back down in his chair.

"Hyperbolic motion. In special relativity, it's a description of…"

"She's talking about faster-than-light travel, Leon," said Quinn, in an attempt to be helpful. "Warp drive."

This just irritated Leon further as it made him seem like the only idiot in the room. And he felt like he was already doing a good job of that by himself.

"OK, yes, I get it. And?"

"Basically, what I'm saying is all that stuff upstairs, maybe even some of what we saw last night… Look, let's at least let him finish his story—and then we can leave."

Leon put his hands out in submission. "Fine. So, there was a spaceship flying around London in World War ll that, somehow, no one noticed. And no one's ever mentioned, even once, in the eighty years since. Then what happened?"

"Yes, right. Exactly that," resumed Quinn, absently checking his watch again, with the same clicking chime as before. "With everything else going on that night, nobody saw it. And, as I said, by then there were defensive batteries all over the place, with orders to fire at anything that wasn't a bird. This was routine by that point. Stuff would fly over the city and hit random targets. And gunneries would try to shoot them down, which, even when they were successful, would often have a similar effect, just with smaller, less explosives pieces.

"But I digress. What we do know for sure is that gunnery placement 372, situated close to Southwark Bridge accidently hit something big that night. And I mean really big, in every sense. Something no one had ever seen before, and something they didn't even know was there until a forty-pound shell collided with it, causing, by all accounts, a gigantic fireball that burned its way straight down and into to the ground, pretty much destroying a section of warehouses, right where your office is today, Leon. Was, sorry."

Leon dismissed the comment. The destruction of his employer's office felt like the least he had to worry about.

"Anyway, long story short: that night the human race accidentally made first contact with an alien species in the worst possible way—by shooting down their ship and, as it turns out, killing everyone inside."

"But nobody knew…" began Izzy, feeling an irrational need to jump in and defend the unwitting action of another age.

"No, of course nobody knew. It was a one-in-a-trillion freak accident. No one even really knew then, at least not for several days. First the volunteer fire crews went in to try to contain and safeguard what was left of the burning buildings. And, with all the Nazi action that night, these guys had their hands full. They weren't paying a lot of attention.

"Then came the specialist army crews, whose job it was to clear the site and also see if they could salvage what they assumed would be a rogue bit of German technology. But what they found instead was a half-buried alien spacecraft. Except of course it wasn't buried. Not exactly. What was it you said—immersed?"

"Fused," said Izzy.

"Right. Fused. Similar to what you guys witnessed last night, the craft had somehow fused with the ground it had crashed into. Naturally, no one at the time had the slightest idea what it was or what to do with it. They co-opted a few select specialists from wherever they could find them. Cambridge, GCHQ, Bletchley Park, but there was still a war on and once they'd established that A, it wasn't German, B, no one was on board, at least no one living that is—they found our new alien friends in much the same state you found Benedict's crew—and, C, they couldn't make it work, Army Special Ops sealed the whole site off. Above top-secret. Officially, it was just one more bomb site in a city that was filled with them. As long as it presented no imminent threat, it could wait until after they were done with the war."

"OK, fine," said Leon. "Let's assume for a minute that's all true. And it happened just the way you tell it. Why is it still here eighty years later? Why not just dig the thing up after the war and take it somewhere? Take it to Area 51, or whatever it's called these days."

Quinn laughed. "Yes, you're right. Area 51. Although I may as well tell you right now, that's not really where we do any of that stuff."

"Really?" Leon couldn't help but feel a little disappointed by this news. He'd secretly been pinning his hopes on Area 51 for a while, if for no other reason than to feel vindicated for all the UFO documentaries he'd consumed. And although, under normal circumstances, he would have dismissed anyone who claimed to have this kind of inside knowledge, he had to admit that Quinn had a pretty good case. Obviously narrowly escaping death from an exploding secret underground bunker helped, but generally this whole story was beginning to sound pretty convincing.

"Yeah, sorry about that," continued Quinn, noting Leon's disappointment. "But the short answer to your question is: we couldn't. You'd have to ask one of the professors for the whys but, basically, we literately couldn't move the damn thing.

"First, it had burrowed all the way down and into the bedrock itself. Merged with it, as you have already observed. And more than that, by doing so it had also somehow transformed the rock around it, to around thirty-forty feet in every direction—and this thing was pretty damn big to start with. That meant we couldn't just cut it out of the ground. It was like trying to tunnel through diamond.

"Then, we tried going around the perimeter of the affected rock and lifting it out but, again, something in the transformation of materials, or in the ship itself, meant it had a shifting density that would go up exponentially in direct proportion to the effort we made to lift it."

"So, the more you tried to lift it out," said Izzy. "The heavier it got."

"Exactly. We just didn't have the technology, or the under-standing we needed at the time to get around any of that. We figured that maybe if we could work out how to power the thing, pull a few levers, we might be able get it to lift itself out, or at least turn off its density enhancer. But who the hell knew what that was, or how long that would take? And, in the meantime—"

"That's what you called it?" interrupted Leon. "A *density* enhancer!? Sounds like a sex toy."

"I don't know, Leon. That's what I'm calling it. I'm sure the boffins have something much more sci-fi appropriate for you. That OK?"

"Fine."

"Great. So, anyway, the simpler option was just to construct a research complex around it, then hide everything away by rebuilding the street above. And if we found a way to move it... But that was eighty years ago. Was it the best idea to keep it right in the middle of London? No. Of course not. But we didn't have much of a choice: there was a war on. People, resources, and technology were in short supply."

"OK, we get it," said Leon. "You have some super exotic stuff that's taken you eighty years to figure out. And although I have, like, a million questions, the thing I really want to know is: who's *we*? And what's with all the killing? Is that what you do with your teams when things go wrong?"

"Oh, you want it all, don't you, my friend?"

"It's a fair question, Greg," said Izzy. "I mean, who do you work for exactly? You're hardly a local boy, are you? And maybe this is the world you live in, and you think it's perfectly OK to sneak around hiding spaceships in the middle of London, keeping secrets from everyone, and killing people with guns. But it's not normal. You know that, right?

"I think the biggest secret I know is that Robbie, my lab assistant, smokes pot on the faculty roof whenever he thinks no one is looking. Or maybe it's that my sister has a crush on a grad, ten years her junior, at work. That's normal people, Greg. All this top-secret 'we figured this, we decided that, we had no choice but to wait until the war was over' shit. Who the hell are you?"

Quinn's watch abruptly made a series of sharp clicks, causing him to look down and press the crown to make it stop. For the first time since he arrived, Quinn actually looked concerned.

"You need to be somewhere?" asked Leon.

"No. *We*. We need to be somewhere else. This gives me a status from the sensors I placed. Looks like we may have company. Time for you to leave."

28

WHO'S THAT GIRL?

C arson's terminal lit up inside her private office as the call came in, throwing shade across the ceiling in long strokes. She opened her eyes and reached across from her reclined position to snap the desk lamp on, then rubbed her eyes to help ease the adjustment. How long had she been out? she wondered. On any normal day, a nap would be unforgivable. But, of course, this wasn't any normal day, she reminded herself sternly, as the call continued to buzz away unheeded. And was likely still far from over.

"Yes," she snapped, hitting the answer button on the screen. The video link sprang to life. "What is it, Milo?"

Milo was Head of Digital Cryptography and Communications, responsible for ensuring digital security across the base. But also, to a lesser degree, for hacking the unhackable, should it ever be required which, often as not, turned out to be more than anyone was willing admit. Officially.

"Sorry to disturb you, ma'am, but you said I should let you know as soon as we had any developments?" he answered, sheepishly.

Carson swiftly formalised her seating position, while her left hand mechanically travelled up to smooth down her already smooth and immaculately composed hair.

"Yes, soldier. That's exactly what I said. What have you got for me?"

"It's not much, but we've managed to unscramble some of the automated wide surveillance capture. Several of the onsite camera systems managed to hyper-sync chunks of data to our cloud vault, *Stratos*, just as they were designed to in an emergency. Just before being totally zeroed out by the blast."

"And?"

"Well, it's only fragments, really. Must be something to do with the initial electromagnetic pulse. And so a lot of what we do have is either heavily compromised or just not that helpful: various gantry ways and empty service corridors, save for the occasional perimeter guard. We have a couple of segments of the Berlin team's incursion but not what happened to them. And some oblique views of the main hall, which are low-grade but good enough that we can broadly make out what happened to the research team. It's not...pretty, ma'am. And, so far, we've got nothing from the primary observation cameras. I'm still trying to figure out why."

"And you're telling me all this, why? There's nothing here that can't just go in your report, to be read by others. Is there anything we can actually *use*?"

"I'm just coming to that. It might be nothing, just an admin error. A last-minute hire who's not been uploaded to the vault yet."

"Just tell me, Milo."

The screen transitioned as several images slid into view, reducing Milo's video link to a thumbnail, pinned to the top-right of the screen.

"We managed to get two, maybe three decent shots of the main hall. At first glance, it's a just chaos: buckled workstations, scattered furniture and equipment. Some of it destroyed. Some of it partly submerged into other pieces of infrastructure, the walls, or the floor. Same with all the people..." Milo hesitated, struggling to find the right words. "Or what's left of them, in some cases. Ma'am, I should warn you—"

"I'm fine, Milo. Just show me what you've found."

Carson remained impassive, as a series of images depicting various grotesque arrangements of humans and hardware rotated around one another. Several seemed to be magnifications or close-crop enhancements of the ones that preceded them. Eventually it stopped and centred on one taken at a high vantage point, overlooking the central-front area of the research gallery, what would have been the primary control position for all the workstations in the room. The stations themselves, and the researchers who worked at them, were scattered much as Milo had described them, while in the far background the heavily buckled but apparently still-active isolation unit housing the ship could just be made out, creeping into frame from the top of the picture.

The lower section of the image was cast largely in shadow, but you could still make out distinct shapes, both organic and constructed. And it was here that Milo paused, circling the section with a virtual yellow marker.

"Ma'am, if you'll look carefully in this section, you'll notice there are a number of personnel in among the wreckage. They're not easy to see on first glance, but we've been back and forth through each screencap and carefully crosschecked everyone we could still recognise against our roster."

"And?"

"And there's an anomaly."

Milo could be heard tapping on his keyboard. The circled area highlighted, as though a light in the image had been switched on, and zoomed in to fill the frame. The initially pixelated image began to recompile as automated enhancement software took care of the detail. Close to the centre of the reframed image was a man, seemingly buried up to his chest.

"That's Miles Benedict," acknowledged Carson.

"Yes, ma'am. It is. We have a couple more 'caps that clearly confirm this. However, that's not all."

Milo quickly tapped through several more key commands. The image jumped back a short distance, revealing two more people, crouched down next to Benedict.

"Who the hell are they?" demanded Carson

"That was our question too. As you can see, the woman's face is reasonably clear, whereas her companion—a man we think—remains in shadow and, in any case, appears to have his back to the camera. So, we ran her through the system."

"Do you have a name for me?"

"We think—"

"Don't answer that. Let's just take this directly to Snark. He'll want to know and it'll save the repetition. No one else, do you understand!? Strictly eyes only. I'll meet you there in five."

"Yes, ma'am."

A short time later they were assembled in Snark's office. Carson stood somewhat formally by the large video screen, joined by Milo, who had installed himself in one of the armchairs to more easily manage his laptop activity and, of course, Snark himself who, naturally, had taken up pole position on his couch, a rattling glass of amber liquid resting in one hand. Macintyre, who Carson had taken the liberty of also inviting on her way up, hovered behind the sofa.

"So, who's that girl?" Snark demanded to know, once he had been brought up to speed on the situation.

"Internal data systems threw up a blank, sir," Milo informed him. "We assumed at first she must be one of the team by the way she seems to be interacting with Benedict, part of his organisation."

"Never assume, Milo," said Snark, magnanimously. "If fifty years of this shit has taught me anything, it's that assumptions really do make an ass of you and me. But, at this point, mainly you. Go on."

"Thank you, sir," responded Milo, patiently. Like many of Snark's favoured motivational techniques, it wasn't the first time anyone in that room had heard this quip. "So, we expanded the search both government and military wide. Still nothing."

"I thought this AI-powered facial recognition stuff was supposed to be good," said Snark.

There were two primary images up on the screen. To the left, a slightly fuzzy image of the woman from the video capture, criss-crossed by geometric lines that seemed to redraw themselves every few moments, and in the centre a constantly recycling composite of faces. They shifted almost too fast to see, as the soft-ware ran through hundreds of permutations a second. On the far right was a tall panel filled with strings of code, topped off by a constantly fluctuating photographic histogram.

"It is good, sir," defended Milo—he personally had made a lot of improvements to the software himself. "With the right starting parameters. But it's not instantaneous. It needs time to—"

"Don't lecture me, kid. Just tell me how long. We're on the clock here. If these two are responsible for compromising our operation in any way, then we need to know, like, yesterday."

"Yes, sir," conceded Milo. "Understood. We've already moved outside of jurisdiction and are pulling in data by geography, starting with the UK and into Europe as single block."

Snark laughed out loud. "My God, don't let the Brits hear you say that, or we'll have a civil war on our hands on top of every-thing else."

"Sir?"

"Don't you read the goddamn papers? Never mind. So, look, aside from who they are, what I really want to know is: Why aren't they dead or melted into their chairs like everyone else?"

Milo looked vaguely panicked by this question, which was well outside his domain, but fortunately Carson stepped in and relieved him of any obligation to answer.

"Pure speculation at this point, sir," she said. "But the only explanation is that they were outside the immediate blast radius. That has to be something in the region of eighty to a hundred and fifty feet. The effect is typically non-uniform. And by our estimation any farther away and they wouldn't have had time to get to Benedict between the initial incident and the whole site going down. The time-window is impossibly tight if you were trying to get in from outside of the whole facility. Wherever they came from, they were already inside the complex during the first blast."

"OK," said Snark, picking up the baton. "So somehow, we have two unknowns at ground zero, moments after zero hour itself. And, aside from an unconfirmed, anecdotal suggestion that there was an explosive device, we have no preceding evidence of foreign infiltration or overt sabotage. And meanwhile, everyone we could have talked to is either dead, or has been blended into the sidewalk."

"We still have Quinn in the open, sir," reminded Carson.

"As far as you know, Frankie. When was the last time he checked in?"

"It's been over three hours."

"Wonderful! Did he stop off for coffee and donuts?"

"No, sir. His comms kit failed in the initial blast. I gave him—"

"But he survived? Incredible luck, I'd say."

"In this case, sir, I'd agree with you. However, his record is impeccable and, despite the circumstantial evidence, he remains low on our list from a suspect point of view. Although I made it perfectly clear it wouldn't stay that way if he didn't come up with something we could use tonight.

"I sent him back into the site for recon, however compromised it was at the time. With the Berlin team still MIA—presumed dead—he remains the best lead we've got."

"Besides our two guests here, you mean," said Snark, pointing towards the screen with his whiskey tumbler hand.

"Besides them."

Just then, the laptop chimed, and the screen froze on an image of Isabella Morton Jones, BSc (Hons), MSc, quickly followed by a string of biographical statistics, including date and place of birth, known addresses, banking affiliations, employment records, and what looked like a Tesco Clubcard. Below these were a series of photographic thumbnails and links under the heading: Known Associates.

They all looked up.

"Bingo!" stated Snark, with a great deal of satisfaction. "What have we got, Milo?"

"We've got a 93 percent match. Isabella Morton Jones, twenty-eight years old, educated in London...still in education by the looks of it. Grew up in Beaconsfield, west of the city. Father was a lawyer, grew up nearby, died 2012—car accident. Mother, originally from North Africa, moved to UK via France when she was five. Still alive. Runs an independent flower business. One sister. Older. Works for a business consultancy."

"What the hell is this!?" yelled Snark.

"Sir?"

"Little Miss Whitebread—this is our terrorist? Our inside man? Our fifth column?"

"With respect, sir," interjected Carson. "No one's saying she's... that either of these two are terrorists."

"What the hell else would you call it!?"

"Undetermined."

"Fine. Yes, I hear you. Then who's she with? And why are they being so chummy with Benedict? I don't like this one bit. Do you think he was turned?"

"Benedict?" replied Carson, with disbelief. "Not a chance."

"I want it checked out all the same. Something's not right here."

"And the guy she's with?" asked Milo. "We don't even know if they made it out of there."

Macintyre made a polite cough. "Sir, if I may," he began.

"What is it, Mac? If it's about the Cardinals again, forget it. The answer's still no."

"No, sir, I just wanted to say: a preliminary report from London just came in. A couple were spotted streetside but still in the operational area, shortly before it went full meltdown. The woman's description matches what we have here."

Snark let out a huge grin.

"You see? That's what I love about this country. We're a team. Perfect. So, we have them in custody already?"

"Not exactly, sir," admitted Macintyre, awkwardly.

"What does that mean? We either do or we don't."

"Well, the report's only just come in. The sighting is several hours old and was initially deprioritized. It was before we had this intel," dissembled Macintyre, gesturing at the screen.

Snark slammed his glass down on the table. "What the hell are you talking about Mac? Just spit it out."

"They fled the scene."

"Jesus Christ. They fled the scene?"

"Ran, I gather. We gave chase but—"

"They fled the scene. They ran. What are you going to tell me next—that they dropped a great big sign saying, 'we like blowing shit up!?' What kind of people are we hiring out there?"

"We lost them, sir. I'm sorry."

The room fell silent, as Snark ran his hands over his forehead and through his thinning hair. He breathed in heavily before abruptly standing and walking over to look at the screen more closely.

Milo found the quiet unbearable, and hardly knew what to do with himself. He rarely had cause to be in the same room as Carson, never mind Snark. And in fact, he had never actually been in Snark's office until tonight. He looked from Carson to Macintyre and back again but they simply stared blankly ahead— they knew from personal experience to wait this out, and not attempt to volunteer suggestions. Finally, Snark turned around and looked at each one of them in turn.

"OK, beautiful people," he said, at last. "Here's what we're going to do. I want you to go back over Benedict. Every detail since he joined the program, and five years before that. Every letter, every phone call made and received, every email and text, every goddamn dinner reservation, if you have to."

"Sir," protested Milo, before he could stop himself from speaking. "We're talking about twenty-five, maybe thirty years of data."

"Well then, you better get started, kid. And that's not all. I want a list of every person in and out of that building complex in the past forty-eight hours—the entire block. Both inside the program, and all of the tenants in the rest of the estate, along with every employee, guest, service personnel, taxis dropping off and picking up, lunch deliveries, the postman, and even his mother, if you can find her. And I want you to go deep on this Jones woman. Everything. Where she's lived, worked, gone on vacation. Her family, boyfriends, girlfriends. I don't care where she came from or what she's doing there, but I don't like her."

"And the man she's with?" queried Carson. "We don't have anything on him yet."

"It's simple, Frankie. Find her, you find him."

Carson and Macintyre nodded their understanding of their orders.

"Sir," the pair said, in unison.

"And then we'll bring 'em both in and find out what they don't want to tell us."

Milo stood, closing his laptop on the way up, and joined the others. Time to go to work.

29

DIVERSION

"Leave?" said Leon, shaking his head as they all stood up. "And go where? Home?"

"Yes," responded Quinn, soothingly. "I mean no, not home, not yet. Look, I know this whole situation is totally screwed up. You don't know me, why I'm here, or what's really going on. I get you've had a rough night and that all this"—he spun his hand in a circle with one finger pointing upwards—"must be pretty scary. I really do. Because whatever you may think of me right now, Isabella Jones, I do still remember what normal looks like."

Izzy smiled fleetingly as Quinn repositioned himself in the kitchen doorway so he could get a clearer view of the frosted porch at the front of the house. He then turned back to look at Leon and Izzy directly.

"Look, I have zero idea how you guys came to be the only people that Miles Benedict could trust with this thing...with his *life*, it turned out, but the fact that he did means I'm going to trust you too. And just maybe, in the less than two minutes we have left, you could do the same."

Leon opened his mouth to remind him about how the whole thing was just chance, but then thought better of it. Perhaps it was acceptance of this new reality or, more likely, the shadowy move-ment he thought he saw over Quinn's shoulder, beyond the porch windows.

"It's not like we really have much of a choice," said Izzy. "So, we'll trust you...for now."

"Great, because there's something I need you to do for me. It's a big ask. And, frankly, I don't really have time to explain it all."

"Why am I not surprised?" said Izzy, casting a look at Leon.

"Does it involve us getting killed? We seem to be on a roll at the moment," added Leon.

Quinn's watch went off again but louder and more insistent. He looked impatiently back down the hall towards the front door, silenced the alarm, and subtly ushered them both towards the back door.

"OK. No more time. This is the deal: I need you to get that data card to the US and I need you to leave today if you can, or tomorrow at the latest." Quinn's voice had dropped into a soft stage whisper.

"The US?" began Leon, too loudly, before ratcheting it down to Quinn's level. "A... You want us to go to the U-S-A?"

"Yes, Leon. I want you to go there. To New York. Go to the Refinery Hotel on West Thirty-Eighth Street. Book a room. Wait it out. I will meet you there on Sunday."

There were definite but subtle noises coming from the front door. It turned out that putting down the latch had been a good idea, but it didn't make them feel any calmer. Izzy unconsciously gripped Leon's arm.

"Jesus, Greg," whispered Leon, through gritted teeth. "You want us to go to New York. Just like that? Like we do it every day. With what!? I don't have a fricking bag of cash stowed at Euston station."

"Well then, today's your lucky day."

He reached into his shirt pocket and pulled out the door key and a book of matches. He handed them both to Leon.

"Mr Wong's," said Leon, reading aloud from the bright red matchbook cover. "What's this?"

"Think of it as a bag of cash. Go there today. As soon as you can. Ask for Mr Wong Junior. Tell them Gary Numark sent you. They'll take care of everything. Now get going."

A sudden rattle from the front door instantly dissuaded Leon from asking who Gary Numark was, or why Quinn didn't just take the stick himself. But then Izzy asked him anyway.

"Why us, Greg? Why not just take it yourself?"

"Something's going on here, Izzy. Even you must see that. I don't know what or why, except that it's all wrong. And they know who I am. So, if they want to go after me to get that data, I'm an easy target, whereas you guys are...unexpected. The thing they didn't count on. You can pass unseen, like a cypher. So, until I know who or what to trust here...it's you."

Izzy nodded, understanding then that, like it or not, the insane events of the previous night were far from over for them. Leon, coming to much the same conclusion, quietly slipped open the back door and gently tugged on Izzy's arm as a motion to leave. They paused briefly and looked at Quinn. A lingering question mark hovered in the air.

"Unless you want to stay behind and do some of the killing?" said Quinn, darkly.

The sound of breaking glass immediately ended any discussion of that.

"I didn't think so," he said, flashing a smile. "Don't worry about it. Just go. I'll hold them off at the front. You can get out over the back wall, behind the woodshed. It's the way I came in."

They nodded briefly and turned to leave. Quinn called after them, quietly.

"Get to Wong's. Don't call anyone. I'll see you Sunday. West Thirty-Eighth Street. We'll make it right."

He turned and softly closed the door behind him.

. . .

Leon and Izzy quickly made it to the back of the long garden, then up and onto the wall indicated by Quinn, obscured from view by what turned out to be more of an ornate gazebo than an actual tool shed. Getting down the other side, however, was something else.

The space between the wall and the rear of the buildings next to it was not only much lower than the garden side but also incredibly narrow. Barely big enough for remedial access in the event work needed doing to either structure, much less to walk down. And as Leon struggled to lower himself into the limited space, he found it hard to understand why the original builders had bothered leaving the gap at all.

However, this thought was quickly dispelled as the sound of a single gunshot suddenly rang out from the direction of the house, causing both of them to involuntarily gasp out loud. And Izzy, who had at that moment been trying to lower herself down with Leon's assistance, promptly dropped straight on top of him, causing him to fall sideways and onto the ground. His face scraped the wall on the way down, swiftly followed by Izzy's bag, and then the rest of Izzy, which somehow sandwiched the backpack between the full weight her body and all of his face as she finally came to a stop. He let out a long groan, through his squashed mouth, to help compensate for both the pain and the ritual humiliation.

"Shh..." said Izzy, rather unhelpfully, Leon thought.

"That's the second time," he mumbled awkwardly, "you've knocked me down today."

"I'm so sorry, Leon," she replied, trying to adjust her position on top of him, causing Leon to make an unintentional noise with each adjustment. "But do you think that was Greg?"

"Shooting or getting shot? It was at least one of them," he managed to say with a wheeze, as her knee pressed into the wrong place, and her bag pushed more deeply into his face, deforming his lips further. The constrained gap and the lack of good leverage made it virtually impossible for her to turn around, or attempt to lift herself off him, especially with one arm partially pinned under her stomach. She decided to shuffle downwards instead and at least get her weight off his face.

"Sorry. I know this is... If I can just..."

"Mnn humm."

"There!" she declared triumphantly, as she got low enough that she was able to free her right arm and use it to push her back-pack off Leon's face and onto the ground above his head. He let out a brief sigh as his lips returned to their normal shape and colour, and he could see again.

What he saw was Izzy's face just six inches from his own. *Man, she's beautiful,* he thought as she smiled at him. What she was thinking he couldn't begin to guess. But in his mind, at least, something seemed to pass between them as they breathed slowly, and the moment paused like a photograph, without either of them saying a word.

A moment later, a police siren cut sharply into their brief reverie, snapping them back to reality. Izzy hurriedly shuffled herself all the way down and off Leon, and they both proceeded to awkwardly shimmy their way back up to a standing position. They found they could just about traverse the narrow space if they stayed side-on, scuttling along the channel like crabs until they reached the end of what turned out to be a long row of mews houses, where a sharp turn to the right opened out into a small, walled-off utility area filled with dustbins and a handful of shredded plastic bin bags. It smelt really bad. And Leon was sure he saw something rodent-like scuttle away as they arrived, but the sound of more emergency vehicles was growing louder. Hard to be sure where they were heading but if it was for Benedict's house, then it certainly hadn't taken the authorities very long to react. So, they pushed on past the wheelie bins, and stepped over the split bags that had presumably been gutted by foxes and rats the night before, out into the street side of the petite dwellings.

Aside from the rotten trash compartment, it was clear they were indeed in a delightful London mews courtyard. Full of ridiculously expensive tiny properties that had originally been designed for horses, and a row of premium badged cars cluttering the cobbled paving, all of which seemed poised to become a liability for Leon and Izzy, should any of their well-heeled owners get curious about what they were doing there. So, without any discussion, they scooted quickly out onto Priory Road next door, and from there turned right and virtually ran the short distance past the church, and out onto Abbey Road: a busy main road at seven thirty in the morning, filled with cars and, by this time, enough pedestrians heading off to work that they could simply disappear from view. Should anyone be looking.

They paused briefly at the intersection, before slipping easily in step with other commuters heading for a bus stop a short way up the road. The 139 to Waterloo was just pulling in.

"Perfect timing," said Leon, giving Izzy a small tap with his hand.

She nodded in agreement, and they half jogged along the pavement to join the short queue entering the bus. Leon tapped his card twice on the reader to cover both of them, and they made their way to the middle standing-room-only area next to the exit doors. They didn't want to risk getting trapped upstairs or at the back of the bus in the event they needed to leave in a hurry. The bus pulled away from the kerb with its customary low rumble. Leon and Izzy looked out of the back window as they left the scene behind, then at each other as the surge of adrenalin and relief hit them all at once. They broke into laughter.

"You really know how to show a girl a good time," said Izzy, as the laughter began to subside.

"Well, I try," he replied. "People underestimate the fun that strangers trying to kill you can bring, so I like to sprinkle a little fatal action into all my dates."

"Oh, is that what this is?" teased Izzy, raising a single eyebrow.

"Ah. Uhm. I mean. Well, when I say date, I...uh..."

"Oh my God." Izzy's face dropped from affectionate teasing to concern.

"What is it?"

"Your face."

"My face!?" Leon really couldn't work out if this was going well or she'd just chosen the worst possible moment to get super honest with him. "What's wrong with my face?"

"Well, not your... let me have a proper look." Izzy physically moved his head into the light with her hands and pushed a fold of his dark brown hair out of the way. Leon's brush with the wall had left some nasty abrasions down one side of his face, and the cluster above his temple still seemed to be weeping.

"I think you cut your head on that wall," she said.

Leon's hand reached up to touch the affected area and came back with blood on his fingers.

"Oh man," he said. "I thought that head pain was just from my hangover. Have you got any—"

But she was already ahead of him and produced pack of tissues from her bag. She pulled one out and gently dabbed the wound, then held it in place for a few moments longer. Leon felt reassured by this that his face as a whole wasn't the main topic of debate.

"Here," she said, and lifted his hand up to replace hers. "Hold that for a while. You might have a concussion."

"Really? What does that involve?"

"I actually have no idea," she replied. "But people always say that in films when someone hits their head. Seems like something we should probably be aware of, considering recent events."

They smiled but were both now thinking of Quinn and what they seem to have narrowly missed. Neither of them really knew how they should react.

"Do you think he made it?" said Izzy, unsure of herself in a way Leon hadn't seen before.

Leon half shrugged, but decided she simply needed to hear something positive.

"Let's assume yes," he said. "He seemed like he knew what he was doing. And he had the advantage of surprise over whoever was coming in. Maybe they were even some his people?"

"But the gunshot…"

The gunshot. Leon had tried hard not to think about that piercing sound. He'd never heard one in real life before but there was no mistaking what it was. Somebody had fired a gun and, despite what he had just said, somebody had taken a bullet. Quite possibly, likely even, to be Quinn, as he didn't seem to have had a gun on him. In which case, he clearly hadn't managed to hold them off as he had promised. This idea left him more freaked out than he wanted to admit. But also relieved because, well, it wasn't him or Izzy lying on the ground. And if Quinn was right, and they really were cyphers, as he had called them, then maybe they really had a chance of getting out of this insane situation unscathed.

But for now, there was nothing more to be said, and they lapsed into silence for a while as the bus stopped and started its way along the busy road.

Forty minutes later they ascended the stairs at London Bridge Tube station and made their way out onto Southwark Street. They had transferred from the bus to the Underground when it became clear that a sizable road reconstruction along Abbey Road, starting at the Beatles crosswalk and going on for who knew how long, was going to keep them stalled in the area much longer than either of them were comfortable with. They jumped off the bus shortly after the crossing and made their way to St John's Wood station via the hospital on Circus Road, deciding on a whim that it would give them some reasonable cover while on foot.

Then, instead of going straight to Mr Wong's as they had originally planned with Quinn, Izzy had insisted they make a detour to her research lab, so she could pick up a laptop and a few of her personal trinkets. Leon had wondered aloud whether this wasn't just like going back into the lion's den, but Izzy was adamant that if they were going to put themselves at risk carrying that data stick over the sea, they should at least find out what was on it.

"But can't we just pick up a laptop anywhere and have a look?" he'd suggested. "We could even pop into John Lewis without buying one and stick it into one of their demo machines."

"This isn't going to be Miles's holiday pictures, Leon. You've seen what they're doing, what he was into. Whatever's on this thing will be heavily encrypted. John Lewis may have really great customer service, but I doubt their training covers high-level cryptography. Whereas I have a lot of custom software that should help us figure it out."

"You seem very sure about this."

"At this point I don't see that we have much choice. Don't you want to at least try to find out what's going on before we get dragged further into this thing than we already are?"

"I do," he agreed, at last.

So, they headed for Izzy's university campus via London Bridge station. Possibly it wasn't the most discreet or even safest approach, and it definitely wasn't the most direct, but plain old curiosity can really get in the way of making good decisions. Therefore, without any kind of discussion, they ended up missing out Waterloo station altogether so they could travel in from the opposite direction—principally so they could try to take a peek at a place they'd spent so much effort trying to get away from only five hours before.

It was immediately clear upon exiting the station that this was not just any old Friday morning in Southwark. For a start, there had been a subtle but noticeable police presence throughout the station complex, that then seemed to permeate the streets above, mixed in with a variety other emergency services.

The air also smelled strongly of burning matter and ash, and faint wisps of dark smoke could be seen high in the air as they cut down into Borough Market. They'd been forced to do this as a police cordon had been set up directly under the iron railway bridge crossing over Southwark Street by the Hop Exchange building. It made the whole thing like a wall, cutting access to both vehicle and foot traffic. There were a handful of tourists hanging about by the barriers, trying to work out if there was a way through or to catch a glimpse of whatever was beyond it. But otherwise, that end of the street was empty and, like a human river, the commuter foot traffic simply flowed into the marketplace.

At Leon's suggestion, they stopped briefly at the first kiosk they saw to buy matching baseball caps as a precautionary measure against being spotted. Although they felt reasonably secure that no one was specifically looking for them, at the same time they didn't think it would hurt to be a little cautious. Izzy's had a Tower Bridge icon on it and the words *London Town*. Bought in haste, Leon thought his did too, until they had popped them on outside and Izzy started laughing.

"Nice hat," she said. "Friendly."

He took it off and examined the front to discover it was a cartoon image of a smiling lamb chop with the words *Happy to Meat You*. He was much less happy than his hat about this turn of events but decided to rein in his instinctive need to start complaining, and they carried on down Stoney Street as it narrowed into little more than an alleyway. At the end, where it met with Clink Street, was yet another Pret, set beside a small raised courtyard, laid with tables. They paused briefly at the inter-section to consider whether it was really worth continuing this way on foot just to catch a distant glimpse of a smoking pile, when suddenly someone called out.

"Dude!"

Leon, recognising the voice, looked up and across to where the shout had come from. Tom Kennedy was sitting at a Pret table with a woman he couldn't quite make out but who looked a lot like Jade-from-Accounts. Tom beckoned them over. The woman appeared less than pleased with this invitation, remaining in a slumped position that matched both the sunglasses drooping down her nose, and the position of her mouth.

Izzy looked at Leon, briefly concerned herself that this may not be a great idea, but Leon seemed to brush it aside.

"It's Tom!" he said, quickly snatching the hat from his head but actually kind of elated to get such a big, friendly dose of normality after the events of the previous night.

"Unless, you know," whispered Izzy, "He also turns out to be a secret government flunky."

"It's Tom...?" he repeated, this time with sufficiently amused incredulity that Izzy realised she might be succumbing to paranoia.

"Maybe you're right." She nodded. "But let's just get takeout, OK?"

"Deal."

They walked up the short steps and over to the table to join the couple. Tom, realising that Leon seemed to be with Izzy in some new way, gave him a hugely unsubtle smile as they approached. Leon, in turn, confirming that the grumpy, perspiring woman was indeed Jade-from-Accounts, gave Tom a questioning raise of the eyebrows. Jade? Really?

"Have a seat," said Tom, ostensibly ignoring Leon's unspoken reproach but not without some visible discomfort. He shuffled his chair sideways and extended a hand to the vacant one on his left. Jade made a reluctant if generally positive noise that didn't seem to involve words.

"Thanks, buddy," said Leon. "But we're not stopping."

"What are you guys even doing here?" Tom's enquiry sounded sincere, but the expression on his face suggested ritual nosiness was at the heart of his question.

"Just passing through," replied Leon, evasively.

"And what happened to your face, man?"

"Oh this?" said Leon, reaching up to touch the side of his now scabby forehead. He'd almost forgotten about it. "I uh...I fell into wall. What can I tell you?" He turned to Jade. "Jade, this is Isabella."

"Izzy," said Izzy, smiling and offering a hand. Jade did her best to return the gesture.

"Really sorry," managed Jade, attempting but mainly failing to sit up. "I have a bit of a hangover."

"Oh, you go ahead," said Izzy, still smiling. "I totally understand."

"Thank you," replied Jade, pushing her sunglasses back up her nose and resuming her former meditation on the universal but transient resolve of those-who-will-never-drink-again.

Leon and Izzy went inside to get coffee and pastries which, despite themselves, they quickly devoured upon their return, much to their own and Tom's surprise.

"You feeling OK? It's like you guys haven't eaten for a week. Have a seat, man."

Leon and Izzy exchanged looks to confirm they wouldn't be saying anything.

"We're good, thanks. Just super hungry," said Leon, licking the remains of a croissant off the tips of his fingers, then finishing the job with a napkin. "What can I tell you?"

"Maybe why you didn't reply to any of my messages last night? Or answer your phone? I had no idea where you went."

"Sorry, Mum."

"No, not that. It was just that when I last saw you, in the lift." Leon's eyes grew wide at this revelation. He had no memory of Tom being there. "You didn't very look well."

"Ohh. Oh. Right. I get you," replied Leon. "No, I wasn't very well. No thanks to you, I suspect." Tom pointed at himself and made a poor attempt at an innocent face that Leon ignored. "I got horribly sick and just went home."

"Ah. The wall. I get it. Well, you could've let me know. That's all I'm saying."

"Sorry, man. I lost my phone," he lied.

"Well, then I guess that's why you're still going into work, right?"

Leon hadn't considered that Tom would question his reason for being there, or that *of course* no one would be going into work today! And although it was obvious to him why, he couldn't be sure what the "official" reason might be and decided it might be better to just play along.

"Shouldn't I? Friday's still a workday, last time I looked."

"Man, don't you check the news?"

"Not today."

"You didn't see they've blocked off all the roads?"

"I thought that was just roadworks," he lied again.

"Then I guess you really don't know. Here," said Tom, picking his phone off the table, tapping it open, and handing it to Leon. "If you'd read your email…"

Leon took the phone and started reading the message. It was a short, all-hands message with the subject: **Studio closed – do NOT come into the office.** It went on to explain how the studio building had been irreparably damaged due to unexpected events and that the business would be reverting to fully remote working starting next week, while the leadership team worked out interim arrangements.

No shit, thought Leon.

It ended by affirming that everyone should take the day off and under no circumstances attempt to return to the building. Then, finally, on what was presumably meant to be a reassuring note, stressing that no one was hurt, the disruption would be challenging but minimal, and that the Hyperion family worked best when "*we all work together to solve the problems that others leave behind.*" Nigel's fricking company mantra. Followed by a number to call if anyone was too distressed by this news or needed IT support—and a link to a BBC news article curiously headlined: London Bridge Has Fallen Down.

Leon looked up. Izzy seemed pensive. Tom started shaking his head. Jade was asleep.

"What the hell's happened to Miles Benedict?" said Tom, half chuckling to himself.

"What do you mean!?" replied Leon, a little freaked out. Tom couldn't possibly know...

"Didn't you see? Miles sent that out. Why not big Nige? Miles loves taking the agency dad role, that haughty prick. He's so old-school."

"Right. Yes. He is," said Leon, trying to play along but, given what he knew, feeling deeply uncomfortable at Tom's remarks. He looked again at the email. It was sent from Miles's account at 6:17. A little over two hours ago. There's obviously no way it came from Benedict, he thought. But why pretend he's still alive at all? Or that no one was hurt? All those dead bodies. He recoiled at the still-fresh memory. And who really wrote the email? "Yeah. Bloody Miles."

"So, my friend," said Tom, leaning back in his chair and placing his hands behind his head as though this whole thing had been his idea. "That means we all have the day off. What are we going to do?"

Leon hesitated. He didn't like the idea of just blowing Tom out but felt they'd already said too much and lingered here too long. This was Izzy's cue.

"Sorry, Tom," interrupted Izzy with a smile. "But I'm afraid I'm playing with Leon today. I promise to give him back in one piece. You can borrow him again next week."

Tom immediately understood. Or at least thought he did, by the impish look on his face.

"Well, I'm going to hold you to that, Jones. But I should warn you, there is a fee."

"Hey," said Leon. "Don't I get a say in this? I may have my own plans."

"No, sorry. Not this time," said Izzy, gently gripping his arm and pulling him away from the group. "Nice to see you again, Tom. And..." She nodded towards Jade but, seeing that she was apparently napping, didn't bother finishing the sentence. Then they turned and headed back into the street.

Tom watched them go for a short while, quite pleased for his friend.

"You never have your own plans, loser," Tom yelled after them, then made a phone-shaped gesture with one hand and held it against his head. "Give me a call!" he shouted, waking Jade up with a start. But Leon and Izzy were already halfway down Clink Street and on their way to the river.

30

BUSTED

"Maybe they simply can't admit to any casualties," speculated Izzy, as they crossed over the last section of the Millennium Bridge towards St Paul's. "Because that would just draw extra scrutiny, which obviously they don't want."

"Maybe so," said Leon. "But why pretend Miles is still alive, writing emails? And who are these people that they can just do that?"

"The same people who can hide a spaceship in the middle of London for eighty years? I don't imagine a fake email is much of problem for them."

"Yes, OK. Fair point. I'm not sure why—I mean, I didn't even know Miles that well—but it just disturbs me that they bothered to do it all. It's stopgap at best. Sooner or later people will notice he's stopped showing up for things. And then what?"

"Maybe that's the point. It's all about controlling the message, right? They've sat on this thing and who knows what else for decades. They had a war for cover, and then lots of time with no one really paying any attention to slowly figure things out. Then something goes wrong in a big way and they're having to scramble to get back in control. It's damage limitation. Making sure no one knows anything and, most important, no one asks any questions. So they use Miles. And they can do it presumably without having to get into a big discussion. It's not like he can say no."

Leon nodded, reflecting on the conversation in silence, as they switched back at the end of the bridge, down the short flight of stairs, and made their way along the riverbank. The sun was out, and the sky was clear. And for anyone not currently distracted by seemingly world-changing secrets, and a bizarre, unexpected, and potentially dangerous task they didn't really want, it was a beautiful early summer's day in London.

"So how far to your lab?" asked Leon after a short while.

"Not far. Fifteen minutes if you stop dragging your feet."

"Hey—"

They walked on at a brisk pace along the embankment, enjoying the warm sun on their tired faces, until they reached the university complex where Izzy's research lab was housed. Like much of the architecture in London, it was a glorious mix of old-world and new. Huge neoclassical columns and porticos, jostling with ornate Victorian revivalist detailing, bustling up against smatterings of clean, modernist geometry and late-century glass-clad boxes that inevitably provided a gloomy footnote to commercial realities and diminishing civic imagination. But somehow it all worked, projecting a heady but studious microcosm of the city in which it thrived.

Izzy decided they should use the library wing to access the campus. Although it was farther away, it was generally much quieter than the main entrance, or any of the secondary publicly accessible doors. They had no particular reason to feel they were being observed, but at the same time it was hard to shake the feeling that they should try not to advertise where they were or what they might be doing.

So, after entering the building, Izzy hesitated to use her student ID to pass the electronic gates. Instead, she was able to convince the security guard she was actually her friend, Sophie (who, she happened to know, was away for the weekend at some kind of horse festival. When Izzy had mentioned this fact to Leon he wondered aloud whether that involved lots of horses gathering in a muddy field to get drunk and watch a series of highly acclaimed horse bands, but it seemed to pass her by. "No, it's showjumping and stuff," she'd said, blankly. He decided not to dwell on it). She explained to the guard that she'd forgotten her pass and, after checking a few personal details, which Izzy knew, he issued her a temporary day pass, and signed Leon in as a guest.

Izzy guided Leon through the library and into a maze of corridors and several stairways that eventually brought them into wing where her lab was located. Robbie was just coming into the room from the opposite side as they arrived. He seemed a little surprised to see them.

"Morning, Robbie," said Izzy, curious about the look on his face. "Everything OK?"

"Good morning," he replied, after a long pause and ignoring the question. "What are you… What brings you here so early?"

Izzy couldn't work out if something was actually up, if she was reading too much into him, or if Robbie had just started his rooftop rituals a little early today.

"Early!? You're a cheeky man. Any coffee on the go?"

She made her way over to her locker at the back of the room, while Leon lingered by the door, wondering if he should say anything or just let them get on with it.

"Not yet," he replied. "I wasn't really expecting you today."

"Why not?" she said, as she dialled the combination lock back and forth, then turned her head back into the room. "This is my friend Leon, by the way," she said. "Leon, this is Robson. He basically runs the place."

"Nice to meet you," responded Leon, awkwardly waving a hand, then sticking it back in his pocket. Robson smiled by way of a greeting.

"I'll put a pot on, then. Back in a minute."

Leon wandered over to the main workbench where all of Izzy's toys were on display. A couple of them were gently moving, their "fingers" opening and closing.

"So, this is what you do?" he asked, leaning in super close to look at one that appeared to have a surgical glove stretched over the endoskeleton.

It whirred and clicked in front of his nose. Izzy came away from her locker with a slim metallic laptop in her hand, slammed the door closed behind her, and came to join him at the bench.

"Yes, that's it. Prosthetic limbs. Well, hands, anyway."

"I though you just wrote the software."

"I do both. Don't get too close to that one."

He looked up, unsure if she was being serious when, before he could react, its fingers and thumb suddenly coiled in, then released, flicking the end of his nose.

"Ow!" he jumped up and back. "It flicked me!"

"I did warn you."

"How does it..." he began, rubbing the end of his nose.

"It's run on AI-assisted software. It has sensors built in at various points to establish limited awareness of its surrounding and reduce risk of accidental damage."

"From noses?"

Izzy smiled. "Especially from noses. Here, let's see if this thing works."

She walked around the counter and placed the laptop down in front of Leon, as Robbie came back into the room. Izzy wavered and closed the laptop again. Maybe not here.

"What have you got there?" said Robbie, heading over to the coffee machine with a fresh bag of coffee grounds.

"Nothing," said Izzy. "Just showing Leon a few of my tricks."

He laughed, opening the lid of the percolator. "Did he get the flick?"

"He did," said Izzy, with a half-apologetic look to Leon, who seemed genuinely stung that he'd been caught out by their shared joke. She turned back to look at Robbie, who was now fumbling nervously with the coffee, spilling half of it onto the floor. "What's up, Robbie? Something seems to be troubling you."

He froze briefly, as though caught out by her question, then carried on, attempting to brush her concern aside with bustle.

"I'm fine," he said, although he clearly wasn't.

Leon looked at Izzy with a question. She nodded and slipped the laptop into her backpack. Something was definitely off.

"You know, Robbie, I think we're going to head off after all."

He spun around.

"You can't," he said.

"Can't?"

"I mean, yet. You can't leave yet—I haven't finished making the... I have biscuits!"

He produced a small pack of chocolate bourbons from his lab coat pocket and attempted to force a thin smile. Even from across the room they could see the sweat beading on his forehead.

"Robbie, you never have biscuits! Either you tell me what's going on right now, or I'm just going to go and we can take this up with faculty next week. You're being weird."

Robbie's face dropped in a mix of guilt and fear. He paused, looking between Izzy and Leon and the main door, as if trying to make a decision. Then he walked over to the service door—the one he had just come through—that led to a utility corridor running between the different labs on the floor, and closed it quietly.

"They came early this morning," he said, somewhat shamefully.

Izzy and Leon both looked at each other, their eyes at twice the normal size.

"*Who* came this morning, Robbie?"

"I don't know their names. They were official. There were two of them. They had badges."

"Police?" suggested Leon.

"No, not police. Security. Agents of some kind. I don't know which, they kind of freaked me out."

"What did they want?" asked Izzy.

"They wanted you."

"Me?" Now Izzy was the one freaking out, silently joined by Leon, who tried to reach out a reassuring hand. She pushed it away. "What did they want me for?"

"That's what I asked them. They were cagey, at first, which I thought was odd. Saying it was simply for questioning. A background check for something. But when I pressed them, they started talking about the gas explosion."

"The one over the river?"

"There's another one?"

"Just tell me what they said."

"That's all they said—that they needed to talk to you. That there might be more to the gas thing, and that you'd become a... What did they call it? A person of interest in their enquiries."

"Shit, Robbie!" she said. "And you believed them?"

"Well, they seemed very serious people. They knew all about you—what you do here, what you're working on. And I just thought—"

"Thought what? That I was involved in something? How long have we fucking known each other?"

Leon tried to cool things down a bit. "Izzy, maybe you shouldn't—"

"No, Leon. Maybe I should. They know who I am! How the fuck can they know who I am?"

"They knew about me too," said Robbie, plaintively. "They said that if I didn't help them out, let them know if I saw you—"

"Oh, what have you done, Robbie?"

"I'm really sorry. I thought I was helping," he said, just as the service door crashed open.

They all turned. A man dressed in black combat fatigues stepped into the room. His sleeves were rolled up, revealing a serpent tattoo circling his right forearm that ended by the crook of his thumb and index finger. The hand itself held a silenced pistol directly out in front of him, supported underneath the pistol-grip by his left. His gaze jumped between each of them in turn and then, before anyone could react, the man pivoted right and shot Robbie in the head.

Leon and Izzy yelled in horror and disbelief as his body instantly slumped to the floor. The man in black put a finger to his lips with his free hand, to quiet them down.

"Shh…" he said, then waved them farther back into the room.

Leon and Izzy nodded reluctantly and stepped away from Robbie's crumpled form.

"You fucking shot him!" shouted Leon, pointing redundantly at the space where Robbie had just been standing.

"I know," said the man, quietly, almost reassuringly. "And, unless you want me to do the same to you, I suggest we all take it nice and easy—and quietly—from here."

Leon and Izzy weren't about to argue.

"Take a seat," he ordered, indicating the high stools next to Izzy's workbench. They sat, compliantly and the man raised two fingers to his ear. "Victor-Charlie-One. Confirm."

They couldn't hear the response, obviously, but after a brief pause the man responded, "VC-One, code 7. I have the primary target."

Leon looked at Izzy. She looked like a ghost. Frozen to her seat, staring rigidly ahead, not blinking. He could hardly blame her. Was Izzy the primary target? But how could she be? Who was she to any of these people? And if she was the target, then what was he? As if to answer his silent question the man spoke again.

"High probability, secondary target also acquired." The man looked straight at Leon. "White male. Dark brown hair. Early thirties. Affirmative."

Leon gazed around the room half expecting to see other people standing there, then looked back to the man and responded by pointing his thumb back at himself and mouthing the words *who, me*. The man nodded slightly, clearly listening to additional instructions on his earpiece.

Leon didn't feel exactly thrilled by this confirmation and,

without really thinking about it, simply defaulted into a defensive, unsatisfied customer mode, which was about all the combat training he had, really, in terms of channelling his aggression in adult life.

"Excuse me," said Leon, but the man ignored him, so he tried again. "Excuse me!?"

This time he lowered his fingers from his ear, obviously annoyed, and looked at Leon.

"Yes?"

"Thank you," said Leon, feigning satisfaction. "Uhm...look, sorry to interrupt your call. I can see you have serious business to attend to with your friend Victor Charlie and everything. But as probable secondary target here, I feel I"—he glanced at Izzy, whose expression seemed to soften as he had begun to talk—"that is to say, *we*—primary *and* secondary target—we'd like to speak to your manager. Would that be Victor?"

"What!?" The man's expression became confused. The people he tended to deal with were either dead or pleading for their life. But this, he didn't recognise.

"Well, it's just that, as the guy on the frontline, I suspect your powers are limited. Right? You have your standard instructions and anything I ask for now, you'd just have to send back up the chain anyway. So why don't we just cut that bit out?"

This just seemed to vex the assassin further. "I can kill right you, how's that for limited powers?" he said, stepping forward to face off with Leon more directly.

Leon, much to his own surprise, only sat up taller and tried smiling at him. While Izzy, who had fully reawakened to what was now happening, wondered what the hell Leon was doing and tried to intervene. She put her hand on his leg, as though to stop him from talking.

"I think what my friend here is trying to say—" she began.

"It's OK, Izzy," said Leon, raising his hands in front of him. "What we have here is a classic service issue. The gentleman here says he can kill us, but it's clear—to me, at least—that he can't.

Otherwise, we'd already be on the floor along with your...friend here." He faltered for a second, as the memory of what had just happened competed with what he was now trying to accomplish. He just silently prayed that Izzy was paying attention. "That means the decision is not his to make."

"Look, mate," interjected the man. "She might like the sound of your voice, but I don't have to kill you to make you shut up."

"Is that in the script? That's kind of rude, you know."

Izzy looked at Leon with some disbelief. Was he actually trying to get them killed?

"Is it, really?" said the killer, folding his arms.

"Look, I realise you're under orders and you just want us to sit tight and shut up until your friends arrive. But I'm *literally* trying to give you a hand here."

Leon suddenly produced the latex-gloved prosthetic hand he'd been playing with earlier, from behind where he was sitting, and held it out in front of him. "Like this one."

Izzy instantly twigged to his plan and casually placed her hand over a numerical keypad on the workbench as, despite his apparent steely focus, the man carelessly leaned in to look at the robotic appendage more closely. Leon pushed it towards him. The hand reacted. Coiled in, then snapped back out and grabbed the end of the man's nose and mouth and squeezed. Hard. The man yelled and seethed as he failed to get the thing off his face. The more he pulled the tighter it gripped. Izzy smiled pridefully at the hand's tenacity, then took the opportunity kick the man squarely between his legs. He let out a roar and his knees buckled but, despite his obvious pain, he still made an unexpected effort to grab Izzy with his free hand. She pivoted at the last second and landed her second award-winning Krav Maga knuckle punch of the day to his gut. He groaned as the wind was pushed out of him and Leon took the opening to grab a nearby fire extinguisher and bring it down across the back of the assassin's head. The man dropped to his knees, with a sorrowful wail, as Izzy reached across the bench and snatched a Biro from a pot of pens. She turned and jammed it into the base of the man's neck. He made a gurgling noise and slumped to the floor.

"Now!" yelled Leon, reaching out and smashing the fire alarm on the wall, enveloping them in an almost painful blanket of sound.

Izzy grabbed her backpack off the bench and they both legged it out of the lab, along the corridor, and down the stairs as fast as their terrified legs would carry them. At the bottom of the stairs, Izzy pulled Leon left instead of right—the direction they had come from—and after several quick turns, joined a concourse that led down to the main faculty entrance. An enormously wide, high, and ornate archway, spanned by a string of electronic barriers at the far end, sat between them and the exit, but all of them were open due to the alarm. The approach was quickly filling up with other people, emerging from different directions, all attempting to leave the building in an orderly fashion, as the wail of the alert required. Leon and Izzy slowed their pace to a brisk walk to merge with the growing crowd, and made their way out of the building onto Aldwych, a semicircular roadway that diverted traffic from The Strand and then north towards Holborn.

Outside the large double doors, a couple of fire-safety officers in luminescent red-and-yellow tunics were attempting to usher people away from the front steps and into different groups and locations. Leon and Izzy narrowly avoided both categorisation and being run over as they shot out across the busy street, then veered left and up Drury Lane towards Covent Garden. They only made it a short way up the road before ducking out of sight, down Tavistock Street, so that they could catch their breath. And so that Leon, much to his own horror and that of two passing tourists in search of Covent Garden's delights, could kneel down on the pavement and throw up.

31

MR WONG'S

Once Leon had recovered his bearings, if not his dignity, they quickly threaded their way up and through Convent Garden towards Chinatown and Mr Wong's. Leon spent half the journey there apologising awkwardly for the vomit ("Really not my best moment."), which Izzy insisted, truthfully, that she did not care about—not least because if it hadn't been him, she would have done it.

"I almost threw up right after he shot Robbie."

"I saw that."

"I still can't believe... Poor Robbie," she winced, fighting to suppress the memory, as they skirted around the piazza and, despite the relatively early hour, a small pocket of tourists watching a unicycling, clown-faced juggler. "He didn't deserve that."

"None of us deserved any of this."

"What I don't understand is how they connected me to this... thing they're doing. I wasn't even supposed to be there."

"We," said Leon, attempting to reassure her that she wasn't alone in this.

"Maybe it's we. But it's definitely me. What did the guy say?

'High probability of secondary target?' To me that means they're not really sure who you are. Maybe we can use that somehow."

"Maybe so."

"I see now why Quinn didn't want us to talk to anyone. And that was before they caught up with us. We need to check it wasn't just a fluke. I'll see if anyone went to my flat. You should do the same."

They stopped off at small kiosk to buy a couple of disposable phones, loaded them up, then tried to find ways to locate or remember the phone numbers they needed. The first call for Izzy was her mum, to make sure no one had paid her a visit, and was immediately relieved to hear she was fine. No unusual callers, she said.

"Unless you count Horace, my regular. Comes in every day to buy a single tulip then sits with it on the bench up by the estate agent to drink his cans of lager. I wonder sometimes why he chooses that spot. Perhaps he used to sell houses," she said.

Izzy suggested it was probably for other reasons, but her mother had already stopped listening, as the shop bell had chimed and she tried to close the call.

"I just wanted to let you know, I'm going away for a long weekend," said Izzy.

"That's lovely, darling. Be sure to get it in the right size this time. Got to go," she said. Then put the phone down before Izzy could correct her.

"Everything OK?" asked Leon.

"She's fine," said Izzy, offhandedly, keen to move on.

She then went to call her neighbour while Leon tried his flat-mate, Nathan, who assured him that not only had they received no unexpected visitors or calls that morning, but that he had only just got into bed after finishing his shift at the hospital at 7:30 and that he would greatly appreciate it if Leon could kindly fuck off and leave him to sleep. Leon was happy to oblige, and reminded himself that he should have known better than to rouse an ICU nurse first thing in the morning, even if it was his brother.

"Maybe I'll see you tonight," said Leon, and left it at that. But just like Izzy's mother, Nathan had already gone.

Izzy's news was much less positive. According to her neighbour Anisha it appeared her flat had been broken into. The door had been busted open and it looked like someone had gone through all her things, leaving the place in a real mess. She added that she'd tried to reach Izzy earlier that morning when she left for work to find the door wide open and nobody at home. This forced Izzy to also lie about losing her phone, but not about her distress at being broken into, which she found difficult to hide, even over the phone.

They cut past the Tube and along Neal Street before skewing left towards Seven Dials, where they found a makeshift row of outdoor café tables by the heptagonal intersection, as Izzy finished her call. She thanked Anisha for her help and concern, and reassured her that she'd be OK, and would take care of everything even though she was, "away for the weekend…"

After the whole thing with Robbie, this news felt like another blow that she couldn't easily walk off. She pulled on Leon's sleeve and indicated she wanted to sit. He nodded but remained standing as he finished his own call and walked up a few paces to the end of the street.

Izzy took a seat on a small two-person bench at the end of the row that faced the memorial seven-faced sundial at the centre of the junction. She just needed a minute to breathe and to think.

Somehow, they knew where she worked and where she lived, while she didn't know the first thing about them. This apparently secret organisation. Run by whom? For what purpose? And she still couldn't figure out how they had connected the dots to her in the first place. Her, but strangely not Leon. They must have been seen somewhere, that's all there was to it, she thought. They're not psychics. Unless…but more likely it was to do the soldiers that chased them down to the Tate. Or maybe they somehow fished Miles out of the ground before the whole place went up, although she immediately knew that was impossible.

Overwhelmed with a feeling of helplessness and suddenly hit by fatigue, she fought back the tears which were threatening their way out. She didn't want to cry. Not now. Not here. Not with... She lowered her head and closed her eyes so that Leon, who was still on the phone, pacing back and forth by the circular junction with a finger in his ear, couldn't see she was upset.

Leon, however, had already noticed. And although his call had finished a short while ago, he continued pacing with the phone pinned to his ear while he figured out what he should do. After all, as intense and terrifying as this whole situation was, it had thrown him and Izzy together in a way he could not possibly have imagined before last night. Until then he had, at best, been hoping he might at some point, maybe, you know, be able to persuade her to go for a pizza sometime. Maybe even check out a movie. But now...? He looked over at her sitting on the bench by herself. Anxious and unhappy about what had happened to them, to her friend, and what might happen next. Just like he was. He decided he was thinking too much, as usual. He walked over, sat next to her on the bench, and put his arm around her shoulder. She leaned her head into his and they just sat together in silence for a while, as the world continued to turn.

One ocean and three-quarters of a continent to the left, Lieutenant Commander Frances Carson burst into the executive bathroom, letting the door slam back against the wall, and then gently close behind her as she marched over to the sink. She ran the tap for a while, staring at her pallid reflection in the mirror, then splashed handfuls of water onto her weary face. She was not happy. It had already been a long day and was rapidly shifting into what was likely to be an even longer night. She was tired and frustrated by a succession of extremely challenging events, from an all-out disaster and borderline international incident, to a bunch of plain old fifty-cent bungling.

She dried her face on a fresh white towel and, reluctant to go back to Snark with yet more bad news, attempted to compose herself as she went back over every step taken to find something she could build on.

Eighteen months of planning and preparation—never mind the preceding eight decades of work—for what was supposed to be a watershed moment in history, she thought. Not just in the history of this agency, but the world, whether they knew it or not. Every member of every team had been vetted, background-checked, and hand-selected, then checked again before they stepped one foot into the deliberately anonymous Washington recruitment lounge, where she and her team would first meet them. And then, after some structured formalities, speak cautiously of opportunity, duty, patriotism, and the chance to make a real difference to the world, before she invited them to join an elite but as-yet undisclosed programme. At which point they would undergo yet another vetting process, only this time with both their knowledge and consent.

And yet, despite all of that, here they were. On what should have been a triumphant night, the programme was lurching around like an injured bear, and creating yet more havoc in its wake as the attempted clean-up had begun. There was nothing to be done but keep moving forward. She took a deep breath, brushed her hair down, and smoothed out her uniform, then briskly left the washroom and headed straight for Snark's office.

She found him there already standing at his desk, poring over a sea of reports and nursing what looked like yet another glass of scotch on ice. Carson had always had a great deal of admiration for Snark. And although his obvious smarts, experience, and ability to quickly grasp strategic imperatives—often on little more than a smudged Post-it note—was a big part of it, she had to confess that it may lie more simply in his singular ability to manage a crisis and chronic alcoholism simultaneously. In any case, he was already in a black mood as she arrived, and he was not made any happier by what she had to tell him.

"So let me get this straight, Lieutenant Commander," he

began, with an unusual insistence on formality. "The London site of one our most prestigious artifacts is in meltdown. Destroyed. And likely unrecoverable, as a result of some as-yet unsubstantiated sabotage. The Berlin team is missing, presumed dead. Quinn is off-the-grid, unreachable—along with whatever intelligence he found at the Benedict residence—and, we may as well presume, also dead, for all the good it will do us.

"Then we have two—two!—random and apparently civilian off-the-books individuals, in the middle of one of the most black-on-black operations in the history of covert actions, affiliated with who-the-hell-knows-what and with—again we must assume—information we need but can't access.

"And on top of all this, we have Jordan Milk. Jordan Goddamn Milk. Running around off leash in Billionaire World, unregulated, and apparently untraceable, conducting all kinds of California-sized experimental shit that we always seem to be too late for. Along with all the motive, means, and opportunity he needs to infiltrate our organization and steal technology he shouldn't know anything about. And yet, despite all this, and all the resources of the U-nited States government, you're telling me that we have no credible way to bring him in and, basically, dick to show for it after a yearlong investigation other than—what—the guy's richer than God!? Outstanding work, Commander. Outstanding work."

Carson cleared her throat and ensured her gaze remained eyes-forward. This seemed to be going slightly better than she had been anticipating.

"Sir, in my—" she began, before his hand slammed down onto the desk and cut her off.

"I'm not done."

"No, sir."

"And now you're telling me that just as we have uncovered and located a highly lucrative thread to pull on in Ms. Isabella Jones, that she and her yet-to-be identified dark brown hair, early thirties, white male companion have somehow evaded what should have been a clean, textbook ghost custody action. And not only evaded, but by all accounts, left the principal asset in need of significant hospitalization."

"That's correct, sir," she replied.

"That's quite a trick for someone who's apparently done nothing in their adult life but book-study and give overpaid executives a little light relief from poor posture, wouldn't you say?"

"I would, sir. Something doesn't add up."

"Something doesn't add up. Jesus Christ, Frankie. I respect the hell out of you, you know I do. But this? This is turning into goddamn amateur hour at the Ritzy. Do I have to get Mac in here? Do I need to go back to Division?"

Snark took a swig of his drink. The ice gently rattled in the glass as he regarded her with an expression she couldn't quite read, other than that his foul mood finally starting to abate.

"No, sir," she said, with all the angry confidence she could muster. *Division*. She was shocked to hear him even bring it up. She had worked too long and too hard to get herself posted here. Made sacrifices. Of friends and relationships. A career she could talk about. A place to call home. A life. More than she should have, some would say. But they would be wrong. If they had been through what she had experienced, what her family... But perhaps she had simply taken his trust too much for granted, she realised. "That won't be necessary, sir. I will do whatever it takes."

Snark stepped back and sank down into his chair with a sigh. He put his glass down on the desk, leaned back, and began to rub the tiredness from his eyes, before returning to his paperwork.

"I know you will, Frankie," he said, at last, without looking back up.

Carson lingered a moment longer, but she knew he was done. She had her orders. Get it done. Whatever it took. No excuses.

She saluted silently, without any response or further acknowledgment from Snark, turned on her heel and left the room.

. . .

Izzy had quietly drifted off to sleep. Her breathing had become soft and regular, like a restrained purr. And although there was a big, exhausted part of Leon that longed to do the same, he was unable to relax in quite the same way. Especially when very serious people seemed to be after them for reasons that still remained a bit of a mystery. On the other hand, he was glad to take a pause. It felt nice to be sitting there and, for the first time since he woke up in the work toilet, not be going anywhere in a hurry. He realised then too that the remains of his hangover seemed to have finally dissipated. He obviously had other bumps and scrapes to contend with but that cloying, sickly feeling was gone. A bit of an intense cure though, he thought, as he quietly watched the commuters and shoppers and tourists go about their business.

Izzy suddenly stirred with a sharp intake of breath and a groan to go with it. Evidently her sleeping brain had momentarily forgotten where she was, while her waking brain had just caught up. She lifted her head up and rubbed her face awake.

"How long was I asleep?" she asked, woozily.

"Not very long."

"Sorry about that," she said, pulling her bag onto her lap in search of a drink. "I don't know what came over me."

"You must have needed it," replied Leon, handing her his bottle to save her the trouble.

She took three large gulps, then handed it back.

"Thank you," she said, seeming to come back to life.

She then scraped her hands through her hair like a comb before sitting up straight and pulling it back into place with a clip she somehow magicked from the ether. Leon smiled at her.

"You OK?" he asked. "You seem better."

"There's nothing like sleeping outdoors, eh?"

"Ready to meet Mr Wong?"

Izzy nodded. They stood up, brushed themselves down and headed directly across Seven Dials towards Cambridge Circus.

"I'm sorry about your flat," said Leon after a short distance. "It didn't sound like good news."

"It wasn't. Seems they broke in and trashed the place."

"Oh, Izzy, I'm really sorry."

"It's OK. After how today has turned out so far... It's just stuff. It can be fixed. I'm mostly relieved they don't seem to have got as far as my mum. What about you?"

"My flat?"

"Your family. Have you spoken to them?"

"Oh, they'll be fine."

"You seem very sure."

"Well, first off, I share a flat with my brother and he couldn't wait to get me off the phone. And as for my parents, believe me, if the slightest thing had happened my mum would have phoned already."

"But it doesn't work. And she doesn't have this number," said Izzy, referring to their newly acquired burner phones.

"My mum?" Leon smiled, anxiously. "That wouldn't have stopped her. If she had to, she would just guess it."

Izzy gave him a curious look.

"When you meet her, you'll know what I mean."

Her eyes widened. "Wait...did you just say *when* I meet her!?"

"Yeah, about that..." said Leon, evasively.

Fortunately for him, however, they had just arrived outside Mr Wong's. A narrow hole in the wall, comprising one door and a narrow ornate window not much wider than the entrance. It was squeezed in at the end of a row of several larger, and more glamorous-looking Chinese restaurants, on a stubby side road running off Chinatown's main drag. Initially taking it for a service entrance, they almost missed it.

"You think this is really the place?" asked Leon, happy to change the subject.

He held out the matchbook in front of him, opening the flap and turning it in his hand in search of more definite clues. Izzy took it from him and did more or less the same thing.

"Dunno," she said, pressing her face up against the steamy window. "Let's assume it is. What's the worst that can happen?"

Leon looked at her. "Really?"

"You're right," she said. Then pushed the door open anyway.

As soon as they stepped inside, a man's voice shouted from the back of the restaurant.

"We're closed!"

There was a sharp band of light streaming in from the half-open kitchen doorway. They could see movement through the gap but otherwise the lights were off, and it was hard to make out where in the small eatery the voice had come from.

"Hello?" called Izzy, into the back.

"Not open," came the voice again, impatiently. "Come back later!"

Leon and Izzy looked at each other, wondering if maybe they should come back later. It was still early. Perhaps it was foolish to think the place would be open.

Suddenly a really pissed-off middle-aged Chinese man stepped sharply out of the gloom and looked at them expectantly.

"What you want?" he demanded. "Restaurant closed. Too early."

He pressed forward and made an arm gesture that suggested the door would be the next best course of action for the two of them.

"Uhm, yeah," began Leon. "I know. But we're not here for food."

"Then what? This is a restaurant. We sell food."

"We're here to see...*Mr* Wong?" tried Izzy, offering the man a big peace-making smile. But it just seemed to aggravate him further, and he let out an irritated sigh.

"Which Mr Wong, lady? This is family business. Everyone here Mr Wong."

"Mr Wong...Junior?"

The man turned without saying anything further and

promptly marched off towards the kitchen, shouting a stream of something indecipherably Chinese.

"Maybe we should come back later," suggested Leon, turning toward the door.

Izzy was about to respond when a small but incredibly old-looking Chinese man, wearing chefs' trousers, black plimsolls, and a curiously tight white T-shirt with the *Fame* logo printed on it, suddenly appeared in front of them.

"Yes?" he said, plainly. It was hard to be sure if he was as annoyed as his friend had been, but he certainly didn't seem happy to see them.

"Mr Wong Junior?" enquired Leon, half looking at Izzy for approval. She responded with an in-for-a-penny look on her face.

"Yes?" repeated the Chinese man.

"Gary Numark sent us?" said Leon, in a half-question-half-statement kind of a way.

The elderly chef simply regarded Leon and then Izzy without any noticeable change of expression before finally responding.

"Two of you," he said, lingering on the words as though that wasn't generally the expected amount of people. "Interesting. You want special or the regular?"

Now they were stumped. On top of not being entirely clear about why they were here, Quinn hadn't mentioned anything about making a choice. Leon looked to Izzy for a little help, but she appeared to be waiting for him to choose.

"Perhaps if you have a, uhm, menu?" he asked. They were in a restaurant after all. But the man remained decidedly unimpressed by this query, and simply waited, arms folded, for an answer to his question.

"Special," said Leon, at last. Deciding that special in this case must be the best whatever it was, rather than just the equivalent of yesterday's leftovers turned into soup-of-the-day. "We'll go for the special."

"Very good," said Mr Wong Junior, briskly. He pushed between them and locked the door before turning around and heading back into the gloomy restaurant. "This way."

They followed him as he wove through the maze of empty tables and into a constricted utility area at the rear, reserved for the single multi-purpose toilet and a tall coat rack. He yanked the coat rack to one side, revealing what turned out to be a narrow door with a numerical lock recessed into the wall. He punched in the code and opened the door to what initially appeared to be a storage area: mops and brooms, a vacuum cleaner, stepladder, and a broken chair. However, beyond this clutter was a heavy dark canvas curtain that opened onto a narrow set of near vertical stairs. More like a ladder, thought Leon, as he climbed over the junk and tried to keep up with Mr Wong, who zipped nimbly upwards like a child in a playground.

At the top was a small landing, with a door on either side, and a shorter but equally steep stairway that switched back in the other direction before disappearing through a small hatch. Wong headed straight up, and they followed dutifully behind to find themselves in a small, dimly lit room with a desk on one side and a camera, tripod, and lighting arrangement facing the wall opposite. On the desk was a lamp, a laptop, a large monitor, and what looked like a very heavy-duty printer that Leon didn't recognise. There were various cables running between all the equipment and snaking across the floor, with no safety coverings or tape. The place was literally a death trap, he thought, as he looked around. It wouldn't take much, he imagined, to trip on one of those and fall headfirst down the hatch they'd just climbed out of.

Wong went over to the computer as Leon and Izzy got their bearings, wondering what exactly they were here to do. Behind them was a small grubby sofa and a low table in front of a couple of windows that, judging by the dirt and grime, had long ago been covered over with cardboard and thick black tape.

"Nice pad, you have here, Mr Wong," said Leon, anxious to fill the dismal silence.

Wong looked up, slightly baffled by the comment, then

crossed over to the camera and yanked down a roller-blind attached high on the wall in front. It had a neutral, blueish colour. He switched on the small umbrella lighting and then the camera itself.

"Who want to go first?" he said.

Leon looked at Izzy. She held out her arm in an after-you gesture, but still he paused. Was no one going to talk about what was going on? What was the picture for?

"Mr Wong," said Leon, after a moment. "I don't want to be difficult. You clearly seem to know what you're doing." Wong's began to roll his eyes impatiently. "But I just wondered if we could take a moment to—"

"Special, yes!?" interrupted Wong, irritably. "Gary Numark special. He not explain?"

"He was in a hurry."

"Fine. I take photo. You get new ID plus operation package. OK? Anything else? I have restaurant to run."

Finally, this whole setup made sense. And Leon could see by the look of relief on Izzy's face that she felt the same way. A fake identity sounded pretty useful after what had happened at the university. And it might even help get them to New York, which until now had just seemed like a bunch of unachievable crazy talk from Quinn. Leon had been prepared to go along with the plan up to a point—after all, what else was he going to do—but it hadn't escaped his attention that, without something like this, they'd probably just get scooped up at the airport. Especially now they seemed to know who Izzy was. And, he suspected, despite his mere *probable secondary target* status it wouldn't take much longer for them to clock who he was. He imagined that people with secret underground bases probably had a lot of people-finding resources to work with.

With the mystery cleared up, Wong proceeded to take them quickly through the required process for creating new identities. And despite their understandable scepticism, it was clear that Wong knew exactly what he was doing.

After taking their photograph, he went over to the computer and took some basic information about their real identities— names, address, date of birth, national insurance, parents' details, that kind of thing. He reluctantly explained in the same blunt manner that staying as close to the truth as possible made for a much better lie. Plus, he hinted, their real information could be used to spoof the system into thinking they were still out in the world, spending money, buying train tickets, eating dinner. Giving them a kind of double cover. Although, based on her own grasp of how integrated networks and AI-augmented platforms worked, Izzy had her doubts as to whether that would be very effective against anyone who was actively looking for them. But what the hell, she thought. It might provide a small buffer while they played tourists with their new passports.

Finally, Wong circled round to asking them if they had any preference for their new names.

"OK. Last question," he said. "What name you want?"

"We get a choice?" said Leon.

"Easier to remember."

Leon was immediately tickled by this idea. Maybe it was because this whole secret identity thing seemed impossible to take seriously. After all, who really comes to a place like this and gets to pretend to be somebody else? Outside of films and TV shows, he could never have imagined that such things were real. Or maybe, as his mind continued to wander, it was growing up on a diet of James Bond films, where Bond would always inexplicably go under cover using his real name. And for a moment, Leon was seriously tempted to try doing the same thing. Instead, he just went for the next thing that came into his head which, in this case, was almost as ridiculous.

"Jason Bourne," said Leon, impulsively. Secretly delighted by his choice.

Wong looked at him blanky. He was used to all kinds of operatives showing up at his door, in various states of mind and body. But these two clowns were something else.

"Jason Bourne," repeated Wong, just to be sure he really had it right.

"Really, Leon?" said Izzy, smiling at his admittedly magnificent choice, but also somewhat concerned that it might somehow come back to bite them. "You can't do that."

"Why not?" said Leon, holding his hands out. "I like it. When else will I ever get to do this? And, anyway, who in the real world is actually looking for Jason Bourne?"

She had to admit, he had a point.

"OK, fine," said Izzy, defiantly. "Then I want to be Hermione Granger."

"What?" said Leon, feeling ever so slightly outdone.

"Not another word from you, Jason," she replied, sternly.

Wong looked up expectantly and waited, but since neither of them showed any sign of backing away from their ridiculous choices, he simply shook his head and began typing the names into the system. Izzy began spelling Hermione for him, but he cut her off sharply.

"I'm Chinese. Not dead," he scolded. "You want make birth-place Hogwarts too?"

"Sorry," said Izzy, raising her hands defensively. "Point taken."

His scowl grew deeper as he returned to the screen and finished inputting all the data. He paused briefly, considering a word of caution, but looked up to find Leon and Izzy were just smiling inanely at him. Screw it, he thought. Their choice. There must be some good reason for them to end up at my door. He pressed submit and slammed the laptop closed.

"We are done. Package ready nine o'clock tonight."

"Nine o'clock!" repeated Leon. "Why so long?"

"It takes what it takes. I got business to run."

"What are we supposed to do until then?"

"Not my problem, Jason Bourne," he replied, smiling for the first and only time. "Come back after nine."

His expression made it quite clear there was nothing more to be discussed and promptly indicated they should leave the way they had arrived. He followed their careful descent back down into the restaurant, muttering in Chinese and closing up all the hatches and doors as they went.

A short time later they were back on Gerrard Street's main thoroughfare, Mr Wong Junior having taken no pains to wave them on their way except to remind them not to come back before nine o'clock. The street was filling up now with a mixture of tourists and shoppers and general curiosity seekers but, even so, after the claustrophobic setting of Wong's identity lab, they were glad to be outside again.

"Well, that was a new experience," declared Leon. "What do you think will happen next? Q coming round the corner with a bulletproof car for us?"

"Invisible car, surely?" replied Izzy, smiling. She then looked at her watch. "What are we going to do though? We need to find somewhere to lay low for the next twelve hours. I don't know about you, but I'm a little tired and could do with a shower."

"Same," said Leon. Then, after a moment, with a slightly awkward smile forming. "I know just the place."

32

FRIDAY NIGHT DINNER

F ollowing a slightly evasive but brief discussion about the joys and complexities of Jewish mothers generally and his North London variety in particular, Leon was able to persuade Izzy that both rest and showers would all be freely available at his parents' house. Or rather, he tried to explain in a straightforward way why it was that, despite everything that had happened to them in the past twenty-four hours, his mum would still be expecting him for Friday Night Dinner.

"But seriously," began Izzy. "You're telling me she wouldn't understand if you had to cancel for some reason? Like, you know, if, say, there was a giant explosion in London that was really a cover-up for a secret UFO programme, and now there are people are trying to kill you?"

"Of course she would understand. She's not crazy," he replied, feeling acutely aware that what he was saying did make her sound a bit crazy. "But she'd still insist we eat something."

So, they jumped back on the Tube at Leicester Square and headed up to North Finchley. A place, Leon asserted, that was so ideal for lying low it hadn't earned a single headline in the *Hendon & Finchley Times* in the last three years, not since it had been obliged to publish a riposte to notable MilkBar user, BluntCACtus37, after they had described the area as, "...implausibly dull, with no decent bars, or takeaways," before warning all potential future residents, "...don't even bother with it, unless you are over forty."

"My dad has that quote framed in his home office," said Leon.

Izzy wasn't entirely sure how she felt about meeting Leon's parents. Not because she was against meeting parents generally but because, well, the whole situation was so weird. Events seemed intent on pulling her and Leon closer together which, to her surprise, she was feeling kind of fine with, happy even, particularly under the circumstances. After all, the alternative of having to navigate any of this crazy stuff on her own filled her with dread. But meeting his parents? On, what, day one? If that's what this was. That felt kind of intense, even after the events of the night before.

But then she looked across at Leon sitting on the opposite side of the carriage, gazing absently into space and decided it would be OK. He was a good guy. And it seemed kind of important to him that they go. Plus, she had to admit, after having her life literally pulled to pieces by a bunch of random unknown forces, there was something genuinely appealing about the idea of a few home comforts, over the spartan, wipe-down surfaces of the nearest Premier Inn. Assuming the Aronofskys weren't all a bunch of sociopaths, that is. How weird could it be?

"Baby cakes, you're early!" shrieked Leon's mum with delight, as she swung open the front door.

"Hi, Mum," said Leon.

"Harry!" she yelled behind her. "Come downstairs—Leon's home."

"Mum, seriously. I saw you, like, a week ago, not last year."

"What's the matter, darling?" she said taking his jacket and brushing down the front of his sweater as he stepped into the house. "My baby comes home for dinner, and I can't be excited? And with a friend!?"

Leon made room for Izzy to come farther into the hallway.

"Mum, this is Isabella."

"Izzy," said Izzy, holding out her hand. "Very pleased to me you, Mrs Aran-"

"Call me Lydia, darling," said Lydia, returning the handshake with a lavish smile. "No need to stand on formality. Very happy to meet you. Although, I have to say," she said, dropping into a conspiratorial tone that was barely any quieter. "Leon's told us nothing about you."

Leon closed his eyes and shook his head, realising he should have warned Izzy more carefully than he had.

"What else is new?" declared Leon's father, Harry, coming down the stairs. "Everything with him is a big secret. Just try asking him what he wants for dinner."

"Dad!" admonished Leon.

He really hadn't thought this through properly, he decided, bristling under his parents' less than tactful remarks. He threw Izzy an apologetic look in an attempt to defuse the situation, but she seemed to be thoroughly enjoying herself.

"Dad, this is—"

"Isabella. Yes, I heard. Very nice to meet you," said Harry, with a much less demanding smile than his wife. He shook Izzy's hand before turning back to his wife. "I thought from all the screaming that maybe Paul Hollywood had stopped by with some cake."

"Don't pay any attention to him," said Lydia, directly to Izzy. "Come in. Come in."

Lydia ushered Izzy through to the kitchen at the back of the house, with Leon and his father dutifully shuffling along behind them.

At Lydia's insistence, Leon and Izzy sat down at a long diner-style table built into one corner of the room, while she busied herself making a pot of coffee and, without even asking if they were hungry, fetching an assortment of noshy items from the fridge for them to eat.

"Leon, you look dreadful," she said, as she placed a box of small pastries on the table, swiftly followed by assortment of bagels, olives, smoked salmon, cream cheese, and egg-mayo with chopped spring onion. "When's the last time you slept? And what happened to your face?"

"Thanks, Mum," replied Leon, "About that..."

But she was already on to Izzy, asking her about her work, where she lived, where she grew up, and other increasingly personal questions that few others would dare to pursue on a first meeting but that, for Lydia, all fell under the category of "...taking an interest in people, Leon. You should try it." Ultimately it was just something he had had to learn to live with, like a speech impediment or sports injury that would occasionally flare up.

Leon did his best to mediate the conversation but as Izzy appeared quite content to share and, to his surprise (and his mother's delight), reciprocate the grilling right back at Lydia, he decided to leave them to it and started loading up a sesame bagel.

Harry, meanwhile, had remained hovering in the doorway, torn between nosiness for this new person in his son's life, his need to get back to work, and, mainly, his desire to eat what was out on the table. He took Leon's submission as his signal to get stuck in.

"I suppose a quick snack wouldn't hurt," he said, mostly to himself, and sidled up to the table to join in with all the bagel-loading.

Eventually the late-breakfasting, and early questioning subsided and, as he helped his mother clear away the things, Leon was able to at least partially explain what was going on: why he was off work (gas explosion version), how it was that Izzy was with him (flat broken into. Which, if anything, horrified Lydia the most. "Do you think they went through your...*smalls*?" she asked, visibly shuddering. Izzy hadn't really considered this, but in the spirit of amity graciously accepted Lydia's kind, if insistent, offer to take her to Marks and Spencer's for a restock), and what they were planning on doing for the weekend (going to New York. Which thrilled Lydia and prompted Harry to grumble about the sinking value of the pound against the dollar). Then, finally, suggesting that they had planned to hang out there for the day "While Izzy's flat gets sorted out."

Lydia was, by now, in her element, and took this as a sign to ensure they (but principally Izzy), felt right at home. But not before they popped to the shops to pick up a kosher chicken and some knickers.

By dinner time that evening, Leon and Izzy were feeling much better and more clear-headed, having managed to grab a few hours' sleep—Leon on the sofa, Izzy in his old room—and get cleaned up. This was just as well, Leon warned Izzy, as the rest of his family was about to descend on the house for Friday Night Dinner.

"Honestly, Leon," said Izzy. "I'm fine with it. Stop worrying. Your mum is great."

"For you, maybe," he replied.

Izzy laughed. "Go down and give her a hand. I'll join you in a minute."

Leon got downstairs just as great uncle Morrie was shuffling in through the front door, ably supported by Caroline, Lydia's sister. He was elderly, and somewhat poorly sighted. And while most in the family would agree he also suffered with *selective hearing,* his voice remained sharp.

"Don't just pull me around like a dog," barked Morrie, to Caroline, as he tugged his arm away from hers. "I can still find my way to a dinner table."

"Jeff's parking the car," said Caroline to Lydia, who was attempting to part Morrie from his heavy overcoat.

"Hi, Uncle Morrie," said Leon. He'd always had a bit of a soft spot for his mum's uncle, even though the man invariably couldn't tell him apart from his brother. Morrie looked up at him.

"You back here again, Nathan?"

"It's Leon," bellowed Lydia, in the manner of someone who felt that speaking loudly and slowly to people in a foreign country was the same as speaking their language.

"Leon? Come here. Why are you hovering on the stairs? You're not ten years old."

Leon came down the last few steps and gave Morrie and his aunt Caroline a kiss on the cheek, just as Caroline's husband, Jeff, came in through front door, huffing and puffing.

"Is someone having a party?" he demanded to know, sloughing off his coat. "The street's full of cars. I had to park round the corner."

Caroline took his coat and told him to stop fussing. He leant over and kissed Lydia hello.

"I'm not fussing. Why does everyone have to have three cars these days?"

Harry appeared at the kitchen door.

"Shall I just bring everything out here into the hall, then?" he said. "We could set up the trestle table."

"We're coming, already," said Lydia, shooing him back into the kitchen.

Izzy came down the stairs a moment later and, after a brief round of introductions, they all made their way into the kitchen where Nathan and his partner, Sam, were already sitting at the table. Everyone took their seats except Lydia, who was busy with the soup pan, and Harry, who went over to the sideboard where a loaf of challah bread was waiting for him under an ornate cloth.

Lydia had already lit the Shabbat candles and filled ten small shot-sized glasses with wine. Harry mumbled the requisite ancient blessings, then distributed the wine and bread to everybody at the table. A mixed chorus of *Shabbat shalom* went up around the table, which Leon explained to Izzy was simply a way of wishing each other peace "...in our lives, and in the week to come," he added.

"Very poetic, Leon," said Jeff, sarcastically.

"Don't be such a prick, Jeff," snarled Morrie.

"Morrie!" yelled Lydia from across the kitchen.

"What?" he responded, with his thin arms raised in outrage. "The boy's right. Where do you get your peace, Jeff, Sky Sports?"

"Someone's got keep an eye on what Arsenal are doing."

"Gah. You can just ignore him, Alice," said Morrie, to Izzy. "That's what we do."

"I make that—eleven minutes," yelled Nathan.

Leon grinned.

"I have it as just under nine," he replied. "Don't forget parking time."

"Of course! Parking time," laughed Nathan. "That's almost a record, Jeff."

Jeff looked less than please by this familiar commentary. Sam leaned towards Izzy to explain, with a subtle eyeroll, "It's how long it takes before Jeff mentions football."

"Gotcha," acknowledged Izzy, still wondering who Alice was.

"I hope you like chicken soup, Izzy?" said Lydia, appearing at the table and handing her a bowl. She passed a second one to Morrie, who grabbed it carefully with both hands, and a delighted look on his face.

"Nectar of the gods," he declared, which is what he always said. Unless it was Caroline's soup, which no one was much of a fan of.

"Oh, I really do," said Izzy, as Lydia and Caroline passed along more bowls until everyone had one, except Lydia herself, who insisted she was simply someone who "...doesn't do soup." So while everyone was slurping and nattering, she took the opportunity to go back to the other side of the kitchen and sort the rest of dinner out.

"What are these?" asked Izzy quietly, to Leon, referring to two small, pale, round dumplings floating in the golden soup.

"Matzo balls," he explained, with a grin, as though that explained everything. "They're the best."

"You know," chimed in Caroline, oblivious to Izzy's attempt at subtle questioning. "You can get a mix for it. Goldman's on High Road does their own. It's fresh. You should try it, Lydia."

"Really?" said Harry, surprised. "Are fresh matzo balls a thing now, like green tea? I wouldn't have thought there was that much demand for it."

"What do you mean, fresh?" asked Sam. "It's made up of ground-up matzos. It's like saying you want fresh cornflakes."

"Not everything good comes out of a packet, Caroline," said Morrie, between two sips. "My Sadie used to make everything from scratch. You couldn't just get it all *online*, or whatever you kids do now."

"Oh, I don't know," responded Jeff. "Caroline's roast potatoes come out of a packet, and they're great."

"Jeff!" rebuked Caroline, more than a little embarrassed by being randomly outed. "What's wrong with you?"

Jeff seemed genuinely puzzled.

"What?" he replied. "I like them. That's what I'm saying. I'm saying I like them."

He looked around the table in search of an ally but came up empty-handed, as everyone suddenly took a deep interest in polishing off their soup.

"You're on your own there," said Harry, plainly, before trying to change the subject. "Morrie, how's that new neighbour of yours working out?"

"Don't ask," replied Morrie. "You should hear him. He thinks he's the first person to have ever had an idea."

Jeff shook his head, trying to figure out why his wife was still glowering at him. "I'm just saying, Aunt Bessie's wouldn't be in business if—" he began.

"Enough!!" Caroline stood up sharply and started irritably collecting everyone's bowls. "I don't know why I stay married to you."

"It's not for the money," said Morrie.

"Watch my china," called Lydia, from across the room.

Jeff shrugged his shoulders and retired into his phone to look at the latest football transfers.

"Matzoballs-dot-com," said Nathan, trying the words out. "There's a business in that. Leon, you should register it."

"Why should I register it?"

"You're in the online business."

"I work in advertising."

"Whatever. Didn't I see on the news that they blew up your office last night?"

"Someone blew up your office?" said Harry, startled by the idea.

Izzy looked at Leon, who gave her a brief, reassuring grip of the arm under the table.

"People didn't blow up offices when I was your age," said Morrie, who believed that no one did anything when he was young. "They were too poor or too busy. Usually both."

"You know," said Lydia, to Izzy, as she reappeared with a platter of delicious-looking roast chicken pieces and placed it on the table. "When Leon was a boy, he tried to blow up the school."

"Oh really?" said Izzy, encouragingly.

Harry started to laugh, while Leon winced at yet another classy story coming out.

"Thanks, Mum, this chicken looks amazing," he said, trying to steer the topic away. But nobody was being steered.

"That's right," said Harry, still chuckling. "He and his friend, David—"

"Daniel," corrected Lydia.

"That's right. He and his friend Daniel, they must have been about seven. They had this whole scheme worked out. They had drawn up a plan of the school. A box of crayons, sandwiches, and a match," continued Harry.

"Sounds cunning," said Izzy, as Lydia returned with large bowl of roast potatoes and another dish of broccoli with almonds. "What were the crayons for?"

"We thought they'd make a good fire accelerant," interjected Leon, quietly.

But nobody heard as Lydia squealed with affectionate laughter.

"We never found out. They were back fifteen minutes later— they were too young to cross the main road by the school!"

Laughter rippled around the table, despite this being a well-worn family story, only to be interrupted by an insistent Jeff.

"Look at this," he demanded.

"Do we really have to hear about Arsenal at the dinner table again, Jeff?" groaned Lydia, as she took her seat and nudged the chicken platter towards Izzy. "Help yourself, darling, to whatever you like." Others had already begun doing the same, spearing a thigh or a piece of breast meat with their fork.

"No, seriously," continued Jeff, pointing at his phone. "Izzy, you must have a twin out there."

"What do you mean?" said Izzy, feeling a chill go down her back.

Jeff turned his phone around to show them a news article with a grainy, blurry CCTV picture of Izzy in close- up. It wasn't clear to her or Leon where the picture had been taken, or when, but perhaps this was what had led them to firebomb her life that morning, she wondered. The fact it had surfaced on the media at all made Izzy's head swim and caused her to clasp Leon's leg sharply. He did his best not to look startled or in pain.

"Looks a lot like you, right?" said Jeff, with his hands raised.

"Leave the girl alone, Jeff," said Caroline. "It's obviously not her."

"I know," he replied, laughing. "I just thought it was funny. We meet Izzy for the first time and then she shows up in the papers! You don't have a twin, though, do you?"

"No, not a twin," replied Izzy, trying her best to sound casual. "At least not that I know of!"

There were a few chuckles. But only a thin smile from Lydia, who was clearly annoyed at Jeff for his total and ongoing lack of awareness.

"Enough with the phone, Jeff, if you don't mind," she barked. "Come on everyone, the food won't eat itself."

"What do they want with her," asked Leon, rather insistently, as the bowl of potatoes landed in front of him. "Whoever she is…" he added.

"Doesn't really say. Just that she's wanted in connection with the gas explosion in London Bridge. Her and…a white male, apparently. Both seen in the area early this morning. No names."

"Busted!" yelled Nathan, with a goofy smile on his face. "I've been telling you all for years that Leon was up to no good."

More affectionate laughter unfurled, mostly from Sam, who could always be relied upon to laugh at Nathan's jokes, however thin. Everyone then started tucking in and enjoying the food. Conversation ebbed and flowed across the table, along with the wine, and the mood generally started to shift away from Jeff's clumsy asides and towards the warm affability and interactions of family life. Except for Leon and Izzy who, despite their best efforts to enjoy the evening and not appear completely freaked out, had fallen a little quiet as they both privately tried to figure out what they should do next—other than jump up and run screaming from the house.

Izzy excused herself from the table as plates were being cleared away and, after not returning for some time, Leon followed her upstairs. He found her sitting on the edge of his old bed, doomscrolling through various news pages.

"I don't know if I can do this, Leon," she said, as he came through the door and closed it behind him. He took a seat next to her on the bed.

"Izzy, you can. You're going to be fine. I know it seems really intense right now, but we're going to get through it, together. I promise you."

"But my picture's in the fucking news! Who the hell are these people that they can do that?"

"I think we know the answer to that question. But it doesn't matter right now—"

"Doesn't matter!? It's not your picture all over the internet. You're just little old anonymous white male."

She sounded bitter and Leon felt awkward that so much of the spotlight seemed to be on her. He also felt a little guilty bringing her here, as though it underscored how untouched he'd been so far. As if he was rubbing it in.

"I'm sorry. I probably shouldn't have brought you here. We should have stayed in town, away from everyone. I didn't mean... I thought... I just—"

She placed her hand lightly on the side of his face, still sore from its earlier fight with a wall.

"I'm sorry," she said, looking intently at him. "I'm just scared, is all."

The muted rumble of conversation and laughter drifted up from downstairs, as they sat wordlessly in the dimly lit room, looking at each other. The noise subsided, as Izzy leaned in and planted a soft, purposeful kiss on Leon's mouth, running her fingers from his cheek into his hair. He responded to her touch in kind, bringing his hands gently around her back and pulling her closer. And just for that moment, they felt completely safe.

Then, suddenly, Nathan shouted Leon's name up the stairs, breaking into their momentary daydream. They pulled apart, laughing at the situation.

"I feel like a teenager again," said Leon, slightly bewildered.

"I know what you mean," agreed Izzy, smiling. "This whole evening...it's been lovely but also so..."

"Exactly."

They laughed again. Leon rubbed his face and head with his hands, to try to reset, then placed a hand on top of hers, which was resting on the bed.

"Look," he began, feeling unexpectedly emboldened by everything. "This whole situation is screwed up. We wandered into the middle of something we shouldn't have. But remember, we didn't actually do anything wrong. We're passers-by. We're total randoms in this. We're, at most, spectators who stood too close to the stage by accident and got *papped*," he said, miming the snapping of a photograph. "And just like those stupid gossip stories that always want to know who's 'stepping out with George Clooney,' or whoever—"

"Oh, George Clooney, is it?"

Leon laughed again. "You know what I mean. They probably just want to find out who we are and what we know. But in the meantime? We have an appointment to keep in New York. And I promise you, whatever happens—what*ever* happens—you will not have do this on your own."

Izzy grinned at him.

"Advertising, right? You're good," she said, playfully, feeling a genuine sense of relief washing over her. She let out a long sigh and gripped his hand. "Thank you."

Nathan shouted up the stairs again. This time, it sounded much closer. He was coming up to find them. They looked at each other and smirked.

"Time for us to leave, I think," whispered Leon.

33

___

TAKE THE MONEY AND RUN

A fter various thank-yous and goodbyes to Leon's family, Leon and Izzy started back to Mr Wong's to find out what exactly an order of two "specials" contained, beyond a new fake passport. Or a real passport, with a fake name. They debated this technicality, among other things, for a while as the Northern line clattered noisily south, unsure in the end whether that subtle difference would really matter should they one day find themselves, say, arrested for fraud. Or worse, Leon found himself pointing out unnecessarily, *international* fraud.

"And you think that's worse?" asked Izzy.

"Well, it certainly sounds worse. Although it probably just involves more lawyers and such. I'm no expert."

"Oh really?" she replied, amused by his need to clarify this.

Despite the simmering fear of what might lie ahead of them lurking deep in the background, they were actually in quite good spirits. The rest and food and, truthfully, the complete normality of a family dinner had gone a long way to show them the world was still, mostly, as it should be.

They eventually arrived back at Leicester Square Tube station and headed directly for Wong's. It was almost 10:00 p.m. and the whole area was buzzing with life. The clubs and restaurants around Chinatown were heaving with people out for a good time, as groups of partygoers, stags and hens, tourists, families, and couples on dates whirled around each other on their search for drinks and food and dancing.

And for a brief moment it seemed to Leon that he and Izzy could be just like anyone else in London on a Friday night. Except that Izzy, in a bid to pass unnoticed, was wearing her baseball cap, sunglasses, a large satin scarf whorled around the lower half of her face, and a pair of oversized 1970s headphones she'd grabbed from his old room before they left, and couldn't look more like someone who wanted to be left alone than if she had a giant sign saying, I Want to Be Left Alone. Whether or not that enabled her to pass by unnoticed, exactly, was another thing. But despite his best efforts, she wouldn't be convinced otherwise until she had her new ID.

"Until I have a way of proving I'm not me," she insisted, "I'm keeping it all on."

There was a short messy queue of people trying to get into Mr Wong's when they arrived. Leon was just wondering if he should nudge ahead and claim they were here for takeout when Mr Wong Junior appeared at the door. He let several people out before ushering in a noisy group of four at the front and then, before turning around, noticed Leon standing at the back. He started shouting something that was hard to make out over the street noise and waving his hand for him to come forward. A few people ahead of them in the line turned to see who he was talking to, causing Izzy to turn the other way, but Leon just grabbed her hand and moved up to the front.

"You late," said Wong Junior.

"What do you mean, late?" said Leon. "You said come after nine. It's after nine."

"Ten past, twenty past, is after nine. Ten p.m. is *ten pee-emm,*" complained Wong. "This our busiest time."

"OK, sorry. Our mistake. Do you have our...order?"

"This way," he grumbled.

There were more people huddled in the tiny lobby inside, but Wong just pushed past them muttering in Chinese and expected Leon and Izzy to do much the same. There were a few gripes, although the little restaurant was so packed and noisy that pushing and shoving just seemed a part of the experience.

This time Wong led them through to the back of the narrow and incredibly hot, steamy kitchen, where there was an equally compact office past the pantry at the far end. Even without the piles of paperwork and assorted restaurant spares heaped from floor to ceiling, it was barely big enough for one person, never mind three. But this didn't seem to bother Wong as he nudged them in and closed the shutters. He pushed a pile of napkin boxes to one side to reveal a surprising large safe, which he then opened with a rapid sequence of numbers. The safe door was several inches thick and made a satisfying *clunk* as it was released. Wong reached in and pulled out a large paper takeout bag, branded in the restaurant livery, with thick, woven paper handles.

"Here, take bag," insisted Wong Junior, handing Leon the bag. It was surprisingly heavy.

"Thank you," responded Leon. "Is there something we need to...?"

"Just don't leave on train."

"Got it."

Wong then reached in again and drew out a sealed brown envelope. He handed the packet to Izzy and closed the safe. She opened it immediately and slipped the contents out: two British passports and a folded sheet of A4 paper. She flicked through the passports and, sure enough, there they were—Granger and Bourne; name, photo, date of birth, and all officially sealed, like a weird fantasy.

"Thank God," said Izzy, literally tearing off the hat and scarf combo. "I'm dying in here."

"You do look pretty hot," said Leon, cheekily.

"Funny."

"What's on the paper?" asked Leon.

"Bank detail," explained Wong, attempting to push them out of the enclosed space. "Bank detail. Phone unlock. OK?"

"Bank detail? What do you—"

"All done. Time to go."

And with that, Wong simply pushed them towards and through the back door of the restaurant, into a pungent, narrow alleyway that ran behind the row of buildings, then slammed the door closed. They were just getting their bearings when it suddenly reopened. Mr Wong Junior leaned out and chucked a small bundle at them, which Leon caught in one hand.

"What's this?"

"Prawn cracker. On the house," said Wong, then pulled the door closed again.

They looked at each other and shrugged. He wasn't coming back.

Izzy popped open the bag of crackers and started munching on them as Leon crouched down to rifle through the bag and find out what exactly a "special" consisted of.

"Jesus," mumbled Leon, as he probed and pulled at the contents of the bag. "Quinn wasn't kidding around."

"What is it?" said Izzy, her mouth full of crackers.

Leon stood and waved a sealed pack of banknotes at her. And in his other hand, a gun. Izzy's mouth literally dropped open, then closed a second later when she felt a crumb of prawn cracker fall from her mouth and realised it probably wasn't a great look. Leon pretended not to notice.

"There must be, I don't know, ten thousand in here. Maybe more, if this bundle is anything to go by. Half of it seems to be in pounds...the rest in dollars."

"What the hell?"

"Exactly. There's a couple of phones and also some...credit cards." He picked one out and tried to examine it in the harsh sodium streetlight leaking from the end of the alley. "Yep. *Black Quartz Bank*. Whoever the hell *they* are. This one's yours, Granger," he said, handing her a posh, metallic card. Izzy held it at the edges with just the tips of her thumb and forefinger as though it were infectious, to examine it more closely. She turned it about between her fingers to see if it had all the usual markers.

"Well, it looks legit to me."

"That's what disturbs me. I don't know about you, but it takes my bank a week to send out a new card."

"Secret agents obviously get special treatment."

"Who knew?"

"Either way, we should probably not hang about in the street with this stuff."

"Totally. But what are we going to do about this?" said Leon, wagging the gun around.

"Put it away! What if someone sees it?"

"Exactly-what-if-someone-sees-it! Maybe we can just give it back." Leon went to knock on the restaurant door.

"Give it back!?"

"Do you know how to use it?"

Izzy popped another cracker in her mouth and shook her head.

"No, me neither. And I don't really want to."

"Well, we can't go back in there, and we can't just leave it in the street for anyone to find."

"You know they lock people up just for carrying these, right?"

"I know they do. We can figure something out. But just not here. We need to rest up somewhere, book the flights. Make a plan."

"Where do you suggest?"

"With this," grinned Izzy, waving her fancy card at Leon. "I reckon we can take our pick."

They toyed with going super posh. After all, the Savoy was only a fifteen-minute walk away - especially once they'd tested the cards at an ATM and found they also seemed to carry a forty thousand pound tab, but in the end, they just headed for the closest nice hotel they could think of, on St Martin's Lane.

Check-in was surprisingly straightforward. Aside from a brief but curious look from the receptionist upon presentation of their IDs, their payment card was accepted with little fuss. As a result, they treated themselves to a junior suite, on a high floor, with a huge bed, a lounge area, and a fantastic view down towards the Thames. They also took up the front desk's perfectly timed suggestion for a bottle of chilled champagne and nibbles to be sent up to their room. Although, naturally, the concierge didn't call them nibbles.

Once they got settled in and cleaned up, which, with nothing more than the clothes on their backs, didn't take very long, and the goodies had been delivered, they set to work.

Izzy broke out her laptop and, using only a customised command-line application, began with a bit of precautionary housekeeping. First, a deep scan on Black Quartz: assets, history, ownership, audit record, market cap, shareholders, and shareholdings in other businesses...

"I'm no expert, but it certainly looks like a real bank," said Izzy, looking over to Leon who, not having much else to do besides watching data scroll up and down Izzy's screen, had opened the champagne and poured a couple of glasses. "A small, private bank, for sure, but still..."

"I'm guessing their client list is equally small and private," said Leon, handing her a chilled glass. "Don't suppose you can just hack a list of who they supply money to? Besides us, I mean."

"If I had more time, maybe. But spooling back across a handful of their investors—presumably equally fake firms, based on their lack of a real data footprint—it doesn't take long before you start hitting up government entities. Mainly US-based as far as I can tell."

"And anyone can just find all that out on the web, can they?" said Leon, equally impressed and amused that she could just rattle that stuff out.

"Hey. Not anyone," responded Izzy, with mock offense.

They clinked their glasses in mutual agreement and took a sip of champagne. It was delicious.

"Plus," she continued, briskly. "The web and the internet are two different things. Anyway, the point is, the banking part may be a little bit fake but the money is real. We should probably just go ahead and use it...but mainly the cash, as it leaves no trail."

"As long as they don't ask for it back."

"What we need is some leverage."

"You mean this," said Leon, holding up the data stick they'd taken from Benedict's house.

Izzy took it and slotted it into the computer.

"That's exactly what I mean."

"Of course, you know Quinn said—"

"I know what he said. But you think, what, we just have a nice weekend in New York, hand over the stick, and we're done?"

Leon nodded reluctantly. "You're right. Even if we promised we never looked at it, who would believe us? And even if Quinn is as cool as he seems about it, whoever sent that guy with the gun will want to know what we know. Or worse."

"I don't like the sound of worse."

"Me neither. Do you think you can crack the files? Maybe it'll gives us the wiggle room we need, for when that moment comes."

"Reckon I can," said Izzy, typing a series of commands into her application. A new window labelled *password hack* popped open, and a string of data started spooling upwards. She slid the laptop onto the coffee table by the couch then turned back to Leon with a mischievous grin.

"It'll take a little while to cook," she said. "How about another glass of that fizz?"

Leon happily obliged. Then a little while became a long while, and several glasses of fizz later, by which time they had become much less focused on password hacking and, finally, much more interested in unlocking each other.

. . .

It was still dark outside when Leon awoke, roused by a quiet electronic alarm. Izzy was still lying close to him, half on her side, with an arm over his chest, sleeping quietly. Her hair still smelled rich and intoxicating, courtesy of the expensively branded products that came with the hotel, and he took a moment to breathe it all in. To seal in the memory of this moment. Whatever he may have been expecting when he woke up in that toilet a mere twenty-four hours earlier, it certainly wasn't this. In fact, he had strongly suspected he'd never see Izzy again after his sickly exit from the party. But now, in the strangest of unexpected circumstances, here they were, cosseted warmly under the sumptuous covers of a luxurious London hotel, with nothing more than the air they breathed between them. On the run for their lives, admittedly, but comfortable and nice-smelling all the same.

The alarm seemed to take on a more instant tone and Leon propped himself up on one arm to see what it might be. He looked across the room, past the scattered luxury hotel robes they'd discarded only a few hours before, to Izzy's laptop, sitting on the coffee table. It was responsible for the noise and he could see there was a blinking notification on the screen.

Izzy murmured next to him, gently awakened by Leon's movement and, at some level, by the alarm. Leon hesitated to wake her properly, wanting to linger in this blissful place they had found together just a little longer, but then Izzy saved him the trouble as she suddenly sat bolt upright and rubbed her eyes awake.

"Dinnertime!" she said, surprisingly.

"Dinner...?" repeated Leon, confused

Izzy smiled at Leon. A huge, twinkly-eyed if tired smile meant just for him. Then she leant over, gave him a sumptuous kiss on the mouth before briskly hopping out of bed and grabbing a robe off the floor.

"Come on," she said. "Before it gets cold."

A moment later they were back on the sofa huddled around

her laptop. The alarm was signalling that Benedict's password had been successfully hacked and they now had access to all his files. A cursory look through his data suggested it was mainly video files, neatly categorised by date and time, and in some cases going back more than a decade.

"Well, your friend Benedict was certainty thorough," said Izzy, as she clicked one at random.

The file opened to reveal Benedict, facing the camera, sitting in a space that looked suspiciously like it might be the (undamaged) lab they found him half-buried in twenty-four hours earlier.

"*Project Helios, phase two, year four, entry twelve,*" began Benedict. He glanced at his watch. "*Two-thirty p.m. Another day, another impatient directive from Snark. As ever, he's dissatisfied with progress. Explaining the latest code initiative to him proved more technical than he was willing to tolerate and I found myself, once again, having to—*"

Izzy stopped the playback and tried another.

"*Project Helios, phase two, year five, entry three,*" began Benedict once again. "*Following a fresh influx of research data from the US team, we were finally able to activate additional power-flow tests on the craft's subsystems straight from the grid, using a jury-rigged coupling. Lighting, environmental, and other auxiliary systems lit up as anticipated but for a much shorter duration than the last batch of tests. We had barely fifteen minutes to evaluate before the main grid went down completely, leaving us to grope about in the dark, both literally and figuratively. And, once again, nothing at all on propulsion.*

"*Despite decades of meticulous scrutiny, and everything the US teams have achieved, the fuller functioning of this particular craft remains stubbornly opaque. Naturally, Snark insists that the problem lies with us, and that if they could just get back to the US facility...but, then, that's precisely the point.*

"*In any case, I'm just glad I'm not the one who has to square yet another power outage with the ministry. Although I fully expect a poisoned missive from Carson regarding—*"

Izzy hit pause once again and tried another.

"*...Pattern analysis continues to suggest there's something in the* *baseline operating code that's simply different than any of the craft they've recovered to date. And, once again, I can't help but feel the problem is in the software, more than it is in the hardware, which we have all but studied to death at this point, with little reward."*

"Video diaries," said Izzy, stopping the playback once again. "Incredibly valuable, I suspect, but there are a lot of them. This could take much longer than we have."

"Plus, of course, there's the deniability problem."

"What do you mean?"

"Well, if all we have is one guy talking on video... I mean it's hardly a smoking gun. It could just be written off as some nut with a nice CGI backdrop."

"True."

"What else is there? What about that?"

Leon pointed to a sperate folder labelled Data Archive that had just scrolled into view. Izzy clicked on it and another window sprang open, revealing a fresh assortment of text files and what looked like scanned documents.

"This might be it," said Izzy, skimming through the list. "Names, reference points, schematics, and tables of experimental data. Bingo. Something here from the US National Security Council asking for...operational field rights—whatever that is—to the UK's Joint Intelligence Committee. Dated February 1948. It looks like there are subsequent amendments in 1958, 1963, '72, '80, and 1987...right up to April 2020. This one's called the Covid memorandum."

"Right—during the pandemic."

"Amazing. This is all potentially traceable and cross-reference-able. Maybe this, plus the video logs, and we really have something."

"What's that folder labelled The Deal?"

Izzy clicked it open.

"More videos."

She opened the file labelled Part 1 to reveal a still frame of three people in a domestic setting of some kind, a lounge perhaps, in someone's home. It was hard to be sure as the picture quality was poor, and the camera was set at an oblique angle, as if it was intentionally hidden from the people talking. However, it did provide a great view of their knees, a low table with some cups on it, and, behind the fuzzy silhouettes, a bay window with a pair of long, elegant curtains.

"Is that Benedict's front room?" asked Leon. Izzy shrugged. "Press play."

"Milk and sugar?" clearly Benedict's voice.

Leon nodded his confirmation to Izzy.

"I'm good, thank you," came the reply. American, female, but clipped and efficient.

A pair of hands—presumably Benedict's—appeared in front of the camera and lifted a cup and saucer away.

"Do you like tea, Mr...?"

"Snark. Linden Snark," grumbled the knees farthest from the camera. *"Thank you, but no. I never really got the taste for it."*

"Well, it's not for everyone," continued Benedict. *"So, how can I help you, Mr...Snark?"*

"Linden will do fine."

"Linden, then."

"It's very simple. I represent a multinational organization with certain...interests. Interests in new technology and materials, processes, cutting-edge physics applications. That sort of thing."

"That sort of thing," laughed Benedict. *"You surely do yourself a disservice, sir. Cutting-edge physics applications? Not something typically expressed so glibly. At least not over here."*

"Maybe so. Apologies if—"

"Not at all. However, I fail to see how I may be of service to you in that regard. I'm not a technologist. I'm not even at the practical applications end of physics really. I'm a theoretician, at best. I dabble in celestial mechanics but—at a push—cosmology, astrophysics is really my field."

"Indeed, sir. I understand," replied Snark. *"But, as such, it's come to my—to our—attention that you may have recently come into posses-*

sion of some intriguing data. Something...out of the ordinary?"

There was a pause in the conversation as a police siren could be heard passing nearby. Leon and Izzy looked at each other.

"This must be how they recruited him," said Leon, pausing the playback.

"Did you know he was a physicist?"

"God, no. Not for a second. I thought he was just an accounts guy. I guess it shows you how context really is everything."

"How long ago do you think this is?"

"Hard to say. I heard he'd been at Hyperion for over twenty years. One of the founders or something? The video quality looks at least that old."

"Let's see if it comes up," said Izzy, and restarted the video.

"Ah," said Benedict, after a moment. *"You must be talking about the recording."*

Snark's knees and the woman's seemed to react with satisfaction. *"The recording,"* they confirmed, more or less in unison.

"The recording," repeated Snark, more definitively. *"We were wondering if you could, maybe, clarify a few points. Perhaps even consider sharing some of your data analysis?"*

"My, doesn't word get around," said Benedict. *"And here I was thinking I was just helping out an old pal. What can I tell you?"*

"Perhaps," said the woman. *"You might begin with telling us how you came into contact with the original transmission?"*

"Pure luck, really. Ran into an old colleague. Kaufman—Mike Kaufman?—tenured professor at Harvard, believe it or not, that chancer. We were at a conference about nine months ago."

"Would that be the International Hadron Symposium?" suggested Snark.

Benedict laughed. *"Comic Con."*

"Comi—" began Snark, confused.

"Comic Con. The international comic book convention? Of course, they do movies and video game tie-ins now but you get the idea."

Snark made a distinct growling noise, and the body language of his knees suggested he was about to stand up but the woman's hand darted into view and seemed to stay his intentions.

"*So, you and Dr Kaufman...*" prompted the woman.

"*We're old Trekkies. What can I say? Anyway, I happened to mention I was working on a study using some old astrophysical data as part of a baseline against... Well, anyway, it piqued his interest. He got very excited, in fact. Asked me lots of questions and promised to invite me in to something he was working on. Something special, he said.*"

"*Something special,*" repeated Snark. "*He didn't say any more than that?*"

"*Nothing. In fact, I never heard from him again after that until—what, six months later?—when I got news of his, uhm...accident. Terrible, terrible business. Then a few weeks later a package arrived in the post.*"

"*What kind of a package, exactly?*" said the woman, briskly.

"*Ohh. Well. Let's just say there was a number of interesting items,*" replied Benedict, sounding like the proverbial cream-eating cat, who'd evidently been waiting for just this moment.

A loaded silence descended on the group once again. This time the blurry figure of Snark stood up and it appeared the woman went to follow.

"*Would you excuse us for a moment?*" she said after slipping off-camera.

"*Take all the time you need,*" said Benedict, generously. He topped up his tea from a pot while they were absent and a few moments later they returned.

"*Our apologies, Dr Benedict,*" she said, as they settled back down in. "*But it appears we have an intersection of interests.*"

"*I thought we might,*" said Benedict, knowingly.

"*In addition to his duties at Harvard,*" added Snark, "*Dr Kaufman was actually an associate of ours working on a number of...specialized properties we are developing.*"

"*I see. And just for clarification then, when you say 'we,' who are you talking about? I think before we go any further, some transparency would be in order.*"

Snark cleared his throat, seemingly reluctant to answer but

spoke anyway.

"*Miss Carson and I work for a non-public-facing branch of the US government. I'm not at liberty to share much more at this point except to say we have exceptional license, and budget, to pursue, let us say, less orthodox lines of inquiry in the interests of national security.*"

"**And less orthodox,**" said Benedict, "*since we're being transparent, could mean what?*"

Another pause.

"*Perhaps it would help you to know that Mike,*" continued Benedict, pointedly. "*That is, Dr Kaufman, was a remarkably studious record keeper.*"

"*What exactly did Dr Kaufman tell you?*" interjected the now identified Carson. "*...in the interests of transparency.*"

"*He told me you were researching extraterrestrial vehicles, Miss Carson. UFOs, I believe, by any other name. Isn't that right? He told me you already had a number of them in your possession. Actual alien craft. But that one, in particular, had become a long-standing problem for you. And that you needed help—my kind of help, dare I say—in solving it. He also said that you had become dissatisfied with what you perceived as his...commitment. That threats had been made.*"

"*Well,*" said Snark, "*He said a lot, didn't he?*"

"*Indeed, sir,*" agreed Benedict. "*He also provided a not insubstantial data set, let's call it, to back up some of the claims he was making.*"

"*And I suppose you have this data set to hand? If, say, someone—yourself, perhaps—were asked to continue the work?*"

"*I could lay my hands on it,*" confirmed Benedict, cautiously. "*If I needed to.*"

Leon stopped the playback.

"Is he talking about...this?" he said, meaning the data stick.

"I think he might be," agreed Izzy.

"Man," barked Leon as he stood up and began pacing the room. "Then that confirms everything Quinn told us. They're talking about UFOs, Izzy! U-F-Os! That thing last night? That really was a flying bloody saucer—right in the middle of London!"

"Well then, we better make good on our promise. And take it

to him in New York."

"And what about the leverage? You know it sounded to me like they killed that guy, Kaufman, for having this stuff—and he worked for them! Imagine what they'd do to us?"

"Already ahead of you," said Izzy, typing commands into her terminal program at speed. "I can set up some kind of dead man security."

"Dead man. Really. Isn't there a better name for it?"

"It's not as bad as it sounds. Trust me. I can probably also set up something to transcribe the video diaries while we're travelling. It'll be easier to analyse the data, if it comes to that."

"Got it. What can I do?"

"Book us some flights, lover," said Izzy, with a wink. "We're going to the Big Apple!"

34

EMPIRE STATE

Leon booked the earliest flight available from Heathrow to
JFK that morning, and a car to take them to the airport.
There were no obvious system flags or errors with their
credentials.

"It almost seems too easy," said Leon, looking again at the
Black Quartz card in his hand.

Izzy nodded. "I guess that's the idea. Assassin kits wouldn't be
much good if everyone got nabbed the first time they used it."

"True," said Leon, smiling at the idea of an assassin kit.
"Which reminds me, we need to leave this somewhere." He was
holding up the gun by the tip of the handle, as if it was infected.

After some discussion they decided dropping it into the
Thames was probably the safest option, and changed their car
pickup to Embankment station, which was a short walk from the
hotel. So less than forty minutes later, just as the faint threads of
dawn's first light were beginning to leak across the sky, they were
quietly zipping down the M4 on their way to the airport, in the
back of a black electric sedan.

With so little traffic on the road at that time of the morning it
didn't take them very long to arrive at terminal five and, as Leon
had taken the liberty of springing for business class tickets, they

were checked in, through security, and drinking another glass of champagne in the lounge less than ninety minutes after leaving the hotel.

"I like your style, Mr Bourne," said Izzy, clinking glasses with Leon.

"Likewise, Ms Granger."

"I'm surprised you didn't go the whole hog and send us first class. It's not like it's our money."

"I certainly thought about it. But—"

"A little conspicuous?"

"Exactly. I mean, check this place out. Nobody would give us a second look here with all this rabble."

Izzy had to admit he was right. The main business lounge at T5 was much larger and plainer than she had expected and also, to her surprise, completely full. Even at this early hour, they'd struggled to find a couple of empty seats. The rest were filled with busy-looking men and women on their phones and laptops, and the occasional couple, or young family, heading for vacation.

"I always assumed these lounges would be quieter, more exclusive."

"I used to think the same," replied Leon. "Until I started doing work trips. Maybe they used to be, but it's been pretty much like this every time I've come here."

"Well, it's easier for us to blend in, if nothing else."

"That was my thought. Easier to hide but also harder for anyone to try anything. The main concourse is so busy with travellers it could be days before anyone noticed an actual dead person."

Izzy smiled, trying hard not to think about poor Robbie as she watched the tiny bubbles rise inside her champagne glass.

Less than an hour later, they were at the gate, waiting to board the plane and Izzy was doing her best to shrug off the gloom and the guilt that Robbie's memory had brought with it. She knew his death wasn't her fault but, even so, was struggling to cleanly separate events.

"You OK?" asked Leon, gently, snapping her back from her thoughts.

"I'm fine," she lied. "Just wondering how long until we actually get to board the plane."

"It won't be long. I'm sure they'll call us soon."

"By seat numbers or class?"

"Class?" laughed Leon. "That's a dirty word these days."

"What do you mean?"

"It's all groups now. Check your boarding pass."

Izzy looked. "It says I'm in Group 2."

"That's business class. First is Group 1. Then it's us and Group 3. Then it's..." Leon looked up at the signage above the queuing lanes. "Groups 4 to 6, then 7, 8, and 9."

"My God, what do you have to have done in life to end up in Group 9?"

"Oh, Group 9 is just for undesirables. Disgraced politicians. Queue jumpers. Lift farters. People who use their phones like a walkie-talkie or have low personal hygiene. That sort of thing."

"I see," said Izzy, smiling now. "And they just let these people on planes with the rest of us?"

"Not necessarily. Often they are made to do grunt work around the airport to qualify for a seat: schlepping all the leaky, non-recyclable waste out to industrial disposal units or cleaning up infestations of rodents from under the terminal building. Picking up animal dung or the bloody remains of dead migrating birds from the runway with their hands.

"They're like the undead of airline passengers. Sometimes they roam the airport grounds for days, or even weeks at a time in the hope that Group 9 will finally get called to board. It rarely happens."

Izzy nodded in understanding. "That's really taking corporate responsibility to the next level."

"Isn't it?" agreed Leon, just as an announcement that Flight 117 was ready for Groups 1 and 2 to start boarding came over the Tannoy.

Izzy gave Leon an excited grin and the two of them sprang up out of their chairs and headed over to the stewards to have their documents checked, before making their way to the plane and onwards to New York City, baby.

A little over eight hours later they were shuffling their way forward in the immigration line towards the automated passport kiosks, with some trepidation. Getting out of a country was one thing. But getting in? That felt like the real test. And for Leon, paranoid even on his regular commute, it felt like entering *The Matrix*: that every fellow passenger, every passer-by, or member of staff could, at any moment, switch out for Agent Smith, who would then pin them to the ground with a series of rapid-fire punches to the body and face.

But, as it turned out, there was no switching out for Agent Smith, or any other robotic sentinels. The automated technology didn't flag them coming through—or at least, if it did, not enough to impede their entry—and nor was there even much of a glance from the weary-looking customs officer who stamped them into the country. After dutifully enquiring after the nature of their visit ("Shopping and a show!"), cursorily wished them a nice day and on their way.

And, with that, Leon couldn't wait to get outside of the terminal building, almost pulling Izzy along by the hand as he quickened his pace towards the exit.

"Are you feeling OK?" said Izzy.

"Fine," he replied, reluctant to admit to another swell of nausea from what he felt was yet one more narrow escape. "Fine. Just excited to get outside and see the city."

Izzy doubted he was being entirely truthful, feeling a little skittish herself after the past thirty-some hours, and equally keen to be free from people who might arrest them. And, soon enough, with no luggage to collect, they were outside the terminal and in a yellow cab on their way to a very rainy Manhattan less than twenty minutes later.

The journey took them along the Interstate 678 North: otherwise known as the Van Wyck Expressway. It wasn't an especially glamourous or obviously interesting stretch of road, passing through large swathes of suburban Queens, filled with a mixture of wet if occasionally charming clapboard housing, industrial units, schools, and hospitals. Not really the stuff of New York dreams and yet, like all trips to a foreign country, the banal suddenly took on a kind of mystic charm all its own: that's not just any old Costco, factory warehouse, hospital parking lot, or railway yard, but an American one—filled with exotic American doctors, trains, and bulk-discount toilet paper!

Initially Leon thought he might try to impress Izzy further with a little Wikipedia-assisted tour of the sights. But he only got as far as discovering that Van Wyck was a former mayor whose most notable legacy appeared to be an ongoing dispute as to whether his name should be pronounced to rhyme with *brick* or *bike*, before giving up and joining her in staring out of the window.

Eventually the 678 turned into the equally functional 495 (the Long Island Expressway, if you're into that kind of thing), which would take them directly under the East River and into what finally felt like New York, proper.

It took less than fifteen minutes to reach the hotel once they were through the Midtown Tunnel by which time Leon and Izzy's excitement had completely displaced their fatigue. The cab pulled up sharply outside The Refinery Hotel on West Thirty-Eighth and, after paying the driver a generous tip for not killing them (they hadn't completely shrugged off their paranoia), they hopped out of the car and sheltered from the rain under the hotel's wide metal awning for a few minutes before going in.

"Can you believe this place?" said Leon, with delight.

"It's fabulous," agreed Izzy, as she admired the hundred-year-old elegance and beautifully wrought terra cotta facade of the once-noted Colony Arcade building, in which the Refinery Hotel now resided.

Inside they were greeted by a long, open passageway comprised of more architectural touches and refinements, that spoke lovingly to the building's historical significance, while contrasting gorgeously with the broadly contemporary interior of glass, white walls, and rich, high-octane artworks that dared you to look at them.

The reception desk was about halfway down towards the main restaurant and opposite a chic-looking piano bar where, even at this hour, Billy Joel's eponymous musician was singing softly for his pleasure. And, while check-in turned out to be an equally warm and delicious experience, none of this quite prepared Leon and Izzy for the exceptionally fabulous views from their high-floor room: the bustling Manhattan streets below were like something out of a movie or a comic book, and Leon half expected to see Spider-Man swing out from behind one building and land on the water tower of the next. And there, crowning it all, despite being several blocks away, was the Empire State Building.

"Quinn has good taste," declared Izzy, standing at the tall picture window after they had finished freshening up.

"I have to agree," agreed Leon, stepping up behind her and wrapping his arms around her waist. She leant back into his embrace, which, although he found lovely, came with the unexpected bonus of her hair going into his mouth as he went to speak. He attempted to subtly push it away with a mixture of quiet blowing and some lip contortions but it just ended up sounding like he was spitting something out.

"Everything OK back there?" said Izzy, partially turning to see what he was doing, and at once solving the problem for him.

"Yes, all good," he replied, attempting to cover for his slight indignity. "I'm just hungry. Are you hungry? We should get something to eat. And then maybe buy something else to wear."

"Good plan. You think we can just go out?"

"I don't see why not. We're not meeting Quinn until tomorrow, and in the meantime..." he plucked the Black Quartz card from his back pocket. "We have a bag full of cash."

But, as it turns out, they didn't get very far with it. Maybe it was the heightened excitement of their "mission," or just the thrill of the Big Apple itself, but despite an effectively limitless credit card, they only made it as far as Vicoletta's EZ Diner on Seventh Avenue, just one block away from the hotel, where the lure of a great big American breakfast turned out to be irresistible. They fell into a booth at the back of the simple eatery and ate ravenously.

"So, have you ever been here before?" asked Izzy, as she chewed on her bacon and eggs. "To New York, I mean."

"Just once. I came with my ex-wife, not long after we finished art school. She had a friend out here and we crashed on her floor for a few days. I came for the art. At least that's what I told myself at the time. She, I found out much later, came for the friend."

"Ah. I'm sorry to hear that," replied Izzy, trying to stifle her morbid curiosity about the surprise ex-wife, and wondering if she was Uncle Morrie's mystery Alice.

"It's fine. It was a long time ago," deflected Leon, scooping a forkful of eggs into his mouth. "And besides," he added, regretting that he'd mentioned Alice at all. "Who can blame her? Her friend had a really nice floor."

Izzy smiled, recognising Leon's desire to brush it aside.

"So, you're an artist? I thought..."

Leon laughed. "Yeah. I wanted to be."

"Were you any good?"

"I was certainly good at getting myself into debt, if that counts. What about you?"

"Art?" laughed Izzy in return. "No. I love looking at it, but I was a science kid through and through. Still am."

"Better for paying the bills though, I would have thought. Or at least, more in demand than another subpar Edward Hopper knock-off."

"Hey, don't knock Edward," replied Izzy, reaching for the ketchup. "I mean, look at where we are now?"

Leon enjoyed her allusion to Hopper's famous painting.

"A couple of nighthawks, is that it?"

"Something like that," said Izzy, hitting the end of the bottle to deposit a fresh shot of ketchup to her plate. "Anyway, to answer your question: yes. It certainly can be profitable for some. But I'm at the research end of it, so the payoff—if it ever comes—is wayyy down the road."

"And New York?"

"No. Never. I always fancied coming here. And almost did a couple of years back but..." she hesitated, wondering whether or not to balance the revelation scales.

"But what?"

"I was going to say, my ex-boyfriend."

Leon did his best to approximate a relaxed smile, while lavishly waving a piece of toast he was holding as if he just loved hearing about ex-boyfriends.

"Anyway," she continued, regarding his apparent largess with some doubt. "He was always too broke. And miserable, frankly. I'm actually happy we never came."

"Oh yes?"

"I much prefer this version of events. Even with the death threats."

Leon grinned.

"Really?"

"Really," she beamed.

"Then here's to this version of events," said Leon, raising his white porcelain coffee mug in a toast. "Minus all the death."

Izzy responded in kind. And they brought them together with a gentle clink.

Early the next morning, Leon sauntered down the short hotel corridor leading from the elevator to their room, whistling a random tune. He was in a great mood. Happy, even. The past few days had been the strangest and scariest of his life but also, in a totally unexpected and, frankly, unbelievable way, the best.

Here he was in New York City with Isabella Jones; a fabulous, smart, and funny woman who, until only a few days ago had been not much more than a fantasy human being he hoped might eventually, one day, you know, maybe, agree go out for a coffee with him. If he ever plucked up the nerve to stop mumbling at her. And now? Now she was lying in their sumptuous hotel bed, in an equally glorious boutique hotel, waiting for him to bring her breakfast. *What could be better than that in this crazy life,* he thought. Except, perhaps, that after Quinn comes by to pick up his goods, and they were done with this nonsense, it doesn't all come to an end. That maybe they get to head out into the city and do some normal-people things. Walk through Central Park, see a show, eat dinner somewhere really fancy. He smiled gleefully as he balanced the cardboard coffee tray and parcel of freshly baked croissants in one hand and lifted the plastic keycard in the other to unlock the door.

"I really hope you like almonds," he called out, as he entered the small suite and the door closed behind him. "Because they looked so great. They smelled so good. I bought a few of them."

He headed through the open lounge area towards the bedroom, his brain feeling like it was firing in every direction, and enjoying every smell, sound, and sensation as he padded over the soft pile rug under his feet. The sunlight poured in through the large picture window, framing the crowning glory of the Empire State Building so perfectly. The faint musical hum of distinctly New York traffic and street noises percolated up despite the double-glazing. The colour of the fresh flowers in the vase on the table. The enthralling scent of the bespoke spa soaps and balms emanating from the bathroom. He was so excited just to see Izzy's beautiful face as he walked into the bedroom.

"You know, I was thinking—" he started to say but then stopped sharply in the doorway.

Izzy was gone.

35

MR BOURNE

Leon wavered in the open door of the bedroom, half-frozen to the spot, the rest of him panicking his prover-bial ass off as he looked upon the empty space. The linen pulled from the bed and seemingly hauled across the floor towards where he was standing. A water bottle by the bed on its side, still faintly dripping onto the rug, and the glass tumbler she'd been using smashed at his feet, presumably thrown. All he could see in his horrified mind was Izzy being dragged from this room, kicking and screaming at her assailants. It terrified him that he wasn't there with her, as he promised he would be. That what-ever had happened, and wherever they were taking her, she would have to face it on her own. And that he might never see her again. Perhaps that more than anything.

The sound of a passing emergency response vehicle screamed its way in from outside the building, snapping him free from his momentary paralysis. *It's a fucking emergency alright,* he thought. *But a fire truck isn't going to fix it.* And he knew, in that moment, that whatever happened next, whatever Quinn may have planned —assuming he damn well shows up—he had to find her. Screw the precious data stick and all the secrets it held. He would burn it all to find her if he had to. And he'd make Quinn, and everyone he knew, help him do it.

How he would do that exactly, he had no idea, but he started by putting the coffees down on the dresser next to him and taking a proper look around the room. No point just running around screaming and demanding stuff be done, he realised. Do what Izzy would do. Take a moment. Think it through. Make a plan.

He went over to the window and pulled open the curtains to let more light in. He could see the room more clearly now and tried to appreciate the scene as it was, with less of the freaking out. Izzy was gone, yes. Taken, clearly. But had it been a violent encounter? And if it had been, was it them or her? He recalled the way she had handled the guy in her lab without any hesitation—sticking a pen in his neck, for crying out loud—and the thought, as gruesome as it was, made him smile grimly as he imagined her giving them all a really good kicking.

After all, of the many great things he'd learned about her in the past three days, he knew she didn't take shit from anybody. And he also knew, from personal experience, that she could deliver a punch to the gut like nobody else. Perhaps, then, the evidence was not as bleak as it first seemed, and he began to calm down. Which was just as well since, a moment later, there was a knock at the door.

He unconsciously stepped back and leant against the window. Who the hell knocks on a hotel door at eight in the morning, he wondered, with no small amount of dread. Is this what happened to Izzy? Did she think it was him, returning? Could this be her? He suddenly wished he still had that gun, even though he had no idea what he'd do with it. The knock came again. This time louder and more insistent. Leon knew he couldn't just hang around hoping they'd go away, but that didn't mean he had to simply open the door like a schmuck and welcome them in. He crept around the bed and picked up the empty water bottle as he passed. He didn't know what he'd do with that any more than the gun, but it felt better to have something more dangerous in his hand than an almond croissant.

The knock came again as he approached the door, followed by a female voice.

"Mr Bourne?"

Leon hesitated and looked through the peephole to see who and how many people might be waiting for him. It appeared to be just one woman. He held the bottle behind his back and gently opened the door halfway. The woman offered him a pleasant but efficient smile.

"Mr Bourne, I presume?" she said.

Leon looked her over and noticed that her hands were folded neatly in front of her. No gun. Otherwise she was dressed simply but elegantly in a T-shirt, dark blue tailored jacket, slim blue jeans and sockless deck shoes. She looked slight but radiated strength and confidence. She held out her hand and Leon instinctively but hesitantly reciprocated.

"Uhm... Yes?"

"My name is Annie. I understand you have a bit of a problem."

Despite his immense surprise at this turn of events, Leon tried not to let it show.

"That's quite some concierge service you're running here," responded Leon.

"I'm not with the hotel. Shall we go inside?"

What the hell, figured Leon, and stood to one side by way of an invitation. Worst-best case, she's there to take me wherever they took Izzy. Best-case, she's there to offer some kind of help. He closed the door after her and they walked through to the sitting area, where Annie took a seat on one of the armchairs.

"You can put the bottle down now," she began, reassuringly. "I'm not here to hurt you."

Leon looked at the bottle in his hand, having half forgotten that it was there, and sheepishly put it on a side table before reluctantly taking a seat himself.

"Then what?"

"Your friend, Miss Isabella Jones, was taken a short while ago by an undisclosed US government agency because, they believe, she has either knowledge or motives that threaten certain...interests, within the broader US intelligence infrastructure. My employer wishes to offer you, shall we say, a helping hand in securing her return."

"A helping... wait, you said *Jones*? I think you must have—"

"I think it's probably better we drop the cosplay fun for now, Mr Aronofsky, wouldn't you say? Just between us."

"But how—"

"How do I know? Let's just say, my employer has certain resources and considerably bigger budgets at his disposal than the people who've been following you around since London."

Leon didn't know whether to be thrilled or terrified by this revelation. On the one hand, here was someone calm, intelligent, and purposeful with no gun in sight, who seemed to know exactly who he and Izzy were and, presumably, why they were here—and at this point he knew he'd be willing to work with Al Capone if it meant getting Izzy back safely—but on the other, they flipping knew who he was...

"Who's your employer?"

"We'll come to that. For now, I just need you to collect your things and come with me."

"What? Just like that?" said Leon, holding out his hands. "You say come with me and off we go? Do you actually know where Hermi... Where Izzy is or not?"

"Right now? No."

Leon stood up abruptly and started pacing.

"Then this is just more bullshit. And I've had plenty of that the past three days."

"Mr Aronofsky—Leon—it's true, I don't know where she is right now. They came sooner than we anticipated and I'm sorry about that. We had hoped—"

"Hoped? That's about all I have to work with. Whereas you show up all cocky and bright, with your just-in-a-day's-work vibes, telling me to go places... You need to be a little bit more convincing than 'we hoped.' I'm only bloody here because of someone like you. Izzy's only missing because of *someone. Like. You.* Someone, by the way, who's supposed to be meeting us here, in this room, today. And it isn't you."

"Leon, I understand you're upset. But, please, try to listen; I said I didn't know where she is right *now*. But I do know where she's going to be. I know where they're taking her."

Leon stopped pacing and turned to Annie directly.

"Then you have to tell me. Enough of the riddles."

"And I will. But first, you have to grab your stuff and come with me. Everything will be explained, I assure you."

They left the hotel five minutes later, straight into a large, black-windowed, high-end Chevy Suburban waiting by the curb. Annie tipped the doorman, then climbed in behind Leon and the vehicle pulled away.

Leon had tried to explain on the way down that they were expecting to meet Quinn there, but Annie assured him that all hotel arrangements, including any rendezvous—planned or unplanned—would be taken care of. In the meantime, they drove on, mostly in silence. Leon tried various ways to find out more about where Izzy was being taken, who Annie's employer might be, or where they were going, but she would not be drawn into further conversation.

"When we're in the clear," is all she would say, without ever elaborating on what *clear* might be.

He attempted to spot clues about their destination as the car turned right onto Fifth Avenue and then again onto West Thirty-Seventh Street, but wasn't sure he'd know even if he saw one. This street seemed superficially like the one he had just come from: a bunch more hotels, office buildings, eateries, fashion, and fabric stores (it was the Garment District, after all), along with that rich mixture of heavily windowed architecture that seemed to loom endlessly into view as they burrowed down the dead straight New York corridor ahead of them. Ultimately, he simply wasn't familiar enough with the city to know where to start, and in less than fifteen minutes they were through the Lincoln Tunnel that ran under the Hudson, and motoring down Route 3, deeper into New Jersey. At this point all Leon's paper-thin, largely movie-based knowledge of New York City came to an end.

Fortunately, however, he didn't have to wait long to have his questions answered. The 3 merged with the 17 North and then a short while later they were pulling into Teterboro Airport, a small airfield that serviced private airplanes.

The car was let through the gate security without any fuss and followed the road up and around the perimeter until it arrived at an unassuming standalone hangar on the far eastern side of the grounds. The SUV drove straight into an open garage entrance that shuttered closed behind them as they came to a stop along-side another black Suburban. Ahead of them in the main hangar space sat a gleaming Gulfstream G700 private jet plane, the main door and stepway already open.

"Nice plane. That where we're going?" asked Leon.

"It is," replied Annie. "Grab your stuff."

Leon picked up his backpack and slid out of the car. He caught the sound of jazz music drifting faintly from the plane when it struck him how strangely normal this suddenly all felt. Until a few days ago, being escorted by a complete stranger, in blacked-out car, to a private plane in the middle of wherever Teterboro was would have been unthinkable. But today, as he crossed the tarmac, it felt like a visit to Starbucks.

"Good morning, Leon!" yelled Jordan Milk, with a grin, as he walked in from outside the open hangar doors towards the plane. "Beautiful day, wouldn't you say?"

"Wait," said Leon to Annie. "That's... This is who..."

"It is," confirmed Annie, briskly, as the three of them arrived neatly at the same time by the steps to the plane. "Leon Aronof-sky, Mr Jordan Milk."

Milk extended his hand, and they shook. Leon smiled awkwardly.

OK, forget about Starbucks, he thought. *But what the hell is a real-life billionaire doing here?*

"Welcome, Leon," said Milk, warmly. "So nice to meet you. I'm just sorry about the circumstances."

"Thank you...I think. Shouldn't you be out building a space rocket or something?"

Milk laughed. "We'll come to that," he said, and extended his hand towards the open airplane door. "Shall we?"

Leon didn't feel like it was a real question and dutifully climbed the short flight of steps where a smiling, neatly uniformed woman was waiting for them. She offered to take his backpack, but he firmly declined, snatching it away as she went to take it from him. He wasn't sure why, exactly, and felt a little churlish for doing it. But somehow, he felt the need to cling on to the only thing he had that was his. The flight attendant looked to Milk, who waved away her concern.

"It's fine, Elena. Our guest can have whatever makes him feel comfortable. Go ahead, Leon."

Leon turned right, through a short galley kitchen and into the main cabin, which smelled wonderful and was laid out more openly and luxuriously than pretty much any room he had ever been in, much less a plane. There appeared to be several bays of facing chairs on either side of the aircraft, separated in the middle section of the cabin by a lounge area, complete with a sumptuous-looking sofa set side-on to the length of the plane, facing an unfeasibly large television. Looking down to the far end, Leon noticed a partial silhouette of someone already seated, facing away from them, and glanced back to Milk to see if he should proceed.

"Go right on through," said Milk, pausing to go over some minutia with Annie and Elena.

Leon proceeded to the back of the plane where he threw his backpack next to the last seat and turned to find Gregory Quinn grinning at him.

"Leon," he said, leaning back in his chair, legs out, and an iced drink in his hand that rattled as he raised it in salutation. "It's good to see you again. I'm so sorry about the mix-up with Isabella."

Leon dropped into the empty seat facing him and leant forward.

"The mix-up!?" he barked, in hushed tones, unsure of the status between everyone on the plane. "Jesus, Greg. Do you actually know where Izzy is? It's the only reason I'm here."

"We do know," responded Quinn, lowering his voice in kind. "Or at least we will, in around"—he looked at his watch—"five hours."

Leon glanced up to see Annie down at the far end of the cabin, finishing up her conversation with Milk and Elena.

"Why does everyone keep saying that? I just want a straight fucking answer. Is she safe or not?"

Quinn held out his hands to calm Leon. "She's safe. OK? If they really wanted to harm her, they would have just left her—and you—to cash in at the hotel. They're escorting her to Nevada. They must think she knows something."

"She does know something. We saw the files, Greg. We saw Benedict's files."

"Ah."

"Yes, ah! What's in Nevada? I thought you said Area 51 was for losers."

Quinn gave him an amused look. "I'm not sure that's really what I said."

"You implied."

"OK. Maybe I implied. My apologies. But in any case, it may not surprise you to know that Area 51 is not the only place to keep things we don't want to talk about. Nevada is a big state."

"It surely is," declared Milk as he and Annie arrived. "It also has more mountains, and more hotel rooms in a single city than any other state in the union. Glad to see you guys are connecting."

They both took their seats on the opposite side of the narrow aisle. Annie next to Leon, facing forward, and Milk next to Quinn.

The plane had already started to taxi out of the hangar, towards the main runway. Elena appeared with a tray of hot towels and handed them out.

"We'll be underway in just a few minutes," she reported, as the group dabbed the warm, beautifully aromatic cloths over their face and hands. "Then I'll be back with your drinks order."

Milk looked at Leon and smiled, then raised his eyebrows.

"Thank you, Elena. I can't wait," he said, then proceeded to lean back in his chair, fold his hands over his stomach, and close his eyes.

36

BLACK BAG

Steven "Mac" Macintyre gazed out of the window of the considerably less sumptuous Airbus C295 military transporter, as it began to cross Kansas's Great Plains. Cloud cover below was minimal, and he had a magnificent view of the vast, open farmland, sliced into thousands of individual plots, with as many shades of brown and green to match. The effect of the gigantic patchwork was almost mesmerising as his brain instinctively sought out patterns and connections, as though he were looking at an enormous game board. And, in that way, he saw how he and his team were part of a game themselves: strategic playing pieces, in a much larger sport he knew they would never get invited to play, any more than a bishop or a knight can control the chessboard they sit on.

This was just a fact. Something that, under normal conditions, he was perfectly fine with. Everyone has a role to play, he reflected, as the ground gently passed many thousands of feet below. And he had his, what some might call a particular *utility*, for when...messier interventions were required. And while he couldn't exactly say he enjoyed that aspect of his work, he fully understood the very real, pressing need it served in a disordered world. And he had always felt proud to serve his country with the unique skills he had to offer.

But there was something off about his current mission he couldn't really place. Maybe it was the way he had been so robustly contained to a strictly domestic operational theatre, or perhaps it was simply dragging civilians into it that soured it for him—although it was hardly the first time he'd ever had to do that—or maybe it was something else. Something about the larger game being played out between Snark and Carson, Jordan Milk, and those damn British folks that he just couldn't see. Or just didn't need to see, he reminded himself. He had his orders. And, as his old unit CO used to tell him, "… successful completion of the mission was always its own reward."

He glanced over at his charge and saw that she was still sleeping soundly on the reclined chair. It was unusual to have such comfortable fixtures on a C295 but, in this case, they maintained a forward section of twelve seats with a broadly domestic fit-out for occasional VIPs. And while she may not be a VIP exactly, nor was this meant to be the kind of black bag job they usually reserved for would-be terrorists. She just looked like a nice kid, to him. Like his sister's kid. All book-learning and nice clothes. A world he didn't really get.

In any case, black bag or not, he just didn't like putting people out for extended periods. He knew from experience that drugging people solely to keep them quiet could spell real trouble or, worse, an afternoon spent filling out a D59-C-for-Charlie "Captive Fatality" report. But the doc had assured him of a safe dose and was keeping a close eye. Plus, they were not exactly in combat conditions, so there was that.

In some ways he wished they were. His mind would stay quieter. He was trained for conflict, not babysitting. A fight was easier to figure out. But he had a job to do. Which reminded him —time to check in. He just hoped it would go better than the last report. Carson had been particularly pissed with him for bringing the girl back.

"You were just supposed to get the intel from her and leave," she had yelled at him.

"There were complications, ma'am."

"Seriously?" said Snark, joining in from a separate line. "A five-foot-whatever inveterate college nerd managed get one past you and your little soldiers? Jesus, Carson, maybe it's time we revaluated our tactical support."

"I would tend to agree, sir," snapped Carson, uncharacteristically. She tended to regard Macintyre and his team as her personal Special Ops unit, so he knew he was in trouble now.

"What I'm saying is," he began again. "We wanted to avoid a repeat of the London capture attempt. But it quickly became apparent how that incident occurred."

"Meaning what?" demanded Carson.

"Meaning the subject proved more able to resist initial subjection than we anticipated. She's had some kind of training, and attempted to subdue one of my team with some hotel stationery. We were obliged to restrain her, chemically, to avoid further damage to the subject, or disturbance to the very public operational setting. Only then did we discover that all her data sources had been locked out with some kind of biometric fractal-modular encryption. Not something we could just crack in the field and leave."

"Speak English, for chrissake," insisted Snark.

"It means she's locked us out," added Carson. "She's encrypted everything. Just her laptop, Steven?"

"No, ma'am. Her laptop and also a data stick we found."

"She can do that?" asked Snark.

"Apparently so," surmised Carson. "Clearly a more capable nerd than we gave her credit for."

"And yet you remain convinced she's operating alone?"

"Yes, sir. Aside from her as-yet unidentified associate, we haven't been able to tie her into any kind of active threat network, foreign or domestic. We still don't know how she got involved in our operation, or why, but unless her cover is exceptional—and I mean unprecedentedly so—our deep background search suggests her presence may be at best...unplanned."

"Wrong place, wrong time—is that what you're saying?"

"Indeed."

"What about the goddamn passport? That ain't luck. She had help. Maybe this associate of hers. Where is he?"

"Still working on it, sir," said Carson. "The passenger manifest from her flight to New York suggested she wasn't travelling alone. He hasn't surfaced since JFK that we've been able to confirm, but I received intel a short while ago that we may now have a lead on him."

"Names? Associations?" said Snark, hopefully.

"I'd rather not say at this time."

"You'd rather not say, Carson?" mocked Snark. "I didn't realize we were at a well-being seminar. Do you have a name or not?"

"Jason Bourne, sir."

Snark roared with laughter. Neither Carson nor Macintyre could quite tell if this was a good thing or not and, despite the video link, managed to exchange a glance.

"Jason Goddamn Bourne," said Snark, letting out a long whistle. "And after fifty years, I thought I had heard it all."

"Sir," began Carson. "There are thousands of actual Bournes out there."

"And yet one just happened to get a seat next Hogwart's preeminent witch? OK. Fine. Whatever. Just find him."

"Yes, sir," confirmed Carson.

"And in the meantime, Mac," said Snark, switching his focus. "Why the hell are you bringing this woman back home with you? I don't know what the hell's going on here with this freak show, but there are too many unknowns."

"Time was against us, sir, and I felt—"

"What was wrong with the local field office?" interrupted Carson, asserting her own authority. This question surprised Macintyre as she had been quite explicit with him that he was not to leave any loose ends in the wild. "A surgically clean trail..." was what Carson had insisted upon. Not a hair, not a fingerprint, not even a bad cup of coffee to remind anyone his team had ever been there.

"As I was about to say, ma'am, I felt it would save further... disruption. In the event she was needed for additional leverage, or to—"

"Unlock the damn encryption," growled Snark. "Fine. I'm not happy about this, Mac. Not one little bit. But you did the right thing. Turns out we may need her after all."

"Just make sure you follow strict quarantine procedures on arrival," added Carson.

"Yes, ma'am."

"She must not be allowed access to the main complex under any circumstances. Or even know it's there. Then, best-case, you can drop her back where you found her when we're done. She'll think the whole thing was a bad hangover that no one will believe."

Meanwhile, drinks ordering turned out to be a considerably longer wait than Elena had so smilingly suggested when Leon and his new associates had departed Teterboro. He couldn't be sure if this was just down to protocol, or simply that they were waiting on Milk, who appeared to doze off as they taxied to the runway and then remained asleep for the first ninety minutes of the flight. Leon just assumed the latter: that billionaires who owned the plane probably get to set the timing of drinks.

In the interim, Leon struggled to pass the time with any degree of comfort. He felt a weird mixture of desperate worry for Izzy, and intense curiosity about exactly what he was doing on a plane with Jordan Milk, of all people. As well as a serious frustration that he'd been dragged to said plane on a promise and, it must be said, no small amount of theatrics, only to watch the billionaire snooze in his chair like his dad on a Sunday afternoon.

And, after ninety minutes, he also felt a bit bored. Annie, who had popped on some headphones and disappeared into her laptop as soon as they were airborne, remained relentlessly occupied in whatever it was she was doing—playing Angry Birds, for all he knew—and Quinn just sat there, eyes lowered but not quite closed, with an otherwise blank look on his face. He was so perfectly still that Leon wondered if he too had just fallen asleep and his eyelids simply hadn't got the message.

It hadn't taken very long for the highly gridded structures of New York's metropolitan expanse to give way to looser and more sporadic formations of smaller municipalities and, eventually, open farmland. With not much else to do, Leon simply stared out of the window, wondering if he'd done the right thing coming to New York at all, or worse, compounded an already bad decision by bringing Izzy with him.

Obviously, she was an independent woman who could think and choose for herself what she wanted to do but, he realised, he'd been selfish letting her come. He should have at least tried to insist she stay behind, he thought. But, despite the constant hum of fear and, he reflected, the high probability that either or both of them could end up dead, he'd simply wanted to spend the time with her. He understood only too well that in the absence of stumbling across an apparently super-secret organisation hidden in the basement of his office and being pursued by assassins, he might never have had so much as a flat white with her, never mind a date. And now where had his needy desire gotten her?

By now the landscape below had evened out into much larger swathes of hill country, with minor pocket towns scattered across the vast countryside and what appeared to be a lot of undeveloped forestry. How nice and sumptuously green—and normal—everything looked from this distance. Leon wondered what it might be like to drive across the country, assuming he ever got out of this in one piece. Him and Izzy in a big American car. Away from all this... He impatiently pushed the fantasy aside realising he had grown exhausted of staring out the window and waiting for something to happen. He slid a foot over and kicked Quinn's shoe. Quinn, apparently not asleep after all, instantly looked up at Leon and smiled, plainly.

"Hey, what's up?" said Quinn.

Leon glanced across at Milk and Annie. They didn't appear to have stirred, but he decided to keep up the urgent whispering from before they took off, despite the background in-flight noises making any such practical murmuring virtually impossible.

"What's up?" repeated Leon, annoyed by Quinn's glibness. "What's up is I seem to be stuck in a plane, with a sleeping billionaire, a virtually mute woman, and you, a—what—agent? Clean-up guy? A spy...a whatever you are, to God-knows-where. Izzy is still missing and no one's telling me a damn thing."

"I totally understand, Leon. But look, it's a five-hour flight. We'll get to it soon enough."

"Easy for you to say," snapped Leon.

"Leon, Isabella is maybe two hours ahead of us—max. Nothing else is going to happen to her. And there's nothing any of us can do until we all get where we're going."

"And where is that, exactly?"

Quinn hesitated, then answered anyway.

"Las Vegas. City of Lights," he said, with a wink.

"City of... Did you just wink at me?"

"Sorry," he replied, raising his hands. "I thought it might help."

"Don't tell me... you have another secret base under Caesar's Palace?"

"Under Caesar's? No, but we do... anyway, no. From Vegas we drive to the facility."

"The *facility*," repeated Leon, in a half-mocking tone, before looking back at the window.

He realised then that, much like the drinks, he wouldn't get much more from Quinn until, presumably, Milk was awake, and everyone was feeling ready to share. He also knew that Quinn was basically right; whatever he told him didn't matter for now. There was nothing to be done until they arrived. He just couldn't stand feeling so helpless. He had no doubt that Izzy could take care of herself, better than he could, for sure, but even so, who'd want to be in that situation alone?

"We thought you might be dead, you know," said Leon, changing the subject.

"At Benedict's place?"

"We heard the gunshot."

"It was pretty close."

"Not your guys, then?"

"Well, let's just say they weren't there looking to make friends. I haven't been able to verify what they were doing there, although I do have an idea..."

"What kind of an idea?"

"It's not good. And I didn't get much time to confirm either way. Not exactly a backwater, that street."

"Not really."

"The police arrived almost instantly..."

Quinn looked at Leon expectantly, for some reason, but Leon didn't really know what to say. It seemed to him that was exactly what the police were supposed to do when shots were fired.

"So, what happened to the whole 'meet me at the hotel' shtick," said Leon after a moment. "Or was this always...?"

"The plan? No. We really were supposed to meet there. Just as I promised. I was going to take the data from you and that would have been it—the last you'd have seen of us."

"Us?"

"But things changed," continued Quinn, ignoring Leon's question. "Seems you guys didn't pass unnoticed after all and my... uhm...employers decided to take a more direct approach."

"One of your employers, wouldn't you say?" added Milk, who had apparently surfaced from his slumber unnoticed and was stretching extravagantly.

"Wait," said Leon. "You actually work for him?"

"Let's just say our interests are aligned," said Quinn but didn't get a chance to say any more as Elena suddenly reappeared with fresh towels, and a tray of sparking cocktails.

"Ah, Elena. Thank you," said Milk, as he took a towel and refreshed himself, taking extra care to dab his eyes. "Perfect timing as always."

Everyone else followed Milk's lead, then gave their food order to Elena, who seemed more pleased to take these orders than just about anyone doing any job Leon had ever seen. He had to assume she must either adore her work, or her boss, or was insanely well paid, although perhaps all three were true. In any case, she went off contentedly to prepare lunch, while Leon and the others supped their drinks and listened to Milk pontificate on a range of topics, seemingly in answer to questions that nobody had actually asked. Leon wondered if Milk had always done this, or just because, as a billionaire, people kind of expected it. Like a modern-day king.

This went on for quite some time with Quinn throwing in the odd point of view and Leon mostly nodding politely, wondering if Milk was ever going to get round to explaining what exactly they were all doing there.

Finally, as they were partway through lunch, and Leon was trying to muster enough appetite to eat his exceptionally delicious piece of black cod, they finally got into it.

"The food not your liking, Leon?" enquired Milk.

"Ah, no," stumbled Leon, feeling slightly embarrassed. "It's not that. The fish is amazing. It's the... It's just that..."

"You want to know what's going on, why you're here..."

"Frankly, yes. I do," said Leon, feeling an enormous weight lift. "This is great and everything," he continued, gesturing at their surroundings. "But my friend is missing. And if this isn't about helping get her back then, I don't know... Maybe you can just drop me off somewhere."

Milk glanced at Quinn, who nodded almost imperceptibly, then back to Leon.

"It is, Leon," reassured Milk. "It most definitely is about

getting her back. And I promise I'll do whatever I can to make that happen. But you have to understand, this whole thing," Milk circled a pointed finger in the air. "It's not *only* about Isabella."

"What do you mean?"

"You know," he began, obliquely. "When I was about, oh I don't know—twelve, thirteen years-old—I was on vacation with my family. Washington State. We used to go up there most summers when I was a kid. My dad had a cabin up there. Still has a cabin up there—he's eighty-five, goes up there half the year, like a damn fool, with his health problems."

Leon nodded, despite thinking this was a bit of a weird tangent. He wondered if it was the billionaire thing again, where they just say whatever they want. Or if it was actually going somewhere.

"Anyway, whatever," continued Milk, dismissing his own commentary with a wave. "We'd go up there for a month or so when school was out. My mom and dad, my two sisters, and me and we'd take that long, beautiful drive up from Oakland. Hang out. Read books. Sleep late. Go for hikes. Fishing. Cook-outs. The whole nine yards. But you know what family's like, right? You love each other, but you drive each other nuts. So anyway, one night me and my sisters, we have this...episode. Started out as a joke I think, but it went too far, and I got real pissed at them. And Mom and Dad? They were no help. Old hippies, both, leaving us to work things out. So I thought: I'm going to show these guys. And even though it was, like, after ten at night or something, I took a bedroll and a bag of chips and went off into the forest by myself."

By now, even Annie had stopped what she was doing, as if she'd never heard this story before.

"I must have walked for an hour, maybe more, until I reached a natural clearing in the trees where I could see down into a river valley below and decided to make a camp, of sorts.

"So, I'm out there, hunched up with my back to an old fallen tree, looking out across the ravine. Kind of regretting my choice as the temperature was dropping, but at the same time it's a beautiful night. Crystal perfect sky above. Crickets chirping. And the ribbons of the Milky Way, clear as day, weaving through the high treetops to the far side of the valley, close to the horizon, where the land began to rise again. Maybe a mile or two away, at most."

"Sounds incredibly beautiful," suggested Annie.

"It really was," replied Milk, reflectively. "But, you know, by now I'm starting to get tired and wondering if I should just lie down on my crummy mat or head home like a good boy, when suddenly there's a weird sound. Subtle. Quiet. But distinct, like an electric hum, somewhere in the distance. And when I look up at the treeline, I see a light. A soft, clear, warm light, bobbing and weaving behind the tops of the tree foliage. For a while it moves gently back and forth like it's dancing, or looking for something. It had the vibe of a search helicopter, except for the curious way it moved, and the humming.

"Then, in a blink, it starts to move in my direction. Slow at first but right for me, like it knew I was there. And part of me wants to run like hell, but the rest of me...? I'm transfixed. Frozen to the spot. I have to see what it is. Then in, like, literally one second it jumps from maybe a mile away and comes to a dead stop over the valley below."

"Oh my God," said Leon, suddenly caught up in Milk's story. "You're above it? What was it? What did you do?"

"Not above exactly. It was still pretty high but far enough away from me that for a moment I could see the craft really clearly. Pretty much a classic flying saucer. With light somehow emanating from the underside and the edges but with no obvious source, like the surface itself was alive. I could still hear the humming but weirdly it hadn't gotten any louder. If anything, it somehow muted the sound of everything else around me, the way snow can after a heavy fall."

"Did you see any..." began Leon.

"Aliens?" Milk laughed. "No, but someone had to be driving that thing, right? There were what looked like a row of small round windows on the top side, where the center rose up from the outer rim of the disk. Sometimes I think I saw a glimpse of move-ment behind one of them, sometimes I think I just imagined it later. The ship was only there for a few seconds and then just as quick as it arrived, the whole thing shot straight up for a few hundred feet, stopped on a dime, then zipped off over the horizon almost faster than you could see."

"So, what did you do?" asked Leon.

"What do you think I did? I ran back to the cabin and woke everyone up—you could see how worried they had been by my little stunt—and I told them what had happened, like I just told you. I ran around like a nut until everyone said they believed me. I'm not sure they all did. But they wanted to get back to sleep.

"By the next morning, it was business as usual. Mom making eggs. My sisters fighting over the remote. Dad sorting out our hiking packs for the day. And by the time we left to head up the trail that morning it had already become family folklore: some-thing I'd get teased about every chance my sisters could get. They still do. Needless to say, I didn't bring it up again with anyone for probably twenty-five years. By which time I was in a position to actually do something about it."

"That's quite the story," acknowledged Quinn, raising his glass. "And here's me thinking you were all business."

Milk smiled. "Hardly," he said. "Why do you think I need Annie so badly?"

"He's not even joking," quipped Annie, as she returned her attention to her laptop.

Quinn raised an eyebrow questioningly at Milk, whose expres-sion remained unchanged.

"So, you see, Leon, what I'm trying to tell you is that you're not the only one with a personal stake in what's happening here."

"Wait, what?" said Leon. "That doesn't even make any sense. I mean, it's a great story and everything. I wish I had a story like that. But how does that even connect? Izzy's not a magical UFO sighting from forty years ago. She's a real person, who's in trouble. You think that because—what—you're richer than God, you can just bamboozle everyone with a great campfire story and we all just go along with you?"

"You're right," said Milk, realising he may have miscalculated. "That was clumsy of me. I apologize. I guess what I'm trying to say, to answer your earlier question, is that getting Isabella back is only part of what we are here to do. And that the other part—the magical UFO part—it means something. To me, personally, yes, but not just to me. This whole thing: it can change the world."

"My world's already been changed quite enough this week, thanks."

"But can you imagine what we could do with that kind of technology?"

"Ultimate stealth bombers?" suggested Leon. "Faster internet? More money for you? I don't think that's going to do it for me."

"Exactly, Leon! That's exactly my point! It's not about the money, or the planes. This stuff, it's been kept under wraps for so long by all the wrong people, with so many stories and hoaxes and so much propaganda that the incredible possibilities, the chance to make a genuinely better world for everyone, it's all fallen by the side of the road in the service of global political brinksmanship. But it's time for that to stop. I've seen these things, Leon. That's what I'm trying to tell you. I know what they can do. And I one hundred percent agree that making a faster warplane is not it.

"These secret government clowns," he caught himself and looked at Quinn, "no offense, man."

Quinn shrugged. "None taken."

"The men in black, the—whatever you want to call them— they've controlled this story for over seven decades, and hogged all the toys and where has it gotten them? Where has it gotten us? They haven't made it work. All this compartmentalized, need-to-know bullshit. They don't even know what they're doing after all this time. You saw that hole in the ground in London, right?"

"Yeah, firsthand, unfortunately."

"Right. They stink at it. More people died. And they're not

about to start sharing now just because they made a great big mess. So, it's time to try something different. And I think you can help me, Leon. You and Izzy. Together."

"But how?"

Milk and Quinn exchanged looks, then Quinn leaned forward across the table.

"I'm going to arrest you, Leon. For conspiracy to commit espionage and smuggling classified government property across international borders."

37

VIVA LAS VEGAS

Snark gazed out across the rippling desert from behind an outcrop of layered igneous rock, which formed part of a natural camouflage for the deep complex below. He was taking a break, trying to put the events of the past thirty-six hours to the back his mind for a while. It had been far from his first international crisis to manage but, even so, he felt exhausted by it. Not just from the lack of a good, unbroken night's sleep, which, at his age, was pretty much standard anyway, but from the incessant vigilance that these black-on-black operations demanded. You're basically never off. Ever. And, in the meantime, it's not as if you could just unload on your buddies after work or, God knows, your wife.

This made him smile ruefully as he thought of each of his three ex-wives in turn and the stream of lies his work required from him. They had all thought he was some international trade and finance advisor, working for the US Treasury. They could never understand, given his position, why they never really had any money. And since he wasn't really a financial advisor, he could never explain it. Perhaps he should have just taken the advice of his old mentor and not gotten involved in the first place. They had all been good women and he had loved them, in his own way. But they deserved better. *We all deserved better,* he thought.

He watched a solitary bird of prey soar above the vast, arid plains below, riding the gently fluctuating thermals that travel the desert regions unseen by mere mortal men. It amused him to think how the bird was effectively violating such a highly restricted airspace, and imagined the hefty penalties it would have to pay should it ever be caught, as he stubbed out a cigarette on the natural rock ledge in front of him. The surface was already heavily bruised by the black marks and smears of its many prede-cessors, and he flicked the butt into a metal canister some ten feet to his right. He wondered briefly whose job it was to empty that container as his stub clipped the edge and fell to the ground, joining a small pile of other discarded butts that had suffered the same fate.

"I always imagined you were a much better shot than that, sir," said Carson, loudly, as she approached him, unnoticed, from a concealed exit door embedded into the rock face. "Did you remember to take your FQC this year?"

"My firearm quals probably expired before you were born, young lady." Snark half smiled, without turning around. "But I can still handle myself."

"Of that, sir, I have no doubt," replied Carson, firmly, as she took up position next to him under the shadow of a looming cliff-edge high above. She felt relieved by the respite it provided from the intense heat of the late-morning sun.

"I thought I'd find you here," she ventured, after a moment of silence. "I wanted to update you."

Snark grunted his acknowledgement without turning around.

"Quinn has just reported in. He has the secondary target in custody."

Snark said nothing. He just leant against the rocky wall, his forearms across the top, worn smooth by many decades of repeated action by who knew how many people. He continued to stare out across the desert basin and Carson waited patiently for an answer, enjoying the additional cooling action of the gentle desert breeze that flowed over the small plateau where they stood.

"Where you from, Frankie?" said Snark, at last. "Midwest?"

"Sir?"

"I figure you to be a Midwest kind of a girl."

Carson hesitated, then relented. "Kind of."

"Kind of," he repeated, slowly, turning towards her. "Chicago?" he said, popping a fresh cigarette between his lips. He offered her the pack, but she declined with a wave of her hand.

"Small town," she replied, as Snark nodded, lighting his cigarette.

"I hear you," he said, taking a long drag. "Leaving it all behind, eh? I get it. Well, I can tell you something; after nearly fifty years of this shit, we're all just trying to get out in front and leave the past where it belongs."

"And have you, sir? Managed to leave the past behind you?"

He thought for a moment and returned his gaze to the open flats far below.

"Look around you, Frankie," he replied, finally. "We're surrounded by the past. This whole...enterprise, if you want to call it that, was built on decisions made in the '40s and '50s. Decisions that inform everything we do here. The rest of the world has moved on, to a place those people simply couldn't have imagined. We're in a different goddamn century, Frankie, but somehow, we're still sticking by choices made by a bunch of old men. Men who were afraid of the future. Because they knew what they had. A world worth protecting."

"And if you had a choice, sir?"

Snark finally turned to look at her. "A choice?"

"To change things. To leave the past behind, as you say, and lift the lid on this whole thing. Let the world know what we're really doing down here."

"The world? Today?" responded Snark, with a bitter laugh. "Hell no. The world's more afraid than it's ever been. Not of the future, because it doesn't see one worth fighting for. And it sure as hell doesn't value the past anymore. The world's run by children now, with their noses glued to their phones, afraid to make the hard choices, spoon-fed, demanding, unwilling to take responsibility but happy to send pictures of their dicks to each other, instead of having a conversation. Like adults. You want to tell the truth to those people? They wouldn't even know what it was if you did. There is no truth anymore, don't you know that, Frankie? Truth is just personal experience. Up for grabs. Up for trial-by-drowning for whoever has the most *Shake-on-its*, or largest cesspool on Twitter. Truth? It's just a passing moment on Instagram to share with a bunch of random strangers."

"So, no, then," said Carson, wryly.

Snark looked at her with a raised eyebrow.

"Sir," she added, concerned she may have strayed too far.

"Oh, what the hell. I'm just an old man having a bad day. And the way things are going right now, we may not even have a choice."

"Perhaps."

A short alert chimed on Carson's phone. She let it pass unchecked for a moment.

"What about you, Frankie?" said Snark, pinching the end of his cigarette between his finger and thumb in an attempt to beat his last poor shot at the trash. He missed again, grimacing fleetingly at his small failure.

"Me, sir?"

"The future. This it for you? God knows I want you to stay—you're the best there is—but you want to spend the rest of your life hiding down here with me? You're so damn young. And all of life, everything we're supposed to be protecting... It's all out there, Frankie, beyond those mountains." He gestured to the far horizon. "Take it from me, there's more to this game than a twelve-story hole in the ground."

"I'll give it some thought, sir," replied Carson, keen to move on. "But as you say, after today we—" she was interrupted by her phone, ringing this time. She answered curtly and fielded a few short comments before closing the call. "It seems our guest has arrived,"

"Has she, indeed. Very good. And you mentioned Quinn has the secondary target?"

"It seems we have the complete set."

"And protocols are in place?"

"They are, sir," confirmed Carson.

"Excellent work, Frankie," said Snark, pushing himself away from his perch. He reached out and lightly touched the back of Carson's elbow. "Let's head back in, shall we? Perhaps today's not a complete loss after all."

"Indeed, sir," agreed Carson as they headed towards the veiled entry to the building.

"Once we're done with these two, we can find out exactly who's been pulling our chain the past three days and get back to doing some real work."

Carson said nothing as they reached the door. A solitary MP on the inside already had it open for them as they approached. He saluted as they passed, and Snark nodded in return.

"I can tell you something, Carson," continued Snark as they disappeared into the darkening corridor beyond. "Whoever the hell it is, I hope their deal was worth it. Because if they're not dead by the time I'm finished with them, they'll be begging me to kill them."

The outer door slammed shut behind them.

"OK, let's go over this thing one last time," said Milk, as the G700 began its descent into Las Vegas's Harry Reid International Airport. "Once we land, deplaning and transfers at the exec terminal will be sharp, and you guys will have to get on your way. If you have more questions, now is the time."

Leon was staring out the window at the baked desert land-scape below and thinking about Izzy, locked up and alone in a bunker somewhere out there in the wilderness. And whether or not he would soon be joining her. *Maybe they'll let us stay locked up together,* he thought, *when they bang us up for life.*

"Leon?" said Quinn. "You still with us? This is important."

"Yes, sorry. Just wondering if I'm going to end the day in jail for the rest of my life. Or not."

"Not super helpful," said Annie.

"I like to plan ahead."

Milk ignored the exchange and carried on with his summary briefing.

"As soon as we land, you, Annie, and Quinn will be escorted to a parking garage, where our technical consultant will be waiting in a civilian vehicle. You'll be driven out to Cobalt Flats where we have a small facility. It's about ninety miles away. Shouldn't take too long. Annie has all the details. When you arrive, she'll hand over the rabbit's foot, and our tech will start—"

"Rabbit's foot?" asked Leon.

"Just a figure of speech. Our tech will start priming the equipment onsite, while you—"

"What kind of equipment? Why does everything have to be expressed so vaguely?"

"Habit, I guess. As I explained, having your own extraterrestrial craft is not something you can just casually drop into conversation. You learn to be extremely careful. It's a very exclusive club. You're now one of maybe nine people in the whole world who know it exists, Leon."

"OK, fine," said Leon, not really feeling it. "The *equipment* will be primed. I still don't get why you don't just reverse engineer it—isn't that what they call it?—into something more useable."

"It's not that simple. If it was, the US Navy would have been flying gravity-powered planes decades ago. They're not—and the government's been working the problem a *lot* longer than I have. But we had the benefit of their head start and we've learned what we can, in the event we managed to get everything we needed to start it up. We actually thought it would take much longer, but it seems the London incident has provided us an unexpected window of opportunity, which I am very keen we don't screw up."

"Yes, OK, so this *craft*, as you put it," said Leon, finally giving in to some interest. Now they were close to landing, he began to feel less locked in by the whole situation and an emboldening mixture of fear and excitement began to overtake his previous feeling of resignation. "Where did you get it exactly? Is it like a book club for billionaires, where you all get together once a month, drink too much expensive wine, and trade highly exotic items?"

Milk laughed. "We don't all hang out with each other. I don't even know many of them. Believe it or not, Leon, we're still just people."

"I wouldn't be too sure about that, boss," added Annie, without looking up from her laptop.

"Thank you, Annie, for your undying support."

"Pleasure," she replied.

"Well, whatever," continued Leon, "I don't suppose they are just laying around the Nevada desert waiting to be found. And based on my extensive armchair research watching *The X-Files* and looking on the internet, I would've assumed the government has long since taken great pains to make sure they got them all."

"They did," replied Milk. "They have. Almost, that is. As I said, we got lucky."

"How, exactly?"

"About seven years ago I kicked off an environmental project, excavating down into a remote area of northern Alaska, taking ice core samples, and looking ... Anyway, they'd been at it a few weeks when they hit something they couldn't cut through, something too big to go around without restarting the whole rig. It was pretty deep in the tundra. Several hundred feet at least. They were about to pull up and restart when the drill dragged up a sliver of strange metal. They might not have even noticed except it was late in the day and somehow it seemed to be generating its own light.

"To cut a long story short, I clicked what it might be and flew out with a small specialist crew to dig it up and transport it out of there before anyone else started joining the dots."

"And did you? Get there in time, I mean."

"We're here, aren't we?" replied Milk, somewhat evasively.

Leon shrugged. He supposed he would have read something about it if the story had ever leaked. But then again, billions of dollars can buy you a lot of silence.

"In any case, it was an astonishing find. Completely intact. It had been down there a long time. Many hundreds of years, so far as we could tell. Maybe even longer than that. But even so a quick wash and a scrub brought it up like new. Literally. Like a car fresh out of the factory. Aside from what appeared to be a little crash damage there was no environmental or mineral effects to the exterior shell. But there was just one problem."

"Which was?" asked Leon.

"We couldn't seem to make it work. Or rather, work out *how* to make it work. I mean we found a way to power up the lights using our own sources, which was great, but the propulsion system—if you can even call it that—forget it. They, whoever they were, must have removed the power source. Maybe they took it with them—there were no bodies to speak of—or possibly both were snatched by locals at the time, who didn't know what they had. It's conceivable they—"

"And that's what you want me, us... I mean, Quinn to steal for you," said Leon. "You want us to just waltz into an ultra-secret military facility, ask if Izzy can come out to play, and then pilfer an alien space-battery for you while they go fetch her?"

"Pretty much," confirmed Quinn, with an open expression as if they were just talking about getting some takeout. Leon realised he really hadn't been paying enough attention when they'd talked about this earlier and, now that he was, could hardly believe what he was hearing.

"Well, I hate to spoil all the happy party vibes here, but d'you really think they're just going to let us do that? If that's the case, why don't we just knock off one of the casinos down there on our way out of town to get us in the mood?"

"Don't say I didn't warn you, Jordan," said Annie, apparently referring to Leon.

"Look, I know it seems like a big ask," said Milk, causing Leon to let out a bark of incredulous laughter.

"A big ask?" yelled Leon. "Jesus. Asking if you can borrow a friend's car to go away for the weekend is a *big ask*. This is... What kind of people are you?"

Quinn, Annie, and Milk all looked at each other in silence for a moment as though this was the first time it had ever occurred to them. It would be faintly comical, thought Leon, if it weren't so serious. And if Izzy's liberty didn't depend on it all going to plan. Or, more precisely, depend on him getting his shit together.

"OK. Fine. So, we're going to get this battery somehow..." he offered, wafting his hands about. This admission seemed to relax everyone, and Milk continued.

"It's actually a bit less simple than just getting a battery."

"Of course it is," said Leon. "Let's hear it, then."

"The battery—or power element to be more precise—is the one part we have. But to actually fly, the ship needs three things. Get one of them wrong or out of balance and you have London Bridge all over again. We think that's where they went wrong."

"That's very generous of you."

"Leon, are you going to play nice or not?" said Quinn. "This could all be a lot easier, you know."

"Sorry," apologised Leon. "I'm all ears."

"So, the element, the power source we have," continued Milk. "We also need the operational code, which I believe your girlfriend has kindly stolen and encrypted for us...and, finally, we need a focusing crystal that appears to both catalyse and channel the power into the craft."

"Kind of like tuning a radio," added Quinn.

"Why can't we just use the one you have?"

"Good question. It's damaged, and has great big crack down the center. It might work. It might not. Our technician says not. But either way it's also a huge risk to go through all this and then roll the dice. Again, I'm not in a hurry to recreate what happened in London. And this is pretty much our only chance to get hold of one."

"Lucky for you, then, that me and Izzy stumbled into this whole pile of ultra-secret crap, isn't it?"

"Yes, actually. Lucky for me. Lucky for all of us. I won't forget it."

"And what would you have done if we hadn't shown up, or played along?"

"I had a backup plan. It would have taken much longer, obviously, and likely cost most of my good fortune, but it was a plan. Of sorts."

"Right. OK. Understood. So, me and Izzy risk getting incarcerated for life, or worse, and you get your spaceship to work. Gotcha. What happens when we get to Cobalt Flats?"

"Oh, that's the easy bit. There, you and Quinn will switch to a new vehicle, where he'll take you into 'custody' and drive you another sixty miles north to the government compound."

Elena suddenly appeared between their seats and interrupted their briefing by announcing that the plane was on final approach and would be landing in around ten minutes.

"I can't wait," said Leon.

The Gulfstream G700 made an elegant landing and taxied to a small standalone hangar tethered to the executive terminal, where the regular wealthy and well-known typically disembarked. It was a small, one-story building on the northeast corner of the airport. They descended the steps from the plane where two vehicles were already waiting. Milk took a moment to shake Leon's hand firmly, before they parted ways, holding his forearm at the same time.

"Thank you, Leon. Really. You don't know how much this means."

For some reason Milk's pressing sincerity touched Leon in this moment. Or maybe it was just the realisation that this might be the last time anyone shakes his hand in a friendly way. Ever.

"Will we…" he started to reply.

"We'll see each other again soon," confirmed Milk, simply, before turning, getting into his car, and driving away.

"Come on," said Annie. "We should get going."

Leon, Quinn, and Annie followed each other into the waiting black SUV in that order. Leon didn't see the driver and nobody spoke to him, but he seemed to know where he was going as the car moved away as soon as the door was closed.

It didn't take very long to clear airside through a large non-public gate, usually reserved for freight. There was a brief conversation and exchange of documents between the driver and a security guard, who waved them on without any fuss. They quickly made their way onto Surrey Street, a road that ran between the airport estate and an adjacent strip mall, then left on East Russel before merging with the main airport roadway that would take them round to the Terminal 3 parking garage.

It was a modern if standard concrete layer cake, rendered clean and bright in the sharp desert sun. After ascending a slow rising on-ramp, it almost took longer to navigate around the garage than it did to get there in the first place. They finally arrived at the rear corner of the last but one parking level. Any farther and they would have been out on the roof. The floor was hardly empty, but the volume of parked cars had noticeably thinned out as they rose up the stack. A dusty, worn pickup truck was waiting for them, the driver partially visible behind the wheel. On the side of the double row cab was a heavily weathered logo that read McGraw Auto Parts in an old-time font.

"We've arrived, ma'am," said the SUV driver, efficiently, as they pulled to a stop.

"Thank you," replied Annie, handing him an envelope over

the back of his seat before releasing the door and climbing out. Leon and Quinn followed suit and made their way over to the parked truck, where the driver had already wound down his window.

"Howdy, folks," he declared, triumphantly, tipping his sun-faded cowboy hat. "I understand you're looking for a ride out to Cobalt Flats."

"You got it," said Annie, moving briskly round to the front passenger seat.

Leon looked to Quinn who was holding the back door open, for him presumably. They all climbed in to find Bryson Hawke, already in the rear seat. They nodded a greeting at each other as Leon scooched across the bench to find himself sandwiched uncomfortably between Hawke and Quinn.

"Pleased to make your acquaintance," said McGraw, splitting the word in two, as they all settled in and he started up the engine. "The name's McGraw. Billy 'Snakes' McGraw. My friends all call me *Snakes*."

"Far out," said Hawke from the back. "Great to meet you, Snakes, man. Why didn't you say before?"

"Well, we was still waitin' on ever'body. Didn't seem right."

"Hey," said Hawke, turning to his two companions. "Which one of you is Leon-the-man?"

"Umm, that'd be me, I guess," said Leon, reaching awkwardly to the side to try to shake Hawke's proffered hand. But Hawke flipped him with a sideways high five and a goofy grin instead.

"Then you," said Hawke, pointing at Quinn, but notably not offering his hand. "You must be the Fed."

Quinn nodded in return. "No, but close enough."

"Whoa!" yelled McGraw, slamming on the brakes. "Nobody said nothin' about no Feds." They were on the garage exit ramp to the main roadway with several cars behind. A couple of them honked their horns. One guy at the back starting yelling.

"He not a Fed, Mr McGraw," clarified Annie, sternly. "No one in the vehicle is a federal agent."

"Well, if you say so, ma'am. Feds is kind of against my creed."

"If we could just get on our way?"

"I was just sayin'," replied McGraw, starting up again and filtering out of the garage to join the traffic heading towards Paradise Road. "I like to know who I'm travelling with, is all. Who's what and who's not, if you take my meanin'."

"I do take your meaning," agreed Annie. "But perhaps you could take mine: this is a private transport arrangement for which you are being well compensated. If you feel it's not to your liking, I'm certain this city has many more options available to us."

Leon looked at Quinn—their whole plan hinged on getting a ride with *this* guy?—and then back to Hawke, who was nodding to some private tune of his own and staring out the window, oblivious to what he'd started.

"Now come on, lady," soothed McGraw. "No need for any of that. Snakes is only too happy to oblige. Let's forget I ever said nothin' and we'll be on our way up the ol' 93 before you know it."

"Good. Then step on it, *mister*. We're on a schedule."

And with that, McGraw tipped his hat, hit the gas, and headed up towards Tropicana Avenue.

It wasn't very long before they were stop-starting their way along the glitzy, nutty, human kaleidoscope of Las Vegas Boulevard; past the architectural brawl of New York, New York's roller-coaster-infused mini-skyline, Aria's refined glass towers and high brand endorsement, Bellagio's faux Italianate lake and fountains, and Caesar's classic iconography on one side, competing with the chaotic string of mass-market retailers and, with a couple of exceptions, a handful of lower-rent properties on the other—all woven together by a foaming mass of human traffic.

As they wove their way along this celebrated avenue of sparkle and shame, Leon couldn't decide what was worse—his uneasy expectations of what lay ahead, or his discomfort at being sand-wiched between a man he didn't entirely trust on one side and an apparently random stoner who smelled of patchouli oil on the other. All while being driven by a man who called himself Snakes for some reason, and directed by an unfathomable, taciturn woman, who appeared to spend most of her time glued to a device.

But then he realised that he would, in one way or another, need to trust these people if he hoped not only to see Izzy again but to somehow make it through the next twelve hours alive. This oddball crew, that an incredibly smart, unreasonably handsome tech billionaire, with all the choices in the world available to him, saw fit to put together in the service of completing a highly dubious mission—with him, it turns out, quite literally in the middle of it all.

As the passing stream of fabulous and not-so-fabulous casino resorts competed for his attention and his money, he had to admit, fittingly, that he didn't feel any more certain about what they were doing than chucking everything he had on a hand of blackjack.

Twenty minutes later, both the traffic and the buildings had begun to thin out as the metropolitan sprawl gave way to the open desert, with low mountains springing up on each far horizon. And soon afterwards, McGraw took the 93 North exit, towards Ely. A place, it seemed to Leon, based on the almost non-existent traffic that accompanied them, that no one else wanted to go to.

"So, what's in Ely?" said Leon, partly out of curiosity, partly to break the deafening silence that had descended on them since Annie had bawled out McGraw for asking a question.

"Ain't nuthin' there," answered McGraw. "Unless you like minin' and old trains." He started chuckling to himself in a way that sounded like a mix of high-pitched hiccups and choking.

"Ohh, hey man, I love trains," declared Hawke, languidly. "Old trains. That's real engineering. Everyone thinks that cars powered the twentieth century. But you know what? Trains built the world."

"Good job we're not going to Ely, then," confirmed Annie.

"So, what is this Cobalt Flats place?" asked Leon. "Or is that a secret too?"

"It's a li'l hole in the ground," said McGraw. "About an hour north."

"Ah. Helpful."

"I think this has all been explained to you," admonished Annie.

"Well, when you say explained..."

"Just think of it as a truck stop," added Quinn. "We'll do a quick changeover. These guys will stay behind, but you and I will head out. New wheels. New story. And off to the old belly of the beast." Then he grinned.

Leon didn't really like the sound of old bellies or beasts, or the look of Quinn's toothy grin for that matter, but he nodded along anyway as if everything was great. Then he returned to staring out the window, and wondering what would happen if he never made it home again. He knew his mum would have already called her sister Caroline three times in anticipation of this. And, naturally, she would also have alerted both the police and the *Jewish Chronicle* as soon as he'd left the country. But never coming home again *ever*? He closed his eyes and tried not to imagine her putting in an extra-large order of fresh matzo balls at Goldman's on High Road.

38

WHO ARE YOU PEOPLE?

L ight poured in from a high, shuttered window, casting long slanted shadows across the wall in front of the bed. A large ceiling fan rotated lazily above. And as Izzy's eyes finally came into focus, she could make out small motes of dust and fibres in the air as they turned and drifted in the unseen currents just ahead of her.

She wasn't sure how long she'd been awake, but it had been a while. Long enough to know she had a terrible headache and a nasty thirst to go with it. If she didn't know any better, she'd have mistaken the cloying sensation for a terrible hangover. Except she did know better and attempted to push the memory of the three men in her hotel room to one side. She had managed to take one of them down, she was sure of that, but then... Did Leon come back? Did somebody find her?

A figure she didn't recognise, or notice come into the room, stepped into view. A woman, neatly packed into a crisp military uniform stood in front of her and seemed to be appraising Izzy in some way, her head tilted slightly to one side. Her right hand rested lightly on her chin, held up by her left as it lay across her chest.

"Finally," said Izzy, after a moment. Her voice slightly hoarse with the dryness. "Where am I? Is this a hospital? It feels like a hospital."

"Good. You are awake," said the woman. "How are you feeling?"

Izzy made a clumsy attempt to push herself up into a seated position. Her body felt stiff and unresponsive, and there was something heavy wrapped around one of her ankles; she probed it gingerly with her other foot under the sheet—a restraint? It was unclear. But if nothing else, she was pleased to see she was still dressed in her own clothes, rather than some nasty, backless gown. So, perhaps not a hospital after all, she thought, despite the trappings of the room. But if not a hospital, then what kind of place chains you to a bed?

"Terrible, since you ask," replied Izzy, punching the pillows behind her into a more accommodating shape.

"That's to be expected. My apologies. You were given something to help you...sleep. Here"—the woman moved around to the side of the bed and poured Izzy a large glass of iced water from a jug on a table next to her.

She accepted it greedily, drinking it down with both hands.

"Better?" enquired the woman.

"Better," agreed Izzy, somewhat resentfully, and wiped her mouth with the back of her hand. "Who are you people? What am I doing here?"

"Did they bring you everything you need?" said the woman, ignoring Izzy's questions.

"Well, that kind of depends on what you mean. First of all, there's been no *they*. You're the only person I've seen since being forced out of my hotel room and apparently drugged. And what I *need* is to get out of here. Is that something you can help me with?"

It disturbed Izzy that the woman hadn't made any attempt to introduce herself, or explain the situation, but she didn't want to let on. Her interlocutor definitely had the look and demeanour of a person who possibly *could* help her, if she was so inclined. Or, she also suspected, make things much worse. Either way, Izzy wasn't holding out much hope. The woman merely regarded her and smiled thinly.

"All in good time," she said, ambiguously. "Have you had enough to drink? It's important to stay hydrated."

She refilled the glass and held it out to Izzy. Izzy looked at the woman directly for a moment, then sharply knocked the glass out of her hand, causing it to smash against the far wall.

"Don't give me the 'all in good time' shit and then offer me a drink. Who are you people!?"

The woman turned her head and nodded at a guard standing by the door, who Izzy only noticed as she did so. Definitely not a hospital, then, she thought, as she watched the guard walk calmly over to the broken glass and begin tidying it up into a nearby wastebasket.

The woman grabbed a chair by the wall and pulled it closer to the bed, crossing her legs as she sat down and folding her hands neatly onto her lap. Cards on the table time.

"Miss Jones," said the woman crisply, dispensing with the vaguely evasive doctor routine. "Who we are is not relevant to this situation, at this time."

"Really. Not even a name, then? Even though you apparently seem to know mine."

The woman smiled once again. "Do you think it would help?"

"It might," said Izzy, rolling her eyes. "I'm not sure who you normally spend your time with but, you know, out there"—Izzy gestured towards the frosted high windows with her thumb—"most people seem to get by with names. It can be pretty helpful in establishing a rapport. Especially with strangers who you want something from. As, I assume, you do from me."

The woman looked faintly amused by Izzy's observation.

"Miss Jones," she began again, then softened her tone. "Isabella...if I may. You are not in prison. We just need a little information from you and then you'll be returned to your hotel. You can call me Frances."

"Interesting. Well, if I'm not in prison, *Frances*, then what the fuck is this?"

Izzy yanked her foot out sharply to the side, causing the chain attaching her ankle to the bed to rattle noisily as it was pulled tight.

"Just a precaution."

"Against what exactly—sleepwalking?"

"Actually, yes," replied Frances Carson, surprising Izzy with her answer. "The tranquilizer you were given is a powerful agent and has been known to have severe side effects on certain individuals—including somnambulant perambulation. As a...guest in our country, we didn't want you to...ah...get lost."

"That's very thoughtful of you."

"We try."

"And now that I'm awake and we're becoming friends...?" replied Izzy, rattling the chain once again.

Carson signalled to the guard with a crisp hand gesture. He walked over and released the padded cuff around her ankle.

"You can leave us now," commanded Carson.

"Ma'am," acknowledged the guard, before picking up the wastebasket of broken glass on his way out.

"Better?" inquired Carson once the door was closed.

Izzy nodded, reluctantly, feeling—and looking—like a scolded teenager as she pulled up her knee and soothed the feeling bank into her ankle with her hands.

"Good. Now, if you're feeling less...restrained, perhaps we can have a nice chat about what you're doing in possession of highly classified US government property."

A mile or so to the southwest, Leon and Quinn were heading down into the lower valley floor on the coarse unmade track that would eventually lead them down into the base's underground parking garage. Leon was now cuffed to the ceiling-mounted passenger handle in the back of the replacement truck from

Cobalt Flats, and was doing his best to look like the reluctant captive he actually was. Having swiftly negotiated their way through the perimeter guardhouse (a direct call to Carson will do that), Quinn was quick to remind Leon that he was now effectively an unrecorded federal prisoner and that from here on out he should say as little as possible.

"I think I got it," said Leon, rattling the handcuffs tethering him to the vehicle.

"And just remember, as soon as we park, you'll be under additional surveillance. Even if you are left alone. Especially when you're left alone."

Leon just stared at the bleached desert landscape outside without answering, wondering if any part of this crazy scheme would play out the way they planned.

"Leon," barked Quinn, demandingly, regarding at him in the rearview mirror. "This is serious. It's Major League time."

"Yes," snapped Leon in return. "Major Leagues. I won't say a word."

The large metal shutters opened as they approached and then duly clattered shut behind them as they crossed the threshold into the parking garage. A perimeter lane guided them into the gloom and an assortment of demarcated parking zones that lay ahead, but they soon arrived beside another security checkpoint before they could make such a choice.

There wasn't much to it: just a medium-sized booth, with a couple of ticketing windows, and a solitary MP inside who quickly dropped his feet off the desk as the truck pulled up. Leon could see a small television in the corner behind him and wondered what he might be watching to pass the time. Sports? News? Prison TV? Not that he'd really taken much notice, but it always seemed to be sports. He wondered if there was a strict etiquette in this line of work that meant they all had to watch the same kinds of things to be accepted in the guard community. He felt a brief pang of regret for all the closeted movie buffs and opera-loving security specialists of this world, obliged to hide their passions under the veil of ESPN and locker-room conventions.

"What do you suppose he's watching?" asked Leon, as Quinn gathered up a couple of items from the front seat.

"What do I think he's watching?"

"Yeah. Do you think security guards have their own TV channel?"

"He's a military policeman, Leon," said Quinn. "Not a security guard. This isn't a shopping mall. Now stop kidding around."

By now the guard was on his feet and coming around the front of his booth as Quinn exited the vehicle and closed the door. They met halfway between and exchanged a few words that Leon couldn't really make out, before Quinn turned back to take him into custody. He yanked open the back door and unclipped the cuff holding Leon's wrist to the passenger handle while simultaneously pulling him out onto the kerbside. Leon was impressed by the skilful manipulation of human cargo and wondered if he trained for that specifically, or if it was just something Quinn had developed on his own. Leons hands were then recuffed tightly behind him. Tight enough that he made an involuntary noise.

"Is that really necessary?" complained Leon. "Where am I going to go?"

Quinn ignored him while the MP looked on with some level of expectation and, Leon thought, an unwarranted look of satisfaction on his face. Behind him, on the other side of the booth, a set of secure-looking double doors sprang open, and another MP walked through.

He was much larger than the first, who was a rather thin, taut man, with a neat, clinging uniform. This one was taller and heavier set, with a broad chest, muscular shoulders, and thick arms that looked like they were fighting with his sleeves for supremacy. He took his place next to the first man, who greeted him with a nod of recognition, and was just able to fold his big chunky arms across his massive chest. Together, they looked like a twenty-first century, gym-enhanced Laurel and Hardy, thought Leon.

"Leon Aronofsky," began Quinn, loudly, and all very official, Leon presumed, for the benefit of his small but smugly satisfied audience. "As a foreign national, do you understand your rights, as I have explained them to you."

"I...do," replied Leon, hesitantly, feeling uncomfortably like the groom at a shotgun wedding.

The two MPs nodded their satisfaction with the proceedings, in unison, and Leon's already meagre hopes for part two of this little piece of theatre decreased accordingly. Especially as Quinn, with his back to the newly formed military duo, had yet to clock who he'd have to contend with.

However, as he wheeled around to guide Leon towards them it quickly became apparent that they were already acquainted. Laurel produced a clipboard from somewhere, ready to document Leon's admission, and Hardy broke into a heavy grin.

"Well, well. The prodigal son returns," said the man in a voice as deep as his body was large.

"Is that what they're calling me now?" replied Quinn, returning the man's smile in kind and placing Leon in front of him for a short inspection.

"We've had a pool going as to whether you'd make it back before Carson sent one of us after you."

"Wasting your money again, Tyrone? I'm like a bad penny. You know that. I always turn up."

Tyrone began to pat Leon down.

"Legs apart, please, sir," he instructed.

"I've already checked him," declared Quinn. "More than once. You think I'd have driven an armed man across the desert on my own without checking him over?"

"You know the protocols, sir. Just doing my job. Turn around please."

Leon dutifully turned around so the policeman could run the flats of his hands down his back, check the folds of his denim jacket (which Leon was seriously regretting now that he was out of the truck's air-conditioned bubble), and gave a tug on the cuffs to confirm they were secure.

"He's good to go," declared Tyrone.

Tyrone's more compact colleague noted something down on his clipboards and presented it to Quinn. "If you could just sign here, sir?"

Quinn obliged. Then as he, Leon, and Tyrone began walking towards the double doors, turned briefly and tossed Laurel his keys.

"Stick it in one of the visitor bays, would you?" he said, as the skinny man caught the keys easily in his free hand. "I don't plan on being here very long."

Tyrone tapped his security card to the electronic pad next to the double doors then hit a large, round, blue door release, with an embossed disabled icon on it. The doors sprang open, and Tyrone nudged Leon through with his huge hand placed firmly on his back, nodding to Quinn that he was free to accompany them.

"Nice to see you've made the place so accessible," said Leon, referring to the blue switch. "I wouldn't have thought you'd get many random wheelchair users down here."

"Not many," confirmed Quinn, as the doors closed gently behind them. "But, you know, government regulations and all that."

"The same government regulations that say you're accountable to your people and not supposed to keep secret underground bases from them?"

"Just keep walking and your mouth closed," ordered Tyrone.

Quinn reinforced this message to Leon with a sharp look of his own that said: *don't screw this up.*

Ahead of them was a short polished concrete corridor, painted in the same bland municipal colours you see in most government buildings, ending in an oversized elevator that reminded Leon of the kind used in hospitals to accommodate the beds. To the left of it was a service door and, on the right-hand side, a set of wide concrete steps that descended out of sight.

Tyrone pressed the call button for the elevator as they arrived. There was no up option, noted Leon. The doors opened sharply a moment later and, just as they stepped over the threshold, Quinn slipped his cane between Tyrone's ankles. The man went down heavily, dragging Leon with him as he instinctively grasped the chain of his handcuffed hands in futile attempt to stop his fall. Leon groaned as the substantial weight of the man landed mostly on top of him and pushed his face into the floor of the elevator.

"Hey, what the—" began Tyrone as he fell, but before he could finish Quinn was on him like a flash, with his right arm curled around the man's thick neck, and hooked into the elbow of his left in a deftly executed chokehold. Tyrone immediately tried to resist but his arms were trapped between him and Leon's back, while Leon groaned under the shifting weight.

"It's OK. It's OK," soothed Quinn, quietly into the MP's ear, tightening his grip. "Don't resist." The man's struggle began to dissipate, as he started to lose consciousness. "There's just something I have to do. I'm sorry. They'll give you a medal..."

"Quinn, you fuuu..." and then he was gone.

"Is he done?" wheezed Leon, weakly, from underneath Tyrone's enormous, unconscious body that, now that he wasn't using it, suddenly weighed twice as much. "Get him off. I can't bloody breathe."

Quinn was able to roll Tyrone's heavy bulk off just enough that Leon was able scuttle out from under him like a beetle. He then pivoted onto his side, breathing heavily, so Quinn could unlock the handcuffs.

"That guy's the size of a fucking fridge," complained Leon. "I don't know how he gets himself out of a chair, never mind how—"

"We can discuss that later," said Quinn, cutting him off. "Give me a hand here. We won't have long."

Quinn peered gingerly around the edge of the partially open

elevator. The doors had started to close but had been halted by the side of Tyrone's giant foot. Satisfied that nobody was coming, Quinn picked his cane up and then, standing on his toes, held it up as high as he could and used the tip to gently nudge the exterior security camera slightly upward.

"OK," announced Quinn. "That should give us a little window to move in. Grab his feet."

Leon did as he was instructed while Quinn moved to the policeman's top end and attempted to lift the man by his shoulders.

"Jeezus," panted Quinn through gritted teeth. The man really did weigh a ton. "You weren't kidding around."

"I know, right?" agreed Leon. "You want me to come up that end?"

"You better had."

Leon and Quinn both grabbed one of his arms and, with considerable effort, heaved his bulk around so his head was facing outwards, then shuffled slowly out of the elevator like a couple of crabs moving a rock down a beach. They reached the service room next door, where they paused to take a breath. Tyrone began to murmur.

"Shit," said Quinn, "he's coming round. Grab his pass."

Leon snagged Tyrone's pass from his elasticated pocket clip and used it to flip the magnetic lock on the service room. The door clicked open, and they awkwardly shuffled backwards into the narrow utility closet that was filled with a variety of cleaning products and tools, including a huge floor polisher that looked big enough to ride on.

"I can see you guys take cleaning very seriously," said Leon, puffing, as they manoeuvred Tyrone's cumbersome bulk past the awkward machinery to the back of the narrow room, where a mountain of plastic-wrapped toilet paper rolls were lined up by the wall.

"Well, that depends," replied Quinn, struggling to position Tyrone's oversized frame into a reasonable approximation of the recovery position. The man let out another groan and began to stir like a man coming out of a very deep sleep. Quinn retrieved the handcuffs from his back pocket, snapping one half to Tyrone's wrist and the other to a thick pipe running up from floor to ceiling. "'Cleaning' here often has another meaning."

Leon watched as Quinn grabbed a couple of industrial plastic containers off one of the shelves and a third from higher up. He quickly measured out several capfuls of liquid from each and mixed them in old pickle jar that he plucked from somewhere Leon couldn't see, then shook the liquid together like Tom Cruise in *Cocktail*, even flashing Leon a grin as he did so. He poured some of the concoction out onto a cleaning cloth, squeezed it out, and just managed to stuff it under Tyrone's nose as he came around.

"You fuuuhhh..." he said, struggling weakly, then was out again just as quickly.

"He likes saying that," observed Leon. "What did you just give him?"

"It's not very friendly, but it'll keep him sedated and out of the way for a few hours."

"Will it...harm him?"

"Unlikely. I mean, he'll wake up with the worst hangover on Earth, but it won't kill him, if that's what you mean."

"That must be very reassuring."

"You do what you can. Now give me a hand getting his clothes off."

"What!?"

39

ROOKIE

A short time later, despite his initial protests, Leon stood in the closet wearing Tyrone's absurdly oversized uniform and attempting to make it appear even vaguely normal. This wasn't easy as, on Leon's much smaller frame, he looked like ten-year-old wearing his dad's clothes. The collar hung loosely around his neck like a noose, and the trousers bagged out like balloon pants.

"I look like bloody MC Hammer at bad fancy-dress party!" complained Leon. "No one's going to buy this. I'm going to be locked up or shot by the first person who sees me."

"Stop overreacting," said Quinn, as he smoothed down the trouser legs and tucked up the hems inside themselves. He placed a couple of binder clips he'd found on the shelves on the inside the hems at the back to hold everything in place.

"It would be a mercy killing."

Quinn ignored him, repeating a similar manoeuvre with the shirt, and clipping it into a neat fold at the back before tucking it out of sight under the belt.

"Hey!"

Quinn stepped back and looked at him. "I think it it'll work," he said, after a moment.

"I'm glad you think so."

"The trick here is not to draw attention. I've done it hundreds of times. You're just another MP going about his business, who no one wants to look at. Policeman make people feel instantly guilty, even here. I'm afraid your Levi's jeans wouldn't have had quite the same effect. Here"—Quinn handed Leon Tyrone's security pass and a small handheld radio. "Clip the pass to your shirt pocket—it'll give you access everywhere you need to go—and the radio to your belt. I've locked the frequency to mine so only you and I can talk, but you'll still receive on the open broadcast channel. Use it only if you absolutely have to."

"Thanks. And this?" said Leon, gesturing at the gun holstered to his side.

"Same goes for that."

"But I've never—"

"I know. But you can't not wear one or it'll stand out. And who knows?"

"I don't find that kind of open question very comforting."

"But just remember, if you do have to use it: you *squeeze* the trigger, not pull."

Leon nodded, unconsciously miming the action with his right hand.

"Ready?"

"As I'll ever be," replied Leon.

They took a last look at Tyrone, who seemed to be sleeping soundly on his little bed of toilet paper, and headed out of the closet, closing the door quietly behind them.

Instead of taking the elevator, as Leon had expected, they headed right and walked towards another security door at the far end of the access corridor. Leon swiped his badge on the door pad and the door unlocked with a satisfying *clunk*.

They walked through and soon found themselves in a spacious no-frills reception area. Two guards were stationed behind the main desk, and to the side of them was a large monitor, with small rotating image feeds streaming from different parts of the complex. One guard ignored their arrival completely, absorbed by some unseen administrative task, while the other looked up with a friendly expression on his weathered, middle-aged face. He nodded at Leon, who did his best to return the simple gesture despite feeling utterly conspicuous, before turning his attention back to Quinn.

"Well, lookee here at what the cat dragged in," said the man, leaning back casually in his chair with his hands behind his head.

"Yeah, yeah, Rocco, I know," replied Quinn. "Lose your shirt again?"

"You owe me a twenty."

"Stick it on my tab."

"Oh, I will. Don't you worry. What can I do you for?"

"I picked up this greenhorn on my way down here," said Quinn, jabbing his thumb towards Leon. "Just posted in from Texas, right, Ty?"

"I, uh…" began Leon, feeling that the sweat must be pouring off him as if he was taking a shower. Quinn never mentioned anything about talking to people.

"I need you to give him the penny tour."

"You should have called ahead, Greg, I would have fit you up with one of our boys."

"I know. But everyone has their orders, right?" Quinn slapped Leon on the shoulder as he said this.

"Don't I know it," responded Rocco, leaning forward and pulling out a sheet of paper from a desk tidy below the lip of the countertop and offering it to Leon. "Here you go, my skinny Texas friend." Quinn grabbed the paper and thrust it into Leon's wavering hand. "The latest in hi-tech navigational instruments: a floor plan. Should tell you everything you need to know. The green square? That's us. The blue ones…ah, you'll figure it out."

"Thanks," said Leon, trying to say as little as possible.

He looked at the sheet, which was indeed a floor plan for just this ground-level section of the base, showing an assortment of different-sized rooms arranged around the outside of a skewed, uneven rectangle, and indicating a number of access points, which he took extra note of. In the centre was a grey area marked *emergency elevator*. He wondered, briefly, what kind of an emergency it might be for.

"Ty, right?" continued Rocco. "As in Tyrone?"

"Uh...yep."

"We already got one o' them. You just missed him not twenty minutes ago. He woulda loved that."

Leon hesitated to respond, but Quinn jumped in. "Yeah, we caught him on the way through. Escorting some civvy dude into the lower decks."

"Down below?" Rocco let out a whistle. "He can't have been a civvy if they let him down there."

"Maybe so. Anyway, look, Rocco, I gotta run, and Tyrone here has some escorting of his own to do. Looking to collect a female—Jones—booked in sometime the past eight hours."

"Jones... I think she came in before my shift," responded Rocco, typing into his workstation. "Let me see... yep, here we go. Jones, Isabella. British national—oh shit."

Leon tired hard not to react but his eyes flicked sharply to Quinn.

"What is it?" asked Quinn.

"Carson's in with her. You sure you're here to collect? There's nothing on the system."

"Orders came direct from the chief."

"Snark? He's there too—in the observation room."

Quinn's expression remained unchanged as he mentally changed gears. He hadn't figured on them being up top.

"Maybe we should..." began Leon, mildly panicking, with no idea what might be at the end of that sentence, or who Carson and Snark might be. Only that they didn't sound fun. Quinn's hand, out of sight of the guards, waved him to shut up.

"Is he really?" improvised Quinn, with a note of irritation. "He coulda saved me the trip. But you know what these guys are like. Saying one thing, doing another."

"Oh yeah," blurted Leon, unexpectedly—mostly to himself—in a broad, nasally approximation of a New York accent. "They act like they can do whatever they like."

Quinn and Rocco both turned to look at him. Who the hell does this rookie think he is, they seemed to be saying. Although Quinn's genuinely surprised face may have been saying something much worse.

"Huh," said Rocco, giving Leon a fresh look over. "I thought you were from Texas."

"Uhm...yeah," replied Leon, sheepishly, his accent buckling a little under Quinn's less than thrilled gaze. "But I, uh, I grew up... north, you know. Brooklyn. *Capeesh*?"

"Capiche?" repeated Quinn, his eyebrows on the rise.

Rocco started laughing. "Capiche? That kills me. Where did you find this guy—1947?"

"What can I tell you?" replied Quinn, with a sigh. He leaned over the counter. "It's not like when we were kids. They'll recruit anyone these days."

"Tell me about it."

Quinn gestured towards the monitor. "Mind if I take a look?"

"Be my guest." Rocco pivoted his screen so Quinn could see Izzy's custody report.

"Hmm," mumbled Quinn, pretending to look it over.

"You want me to call through? I can call through," offered Rocco.

"Nah. That's OK," said Quinn. "Snark's in observation. I'll go talk to him direct." Rocco's eyes darted questioningly to Leon. "And I'll take the kid with me. It wouldn't hurt him to meet the boss before he says something really stupid."

Rocco chuckled again. "You got that right. Good luck, Ty-*rone*."

Leon smiled awkwardly and nodded his thanks as he and Quinn turned set off up a short flight of steps and around the corner into a long corridor.

"*Capiche*!?" whispered Quinn, harshly, when they were out of earshot.

"What do you want me to say?"

"Nothing. That's what I want you to say. You need to be as unmemorable as possible. The less you say to anyone here, the better. And what's with the Dustin Hoffman thing?"

"The accent?"

"Yeah. The goddamn 'accent,'" stressed Quinn, mockingly, while adding air quotes with his fingers. Leon went to answer but Quinn cut him off. "You know what, never mind. Show me the floor plan."

Quinn took the plan and pulled Leon into a small utility area up ahead. There was a rack of stationery on one wall and a standard office printer on the other. He took the map and laid it out on a narrow worksurface and grabbed a pen from the rack.

"OK, this is what what's going to happen," he said, scribbling a couple of circles onto the plan to indicate prime locations, and using his pen as a pointer. "We're here, right?" Leon nodded. "And Izzy is being held here in room 23." He jabbed at the second circle, located on the far right of the rectangular layout where a cluster of seemingly paired rooms—one regular size, one narrow—were designated AA-15 to 25.

"And the small ones are the observation rooms?" asked Leon.

"Right. So, I'm going to go talk to Snark and you're going to wait here"—Quinn indicated a square room at the far end of the plan labelled *Snack Room*—"until I give you the signal."

"Who is this Snark?"

"Director of the program. He runs this whole place."

"Ohh. Now I get the look. And Carson?"

"She's my boss. She may also... Look, it doesn't matter. I'm going to go talk to Snark and Carson and get them to leave. When I'm done, I will signal you with a triple click on the radio and that's when you make your move. Once you have Izzy, you take the emergency elevator down to sub-level six. Turn right out of the elevator—not left, right—follow the corridor until you get to the hangar bay. You shouldn't have any trouble finding it. It's signposted."

"Helpful."

"Government building," said Quinn, raising his hands. "You got it?"

"Izzy. Lift...I mean, elevator. Turn right. Hangar bays..."

"Do not turn left."

"What's left?"

"Leon!"

"I got it. I got it. Turn right. Hangar bays. Steal one of the most closely guarded secrets of the twentieth century. Then leave the way we came in."

"That's it. Questions?"

Snark was observing the conversation between Carson and Izzy from behind the two-way mirror fixed to the wall of Izzy's holding room. Something about this young woman didn't add up for him. Despite Carson's insistence that she was apparently at the heart of some elaborate scheme, nothing about this Isabella Morton Jones, her background, her demeanour under Carson's scrutiny, or her story felt off-key to him. Quite the opposite. He had the distinct impression she was actually telling the truth, which in his business was something of a novelty. And after five decades of watching people sweat it out in rooms like these, Snark had developed a pretty keen sense of what professional liars and thieves did under pressure.

To him, this woman was just a regular Joe, displaying all the guile and indignation of someone who had accidentally picked up the wrong coffee order at Starbucks. And if the background reports were anything to go by, he expected much the same from her companion when he arrived. Yes, they had accessed classified data. They'd seen things that had been carefully hidden over many decades. And yet what did they really know? They were tourists who'd taken a wrong turn down an interesting side road in a foreign city. If that really turned out to be the case, he decided, he'd have to put a stop to this and find a way to send them back to their little lives without any legal blowback or inter-ference from the press. He'd done it before.

Just then his phone chimed. A message. Quinn was in and ready to debrief.

"Finally," he said out loud. "Something we can actually work with. Enough with this amateur-hour shit."

He responded by sending a message of his own to Carson, telling her to close out the interrogation and meet in his office in five minutes. He stood up and left the room, as the grilling continued next door.

"I told you three times already," said Izzy, with no attempt to hide her frustration. "I am not working with anyone. I'm not affili-ated with anyone. Or even, as you put it, sponsored by a clandes-tine intermediary, or hostile third party. I just went to an office party. Randomly, I might add—I wasn't even planning on going until the last minute—where I had few drinks, listened to some speeches, danced badly, and got accidentally locked in a base-ment, where I fell asleep."

"And then?"

"Just what I said: I got rudely awoken when some apparently secret lab explosion broke open the walls of the room. And, yes, the lab was full of... I don't know what the hell it was. And I don't want to know. I never want to see it again. I was just glad to get out of there in one piece."

"I bet you were. And yet instead of going home to try and forget about the whole thing, you somehow acquire a couple of fake passports and travel to the United States. Tell me again; why you would do that?"

Izzy let out a long, frustrated sigh.

"Like I already told you: a man showed up at my college lab looking for me and killed one of my friends right in front of me. Killed him. With a gun! And just as I get away from that, my name and face starts popping up on the news. Is that going home and forgetting about it? I don't think so. I was terrified. I ran. How many more ways can I say it?"

"Let's find out," demanded Carson. "And this time, don't miss the part where you tell me all about Leon Aronofsky's handler."

Izzy laughed out loud.

"His handler!? Do you actually know anything about him, or are you just making this shit up as you go, the same as you're doing with me? I don't know who you work for, or what you do for a living, but you know, out in the regular world, where real people live, not everyone is—"

"Let's talk about the data, then, shall we?"

"The data...?" began Izzy, looking at her nails in a clumsy attempt to be casual.

"Enough games, Miss Jones. We know you have it. A system flag went up the second you accessed it in London." Izzy's face instantly betrayed her regret to Carson. "Oh, yes, that's right, my dear," continued Carson, condescendingly. "We had you at hello, as they say."

Izzy was quietly seething. She chastised herself for such an epic schoolgirl error. Of course there'd be embedded tracer code. Anyone would know that. And she wanted to actually kick herself for not taking even rudimentary precautions. She should have parsed the connection through an encrypted network but hadn't even bothered spoofing it with a bog-standard VPN. What the hell was she thinking? Then she winced, as she remembered seeing Robbie go down in a mist of his own blood. It had been a tough day.

"How you got it, we don't know. And, at this point, we don't much care. The fact is, it doesn't belong to you and we just want it back."

"And yet..."

"And yet. Look, I can make this really simple for you. We already have you here under guard and, shortly, your friend, Leon—"

"Leon..." gasped Izzy, involuntarily.

She'd just assumed he, at least, would have somehow been safe buying pastries. But of course he wasn't. It just hadn't occurred to her until that moment that they might try to... Oh screw it, she thought, at last, her resolve doubling down. And screw them. She'd had enough of this woman. They want the data? When she and Leon are safe. And maybe not even then. In the meantime, they can bloody well work for it.

"Yes, I thought that might hurt a bit," said Carson, smugly. "We have Leon in custody and, if he's not here already, it won't be much longer. The fact is, nobody knows you are here. And there are no outside lines for you to access. No one to call, so to speak." Carson paused to let that thought sink in a little further. Then offered her terms. "So, here's how it will go: we'll have a nice little chat with Leon when he comes in. Just like this one. His story matches yours? Two points. You then hand over the data—in full, and unencrypted—another point. We sweep it for any deletion triggers, binary markers, or any other *gifts* you may have left us with and if it all checks out—full house. You get to go home. Or back to wherever. We might even throw in a seat upgrade for you, just because we're that nice."

"Well, that is kind of you."

"We try."

"And if I don't comply? Or you find some software glitch you don't like?"

"Then we switch to plan B. It's a lot simpler really. We take you and your friend out into the desert and put a bullet in your heads. Leon first, and then, when you've handed over the goodies, you."

"Hmm. That's a lot to think about."

"Isn't it," agreed Carson, absently, as she looked at a message on her device. Her thumb tapped a three-digit reply and she stood up, pocketing the phone and straightening her neatly buttoned jacket with a sharp tug. "Just don't take too long, Isabella. Mr Aronofsky will thank you for it later."

Izzy watched Carson walk towards the door and deactivate the lock with her security card, while her fingers tightened into a fist under the sheet.

"Frances?"

Carson turned. "Yes?"

"I appreciate the offer. I really do. But is it possible you don't have all the facts? It's important to proceed with all the information, don't you think?"

"Oh indeed. And what is it you *think* we have overlooked?" replied Carson, almost biting the word out of its sentence.

"Well, here's the thing. I know it feels like you hold all the cards right now. And maybe you do. That must be a good feeling. But while I might have been a little clumsy when I opened up your files, once I saw what they might be...I did take a few precautions of my own. I figured this isn't the sort of thing that people like to leave lying around, and it wouldn't be long before someone showed up looking for it."

"Really."

"Yes, Frances, really. I mean, some guy had already pretty much tried to kill me only that morning—one of yours, I presume?" Carson didn't react. "So, I encrypted the data, backed it up to my private cloud, and installed a dead man's switch."

Having adopted a faintly amused expression until this point, Carson subtly raised a single eyebrow in response to this declaration.

"A dead man's switch," she repeated, dubiously.

"I'll make this really simple for you," continued Izzy, parroting Carson's previous tone. "In addition to my own custom-made biometric three-stage verifications, I geo-locked it to a number of specific times and locations. It can't be hacked...at least not in the time you have, and it can't be spoofed.

"If I don't personally check in precisely at the time and place that I set within the, what"—she glanced at the clock on the wall and made brief mental calculation—"next nineteen hours, everything gets released. Every media outlet, social network, and newsfeed on the planet: names, places, dates, budgets...all your dirty little secrets. Oh, and then all the core experimental data—the stuff I assume you really want—gets wiped."

For the first time since Izzy awoke, Carson's seemingly

unbreakable air of confident self-satisfaction missed a beat. A flash of anger seemed to pass across her face. And then it was gone.

"We'll see about that, young lady."

Then she turned sharply and left the room. The door closed behind her with the solid, unmistakable click of an electronic lock falling into place.

40

MOLE HILL

Snark literally ran into Quinn coming from the other direction, as he stormed around the corner from the holding rooms, and they each backed off a step in a bid to reclaim some dignity.

"What the hell?" shouted Snark, which is how he tended to reclaim any moment. "Watch where you're going, soldier."

"Sorry, sir," replied Quinn, stepping farther to one side. "I was in a hurry to catch you."

"I see that. But I thought I told you to meet at my office."

"Yes, sir. You did say that."

"Then why in the hell are we talking now?"

"I thought...never mind. I agree, sir. Your office would be the best place to discuss things."

"Very good."

And with that, Snark pushed on with the hard, purposeful stride of a much younger man, expecting Quinn to follow.

"Will Carson be joining us, sir?" asked Quinn, as he got in step.

Snark was heading down the short stairway into the reception area Quinn had left only five minutes before. Rocco and his friend were still at their posts, but gone was the friendly banter. They both stood sharply and saluted Snark as he and Quinn marched through the open area towards the exit. Snark, as usual, ignored the etiquette.

"She damn well better be. I've just watched her roasting some poor English schnook we pulled in for almost no goddamn good reason. And we've been waiting for you to show up for nearly three days."

"Yes, sir. Would that be Miss Jones?"

By now they were outside the holding annex by the main elevator, with Snark jabbing at the call button with his meaty finger. Quinn was acutely aware that Tyrone was still tied up in a small room ten feet away. He expected him to stay asleep for a couple of hours but, even so, janitor-cupboard cocktails were far from an exact science. He also knew that Leon was waiting on a signal from him but couldn't risk an explicit message to let him know things had changed. He needed to delay until Carson showed, and he could be sure the area was clear. Then the elevator arrived with a friendly *bong*.

"Yes, you know her?" said Snark, as he stepped on board.

"Only by name really," he lied, lingering by the open doors. "I just brought in Aronofsky. They know each other. She came up quite a bit."

"I bet she did. Carson seems to think she's at the center of this whole catastrophe."

"Personally, sir, I very much doubt that."

"I'm inclined to agree, despite the data breach she's been carrying around like a souvenir. Are you going to stand out there all goddamned day long, or get on the fricking elevator?"

Quinn hesitated and looked back up the corridor. He'd figured that if Snark was done observing then Carson couldn't be too far behind, but there was still no sign of her.

"I thought Carson might be bringing up the rear."

"Forget about her. She knows the way."

"Yes, sir, it's just—"

"Did something happen to you in London you haven't told us about? Get on the goddamn elevator!"

Quinn got on the goddamn elevator and Snark punched the floor to sub-level 6. The doors had just started to close when there was a commanding shout from some way off.

"Hold the door!"

"Jeezus," growled Snark, as he pushed the open button and gave Quinn a withering look.

Quinn leaned forward to look outside just as Carson appeared. A little breathy but otherwise her usual brisk and efficient self. She offered Snark a thin smile as she joined them inside.

"Thank you, sir," she said, mechanically.

Snark nodded and hit minus six again. The doors closed and the elevator began to descend. The three of them stood neatly in a line, with Carson in the middle. Quinn stepped slightly to the side as he casually dropped his right hand to his belt, in search of his radio. His thumb reached over the send button and he pressed it: one, two, three times.

"All done with the ritual flogging now, are we, Frankie?"

"Sir?"

"The girl."

"Yes, sir. It seems she's decided to play hardball after all."

"How so?" asked Quinn.

"She has the experimental data locked up. You heard about that?"

"I heard."

"She doesn't really know anything useful," insisted Snark.

"She's hit us with a dead man's switch. So she says. How's that for not knowing anything?"

"Shit," said Quinn, staring at the numbers ticking down on the display as it reached sub-level 6. The elevator pinged its arrival and the doors slid open.

"We don't acquiesce and she—" continued Carson but Snark

cut her off with a raised hand, then pointed farther down the hall. She understood. Not in the open.

"My office," he said.

Once inside he walked over to a side cabinet where his liquor had been relocated—the coffee table was stacked with paperwork —and started fixing a fresh drink. He turned and offered a glass to his subordinates, but they both politely declined.

"Take a seat."

"As I was saying, sir," began Carson, "she's installed a dead man's switch. We don't play nice, and it releases everything to the media."

"She's bluffing," offered Quinn.

"You think this is the first time someone's tried this, Carson?"

"No, sir."

"No, sir," repeated Snark. "She's smart, I'll grant you that. Clearly, she's smart. We should probably recruit the hell out of her. But she's also scared. She's a civilian. And this whole Gestapo shit you're giving her is making it worse. But right now we have plenty more important things to deal with."

Snark rubbed his eyes and readjusted the rolls of his sleeves.

"But the data, sir. We need it," exclaimed Carson.

"Look, I doubt she knows what she really has. How could she? She's putting on a good show. Good for her. Play along. Do what's necessary to get hold of it and, unless this Aronofsky kid has anything new to add, let's cut them loose. We're t-plus three days since our world went to shit and no closer to working out how or why."

He then turned squarely to Quinn.

"So, what have you got for us, Captain?"

The second Carson was out of her room, Izzy was off the bed and padding about her cell looking for something, anything that might help get her out of there.

Her half-bluff seemed to have bought her a little wiggle room, she reckoned, but it wouldn't last. And while she did have to perform a digital check-in, she hadn't had time to actually set up the universal media release, and nor was it really geo-locked. Instead, she was relying heavily on her hacker friend, Ludovika, who on Izzy's failure to check in, would receive a cryptic data packet and a hastily written coded message, to do the dirty work for her. Worst-case, she also had an encrypted backdoor she could use. But she wasn't about to admit to any of that. She'd taken a gamble this Carson woman wasn't clued up enough to know the difference and won—for now.

But she also knew, if her tech guys could get past her encryption, however unlikely, then it probably wouldn't take them long to unhack the rest. And then it really would be *adios amigos.*

Izzy headed over to scrutinise the mirror, running her gaze and fingers along the edges to see if it backed onto another room. She'd seen enough movies to know that the mirror probably wasn't there just for her to check her hair. But it was hard to be sure. She flicked off the lights and pulled on the shutters, then pressed her face right up to the glass; she thought she could just make out the shape of something. A couple of chairs maybe? Whatever it was, it didn't seem to be people-shaped. So, if nothing else, Carson hadn't just nipped next door to watch her squirm, or check how many times she used the bathroom.

The rest of the room was pretty spare. Izzy dragged the single chair over to the high-set window and stood precariously on the back of the seat. She could just about see over the lip of the glass, making out the edges of some nearby dry rock formations and an achingly blue sky. But otherwise, the window was completely sealed, like an office building. She wasn't surprised. She jumped back down and looked around for something else she could use when, abruptly, there was a noise coming from the door.

"Shit," she said, quietly. Then spotted the water jug next to the bed, as the door lock clicked open and the light above turned from red to green. She had to do something. She lurched across the bed to grab the jug and managed to get back behind the door just as it opened.

A wide stretch of light cut into the darkened room from the open doorway and a man stepped into the room.

"Hey," said Izzy. The man turned and she chucked the half jug of water into his face. He reached up in surprise, and Izzy let him have her full, closed fist, straight to the diaphragm. The man let out a heavy groan and she raised up the water jug to deliver part two, just as he buckled over and sank to the ground. A slice of disappearing light from the closing door ran across the man's face as he reached the floor. It was Leon.

"Oh my God, Leon," said Izzy, dropping to his side.

"What is it with you?" he wheezed, trying to catch his breath.

Izzy wiped Leon's scrunched-up face with her sleeve, and kissed him ardently, as mix of surprise, guilt, and straight-up relief at seeing him here, pulled at her all at once.

"I'm so sorry," she said, stroking his hair. He attempted to get himself up into a sitting position as Izzy, shocked by his arrival, slipped into overdrive. "I just thought they... My God, Leon, you have no idea, they grabbed me...they, they drugged me—they drugged me, Leon—I woke up here, chained to a bed, this woman, she kept asking me questions, she knows, she knows everything about—"

Leon held up his hands to slow her down.

"It's OK," he said, and reached for her hand. "I'm here."

"But you don't understand, they're going to—"

Leon leant forward and kissed her. "I'm here, Izzy," he whispered. "Just as I said. Whatever happens."

Then she kissed him back, harder, and for a brief moment their emotions at seeing each other again overwhelmed, and their kiss erupted into a storm, as they clawed and grabbed and stroked at each other's hair and faces, as though to life itself. And then the moment subsided, just as quickly, and they fell into laughter. The combination of sheer relief and the total absurdity of the situation they were in hitting them all at once. Izzy sat back, finally, brushing her hair from her face.

"Thank you," she said, after a moment. "For being here, with me. However you did that...and wherever here is."

"Somewhere in the Nevada desert, I believe."

"Seriously? But we were...in New York. Why bring us all this way?"

"Technically, they didn't bring me."

"They didn't...? I kind of assumed... Wait, then what the hell are you doing here, Leon?"

"I have a lot to tell you," he said, looking about the darkened room. "But not here."

"And why are you wearing your dad's clothes?"

"Oh, it's worse than that," replied Leon. He stood up to reveal the baggy, blousy truth of his makeshift borrowed trousers. Izzy barked out a laugh then clamped her hand over her mouth to quieten the noise.

"Now I finally know what Hammer Time is!" declared Izzy, in a stage whisper.

"Shh," said Leon, smiling, and offering his hand to help her up from the floor. "Or I'll just go back out and leave you here."

"Just see what happens if you try..."

They took a moment for Izzy to grab her shoes and arrange the bed pillows in the shape of a person, in case anyone looked in. Then, after cracking the door open to confirm that the corridor was empty, they slipped quietly out of the room.

Leon pulled out his floor plan and pointed right, explaining that they needed to get to the elevator unseen. Izzy quickly pointed out how conspicuous they were—especially now that Leon was all wet from the chest up.

"I don't imagine that goes unnoticed in a military bunker," she said.

After consulting the map, he saw there was another utility closet around the corner where they could briefly take stock and see if there was anything they could use for cover.

Once inside, they found a unit stacked with folded grey-blue janitorial overalls and a lot of the equipment to go with them; brooms, mops, sprays, cloths, an eclectic floor polisher, and various industrial-sized canisters full of cleaning products. Plus, another wall-sized stack of toilet paper rolls.

"These guys must have a real problem down here," said Leon, nodding at the stack.

"How do you mean?"

"There's another room full of these just outside the main door. Remind me not to stop at the canteen on the way through."

"Got it."

They changed quickly, without any fuss. Izzy scraped her hair back and pinned it under a cap that formed part of the uniform. Leon did the same, but with less hair scraping, feeling a huge relief to be out of that absurd-looking military costume. They tucked Izzy's clothes—plus the gun Leon had been carrying—into the bottom of a large, wheeled bucket, and jammed a mop into the holder on the side. They couldn't risk her stuff being found, and figured the contraption would also make a good prop. Leon popped on a workman's belt he found hanging off the back of the door and loaded it with a few items from the shelves. Cloths and a couple of sprays.

"You think that will help if you get into a polishing quick draw with someone?" teased Izzy.

"Better that than a gunfight," replied Leon. "Now, remember—don't look at anyone directly but don't look away either."

Izzy nodded. "You ever going to tell me where we're going? Or why it's not just the exit, so we can get the hell out of here?"

"As soon as we're somewhere they won't be actively looking for us. Ready?" asked Leon.

Izzy wasn't ready. Neither of them were. But they also knew they couldn't just hide in a closet hoping it would all go away, and so they set off down the long corridor, pushing the mop and bucket ahead of them like a shield.

Eventually, Leon knew, it would bring them back to the main lobby and presumably Rocco, which obviously he wanted to avoid. Instead, he diverted to the emergency elevator halfway along. They passed a few people on the way but were roundly ignored by all of them, even when Leon, looking back to check as they turned a corner, accidentally clanked the bucket loudly into the wall.

"Nicely done," congratulated Izzy.

They came to a large double-wide elevator, similar to the one Leon had been escorted to by Tyrone. However, this one had striped red-and-yellow hazard detailing around the edges and a large sign across the doors that read Emergency Access Only.

"Do you suppose this is alarmed," asked Leon, "or just for show? You know, to dissuade people from using it when the main lifts get congested at home time?"

"You reckon they have home time here, like a regular office?"

Leon shrugged then, as he pondered his own question, Izzy nudged him.

"What about that one?"

A short way to the right, recessed farther into the wall, was a smaller, standard elevator. It had a much plainer sign that read Maintenance Only.

"That has to be us, right?"

They walked over and pressed the call button. Nothing happened. Then Leon remembered the security card. He brushed it against the keypad and the button lit up.

"Where did you get that exactly?" asked Izzy, pulling it towards her. "Tyrone?"

"Yeah, about that," began Leon, as the elevator pinged its arrival. The doors slid open and they stepped onboard. Leon pressed minus-six and, working backwards from when Quinn subdued Tyrone, took this as his cue to start filling Izzy in on Milk's insane plan.

· · ·

"So, let me get this straight," demanded Snark. "You're trying to tell me this whole thing is an inside job—one of our own did this?"

"I am saying that, sir, yes," replied Quinn, leaning forward on the couch. "Maybe not orchestrated from here, but someone on the inside is helping out. Had to be."

"That's ridiculous, Greg," snarled Carson, "and you know it."

She stood up and made her way over to Snark's drinks supply.

"Bring the bottle, Frankie," said Snark. "And some ice."

"Normally, I would agree with you, ma'am," continued Quinn, looking up, "but I've had a lot of time to think about this the past couple of days and there's just no other way. Too many coincidences. Too much insider knowledge. It would require an astounding level of infiltration: a mole, or several working together. Frankly, either seems unrealistic to me give the controls we have in place. And yet, here we are."

"Here we are? Do you know how deeply we vet people in this organization?" said Carson, returning with the bottle and two more glasses, one filled with ice.

"I think he just said he did, Frankie," said Snark, surprised by Carson's uncharacteristically reactive comeback.

"Yes, sir," replied Carson, distributing the ice between the two fresh glasses and Snark's third. "Apologies, Greg. I meant that as a statement, not a question. But, even so, it's a lot to come in here after being MIA for three days and start throwing shit around as you waltz in the door. If I didn't know any better—"

"Frankie…" warned Snark. "We're all trying to figure this thing out."

"Look," stated Quinn. "Don't just take my word for it. You can check the facts for yourself. Firstly, this thing is about access. Access to the London site, yes—and that's huge by itself—but not just that. Access to the technical schematics, access to the research, and the past thirty years of testing data—whoever planted the explosive knew exactly where to hit us. Anywhere more obvious in terms of impact and it would have been found in any number of regular sweeps. But that's just the point: the actuation servers? The complete opposite of obvious—I'm not even sure it occurred to us—and yet, weirdly, turns out to be the perfect choice if you wanted hit something seemingly non-critical that would have such a devasting effect. That's no lucky guess. You'd really have to know this stuff, inside out.

"Secondly, the clean-up squad gets cleaned? Come on. I was there, dammit. I saw what they did to Manchego and his team, and it wasn't pretty. Take those guys by surprise? Forget about it. I've worked with them in the field. More than once. Not a chance. Not unless...someone knew—in advance—where, when, and what they'd be doing. They were set up. They had to be."

"Who ordered the team onside, Commander?" asked Snark.

"I did, sir," responded Carson.

"And who else knew about your orders?"

"Just Macintyre. Standard procedure. They're his team, ultimately, sir. They all are."

"Mac? Jesus Christ. Mac? It can't be him. Do you have any idea how long he's been with me?"

"I do, sir," confirmed Carson.

"Well, if it's Mac, then we really are fucked," declared Snark. "He knows where all the bodies are buried." Quinn looked at Snark, as the idea infected the air like a bad smell. "Metaphorically speaking, of course," he added.

"Now wait a minute," responded Quinn, his hands held out in front as though to physically stop Snark from moving. "Nobody's saying—"

"Who else, then Greg?" demanded Carson. "You said it yourself. He's perfectly placed to make this happen."

"That's not what I—" protested Quinn, but Snark cut him off.

"Commander, I want you to take Mac into custody now. But do it quietly. We don't want to scare the henhouse—especially if it turns out not to be him. But if it is, hell, I want to know who got to him and when, and then I want both their heads on my desk by the end of the day."

"Sir," insisted Quinn. "I must advise caution. Or we risk showing our hand too soon."

"Caution? And give Mac a chance to drive another train through the middle of this operation?"

"And if it isn't him?"

"He's a big boy. He understands how the game is played. If it isn't him, then he'll be first in line to help us hunt the bastard down, whoever it turns out to be. You have your orders, Lieutenant Commander."

"Yes, sir," confirmed Carson, placing her glass back down on the low table. "What about the Brit woman and her boyfriend? Quinn just pulled him in."

"They'll keep. Cleaning house is our priority right now."

Carson stood up and went to leave.

"And Frankie?"

"Sir?"

"I mean quietly. Off the books quiet. Do it personally if you have to."

"It's done, sir," said Carson, then turned and headed for the door.

"Anything else from you, Quinn?" said Snark, adding another finger of whiskey to his glass.

Carson paused at the open door as Quinn went to answer.

"Problem, Commander?" called Snark across the room.

Quinn turned to look at her.

"No, sir. It's just...if... What I mean, sir, is, what if Mac... *resists*?"

"He won't."

"But if he does?"

"Then you put him down," said Snark, without hesitation. "Like any rabid dog."

Carson gave a reluctant nod and let go of the door, as Snark turned his expectations back to Quinn.

"There was one more thing, sir," he began, quietly.

Carson strained to hear what that might be, as the door closed behind her. But she had her orders. She turned suddenly and strode purposefully down the corridor towards the operational mission area.

41

FUTURISTIC BAGELS

"And you didn't think to say no?" said Izzy, as they made their way cautiously along a string of concrete-lined corridors, on their way to what the signage referred to as the Main Hangar Complex.

They'd been catching each other up on events as they went along, passing various labs, offices, and engineering rooms as best as they could tell from the occasional open door, or unshuttered window. Some had a lot of people in them, crowded around a variety of objects they couldn't make out, while others only a handful; and in those cases, they were often engaged in some solitary activity or other. It was an industrious organisation, reflected Leon. His work environment, by comparison, felt more like a student dorm. Or used to feel, he corrected, unsure of what might be there if he ever went back.

The passageways themselves were relatively quiet, and anyone they did pass seemed intently focused on wherever they were going. Either that, or they were simply uncomfortable engaging directly with the janitorial staff, which, given what they were up to, he really didn't mind.

"To what," replied Leon. "Stealing the crystal or saving you?"

"Saving me? I'll have you know my fists are registered

weapons at Newington Green's Arts Shack. Every Tuesday evening, seven-forty-five 'till nine, I let 'em out for a nice run." Izzy mimed her signature gut-busting move. "I'm top of the class at taking down a bag of sand."

"Hey, you don't have to convince me."

"Sorry," said Izzy, regretting her showy display. "Go on..."

"Well, whatever you want to call it, I didn't much like the idea of sitting around in New York by myself waiting for you to show up, or worse, going home and sorta, kinda, just hoping that Quinn would come through. When I saw that you'd been taken, I was terrified—for you and me. Then Milk offered me a way to help. I had to do something."

Izzy smiled and placed her hand on his chest. "You're sweet," she said. Leon smiled back. "You're also an idiot," she continued, this time whacking him with the same hand.

"What!?"

"For wilfully putting yourself in danger. You could have been killed. You might still be killed. You know that, right?"

This, Leon had not been expecting. "Yes, OK, maybe, but—"

"You also forgot about our ace in the hole. It buys quite a bit of protection."

"Which is what again?"

"Benedict's data hoard."

"The one you pretended to set up as a time-bomb?"

"Exaggerated, not pretended."

"Well, that might be your ace in a hole, little Miss Steve Jobs, but I don't have the chops for it. I can barely reset my own password. All I had was a choice between sitting around on my hands, worrying, maybe for the rest of my life, or coming to find you. I chose you."

Izzy's face blossomed into a beaming smile. "Thank you. I take back what I said."

"About being an idiot?"

"About being killed."

They turned a corner and ahead of them were a set of industrial rubber-sealed double doors, marked with a sign that said Controlled Area—Containment Protocols Apply. They peered through the small, square, wire-glass windows to check no one was on the other side, and then again back around the corner to make sure there weren't any surprises coming up behind them. The long corridor was empty.

Leon activated the door mechanism with his keycard and they pressed ahead, keeping the mop-bucket-trolley on point. Almost immediately they found themselves in front of another set of matching doors. These also had a security pad to one side, except this one appeared to be inactive. Leon tried the card a couple of times, but nothing happened and the doors remained firmly locked.

"Great," said Leon, rattling the doors for a third time. "We're stuck before we've even got started."

"Wait a second," said Izzy, indicating the doors they'd just stepped through, which were still drifting to a close. As they did so, a rotating mechanism could be heard falling into place, along with the short, inverted huff and whine of a vacuum forming somewhere, apparently sealing the doors shut. A red light on the second control panel lit up. "Airlock," established Izzy. "Containment protocols? Try now."

Leon flashed his card and the panel switched to green, releasing the second set of doors. He looked at Izzy. "Ready?"

"Ready."

They moved slowly into the chamber ahead, which at first seemed like another, much wider corridor, only with nothing overhead. Nothing close, anyway. High walls that ran on for perhaps twenty or thirty feet ahead and then, above them, an incredibly high ceiling that clearly spanned a much larger, cavernous space beyond. There were various mechanisms, gantry ways, pipes, cables, and rows of stadium lights in regular intervals suspended from the roof that seemed to run on much farther than they could see.

At the end of the walkway, they encountered a wide row of tall industrial shelving filled with electronic equipment, and obscuring their view of whatever lay ahead. Up close it became clear to Izzy that the components were in fact a mix of densely layered parallel computing modules and operational servers.

"Careful," warned Izzy, holding out a hand to slow Leon's progress. "Wherever you have custom, high-end computer installations, there's sure to be a nest of geeks close by."

"Got it," said Leon, not entirely sure if Izzy was joking.

"Take it from me: you don't want to surprise them. They can get pretty vicious."

He nodded and parked the wheelie-bucket carefully by the wall but kept hold of the mop as they dropped to a slow creeping pace. "What if—"

"Shh." Izzy raised a finger to her lips and they both pressed themselves into the wall.

A man with waxy-looking shoulder-length hair and a lab coat appeared from the left and paused partway along the row of equipment to check something out. He had a notebook with him, which he referred to several times before pulling out a circuit board from one of the stacks. He checked it over, turning it in his hands, blew on it, and replaced it into a higher slot on the tower. He pressed several buttons on a small, thin control panel below, then noted something down on his pad before moving off and out of sight.

"I told you," whispered Izzy, firmly.

"And I believed you," whispered Leon right back.

They stayed close to the wall and began gingerly making their way up to the intersection at the end of the walkway. At the last two feet they stopped and, crouching down, carefully peered around the corner, one head above the other. The hangar space they were in turned out to be at least as wide as it was high. To the left, close to the far wall, were a cluster of workstations. Perhaps fifteen or more desks, with only three people working at them that they could see.

"Not very busy," murmured Leon. "Maybe everyone is at lunch?"

"Not busy is exactly what we want."

"And why is everything so insanely clean?"

On their right, way past the racks of computer equipment, was a series of tall storage bays, enclosed behind a cage. It was hard to be sure what was there. Barrels containing who-knew-what-kind of hazardous material (lots of warning stickers) and, beyond that, layers of utility shelving that appeared to store various translucent containers, stacked on top of each other. Then, piled high against one side of the cage, were blocks of raw materials—plastics, metal, wood. In a strange way, the whole place reminded Leon of his local DIY box-store but on an insanely different scale.

"I think this place is some kind of super hi-tech industrial lab," observed Izzy.

"Yeah, that's what I was going to say," pretended Leon.

"It wouldn't surprise me if there were machine shops back there," she continued, referring to the bays lined up on either side of the highwalled entrance they had just crept along. "Just look at this stuff. No wonder it's so clean. I bet they can make anything here."

"But why? I get that a hangar would have maintenance stuff, but this seems a bit overkill, don't you think?"

"Backwards engineering," suggested Izzy. "If what you say... If what Milk says is true, then this whole place will be dedicated to studying the ships, working out how they function. And then trying to recreate the technology. All this kit means they can prototype whatever they need and test as they go. It's like an Emerald City version of my little college lab back home," said Izzy, fighting off a flashback of poor Robbie hitting the floor.

"From *The Wizard of Oz*? Just as long as there are no flying monkeys to go with it."

"Not a fan?"

"Little fez-wearing flying monkeys!? Are you kidding me? Terrifying. Come on, we can't lurk here all day."

They scooted across the aisle to the server racks and headed right initially—away from the people working—towards the equipment store. It turns out Izzy was spot-on with the workshops: at the back of the hall was a row of large glass-fronted machine rooms, containing drills and lathes and milling machines, and other specialised equipment Leon didn't recognise. All of it beautifully clean, like an engineering museum for the super-rich. Milk would love it, thought Leon. And on the level above them—the hangar was at least three stories tall as far as he could tell—was a row of what looked like offices or observation rooms, where someone appeared to be observing them.

"Start cleaning," snapped Leon, dropping the mop from his shoulder to the floor and running it vigorously along the base of the nearest rack.

"What?"

"Start cleaning," repeated Leon, his heart picking up the pace. "Someone's watching us."

He made a motion with his eyes towards the gallery above. Izzy glanced up and could see there was indeed a figure standing there looking out, but whether it was at them, she couldn't be sure. In any case, she grabbed a cloth and a spray from Leon's utility belt and joined in, enthusiastically dusting and wiping the surface of a nearby console. They maintained their little charade as they shuffled along towards the end of the row when, suddenly, a man's voice called out from somewhere behind them.

"Hey, you!"

"Just keep moving," said Leon, his faux mopping revving up to feverish pace as he tried to clean his way to the corner, and out of sight. Izzy, only a step behind, was giving the shelves a similarly theatrical swirl of the yellow dustcloth.

"Hey," came the voice again, much nearer this time. Neither Leon nor Izzy dared look up from beneath their caps but the voice persisted. "What are you doing down here?"

Leon froze, at last, his mop locked to the floor at a jaunty angle, as he steeled himself for what was surely about to be a very difficult conversation. Izzy, not noticing that he had come to a halt due to her own overzealous polishing, bumped straight into the back of him.

"What are you two doing?" came the insistent voice again, plainly irritated this time, and now only a few feet away.

Leon looked up slowly, attempting nonchalance, while feeling the exact opposite, as Izzy turned about and smiled gamely at the man.

"Hello," she said, pleasingly, forgetting for a moment that in this setting her accent stood out as if she really was Hermione Granger, about to serve tea.

It was clear this unexpected sound confused the man standing in front of them, who turned out to be the same lanky-haired, lab coat-wearing dude they had seen when they arrived. He still had his notepad and, now they were three feet from him, a name tag that said Dr. Robert Maze.

"Uh, yah," interjected Leon, attempting to direct the man's puzzlement away from Izzy's cut-glass greeting with the same mangled Noo-York accent that he'd attempted previously but with added Rocco. "What can we do yer for?"

It seemed to work. "You know, I called maintenance nearly an hour ago," complained the man.

"Uh-huh."

"About the spill in lab four?"

"Lab four? Oh yeah, sure," agreed Leon, ratcheting up the *Midnight Cowboy*-era Hoffman. "The spill. Right. The supervisor said—"

"So, what are you doing over here?" demanded Dr Robert Maze.

"Just...you know, cleaning."

"We like to clean," said Izzy, joining in with the accent fun, if slightly less successfully than Leon, which wasn't an easy feat.

"Everyone's got to have a hobby, I guess," said Maze, not entirely convinced but impatient to get his needs met. "Let's go."

He led them back along the wall of computer servers to the

opposite end of the concourse where the workstations were laid out. Behind this wide bank of desks was another series of glass-fronted work rooms—labs, as Maze had called them—similar to the workshops on the other side, except these were clearly set out for much more refined analysis-based activity. Whether biological, chemical or microelectronic analysis Leon couldn't really tell. But there were various configurations of stainless-steel benches, glass-doored refrigerated units, shelves laden with steel canisters, glass jars, and plastic storage boxes of various sizes, along with a warren of pipes and extractor vents in all four bays. Leon noticed the familiar shape of a handful of microscopes in one, and another that seemed to have at least one bench dedicated to small electrotonic components but otherwise much of the equipment struck him as strange, exotic even.

Each lab had a couple of people working in it and, much like their machinery-based counterparts on the other side, appeared to be immaculately clean. Except, that is, for number four. Lab number four had a large swathe of speckled, oily-looking haze over the inside of the glass wall, as though something had sprayed across it.

"Well," began Maze, with something approaching a smile creeping across his face. "You said you liked cleaning."

Leon and Izzy, however, were now looking in the other direction. With their mouths open. From this raised vantage point, they had a clear view of the rest of the hangar, which turned out to be an immense cavern—part natural formation, part man-made, reinforced structure, with straight concrete walls on either side, and a row of thick columns that ran down the centre of the stadium-like enclosure at regular intervals—going back much farther than they could make out. It was also deeper by perhaps thirty or forty feet below the level they were standing on, with a metal safety rail running along edge of the floor area. And, on the far left-hand side, behind the workstations, was a set of metal stairs that descended out of sight.

This hangar was unlike anything either Leon or Izzy had ever seen before. Not just because of its size but because, right there, running neatly down one side of the hangar floor were what appeared to be twelve spaceships. Not NASA rockets, or variations on the space shuttle, but twelve extraterrestrial crafts of various sizes and configurations.

And while most of them were, yes, broadly saucer-shaped, from this high angle more than half of them looked, to Leon, more like huge, metallic, futuristic bagels—complete, in some cases, with a hole in the middle where technicians had apparently removed some mechanisms from the central section of the vehicles. In a couple of cases the detached componentry was sitting right next to its craft, on small scaffolded platforms.

"First time down in the crypt?" said Maze, with something of a paternal smile. "I can always tell."

"What?" replied Leon, not quite able to pull his gaze away.

"First time down here, I nearly crapped my pants," continued Maze, pride swelling in his voice. But then, after neither Leon or Izzy seemed much impressed with this confession, added, "but in a good way."

"Really?" responded Leon, finally. "There's a good way to crap your pants?"

"Sure. Well, you know what I mean. These babies are quite something to see, though, ain't they?" Maze began to laugh. "I love seeing people's faces the first time. Always the same. Hey, Sandy," Maze called across to his colleagues at the workbenches. A woman closest to them looked up. "We got ourselves a couple of newbies."

The woman shrieked with delight. "You two just in from Kansas?" she laughed. Leon and Izzy tried joining in, although without any real idea what was so funny. "Bob, let me give 'em the show. You did the last one."

"Sure, why not," agreed Bob, turning back to Leon. "Once they've cleaned up here. You two reckon you're up for a closer look?"

"Oh yah," said Leon, remembering why they were here. "I mean, who wouldn't, right?"

"OK then, back to business," said Maze, as he went to open the lab door.

A truly disgusting smell immediately slapped them all in the face, causing the trio to recoil.

"Yeah," acknowledged Maze, seemingly embarrassed by the stink, as though he personally had made it. "A bit of a biohazard, as they say. Sorry about that."

"What the hell is it?" asked Izzy, dreading being locked in a room with the awful fug.

"Uhm...classified," was all Maze would admit after a pause. "But safe enough. Grab me when you're done and I'll have Sandy take you down."

Leon and Izzy both nodded. Maze walked away and they slunk reluctantly into the foul-smelling hermetically sealed room.

42

MAC AND CHEESE

S teven Macintyre was in a breakout room at the rear of the main operations area, finishing up a tactical briefing with his team, when the door snapped open. It was Carson. He briefly noted the MP hovering behind her but dismissed it just as quickly.

"Lieutenant Macintyre," said Carson, bluntly, not moving any farther into the room. "A quick word, if I may."

"Sure," agreed Macintyre, lifting his foot off the chair he'd been leaning it on. "Just give me a moment to—"

"Now, please."

Macintyre's team descended into a jeering rabble at this, whooping and calling him out as though this was high school and he'd been summoned to the principal's office.

"I told you not to cheat on that term paper, boss," called out a man at the front.

"Alright, fellas, that's enough," said Macintyre, good-naturedly but clearly asserting his authority. "Back to work."

The group quickly grew quiet again as Macintyre reached the door. Carson greeted him with a thin smile and stepped back to let him through.

"What can I do for you, ma'am?" asked Macintyre, glancing

briefly at the MP, who stood to attention, staring into the middle distance.

Carson appraised Macintyre for a moment, waiting for the door to close, before addressing the MP directly. "Officer," was all she said. The MP stepped forward and placed his hand on Macintyre's upper arm.

"This way, sir," he said plainly.

"What the hell is this, Carson?" growled Macintyre, yanking his arm from the MP's grasp.

"Don't make a scene, Mac," instructed Carson. "And you can address me as Lieutenant Commander. You'll have plenty of time to lodge your protests. Officer, take him through to the brig."

"The brig!? Jeezus. Look, if it's about bringing the girl here, I know I broke protocol but I hardly think—"

"It's not about that, Lieutenant," snapped Carson, cutting him off. "Officer?"

Once again, the MP attempted to coerce Macintyre, and once again he pulled away.

"OK, alright. I'll come. Whatever this is, there better be damn good reason for it or I'm going straight to Snark. Your ice-woman routine might work with the others but I see right through it, *Lieutenant Commander*. Maybe it's time we finally discussed New Mexico," he threatened.

Carson's jaw tightened briefly, but she said nothing, then turned and led them away towards a large set of double doors at the back of the room.

When they arrived at the brig, Macintyre was checked in with the duty officer and placed in a holding room. Carson instructed the MP to wait with him, then left.

The officer took up position by the door, keeping his eyes firmly ahead. They didn't talk. More than an hour passed like this, in silence, with Macintyre chewing on various emotions from outrage and anger to confusion, frustration, and even amusement as he tried to sift through all the possible reasons that might have brought him here. It couldn't be his blunder with the English girl, however clumsy that may have been, or Carson would have acted much sooner. He knew that much.

But could something have come to light about Manchego's team, he wondered. Some anomaly about their failure that linked directly back to him, or a breach in Manchego's hack-job operational protocols that would finally throw him under the bus for good? It wouldn't be the first time. There'd been a lingering fog of suspicion following him and Manchego ever since the Guatemala screw-up in 2016, where several key targets and a large sum of cash disappeared. Manchego liked to play things loose, especially back then, and was often in the habit of kicking up shit for people around him. They may have been cleared at the time—officially— but that stink never leaves you in this business, Macintyre reflected. Maybe someone was able to make a connection, a link between himself and... But even if that were true, surely that could just be handled once this London incident was closed off? Priorities, and all that.

So, what did that leave? Could it finally be, he speculated— just as he'd intimated to Carson—about New Mexico? He thought they'd had an understanding. But, despite all assurances, he should have figured this day would come as soon as he'd laid eyes on those documents at the county archives. Except, after five years, would she really choose now, this moment, in the middle of an international crisis, to tackle it?

Perhaps he shouldn't be so surprised. He knew how she operated. She was well practised at playing the long game, just as those old files had suggested. Little Frances Carson—or Frances Cordova, as she had once been: a hick farm girl, with a past and a record she wanted to leave behind. He still admired how well she had hidden it all—and he'd told her at the time—behind her affected northeastern educated manners, her mother's maiden name, and an exceptional military track record. It can't have been easy. But, even so, she'd been able to ride Uncle Sam's pocketbook all the way to the centre of its rotten, black-on-black heart.

The door to the holding room swung open and Snark

marched in, followed by Carson and a slightly nerdy-looking man with flat, dark hair and thick glasses who introduced himself as his provisional legal counsel.

"I don't need legal counsel," protested Macintyre, waving the handshake away.

"Jesus Christ, Mac," began Snark, as he pulled up a chair and placed it across the table from Macintyre. "What the hell are you doing in here?"

"Sir?" responded Macintyre, for a moment taking Snark's question at face value. "I, well—"

"Don't interrupt me," yelled Snark, causing the lawyer to literally jump backwards and place himself awkwardly next to the immobile MP, looking like he might even grab hold of him for balance. Cason took up a more leisurely position in the corner and remained standing with her arms folded.

"How long have we known each other?" Snark continued. "Don't answer. Too damn long. I handpicked you, Mac, from that little chickenshit outfit you had going back east. I took you out of that sideshow and put you at the center of the most crucial operational theater this country has ever built. I nurtured you. I promoted you. I *trusted* you. And this is how you repay me!?"

Macintyre was reeling. He had no idea what Snark was talking about but he also knew the man wouldn't come down here to personally tear him apart for no good reason. He wanted to answer, but didn't know where to begin. In many ways Snark had been, just as he said, more than a mentor and it pained Macintyre to find himself unable to respond. Then Carson approached the table and saved him the trouble.

"Lieutenant Macintyre, we have good reason to believe you were instrumental in the sabotage of the London project. And, to speak plainly, if you want any hope of seeing daylight again, you better start talking."

Macintyre laughed. So that was it. He had no idea where this had come from but if this was the full extent of Carson's gambit, then it really was New Mexico time.

"Good reason? Come on, Carson. Surely you have more than *good reason* to drag me down here. Some evidence, for one thing."

"Cut the laughing clown act, Mac," said Snark. "We're not in Guatemala now. This is serious."

"Is this about Manchego? That guy. I should have canned him when I had the chance."

"Manchego is dead," said Carson.

"Yeah, well, that's never stopped him before."

"Sir, if I may?" enquired Carson to Snark.

"You may."

Carson walked over to a large wall monitor and flicked it on. She tapped a few on-screen items and the interface rearranged itself to present a number of layered documents and video files.

"What the hell is this?"

"You wanted evidence."

Snark observed Macintyre's expression as it registered genuine surprise. Whether it was because he had no idea what he was seeing or that he never expected something like this to come to light wasn't clear. It didn't really matter. In either case, this whole discussion and the implications of the evidence Carson was flicking through made him roil with discomfort and rage. There was a rat in the kitchen and his unforgiving need to eradicate it vied only with his feelings of complete betrayal. He had barely held it together when Carson had come to him before this meeting to take him through the documentation she'd evidently been assembling in secret.

"I had Milo run down the numbers."

He'd been able to channel it into surprise of his own as to why she hadn't mentioned it in their earlier discussion but only just. Carson had insisted that it was necessary, agreeing with Quinn that to have come to Snark too soon would have risked playing their hand, and giving Macintyre time to run for cover. The fact Quinn had reached a similar conclusion, she said, meant it was time to bring her own suspicions into the light.

"Evidence of what exactly?" Macintyre demanded to know.

"We have transmissions. At least seven separate encrypted messages sent over a period of six months to someone in our off-books Obsidian unit."

"That's it? It's my job to speak to these people. You do know that, right?"

"I'm not done. Yes, it's your job, but we have established protocols for that. As you know, all comms traffic in and out of our systems is uniquely encoded—for content, duration, user identification, and destination accounts. We can track every login, every keystroke, and every pause while you scratch your ass."

"Oh, I bet that's come in real handy," said Macintyre, folding his arms.

"You weren't clumsy, I'll give you that. You used different work-stations, different shift rotations, and you somehow managed to spoof the ID tracking to obscure both the login and the transmission. It would bypass any conventional system sweeps and if we weren't specifically looking for it, you could have gone unnoticed for years. I'm guessing you thought you'd be long gone before any of this came to light. But then we had a meltdown and you're stuck investigating yourself."

Snark was visibly fuming. His body language mirrored Macintyre's, leaning back in his chair with his arms folded. But whereas Macintyre seemed annoyed, petulant, frustrated, indignant even, Snark was clearly enraged, red-faced, and breathing hard, like a dam waiting to burst.

"If I was so damn clever," responded Macintyre, "then how in the hell can you possibly know it was me?"

"Entry codes, you goddamn double-crossing perfidious bastard!" exploded Snark.

"Alleged," offered the lawyer, meekly, who had by now slithered to a chair in the corner.

"What?"

"*Alleged* double-crossing perfidious bastard...sir," repeated the lawyer, ducking back behind his open briefcase.

"What the—" growled Snark, who started to rise from his chair.

Carson placed a calming hand on his shoulder, which he shrugged off but sat back down anyway.

"Yes, entry codes," said Carson, picking up the thread. "You forgot one little detail."

"My ID badge."

Macintyre's face seemed to sink with a look of confused resignation.

"That's right," confirmed Carson.

She clicked one of the video files that appeared to be looped CCTV footage of Macintyre using his badge to clock in and out of a number of security doors, then cutting to him at various different workstations—all time and date stamped in the top right-hand corner of the frame.

"We have checkpoints for a reason. From the gates on the main highway, to the restrooms at the end of the primary hangar bay, no one can simply move about this base unseen."

43

HACKING IT

Fortunately, Leon had taken the opportunity to grab the wheelie bucket when they passed the main entrance with Maze because once the lab door sealed behind them Leon and Izzy were confronted with a horrendously glutinous organic-looking mess spread over a large portion of the floor. It was hard to work out where it had come from exactly, or even what it was made of. The obvious candidate, based on the spray pattern, was a long steel workbench in the middle of the room. But there was nothing substantial on top of it, just more disgusting smelly goop.

"It looks a bit like an oversized autopsy table," said Izzy.

"Is that right, Agent Scully?"

"Funny. But look at it: built-in sink, taps, drainage channels. I wonder why it's so long?"

"You're not going to tell me you studied medicine as well?"

"No, no, but my friend Ava did. Does. She's specialising in forensic medicine. She took me down to the morgue once. It looked a lot like this room. Smelt a bit like it too, although not quite as disgusting."

"It looks like they dragged something off the bench," observed

Leon, pointing out some smeary drag lines of sludge streaked across one side.

He walked around the table to follow the pattern and could see that whatever it had been had dripped its way over to a large steel hatch mounted in the wall marked Biohazard. A steel handle ran across the top of the panel like an oven and there was a stack of three palm-sized push-buttons to one side marked Incinerate, Freeze, and Stop.

Just then there was a muted thumping on the glass wall behind them. They turned to see Maze standing on the other side. He was pointing to where Leon was standing and saying something that was impossible to hear properly through the thick, sealed walls. He then grinned and gave them a thumbs-up signal.

Leon and Izzy looked at each other then back to Maze. They returned his gesture and smiled back. Maze looked pleased with this result and raised his other thumb to match the first to signify success. He then turned and wandered off.

"I guess he really wants us to use this," suggested Leon.

"OK," began Izzy. "Why don't you make a start with cleaning up the...goo, whatever it is, and I'll check out that terminal over there. See what I can find out. Chuck me the keycard."

"Wait, so I clean up this repellent, sickening mess all by myself and you get to sit over there all nice and work the computer?"

"Happy to trade. How are your hacking skills Mr I-Can-Barely-Reset-My-Password?"

"Fair point."

Leon tossed Izzy the security pass, then walked over to the table, rolled up his sleeves, and began reluctantly spraying down the surface of the table using a retractable hose mounted into an attached sink unit.

Meanwhile Izzy used the keycard to log in to the computer and see what she could see. It quickly became apparent that the system was structured around federated gatekeeping. Presumably everything here was compartmentalised and need-to-know, she figured, as she tapped away at the keyboard, navigating the few menu trees available.

As Tyrone evidently only had Level 2 access, these were pretty much limited to Web, Settings, Help, and one special item— doubtless his only job-specific feature—Main Building Access. She tried Web first, just to see, but wasn't surprised to find it opened a locked-down browser application and a drab, poorly designed intranet; the main features appeared to be a live feed from the White House Briefing Room, along with a backlog of daily presidential news items, a new video update from The Office of Linden Snark, a calendar of upcoming actions, and an invitation to enter this month's Service Personnel Incentive Program (win additional canteen tokens just for signing up!). She declined to enter and likewise decided not to explore Tyrone's timesheets or request vacation for him, before closing the application window.

"Poor Tyrone," she sighed.

She tabbed through the remaining settings and, again, was confronted with some fairly useless items, though Building Access showed some promise. Again, his limited clearance meant there wasn't much in the way of things he could actually do on his own —primarily just check the listings of all personnel who had access to different areas of the base. In terms of actual functionality, he had powers to deny access to any individuals below Level 3, and request—not activate—access for new team members or issue restricted day passes for approved guests.

"Hmm," she muttered. It wasn't much to work with but the fact he could initiate something, even just a simple guest pass, gave her an idea. She went back to the settings menu and, using a couple of non-standard key commands, it didn't take her long to activate a buried command-line access terminal. This would let her sidestep the frontline user interface by entering code-based system commands directly and, depending on how deep the security protocols went, would theoretically give her access to other areas of the network. How much access would depend on how much the original system programmers anticipated a hack from within.

Leon had moved on to the floor around the main steel bench. Noticing there was a drain in the floor underneath the table, he thought he might get away with just using the spray but quickly realised the matter strewn across the floor was much lumpier and more glutinous. He looked about for something that might help with the onerous chore and noticed there were some steel-backed clipboards hung on the side of the bench. He decided he could use them as a makeshift scoop and began unenthusiastically scraping up wads of the monstrous red-and-brown crap and dropping it into the wheelie bucket (having remembered to remove Izzy's clothes and the gun of course).

"I hope you're having as much fun as I am," he said.

"Actually, I might be on to... Yes! I'm in," replied Izzy.

After testing out a couple of baseline *system calls* Izzy realised she could use the guest setup function to piggyback her way into the primary operating system and, from there, to the rest of the network. Naturally most of this was still heavily gated but to get started she only needed to trigger an IP tunnel to the outside world; that would allow her direct access to a specific address on her own private server and, from there, she was able to download a small command-line programme of her own design. This allowed her to use this terminal to navigate the rest of the base's network.

Leon happily stopped what he was doing and came over to see what Izzy had found.

"What have you got?"

"I think, maybe, I might have everything. I've got some security gates to get through for the really juicy stuff but, even so, I now have top-line access to a lot of their open comms, projects, and data feeds, including a bunch of live mission files. Look, here's something about London. See the date? That was initiated four days ago. That's us."

"That's great, Izzy but—" he looked up to see what everyone

outside the lab was doing. Maze was standing next to his lady friend, Sandy, and chatting animatedly about something. It looked a bit like he was flirting with her. "We may not really have the time to go through all this now. That guy will be back anytime soon."

"I don't need time. I'm going to set up a drain."

"What's that?"

"In hacking terms, it's small programme that will allow me to syphon off their data to another location."

"Are you crazy!? Don't you think we're in enough shit as it is? If they find you doing this, they'll kill you. Or worse."

"It's OK," said Izzy, placing a reassuring hand on his arm. "They won't find me. This kind of thing is almost impossible to set up from the outside, which is where most hackers usually get caught, but I'm not on the outside. I can install this cheeky little bit of code that will essentially drip-feed their data back to an external secure server a single byte at a time. Ones and zeros, Leon. That's all this is. It'll mingle with all their other outgoing traffic, like a bug on the windscreen of your car. It's a slow process, but that's the point. They won't even notice. And then, in a few days, we can begin recompiling."

"And then what?"

"Then nothing. This is about insurance, for us. That's all. To keep us alive."

"OK. Got it. I'm into staying alive."

"We can decide later if we want to do anything with it. Your friend Milk might want a look-see, for one."

"He might. Speaking of which, is there anything in there on the crystals that Milk could use?"

"There'll be something," began Izzy, as her hands moved back over the keyboard and began typing. "You better finish cleaning that crap off the floor before the guy comes back."

"Hmph. The glamour. Can't you set up a cleaning robot or something? I thought you were good at this stuff."

Izzy gave him a look.

"OK, OK." He held up his hands, went to return to his task, then stopped. "Wait a minute."

"What?"

"They promised us a tour, right?"

Izzy nodded.

"But we don't both have to go. It doesn't even make any sense for us to do that. I can do it. You stay here and finish...whatever it is. Then, if you set up a distraction while I'm down there, I'll grab the crystal and we're outta here. Somehow. See what you can find."

"I'm on it."

"I'll finish incinerating the sludge, then go outside and make up some BS about you being claustrophobic or something, and needing to finish up."

They set to work. Leon, scooped up as much of the stinky matter as he could and dragged it over to the biohazard unit. The door opened vertically to reveal a chute mechanism, into which he was able to feed the gory mess. He hit the incinerate button. A red light went on above it and there was an instant roaring sound, followed by sharp hiss of gasses escaping and the whine of a vacuum forming. The machine beeped. The light turned to green. He opened the door to see what had happened, releasing a chilled vapour into the air. Inside the unit was sparkling stainless steel clean. The whole thing had taken thirty seconds.

"Wow," exclaimed Leon. "We could use one of these in the office kitchen."

He thought of the grim calamity of mugs, dishes, and food waste that would build up there by the end of most days, and the regular emails from Lauren, reminding everyone to clean up after themselves. Then he remembered there was no office kitchen anymore.

He made two more trips like this as Izzy tapped away at the computer. He had just finished hosing down the last of the residue and was about to mop up the remaining liquid when Izzy called him over.

"I think found it," she said.

On-screen was a series of schematics, detailing the layout and some technical details of one of the ships. At the top right of the window was a file annotation that read: CE/I9I6951225I87 | OBJECT#5, GOBI DESERT, 1977. Izzy scrolled and panned about the main image.

"As you can see, it's a pretty simple circular configuration, on two levels. You want the top level, which is where you enter the craft. In any case, everything appears to be oriented around the central core—the engine, I assume. If it has an engine—with what seem to be some kind of control stations arranged at regular intervals around the clock, except in two areas." She pointed at the right-hand side of the plan. "One here, where you enter, let's call that six, and the other on opposite side–twelve o'clock— which, if I'm reading this correctly, is a structure that houses the crystal."

"Got it."

"It should be pretty straightforward. Walk on. Follow the floor ring around to the other side and bingo."

"Grab the rock and leave without being noticed. Sounds so easy."

"Doesn't it?"

Three levels up from where Leon and Izzy were considering the merits and relative ease of stealing an object from a top-secret government base, Macintyre, Snark, and Carson were sitting in momentary silence as Macintyre looked from one of his accusers to the other in complete disbelief.

"But this is ridiculous," said Macintyre, finally. "This just isn't true. I don't care what those logs say. Linden, please, you have to do something."

"My hands are tied here, Mac. What the hell did you expect— a pat on the back?"

"Lieutenant Macintyre," announced Carson. "I am placing you

formally under arrest pending further inquiry, where your obvious guilt will be clearly established."

"So-called obvious guilt is not strictly admissible, ma'am," suggested the lawyer.

"No, that's right, Stefan. Courts prefer the kind of guilt that dawns on you slowly the next day, after you've had a nice sleep and chance to think on it. Like a good movie."

"Uhm, that's not quite what I—"

"This is complete bullshit, and you know it," protested Macintyre, turning to look directly at his appointed legal counsel. "God knows what would have happened if you hadn't been here."

The lawyer nodded, went to say something, then clearly changed his mind and instead simply suggested, "We can pick this up afterwards."

Macintyre looked away dismissively.

"Bullshit or not, Mac, what I know for sure is we have a Level 6 security breach in this organization and, as a result, are now in the middle of a highly sensitive investigation of a catastrophic international incident in which, it turns out, you, your orders, and the people who work for you somehow form a central part. I need to find exactly what and why and we can't just have you roaming the halls, giving out tickets, while I do it—and you damn well know it. So, unless you have anything helpful to add at this point, we have real work to do."

"New. Mexico," said Macintyre, breaking off each word.

"What?"

"New Mexico. I think now might be a good time to discuss it, wouldn't you say, Lieutenant Commander Carson?"

This unexpected segue momentarily piqued Snark's attention, but he suspected Mac was just reaching. Then Stefan the lawyer woke up again.

"Lieutenant Macintyre, perhaps it would be best if we—"

Macintyre waved him away.

"Is this even relevant?" enquired Snark to Carson. "What's New Mexico got to do with anything?"

Then Carson, whose jaw was locked so tightly it looked like it might actually crack her teeth, managed to interject before Macintyre could say anything more.

"It's nothing, sir. Macintyre's babbling. He tried the same with me when I took him in. I can fill you in, if you require."

"That won't be necessary, Commander," agreed Snark, his patience for this decidedly uncomfortable and time-consuming situation having reached an end.

"Officer, remove this man and place him in a cell," ordered Carson.

The MP moved swiftly from the door and took out his cuffs to secure Macintyre, who visibly if stoically resisted as the restraints were locked into place.

"Linden," howled Macintyre as he was pulled back by the MP, his chair tipping onto its side in the process. "Sir! I can't believe you're just letting this happen. I would never—"

"Take him away, soldier," snapped Snark to the MP.

Macintyre was escorted briskly from the room, followed by his lawyer who scuttled after him like a labrador chasing a ball.

"Well, that was a complete shit-fest, Carson," growled Snark, picking up the fallen chair. "I was expecting you to have the situation more under control before bringing me down here. He had no idea what was going on, that much was clear."

"Indeed, sir. My apologies. I hadn't yet had the chance to bring him fully up to speed. I wanted to brief you first. And then you... Then we came straight here."

"You better be sure of your facts on this one, Commander."

"I am, sir," replied Carson.

"Because, if I didn't know any better, that felt a lot like an ambush. And what was all this New Mexico shit?"

"As I said sir, it's nothing. When I brought him down here, he tried to convince me there was a connection to a heavily sponsored survivalist cell based out of New Mexico, looking to initiate the 'Next Great American Revolution,'" explained Carson, adding air quotes at the end. "Something like that."

Snark roared with laughter.

"Survivalists? Does he expect us to believe that a bunch of redneck farmers and gun-loving kooks would be capable of... sponsorship or not, they couldn't even conceive of an intervention at this scale, much less carry it out. We've wasted enough time here. Keep Mac on ice until we've finished cleaning house and then we can get into it with him."

"Yes, sir."

"Where are we at with these two kids?" said Snark, opening the door and holding out his hand as an invitation for her to leave. She took it and he followed her out into a busy corridor.

"Just about to check in on that, sir. They're currently being—"

Just then her phone chimed. She looked at the screen, then gave Snark the I-have-to-take-this look. He nodded.

"Come find me when you're done," said Snark.

Carson acknowledged his request and he walked away. She lingered, watching him go as she answered the phone, unconsciously putting her free hand up to her other ear to close off the external noise.

"Yes?" she said. Then, after a moment of listening, exclaimed, "What?"

Realising she'd been quite loud, Carson looked around to see if anyone had noticed, then repeated herself much more quietly before setting off sharply in the opposite direction to Snark.

"Lock the infirmary wing down now. Nobody enters or leaves until I arrive."

44

CRYSTAL BALL

Leon sheepishly exited the lab, leaving Izzy to install her drain program and figure out a good distraction to cover their exit. He approached the workstations where it appeared Maze was still trying to chat up his colleague Sandy. To look at the two of them you'd think this guy was headlining at The Comedy Store, as Sandy seemed to find everything he said hilarious. But it was equally obvious to Leon that their co-workers at the other desks were much less impressed by him. Leon wondered if he might be risking some unwanted attention himself by suggesting a quick *house tour*, but then Maze noticed him and stood up from his perch on the edge of Sandy's desk.

"All done?" he said, stepping away from the desk and unconsciously buttoning his lab coat in an attempt to reassert a touch of formality.

"Almost. My, uh, colleague's just finishing up."

"Very good. Excellent. Sorry it was such a stinker." He made a face. "It happens."

Leon nodded sagely, as though he knew just what Maze was talking about but decided to move on. "I was just wondering... If it would be, you know, uhm, possible to..."

"A tour? Yes, of course. Sandy will take you down. It'll have to be a quick one though as we have some tests scheduled."

"That's no problem. We have a schedule of our own to keep."

"Of course, of course. How long will your co-worker be?"

"We don't have to wait. She told me to go on ahead. She's not" —Leon looked around, pretending to see if anyone else was listening, then dropped to a whisper—"really a fan of, you know... She's more of an...*American Made* kind of girl. She drives a Chevy."

Maze chuckled. "It's been a long time since you could really say that, about anything. But I get what you mean. Sandy, do you want take our friend here down to take a look at some of our, uh, classic cars?" he winked at Leon.

"Love to," said Sandy, springing up from her desk.

She directed Leon to the stairway by the wall and they headed down to the cavern floor where it quickly became apparent to Leon, as they walked along the centre of the hangar floor, just how big the spaceships were. He had expected them to be more like a large truck or small plane—and a few of them were—but most of them were more like 747s. Up close they looked insanely large.

"Man... They're so big," said Leon, pausing for a moment to take it in, and forgetting himself in the process. "Like giant boulders. Hard to believe they can fly."

"Where did you say you were from again?" said Sandy, seeming to eye him with a touch of suspicion. He realised his accent had dropped and quickly pivoted to provide some cover.

"You know, my mom was British. She thought everything over here was big." He snickered at the fake memory. "Even the UFOs it turns out. She woulda loved this."

Sandy smiled, her bubbling doubts assuaged for the moment. "UAPs," she corrected.

"What's that?"

"Don't they brief you guys anymore? Strictly speaking they're called UAPs nowadays - Unidentified Aerial Phenomena."

"Oh, yeah, sure. That makes all the difference."

They both laughed.

"How about this one?" asked Sandy, extending her hand towards one of the smaller craft on their right. "They may be different in size. But aside from a few special configurations, they're not really that different from each other."

"You seen one, you seen them all—is that what you're telling me?"

"Something like that."

The circular ship they were standing next to was not much wider than the length of a school bus. It sat on four stout legs that protruded from underneath that, in turn, was balanced on a clearly human-made scaffolded platform. Sandy flipped a couple of switches on a nearby portable console and an opening appeared in the otherwise seamless exterior, which extended out, like a ramp, from underneath the vehicle, unfolding from the central core of the ship.

"Make yourself at home," said Sandy.

Leon hesitated. He kind of thought she'd walk him in, given her earlier excitement, but now she seemed to be weirdly hanging back. What if she planned to lock him in there? He just hoped that Izzy was still in control of things upstairs. They'd estimated fifteen minutes from his descent before she was to start ringing some bells.

"Go ahead," urged Sandy. "It won't bite you."

Leon looked at her, then turned and began self-consciously making his way up the ramp. As he ascended the relatively short distance, he couldn't help but marvel at the singular smoothness of the vehicle. The metal shell—if it was metal—appeared to be just a single uninterrupted sheet of material, with no apparent seams or rivets or joins of any kind that he could see. Even where it split to accommodate the entrance ramp he was walking on, or for a series of what he assumed were lights along the outer edge, there was no obvious sign of componentry or mechanisms. It was unclear how one element fitted to another.

As he got closer to the actual entrance—as wide as but not as tall as an average door—he noticed a number of small, slatted vents in blocks of three that ran around the underside like a clock face. But even though there was a rounded rectangular border demarcating the edge of each block, the effect was the same: no joints, or screws, or welds that he could see. He reached out to touch one as he passed, and the surface felt more like incredibly smooth skin than metal. It had a warmth to it and even seemed to deform slightly under pressure, before returning to its previous state. It gave him the creeps, and his hand instinctively recoiled.

Then, just as he was about to cross the threshold, he felt something else, a tingling, slightly cloying presence of something he couldn't see. It seemed to envelop him as he pressed forward, almost as if he was pushing through a watery membrane. He immediately stepped back and shook himself off, feeling like he should be wet. But he wasn't. Sandy squealed with laughter.

"That's somethin' else, right? Not quite metal, not quite something organic."

"Not quite something I want to feel again. What is it?"

"Closest we've been able to tell, it's like a force field. Although I'll be damned if we can figure out what generates it."

"Really? How long have you had these things?"

Sandy placed a finger to her lips and made a *shush* sound.

"Above my pay grade. And yours, I'm pretty sure of that. They have their own sweet way of parcelling out information around here, and not all of it makes sense. But what I can say is, it's a lot longer than you think. You wanna go in or not?"

Leon made a face at the thought, but she was up the ramp like a rabbit, tugging on his sleeve.

"Come on, it's fine once you're through."

And a moment later she'd proved her point, as they passed the through the sticky, invisible field surrounding the ship.

"Eww," said Leon. "That does not feel good."

"You get used to it. But if you think that's weird, come see what they use as a toilet."

· · ·

Back in the lab Izzy was able to partially observe Leon's field trip by tapping into the security cameras. She hadn't been surprised to find the entire base was under constant observation in every room and at every door and intersection across the complex, but she was surprised that the main hangar—surely the home of their crown jewels—had such limited coverage. She suspected there may be an additional security subsystem she didn't have time to get into, but by her count she'd only been able to pull up six discreet camera feeds covering the entrance, storage area, labs, and workstations where Maze's gang were hanging out, and two views of the primary hanger deck—one looking forward from the upper level and another at the far end facing back. She was also surprised, given the size of the camera network, that they hadn't been picked up by now but took it as a sign that either most of the surveillance was passive, or that they were simply watching and waiting to see what she and Leon were up to before making their move. Izzy fleetingly imagined that Carson woman and a bunch of her goons appearing from behind a metaphorical curtain just as they tried to leave. *Surprise!*

She dismissed the thought and refocused on looking for something that would provide a good diversion. The fire alarm crossed her mind again but in a secret subterranean setting she couldn't assume they'd just file out neatly into the street. Especially as there was no street. Environmental controls? Would take too long. Main power? Getting back to the surface might be difficult. Trigger a system-wide reboo—wait a minute... She flipped back to Craft Management, where she'd found the schematics before. Clicking the main menu item brought up a full catalogue of the twelve ships they'd spotted below. Each one had a picture and a file annotation similar to the Gobi Desert ship, along with some associated schematic files. But there was something else she'd missed the first time: Operation and Maintenance.

"This can't be..." she muttered.

But it was. Clicking it opened up a new set of features and functionality that appeared to give her some limited remote access to the ships. Or at least three of them, as the other nine were greyed out and variously labelled Offline, Maintenance Mode, or System Error. However, one of the three was firmly lit up in green, reading Online. A quick double check with the camera feeds confirmed this was the one Leon was on. She clicked the status button and the screen updated to reveal a schematic overview of the ship, with a few key areas highlighted in green and amber and, underneath, a row of fluctuating data sets that could be adjusted with an up or down arrow. The bottom third of the screen was comprised of a series of physical controls for the ship: power levels, direction and attitude adjustment, altitude, and acceleration. Plus, an additional panel that read Transitional State, with a number of functions and dials that Izzy didn't recognise.

"Bingo."

Izzy glanced up from the screen to check that Maze or one of his gang wasn't about to barge in, and set to work.

Leon did his best to share Sandy's enthusiasm for extraterrestrial pooping but had to step away when her uncomfortably lurid description gave way to an equally needless mime. Some things are definitely better left unseen, he decided, and wondered just how long she'd spent down here studying these things.

"But there's more," insisted Sandy, as she dismounted.

"Oh, I think I've already seen more than I expected. But thanks. I probably need to be getting back. Mind if I just finish looking around before I go?"

"Uh, yeah, sure," agreed Sandy, with some disappointment. "I'll tidy this up. It's basically a circle, so you'll come back around. I'll meet you by the door."

No sooner had Leon set off than the ship suddenly seemed to power up, producing a subtle fluid sensation underfoot, like an elevator coming to a stop, and a hum that seemed to ripple through the ship—and him. He froze, placing his hand on the wall for balance, and waited to see if anything else was going to happen. But then the power surge seemed to drain away again just as quickly, dimming the ambient light-emitting walls in in the process.

"Hey are you OK?" shouted Sandy from the alien toilet.

"What was that?" called Leon in return, although he had a pretty good idea what that was, while praying that Izzy wouldn't accidently kill them.

Sandy's head poked out from the doorway. "That was not supposed to happen. Someone triggered the main power systems."

"And that's bad?"

"It isn't good. Not when we're inside the hangar, in inspection mode. I'll go take a look. You should probably finish up."

Sandy darted out of the loo and headed for the main door. As soon as she was out of sight, Leon headed in the other direction. He moved quickly around the central core, past a couple of unfamiliar panels and control surfaces until he located a more robust-looking floor-to-ceiling unit projecting out from the hub.

"This must be it," he murmured, as he examined a smooth, smoky glass panel occupying the central third of the front fascia. Again, there appeared to be no visible seams between the metallic part of the structure and the glass, if that's what it was. He touched the surface; it certainly felt like glass—hard and cold—but with a quality similar to the exterior of the craft, slightly distorting as he pressed it with his finger.

He could just make out a tall cylindrical appliance behind the translucent surface. It was recessed some way back, with a large octagonal donut-shaped mechanism in the middle, housing a faintly illuminated crystal-like object about the size of an orange. It seemed to shimmer and shift in place, as though it wasn't quite there.

The ship abruptly sprang back to life but more forcibly than before, causing Leon to stumble backwards as the floor dropped on one side. He was just able to stop himself from falling thanks to a rail above his head when he heard Sandy calling again from outside.

"Hey are you OK in there, buddy? You need to come out now."

"I'm OK," called Leon, fretting slightly that he wouldn't get another crack at this. "I'm coming."

The quiet hum had also returned, pulsing steadily as the ship gently returned to the horizontal, seeming to rebalance itself. Leon noticed that the light emanating from the crystal ebbed in time with the sound, as he ran his fingers around the edge of the glass panel looking for a lip, or a switch, or anything he might use to open it. Then he spotted a small round-cornered rectangle right above where the glass fused with the metal surface. It looked similar to the ones he'd seen outside but instead of three vents there was a configuration of geometric lines and dots that seemed to relate to one another. A label, perhaps, thought Leon, as he reached up and instinctively placed two fingers on it. The shape glowed briefly under his fingertips and then, a second later, the translucent surface slipped downwards with a gentle hiss but not into any kind of slot that Leon could make out. It just got smaller until it disappeared completely.

"Do you need help?" came Sandy again. "I'll come up."

"No," shouted Leon, too quickly. But before Sandy could react, the ship suddenly lurched hard to one side, throwing Leon off his feet this time.

"Whoa, Izzy," he said aloud. "What are you doing?"

He tried to pick himself up when the floor pitched again in the opposite direction, rising up rapidly to meet his face. His cheek and mouth smooshed against the hard floor as he fought against the upward force of the vehicle, and he was reminded of his rude awakening just a few days before.

Outside Sandy was shouting and frantically tapping away at her control panel as she watched the craft scoot sideways off its stand, knocking the scaffold to the floor, and then rise vertically in a straight line a second later, before stopping just short of the high ceiling.

This triggered a proximity alert, which fired off a siren and string of amber warning lights that strobed their way around the hangar walls.

"It'll be OK! Hang in there!" shouted Sandy, although she had no idea whether Leon would be OK, since according to the dials, the inertial compensators were offline. She pictured him squashed into a pancake as she hammered at the comms switch, trying to get Maze's attention.

"Bob! Bob, are you seeing this? We have an unsanctioned craft excursion. Are you doing this?"

"I'm not doing it," he shouted back over the radio. "I thought you were."

He ran from his desk to the rail along the edge of the upper gallery and watched helplessly as the craft seemed to fling itself randomly about the giant cavern, somehow narrowly missing the walls, the central columns, and the other craft.

"The cleaner's onboard," hollered Sandy.

"What!?"

"The cleaaan-errr! I can't get the compensators online."

"Oh Jesus," snapped Maze, jumping back to his workstation and furiously tapping in commands. Some of his colleagues took his spot by the railing to see what was going on until Maze looked up. "What the hell are you all doing?" he yelled. "Get back to work!"

His team scattered back to their stations like bugs from under a rock.

Izzy could hear the commotion outside and began typing faster, certain she'd get busted at any minute, as she toggled one switch and then another trying, like Maze, to get it to stop. She wanted a distraction, not a train wreck. She hadn't been certain her idea would even work but also found herself slightly confused, as she was sure from Leon's description that the crystal was needed to control the power. And if he had the crystal then... Oh.

"Crap."

Inside the ship Leon was getting tossed about like pocket change in a tumble dryer, sliding across the slick floor from one side to the other, then falling into a clumsy pile of arms and legs as the ship took off in another direction. He thought he might be about to throw up when the ship abruptly came to a halt.

"Ohhh man," he groaned, grabbing at a seat-like pedestal fixed to the floor and taking a moment to catch his breath. At least he assumed it was a seat. He really had no idea. Nor was he certain if they had actually stopped moving, as the inside of his head continued spinning in every direction. Either way, he didn't think he had much time before someone unfriendly came and took him out of there.

He crawled painfully over to the cabinet where the crystal was presumably still doing its thing and cautiously got to his feet, holding fast to the unit's unfeasibly smooth edges for balance. The large gem appeared much brighter now without the glassy shield but the drifting in and out of focus persisted. For a brief moment, Leon wondered whether it would be safe to touch but dismissed the thought as he reached in anyway and snapped it out of its cradle. The overhead lighting immediately dimmed and the ship, which unknown to Leon was suspended close to the hangar ceiling, dropped like a stone.

45

PANCAKE MIX

By now Izzy was caught up in the horror show of what she had started but didn't seem able to stop. It wasn't clear how, but she seemed to have triggered some kind of shakedown programme—a pre-configured set of stark manoeuvres that the ship was now trying to exercise in the limited space available. But even as she fumbled to wrest back control, Izzy couldn't help but be impressed by how the ship seemed to exhibit a kind of environmental self-awareness, as it zip-zapped its way around the web of support columns, hanging gantry ways and pipes, uneven walls, rock formations, and, of course, the other ships and yet avoided touching any of them.

Forget all the military applications, she thought, if they could just get that one feature to work in cars alone, imagine all the lives that would be saved? What the hell have they been doing down here all this time? It felt like such a waste.

Her thoughts were sharply interrupted by muffled shouting coming from outside the lab, and quickly realised that whatever she was trying to do, Maze and his team must by now be doing the same thing. If anything, she was probably just making things worse, and it wouldn't take them long to notice.

She surrendered her hands from the keyboard, got up, and

walked over to the lab's glass wall just in time to see the ship slow to a sudden but gentle stop high up in the cavern's ceiling. Izzy let herself feel a great sense of relief; perhaps Leon would be safe after all. Then she screamed as the ship's light-emitting skin suddenly dimmed and the whole thing dropped out of sight.

At that same moment, Sandy finally managed to flip on the inertial compensators, yelping as the indicator toggled to green. This not only saved Leon the trouble of dying prematurely but also saved the ship (and him) from being pasted across the hangar floor. She watched as it fell sharply and then, at the very last second, pulled to an improbable stop an inch from the ground. She activated the landing system and three angled pillars emerged from underneath the craft, pushing it gently up into a parked position, some five or six feet up. The door-shaped aperture slid open and the ramp unfolded, meeting the ground towards the outer edge of the ship.

A moment later, Leon tumbled into the opening and staggered down the ramp, like the proverbial sailor on leave. Sandy ran over to meet him.

"Oh my God, are you OK?"

Leon held up a just-give-me-a-minute hand. She guided him over to the control area where he could take a seat next to the main console, and went to grab some water from a nearby cooler while he caught his breath and waited for his head to stop spinning.

"Thanks," he said, weakly, taking the small cup of water and drinking it down in one hit.

"Do you have any idea how lucky you are?" said Sandy.

"I don't feel very lucky," responded Leon, clutching at his right arm, which ached noticeably more than the rest of his horribly aching body. "What the hell was that?"

"You know, I really have no idea. We have safety protocols for that kind of thing."

"Oh yeah?"

"Oh yeah," said Maze, definitively, as he suddenly appeared

next to them, trailed by a bunch of his troubled-looking acolytes and, some distance behind them, Izzy, who was rattling down the metal stairs, a cloth and a bottle of cleaning spray in hand. "What the hell, Sandy?"

"You think that was me?" barked Sandy, looking genuinely hurt.

"Who else?"

"Jesus, Bob. How can you...? I opened the doors, let him have a look around—that was it. I've done it a thousand times."

Maze walked over to the main console and started to hit the controls, clumsily, like a toddler playing with a My-First-Kitchen toy.

"Well, I sure as shit didn't set that to go off. And it wasn't any of these clowns." He swept his arm across the group behind him, who immediately began trading puzzled he-must-mean-you expressions with each other, like a pack of lab coat-wearing penguins.

Izzy hovered at the back of the group, trying to get Leon's attention with a wide-eyed did-you-get-it raise of the eyebrows, and Leon responded with a subtle nod and a we-should-probably-get-out-of-here-side-eye look of his own. He pushed himself painfully from the seat and attempted to shuffle off quietly behind Maze, as the pack drew in awkwardly to watch the man play.

"I think we should probably leave you to it," suggested Leon to Sandy, with a gentle thanks-for-everything squeeze of the shoulder. She cut him a glance and a brief smile in return.

"Sure. And again, really sorry about—"

Leon waved her apology away. "It's fine. Good luck with all the, uh...stuff."

But Sandy's attention was already gone.

Leon and Izzy circled around the edge of the group, fleetingly grabbing hands as they met and turned back toward the stairs and the way out.

"Well now, isn't that sweet," declared Carson, stepping out from behind the supporting scaffold of a much larger craft just ahead of them. She was accompanied by two of Macintyre's former tactical unit, who had perfected the standard henchman blank look, while clutching semi-automatic weapons securely across their chests.

"Frances," said Izzy, disarmingly, as though she were running into an old friend at a party.

"Isabella," countered Carson, with much less warmth. "And Mr Aronofsky, I presume? I don't believe we've had the pleasure."

Leon smiled awkwardly and held out his hand. "Leon."

"I don't think so," said Carson, as she stepped forward, declining to take up his greeting.

Leon and Izzy shuffled backwards to try to maintain the distance, while Maze's group parted to let them through until their backs were against the main console next to Maze, who finally looked up to see what was going on.

"Ah, Commander, you're here," he began. "Excellent. Although you really should have let me know you were coming. We've had a bit of a situation."

"I should say you have," replied Carson, bluntly. "And when were you planning on telling me about it?"

"Well, I, uh...after we, that is to say, once I had—"

"Covered everything up?"

"No, of course not."

"Never mind. We'll discuss it later—along with why you thought it was OK to let two unknown Level 2 support staff have first-hand access to our primary operational area," said Carson, indicating Leon and Izzy standing left and right of the work-station.

Maze looked momentarily confused. His open mouth wavered as he gathered his reply, but Carson jumped in before he could say anything.

"Take your people and return to your stations. I expect a full report, Dr Maze, in one hour. And your resignation. I'll decide then which to accept."

"Ma'am, if I may. I just need to—"

"Now, Doctor."

The guards stepped to either side of the group and used their weapons as less-than-casual pointers to direct them back towards stairs. The penguins shuffled off obediently, muttering quietly among themselves as they went, reluctantly followed by Sandy, and then Maze. He paused briefly by Carson as though to say something else but quickly thought better of it as her expression darkened. He bowed his head and scuttled off after Sandy like a good little scientist.

Leon and Izzy meanwhile had taken the opportunity to step around the edge of the boxy workstation so that it formed a barrier of sorts between them and Carson's unwelcome wagon.

"You know, I have to hand it to you," said Carson, finally, when she was sure the others were out of earshot. "It's not easy to navigate your way down here, even when you have permission to do so. Much less by accident."

Leon looked at Izzy, then back to Carson who stood facing them unsympathetically, with her arms firmly crossed.

"Well, we just kind of pressed 'down' in the lift," offered Leon. "We thought it might take us to the street."

Carson regarded him with some obvious doubt.

"I'm not sure—" began Izzy.

"Let's just cut the shit, shall we? Whatever you're doing down here, you had help. I want to know who. And I want to know now. Or we can just dispense with the pleasantries and my friends here will take you out the back"—she nodded to the far end of the hangar bay—"and shoot you."

Izzy glanced down and noticed that Maze had left the fleet's primary controls unlocked and in full diagnostic mode.

"You seem to be forgetting our arrangement," replied Izzy, placing her hands as casually as she could on top of the console to hide it from Carson, while nudging Leon with her foot.

Carson let out a caustic laugh, "Arrangement!"

"That's the way out, then, is it? The back of the hangar?" enquired Leon, with faux innocence. "Izzy, you were right to come down here."

Carson seemed genuinely troubled by this question. Could he really be this stupid?

"No, Mr Aronofsky. That is not the way out. Not unless you want to leave here in a box."

"I can't say I really fancy that."

"I didn't think so. Any other pointless questions on your mind, or shall we get on with it?"

Izzy slowly moved her fingers across the touch screen while they talked, pulling up the ship inventory and power status, double-tapping Leon's foot to keep it going.

"You know, if you don't mind me saying, you seem very angry," suggested Leon. "I mean, we've only just met."

Carson let out a sigh and looked at her watch. She understood these two were effectively civilians and that playing nice might be more effective than going straight for the gun to the head. After all, fear of death can paralyse as well as motivate, but Aronofsky was really pushing it.

"No, I'm not angry. I'm busy. I have responsibilities you cannot begin to imagine. And I don't have a lot of time."

Carson signalled the man on her left, who took three steps forward, yanked Leon into a neck hold, and placed his service revolver against Leon's temple.

Despite her intense fear, Izzy used the distraction to activate three of the ships. A subtle but palpable electrostatic hum roiled around them then quickly retreated as Carson looked about to see where it was coming from. She turned her attention back to Leon who was now squirming and shouting.

"Whoa. Hey, get off me," shouted Leon, fidgeting awkwardly under the soldier's iron grip. "What are you doing?"

"What I should have done from the start," replied Carson, turning her attention back to Izzy. "Miss Jones. We may have an arrangement, as you put it, but as far as I'm concerned, your friend here is not part of it. So, I'm going to make this very simple for you: tell me why you are down here and who helped you, or I shoot your friend. And then we'll get to work on you. There are worse things than being killed, I assure you."

"Why the hell are you doing this?" said Izzy, moving her hands carefully back across the screen as she spoke.

"Yes," muttered Leon, through clenched teeth and the henchman's headlock. "Why are you doing this? It's really very uncomfortable."

"I mean, what are we to you?" continued Izzy. "Nothing. Nobodies. We were in the wrong place at the wrong time and that's it—just as I explained to you. Three times. And yet you seem to have some fixation on—"

"Twenty-three years."

"What?"

"You have no idea what we're doing here, do you."

"Hiding alien spaceships from the rest of the world?" said Leon.

"Spaceships," she scoffed. "Is that the extent of your imagination? It took me twenty-three years getting here. To this place. And you have no idea what it took—what I had to do—to pull myself out of a no-name shithole you can't imagine, just for a chance at the US Naval Academy. Never mind the seventeen years of eating more shit and saying thank you that followed. And you think that it's just about spaceships?

"Don't be so naive. I lead one of the most important operations ever undertaken by any institution in the history of this country—maybe even the world. A place so important, by the way, that not even the president himself knows it exists. And yet you two wander in here like a couple of vacationing teenagers in a shopping mall, buying useless junk for your equally useless friends back home. You think I'm just going to let you come in and piss over everything I've worked for just because you got drunk at some party?"

"Technically," mumbled Leon stoically, "you brought us here. We would have been quite happy to stay at home with our hangovers and watch *Columbo* on the telly."

"We were just trying to get out of here," added Izzy. "You would have done the same."

"I wouldn't have done the same, Miss Jones. I wouldn't have taken things that didn't belong to me and then tried to use them for blackmail."

"Oh right," growled Leon. "Sure. You would have just rolled over like a puppy. Or is your seventeen years of shit-eating just a nice story?"

"Travis?"

Travis, who turned out not to be a question but the man gripping Leon around the neck, took this as his cue to pull back the trigger on his gun and push it harder into Leon's head. He looked at Carson and awaited the signal, while Leon pulled and yanked at the arm of his immovable captor.

"Jeezus," he squawked.

Izzy punched a large dark green switch labelled Activate at the top of the screen. Seven of the twelve craft icons below lit up in turn and, for just a second, there was a muted, electrified silence, as seven alien power systems went online at once. The three of them looked at each other. Then, just as Carson went to speak, the hangar erupted into a booming, technology-defying chaos.

All seven active ships yanked instantly away from their scaffolded platforms, scattering the supports, poles, and beams behind them like a handful of straw. The noise of the collapsing metal structures was deafening as the ships pulled away in different directions and began performing a series of mindbending geometric manoeuvrers, cutting across and around each other at unfathomable speeds for such an enclosed area. A siren began wailing, and the emergency orange lighting kicked back in.

Travis reflexively let go of his grip as the uproar began and Leon didn't wait to be asked before heaving himself away from the man's monstrous arms. He dropped to the ground and pulled Izzy down with him, just as a thick metal pole sheared its way past like an iron javelin, taking some fleshy parts of Travis with it. The rest of him fell to the ground in a bloody heap where Leon had been standing only a second before.

They managed to push themselves under the workstation just as the last of the collapsing metal pieces came to a rest. Above them the hum and swish of extraordinary otherworldly vehicles continued and, beyond that, the shouts and cries of Maze's team as they presumably rushed to put an end to Izzy's unplanned lab experiment.

"What the hell did you do?" said Leon

"I'm not sure. I kind of pressed everything and hit go."

They looked at each other and then, grimly, at the bits of Travis spread out on the floor in front of them.

"Good job," nodded Leon. "Let's get out of here before his friends start showing up."

They stuck their heads out either side of the console to find the area around them was a mess of deconstructed scaffold, like a life-size version of Pick-up Sticks. Staying on their hands and knees in case the craft weaving above them clipped the mad nest of metal poles and supports surrounding them, they made their way carefully forwards, doing their best to avoid Travis's remains. They quickly came upon the prone bodies of Carson and her other henchman, partially obscured by a couple of intersecting pylons. One of the pylons had apparently buried itself into the back of the man's head, while Carson, though trapped by a long beam across her back, appeared to be physically unharmed. Leon noted that, unlike her companions, she was still breathing. Presumably unconscious.

Izzy gave him a look. "Should we...?"

"Are you kidding me?"

"Sorry," replied Izzy, shaking her head. "Habit."

"She has people. I'm sure she'll be fine, once they can get to her."

They continued on, crawling for the most part, or climbing

carefully over, under, and around the fallen structures, until they'd cleared the main area. Even then, they stayed low to avoid the spacecraft that continued to swoop and buzz above them. Once free of the chaos, they made their way across a narrow perimeter walkway to the stairs that led to the mezzanine above. They took shelter in the space under the metal steps and, crouching with their backs to the wall, looked back across the cavernous space to watch the most unlikely airshow anyone had ever seen.

"Who are we ever going to talk to about this? No one would believe it if we tried."

"I look forward to being able to try," said Izzy, apprehensively. "It means we survive."

"Oh shit," yelped Leon. "Quinn."

Izzy then gave him a very different kind of look.

"I'm doing it, already," he said, holding up his hands. He unclipped the radio Quinn had given him, along with instructions that holding down the send button would produce a squawk of white noise across the network. All Leon had to do was perform the agreed tapping code ("On no account should you try to speak. It could get me killed. And you. Very quickly."). In this case, three sustained clicks, followed by three rapid ones: we have the object, send instructions.

"Is that it?" asked Izzy.

"Security," he replied. Like that explained everything.

"You aren't going to speak to him?"

A long moment passed, as he regarded a confused and frustrated Isabella Jones in awkward silence. Then, suddenly, her patience seemed to run out and she went to grab the radio.

"I'll speak to him," she snarled.

"You can't," replied Leon, pulling the radio away from her grasp.

"What are you doing?"

She stretched again for the walkie-talkie, and again Leon held it out of her reach. Then Izzy lunged at him, pushing him onto his back.

"Give. Me. The radio," she insisted. But still he kept his arm outstretched and away from her clutching hand, even as she writhed and climbed over him to get at the device. Leon fought her advance, pushing himself awkwardly along on his back by twisting under her weight and stiffly paddling his heels on the hard concrete floor.

"Stop, Izzy," he called out from under her.

"You stop," she said, angry now and actively fighting his resistance. "Gimme the radio."

"No. You can't. You'll blow his cover," he shouted in return.

But she wasn't listening and, shifting her weight as he tried to slide out from underneath, sat up with her knees either side of his thighs, and started pounding his chest with her fist.

"I need to get out of here, Leon." Her anger shifted into something else.

"Whoa," said Leon. He let the radio drop behind his head and caught her fist before she could land another blow. She lifted her other hand to compensate, but he grabbed that too and she immediately began pulling and struggling to free her hands from his grip.

"What the hell are you doing, Izzy?"

Suddenly all the fight went out of her, and her hands dropped.

"I need to get out of here," she repeated, her voice beginning to crack. "I killed those people. I killed them, Leon. I need to…" her voiced drifted away and her eyes closed.

Realising finally what was really going on, Leon let go of her wrists and gently pulled her to him instead, letting her head come to a rest on the chest she had been thumping only a moment before.

"I killed those men, Leon," she whispered.

"You didn't kill them," he responded, softly stroking her head.

"Didn't you see what happened to them?"

"Oh, I saw alright. I saw two dead people who were just about to shoot me in the head. And then probably you too, once you'd given that woman what she needed."

Izzy breathed quietly, her face lit up intermittently by the strobing emergency lighting and the otherworldly craft passing by.

"I think I'm done with all this," she said, wiping the dampness from her eyes. "I just want to go home."

"I know," said Leon. "Me too. We'll get there. I promise."

Leon's radio suddenly came to life. Two noisy clicks. Then two more.

"Stand by," came Quinn's hushed voice over the speaker.

"And there's our ride," said Leon.

46

SCOOBY-DOO

S nark stepped up to the balcony running along the front of his office. He clutched the rail and his knuckles were white. Behind him stood Quinn, observing passively, as they faced the giant mission control screens on the opposite wall, and looked over the workstations below. Snark's face, lit intermittently by the orange emergency lights, wasn't a happy one.

"Deck Officer!?" he shouted. Partly because of the din of the alarm but mostly because he was furious. "Deck Officer!"

A uniformed woman standing over a station below, conferring with two seated colleagues, jerked her head up to see where she was being called from. She snapped to attention as soon as she saw it was Snark.

"Sir?"

"Turn that damn noise off."

The officer, Keynes, looked over at a man to her right and made a slashing motion at her neck. A moment later, the klaxon stopped its wailing.

"About goddamn time," bellowed Snark, mostly to himself, as he turned and headed down the stairs to his left. Keynes moved away from her post and headed to meet Snark as he stepped onto the main floor, quickly followed by Quinn. They assembled next to a harried-looking junior analyst who did his best to pretend to look busy, despite the loud, high-ranking conversation unfurling next to him.

"What the hell's going on?" demanded Snark. He could see what was happening on the screens as well as anybody but as always preferred facts over speculation. "There's no drill planned for today."

"No, sir," replied Keynes. "We seem to have a situation."

"No shit we have a situation. Like we needed another one. Is that all you've got?"

"We're still gathering data, sir, but I've spoken to Maze. It was an unplanned test of the fleet, he maintains. But his team is all over it."

"Is that right? Unplanned or... Where's Carson?"

"Sir?"

Snark rubbed a hand over his face and sighed. "It's a simple enough goddamn question, Keynes. We have a master alarm going off. Where is she?"

"Nobody knows, sir," replied Keynes, taking a step back sheepishly.

"What do you mean *nobody knows*?"

"She went to investigate something in Hangar 17 not long before the alarm sounded and hasn't reported in since."

"Hangar 17..." repeated Snark, shifting gears. "What the hell was she doing down there? We're still in the middle of cleaning up the London incident. Quinn, what do you know about it?"

Quinn's radio kicked out a series of static clicks at the same moment, and he felt momentarily snared by the competing demands for his attention.

"Well?" repeated Snark, impatiently.

He decided to act dumb, which wasn't far from the truth. He couldn't be sure why Carson would be down there—an unlikely coincidence at best—and whether that represented a material danger to Leon and Izzy, despite the coded signal suggesting otherwise.

"Me, sir?"

"Yes, you. Jesus. Do I have to have to get out and push this thing uphill myself?"

"No, sir," said Quinn, calmly. "Of course not. It's just... Perhaps I should go and investigate?"

"As a matter of fact, yes. I want you to go and find out. Carson has no business being down there today, and we certainly don't need any more underhand BS after Mac's unilateral bid for emancipation. But I'm concerned this action may have...additional implications. I'm putting the base on silent lockdown until we find out what's going on. No one in or out. No external comms. Nothing. Keynes, see to it."

"Yes, sir."

Keynes scurried away to carry out her orders. Quinn hesitated.

"What are you waiting for," said Snark. "A goodbye kiss?"

"Just wondering if I should take a team with me."

Although he really wasn't wondering and didn't want to, as it would be yet more people to lose. But it was protocol. Fortunately, Snark seemed to be on his wavelength.

"Let's just keep it small for now, shall we? And when you're done there, I want you to check on our...guests. Carson was getting a bit frothy with them earlier, and whatever she may think they've done—even if she's right—they're still civilians."

"Understood, sir," agreed Quinn, pleased with this additional leverage, and he turned to leave.

"And Greg?"

"Yes, sir?" said Quinn, turning back.

"Don't fuck it up."

Quinn left the mission area and jogged down the busy corridor to the main elevators, signalling to Leon to stand by as he waited for the elevator to arrive. Certain that Snark would be monitoring events closely, he needed to demonstrate appropriate intent and took the elevator down to the hangar level while he considered the best way for everyone to come out of this in one piece.

The lockdown was an additional challenge he hadn't antici-pated, but perhaps it was also an opportunity he could exploit, assuming he could set things up right and Leon didn't blow it. He tapped his earbuds to make sure they were on and called him again on the radio as he exited the elevator and headed for the main hanger bay.

"Leon, are you there? Come in."

The line crackled then Leon answered. "Thank God," he said. "We thought stand by was all we were going to get."

"Where are you?"

"We're still in the bloody hangar. It's a literal train wreck down here."

"Are you hurt?"

"No, we're fine. Just trapped. There's no way out that doesn't involve us getting shot."

Sitting up now, under the stairs, with their backs against the wall, Izzy nudged him:

"Tell him about Carson."

"There was a woman. Carson—"

"I know," interrupted Quinn.

"You know?"

"Yes, I know."

"He knows," said Leon to Izzy.

She nodded. "But does he know she..."

"She might be dead," blurted Leon.

"Shit."

Quinn stopped walking. He could see additional guards had been posted outside the hangar doors at the far end of the corri-dor, and mentally added them, along with a potentially dead Carson, to the list of problems he had to deal with.

"She's dead? How?"

"I said *might*. May-be-dead. She certainly wanted to kill us. She tried to—"

"Is she dead or not, Leon?" barked Quinn, louder than he meant to, causing the guards to look his way. He waved them to stand down, then turned away to speak more quietly. "It makes a difference to how things play out from here."

"Well, her friends are definitely dead. And if she isn't... Look, Greg, she wanted to kill us, OK? We did the best we could to avoid that and we got lucky. She didn't. We didn't wait to give her a health check. Are you going to help us or not?"

The guards seemed to be taking more of an interest in Quinn, and why he was hanging around a highly restricted area during a lockdown. One of them left his post and began to approach.

"OK, Leon. Alright. I get it. Here's what I need you to do," said Quinn, before providing them details of an off-the-cuff exit strategy via an emergency stairwell at the back of the hangar. Presumably the one that Travis had planned to use as a murder room, only thirty minutes earlier.

"And remember," he continued. "The base is now on lockdown. No one officially knows you're on the loose yet, but it won't take long. Don't go off-plan or try anything funny until you get my signal."

Quinn then proceeded to redeploy the guards—on Snark's orders—before entering the hangar itself. Naturally, they both made an initial show of loyalty to Carson by attempting to stick around, but Quinn didn't have to insist very hard to make them leave.

Once inside it became clear that Maze and his team had manged to bring the technical exercise, as it would later come to be called, under control. The previously active ships were now quite stationary at various heights and locations around the stadium-like space, with a couple at the far end just coming to a sharp but gentle halt as he walked in. The overall effect was quite eerie, thought Quinn. Like an array of giant sci-fi-themed Christmas decorations with the tree suddenly removed. Maze approached Quinn as he made his way across the concourse toward the workstations.

"Quinn, thank God it's you," began Maze, directly. "And not one of Mac's regular goons."

"I guess I'll take that as a compliment."

"You should."

The two men shook hands.

"What the hell have you been doing down here, Bob?" said Quinn, making a show of peering out across the hangar floor. "The old man is not happy about it. Not today."

"Oh God," responded Maze. "He's really going to fire me this time, isn't he?"

"You know he might. And who could blame him? After the past seventy-two hours, losing our jobs might turn out to be the least of our worries."

Maze immediately started to wring his bony hands as he glanced over to his team and then back to Quinn, speaking more quietly this time.

"You really have to do something, Greg. Between you and me, I think we were hacked."

Quinn started to laugh. "Hacked? Is that what you're going with?"

"You don't think it's possible?"

"Possible, yes. Always. But likely? And here, in this place? You know the only way that's plausible is with some kind of complicity or compromise from the inside, and either way you come out covered in stink. Snark will start handing out prison time like candy."

"I know, I know. It's just that... We had some kind of a breach down here. Did you know that? A pair came in posing as a maintenance crew. Carson was dealing with it personally."

"Yes, that's why I'm here," lied Quinn. "Now where is she?"

Maze looked even more uncomfortable, if that were possible.

"Better if I show you," he said, and led Quinn over to the waist-high guard rail running along the edge of the research area and overlooking the main hangar.

"Jesus, Bob, when you throw a party..."

From this high vantage point, the carnage of busted scaffolding, platforms, poles, and equipment looked like someone had chucked a concussion grenade into the middle of the floor. No overt material damage, but everything not bolted to the floor was busted apart like a hurricane had torn through the place.

"I know, it's a real mess. Fortunately, the ships can hover there indefinitely while we clean the place up."

"Fortunately," repeated Quinn. "And Carson's somewhere down there?"

"Presumably. We...uhm...haven't had a chance to investigate."

"Well, let's hope she's not dead, eh, Bob?" said Quinn, unimpressed with Maze's priorities.

"Of course, of course," replied Maze, awkwardly. "We'll get straight on it."

"Forget it. I'll go take a look myself. In the meantime, I want your team to conduct a damage assessment and organize a cleanup crew A-SAP. But nobody comes down until I've cleared it."

"Yes, sir," agreed Maze.

Quinn headed towards the stairs leading down to the hangar floor when Maze called after him.

"Uhm...sir?"

"Yes?" said Quinn, looking back.

"There is one other thing."

"I'm listening."

Maze walked over to Quinn and lowered his voice conspiratorially.

"We have a prime system error on one of the ships."

"Meaning?"

"Well, we can't be sure without checking physically, but we think a control unit has been physically removed," said Maze, with some expectation that Quinn would know what he was talking about. Quinn merely raised his eyebrows in anticipation.

"It's possible one of the, uhm, fake maintenance people took it. Without that, it's useless. Just a ton of exotic material. If someone were to get their hands on it…"

"I get it," said Quinn, not really getting it, but assuming this was the item Leon came for. "I'll take a look."

Maze nodded gravely and Quinn headed down.

Once below, he began to comb carefully through and around the wreckage, but it didn't take long for him to locate Carson and her thugs. Or what was left of them. Movement at the far end of the hangar caught Quinn's eye and he looked up just in time to catch a utility door closing. Leon and Isabella, he had to assume, and left it there as Carson began to groan.

"Frances?" said Quinn, gently. He moved across to where she was lying face-down, with her head towards him, and placed a hand on her neck. Her pulse was slow but steady. She made another noise, this time it sounded more like words, more like a protest. "Frances?" he said, again. "Are you OK? It's Quinn."

Her eyes flickered open. "Quinn? Goddammit." She immediately tried to move but struggled under the pole and other debris that had fallen across her back.

"Whoa. Careful. Don't struggle. You might be injured."

Carson let out a frustrated bark, as she tried to push again against the weight. "I'll goddamn injure you in a minute if you don't help me. Get this shit off a' me."

"Well, hello to you too," said Quinn, looking around to assess the risk of lifting the pole without disturbing the rest. Carson's eyes followed his inaction with growing frustration.

"Quinn!"

"Give me a minute. You want me bring the rest down on your head, go ahead and shout some more."

"Just make it quick. I can't even turn my head. What about the others?"

"The others?" feigned Quinn.

"Your British friends were here when the place came apart."

"Really? What would they be doing down here?" said Quinn, continuing to play dumb.

He shifted his weight and leant across the splintered remains of a laminated MDF board to get a grip on the metal pole pinning Carson to the floor.

"Are they here or not?" spat Carson, through gritted teeth.

"I don't see them. Now hold still."

Quinn shifted again, then carefully, slowly, rotated and lifted the pole up and away from Carson's back, like the ultimate game of Jenga. Carson made a noise as the weight was lifted and rolled painfully to one side before using her arms to push herself up into a seated position. She refused Quinn's hand and, finally, awkwardly was able to stand.

It was obvious to Quinn that she was in some amount of pain, but she certainly wasn't about to admit it. Her gaze fell on Travis with a barely detectable wince as she brushed down her uniform with her hands.

"So much for Travis's vacation plans this year," she said, bluntly. "Where are the others?"

"You mean Hicks?" replied Quinn, gesturing at the other soldier who, aside from the metal shaft skewering his head and holding him in a bowed position, looked as though he were kneeling in prayer.

"What's up with you today, Greg?" snarled Carson. "I mean the Brits. The goddamn Brits. Where the hell are they?"

"I don't know, ma'am. As I say, I didn't—"

"Fine, whatever. We don't have time for this. They can't have gone far. Initiate lockdown."

"Already done."

Carson went to respond but realised the world had not stopped just because she had, and simply nodded.

"Snark sent me down here to find out what you were doing," continued Quinn. "He has...concerns."

"I should say he damn well does. We had—have—an incursion. Do you realize that? Right here. In a place that officially doesn't even exist."

"Well, you say incursion, but if you mean that British pair, then technically we brought them here ourselves. That's a hell of an infiltration plan for a couple of civvies."

"You may say civilians. I say hostile operatives."

"Those two?" laughed Quinn. "And their plan was, what? To spend years biding their time in obscurity, in the hope that at some point we would simply pick them up and take them where they wanted to go? Let's just say that Snark's prime concerns are not really with Shaggy and Velma."

Carson looked blankly at Quinn.

"Scooby-Doo?" he offered, by way of an explanation.

She shook her head. Something had changed she couldn't place and she didn't like it. Perhaps it had been a mistake to come down here and try to cover the situation herself, but who else could she trust to get it done? Clearly not Quinn who might have been her first choice after Mac. And now it was clear there were unspoken questions in the air. She'd be able to bring Snark around, she was sure of it. But Quinn's passive and not-so-subtle insubordination might be a problem. He was too visible to simply push aside, especially right now. She'd have to bring him in somehow, then deal with him later. Perhaps, at this point, the only way out was through.

"OK, fine," she said at last, ignoring Quinn's remarks. "I say incursion, you say dinner guest. We can debate later. Right now, we need to figure out what they were doing here, and they need to be found, for their safety and ours. OK?"

"Well, this may be nothing..." began Quinn, hesitating. He could feel her suspicion growing, but knew he needed to throw her a bone.

"What?"

"Maze said a part from one of the ships was missing."

Carson's eyes grew more intense.

"And you're only telling me now?"

"You were unconscious before. And besides, I thought it was Maze geeking out over his toys."

"Just tell me."

"He said a control unit had been removed."

"A crystal?"

Quinn shrugged.

"Jesus, Greg. If they've got their hands on..."

"Who's to say it's even them?" interjected Quinn. "Look at this place. Maybe it just fell out."

"It's them. I know it is. Those little shits. Are you going to help me or not?"

"Actually, Frances, I will help you."

"Thank you. With Mac incarcerated I need you to take command of his team. Can you do that?"

"I can."

"I want guards at every entrance and every exit, with a check-in every fifteen minutes. I want you to go floor by floor and room by room. Every lab, office, and equipment store. I want every janitorial closet and every bathroom checked. I don't care who's in there or what they're doing. I want them found."

Quinn did as Carson asked. And not simply because she ordered him to, but because her reaction confirmed all his suspicions and he needed time to act. He also needed the operational latitude if he was going to exfiltrate Leon and Izzy from the compound.

He and Carson quickly parted ways, leaving her to rebuild bridges with Snark, while he headed for the tactical officer's room. Once there, he assembled the remaining squad leaders and issued orders and a plan as per Carson's directive, with one exception; that all status reports go through him, rather than direct to Carson. He needed the intel first-hand, but it also freed him from direct tactical command to move about the base unhindered. This would prove particularly useful as his first step would be to go and see Macintyre. Something about him being in custody smelled bad from the first, and he was determined to find out where the stink was coming from.

Tactical units had already begun installing themselves at key intersections and points of ingress throughout the complex as Quinn made his way across to the brig. He knew that dedicated security personnel would already be moving steadily upwards, floor by floor, in search of Leon and Izzy. But he figured that as long as they stuck to the plan, they had enough of a head start to make it to the surface level ahead of any search party. The real trick would be exiting the building unseen.

47

FIREWALL

An armoured Jeep screamed its way up and out of the lower level of the parking garage, rapidly pursued by another black-windowed four-by-four and three other dusty sedans some ways behind. It easily managed to avoid the automated tire spikes lying in wait across the exit roadway by mounting the narrow pedestrian sidewalk, taking out most of the guard booth on its way past, and scattering the three guards sitting inside it. Two of them were just able to pull out their sidearms in time and fire after the Jeep as it made short work of the red-and-white boom barrier ahead of the exit ramp, before busting its way through the closed metal shutters disguising the main entrance.

The perforated metal coverings—designed for concealment more than protection—shattered and splintered as the Jeep momentarily left the ground and smashed through the metallic skin, before landing heavily on the unmade road outside. Its wheels ground out a cloud of dust and gravel as it dropped gears and sped away, skidding out of sight around the first bend, immediately trailed by the second off-roader.

Only two of the three remaining pursuit vehicles made it through the busted opening, the third having come unstuck by the ruined guard booth, where a poorly judged maneuverer—in an attempt to avoid killing one of the surviving guards—kicked it over on its side and into the concrete wall. They were immediately joined by five additional cars pounding their way up the service road from farther along the valley floor and, together, they piled around the sharp curve in the road in a clumsy, erratic convoy.

Up ahead, the armoured Jeep, seemingly oblivious to its growing tail, continued its rapid ascent up the dirt road, narrowly avoiding catastrophe at every hairpin bend and sending a dense, bilious cloud of dust behind it, ensuring that three of the eight vehicles in pursuit were not so lucky. Finally, the gritty four-by-four leapt over the humped ridge at the very top of the slope before it evened out and accelerated into a more or less straight run towards the perimeter fence.

The security checkpoint that comprised the main gate had already been mobilised. The gates were locked, the booms were down, and two security vehicles had been parked at right angles across the road access in and out. A squad of armed guards flowed out of the guardhouse and positioned themselves behind the cars, taking aim with variety of automatic weapons and handguns. The black-windowed Jeep approached them at speed, with no apparent sign of slowing, even as the pursuit vehicles finally closed the distance, cutting through the dusty haze and spreading out behind it. A megaphone-enhanced voice squawked out from the guardhouse.

"Approaching SUV—Stand down!"

The SUV did not stand down and continued driving forward at speed.

"SUV, I repeat, *stand down now*! We have *orders to fire*."

The armed guards took this as their signal to lock and load their weapons, as the Jeep hit the final stretch of the road. Another two cars appeared from east and west of the guard post and, in unison with the other pursuit cars, began closing in on the speeding vehicle like numbers on a clock face.

"S-U-V, *this is your last warning. Stand down or you will be fired upon.*"

The guards raised and aimed their weapons. The Jeep seemed for a moment like it was really going to pile right into them when, suddenly, it jammed hard on its brakes, turned, and skidded sideways to a halt six feet from the guard position. The pursuit vehicles all followed suit, grinding to a stop in a wide rough circle and, as the dust moved thickly around them, more armed guards immediately exited the vehicles and aimed their weapons at the Jeep.

"*Driver,*" came the voice again. "*Exit the vehicle now! Keep your hands visible. I will not ask a second time.*"

Thirty seconds seemed like an hour as the air fell silent in anticipation. Several of the armed guards took the opportunity to reposition themselves and brace for action. Two birds of prey glided on the desert thermals high overhead. The dust began to settle. A squad of guards peeled away from the main cordon and positioned themselves in a semicircle around the front of the vehicle. The driver door of the black Jeep cracked open.

"Report, goddammit," shouted Snark from across the mission room. "Why are there armed guards rooting around in the fucking john?" Snark still had paper towels in his hands.

Keynes was about to answer when Carson appeared.

"My apologies, sir," she said, approaching Snark appeasingly. "But we felt, that is to say, I felt, we needed additional security sweeps."

"More sweeps? Well shit, Carson, my ass now feels pretty goddamn secure. That's a hellava gift. I'll be sure to tell my doctor at my next colonoscopy. Meanwhile, does anyone around here actually know what a silent lockdown is?"

"The situation has continued to...evolve, sir," said Carson, plainly.

"Which means what, exactly?"

"Our British guests have gone AWOL. We believe, as I suggested earlier, that they have an additional agenda for—"

"Christ Almighty, Carson. Is that what you were doing down in Hangar 17?"

"Yes, sir."

"We have people for that. I needed you here."

"Yes, sir," agreed Carson. "It was an oversight, on my part. I thought I could deal with it more effectively if I—"

"And yet here you are. Empty-handed. And you look terrible, by the way. What the hell happened? They offer to make you tea or something?"

"Sir," interrupted Keynes, before Carson could respond adequately.

"What is it," he snapped.

"We have a report coming in of a vehicle breaking out of the main parking garage. Possibly more than one."

"There you are, Commander," said Snark, pointedly, as he folded his arms. "Everything at your fingertips without even having to leave your chair. We'll have words about your little field trip when this is done."

"Yes, sir," responded Carson, uneasily.

"Put it on the main viewer," commanded Snark.

A second later most of the giant screen array at the front of the mission room was filled with a live exterior camera feed. A vertical strip on the right-hand side contained a stack of feeds from different angles and locations. Each of them presented a looping version of the car chase happening aboveground, with different timestamps—from the vehicle breakout at the base, then progressing upwards as the cars hit each bend and intersection along the dirt road, culminating in the main screen which was dominated by an aerial view of the perimeter guard post. A drone, Snark speculated, as he watched the lead vehicle tear its way up from the bottom-right of screen and skid artfully to a stop a short way from the shielded guard positions.

For a moment the view was obscured by dust as each of the

pursuit vehicles ground to a sharp stop in a wide, rough circular formation around the lead SUV. The mission room's normally constant activity went still as everyone waited for the air to clear.

"This should be good," said Snark, leaning back onto the edge of a desk, as the breakaway company of guards repositioned themselves around the car.

"Who..." began Keynes.

"Quiet," barked Carson. "They're coming out."

They watched in silence as the Jeep door opened a third of the way, and two empty hands emerged from the gap at the top, followed slowly by raised arms and a body of a man in black fatigues. He stepped carefully onto the ground and faced the command post. The men surrounding the vehicle immediately raised their weapons.

"I can't see his face from this angle," growled Snark.

"Sir, I'm not sure—" began Carson

"Move the goddamn camera."

"...if that's really Aronofsky."

The camera view stayed put, but indistinct radio chatter began crackling in over the speakers as the apparent standoff continued. Snark could hardly believe what he was seeing. By now, the driver should be on his knees and in custody, but instead it seemed as if he was talking to the group of soldiers poised ready to shoot him. He watched incredulously as another soldier stepped sharply from the door of the guardhouse, marched around the cordon, and cut briskly through the armed perimeter to approach the man standing by the car. The driver stepped clear from the open car door to meet him and the two men faced each other for a moment. Then the second man saluted the first, who lowered his arms and responded in kind. The armed guards surrounding the vehicle immediately stood down and holstered their weapons.

"What the hell?" exploded Snark.

"Report!" roared Carson into the radio.

There was a brief crackle of static before a voice came on.

"It's Lieutenant Macintyre, ma'am."

"What!?"

Carson's eyes rolled wildly around the room. She had trouble conceiving how or why he'd be there. He should be locked up. He was locked up—she'd made sure of that personally—and yet, here he was. Which means he'd either broken out, which was at best extremely unlikely, or he'd been set free on someone's orders. There was only one person on the base whose authority exceeded hers, but he was standing next to her with his mouth open. That could only mean someone with authority to act...Quinn. Goddammit. She should have exercised more control over his access once the Benedict lead was shot to hell. Or she should have just taken him out of the equation completely, as she'd promised herself she would.

A rage exploded inside her that she could barely defend or contain. She knew she had to get out of there before Mac started talking, or Snark began putting things together on his own. And she had to find those damn British kids. They couldn't have gone far on their own. Bringing them in was a mistake from the start, she decided, but if she could get to them first, they might give her the leverage she needed.

"Yes, ma'am," confirmed the radio. "Do you want us to hold him? He insists he was—"

"Check the vehicle. Now, soldier. I want every inch of it combed. And every other car behind it."

"Ma'am?"

"Bring him and everyone in if you have to. We have two foreign nationals unaccounted for and I want them found A-SAP. I'm coming down myself."

"Commander," warned Snark.

Carson hesitated. She hated what she knew she was about to do. Despite everything, Snark had been good to her, treated her with respect, and even kindness at times. But too much had slipped from her direct control in the past three days. And he wasn't a forgiving man. If she didn't bring this whole stinking mess back on track, and quickly, then it was over. Her plans destroyed. Like the life she should have had. And she couldn't allow that to happen. Not this time. Or everything, all her work, and all her sacrifice, would be for nothing.

"I'm...sorry, Linden," she offered, after a moment.

A brief look of confusion followed by hurt rolled across Snark's face. He knew, then, in that exact moment, that she was about to cross a line. And for just one fleeting moment, he might almost have gone along with her, whatever she had planned, such was his admiration of the young officer. But his decades-long resolve, ambition, and duty quickly reasserted itself.

"Linden, now, is it?" he said, pointedly. "We really have reached a crossroads. Do not go down there."

"Sir, I..."

Snark subtly nodded at a nearby MP, who stepped forward in response to his unspoken orders.

"I don't know what the hell you think you're doing, Frankie, but I'm warning you. If you take one step away, I will not hesitate."

Carson suddenly reached for her sidearm and aimed it directly at Snark. He braced himself but didn't move. The MP reached for his own weapon but wavered as Snark gave him an almost imperceptible shake of the head. He waited, along with everyone else in the room, paralysed by what they were seeing.

"Jesus Christ, Frankie. Do you realize what you're doing?"

"Regretfully, sir, yes. I do."

"If you lower your weapon now, Frankie, we can work this out. Whatever it is, whatever's going on, we can work it out," Snark offered, gently, taking a step toward her with an open hand.

She responded by gripping her pistol still more tightly, her eyes darting around the room as she tried to assess the inevitable threat and where it would come from first. Probably the MP, of course, but she couldn't just dismiss the possibility of another eager, dutiful colleague.

"I know you believe that, sir, but please, don't move."

She really didn't want him to give her a reason. Snark stopped moving, though his hand remained outstretched.

"If you go through with this, Frankie, if you leave this room, I won't be able to help you."

Carson looked at him sadly. Underneath all the bluster and fury was a good man, a decent man, out of time, trying to do the right thing. He'd taught her so much. But none of it mattered now. He'd never think of her the same way again, assuming he was even willing to listen.

She suddenly regretted forcing herself so deeply into a corner, so abruptly, and dragging him along with her. But it was only a matter of time. Now or later, she knew, there was never going to be any going back. She thought about the Jones woman and her friend Aronofsky, who'd somehow pushed their way to the front of the line with little more than string and brown paper to work with. It had to be now.

She sprang forward, grabbed Snark's open hand, and yanked it up, around, and behind him. He yelled out in pain and the MP took a step forward with his weapon raised. But he was too slow. Carson already had her own handgun dug into the fleshy underside of Snark's jaw.

"Nobody moves," yelled Carson, as she began to step unevenly backwards, half pulling, half guiding Snark, who remained firmly in her grip. "Especially you, soldier."

Snark waved the MP down with his free hand.

"Do as she says," he ordered, through gritted teeth. He didn't really believe she'd go through with her threat but the betrayal cut deep, and he couldn't bear to take the chance.

On the main viewscreen, soldiers could be seen acting on Carson's orders, searching all the vehicles by hand, and rounding up the drivers into a loose group behind Mac. But all eyes in the room were on Carson and Snark as she slowly manoeuvred him backwards to the main door. Beside it was a small control panel with a large red push-button switch in the middle. The label, embossed into the metal plate, read Firewall Protocol – Emergency Only.

Snark saw it as the door behind Carson slid open and knew

immediately what she planned to do. The Firewall Protocol was a hangover from the cold war designed to effectively seal off the command centre in the event of a nuclear strike. He tried to call it out but was a moment too late. Carson threw him forward into the room as her arm reached out and hit the big red button. And a second later they were separated by a bulletproof, hermetically sealed glass door as it slammed shut between them, the motorised locks whining into place. She knew it wouldn't take them long to deactivate—perhaps ten minutes at best for the system protocols to reset—but it would be enough time to get where she needed to go.

Snark recovered his footing and turned to look at her, firmly shrugging off several people who had rushed to his aid. And for a still moment they regarded at each other through the glass, as though waiting for a signal that Carson knew would never come. She straightened her back and gave him her most respectful salute. Then she turned and ran.

48

UP AND OUT

Leon held out his hand to support Izzy as she climbed up and over the last rungs of the metal ladder pinned to the inside of the emergency exit shaft: a narrow, more or less vertical channel, excavated from the bedrock that ran from the rear of Hangar 17's cavern and climbed all twelve levels up to the back of the parking garage. It had been a hard climb, made tolerable only by a handful of natural stops imposed by changing rock density that created a narrow shelf, and forced the ladder to restart its ascent on a different wall. Their hands, arms, and legs began to hurt well before they reached the top, but they knew they had to keep going.

The top of the shaft opened out onto a small rocky landing, big enough for perhaps five or six people at any one time, like a small elevator car. There were a lot of old cigarette butts on the floor and a collection of crushed beer cans scattered next to the wall.

"This must be where all the cool guards come to hang out," observed Leon, dryly.

"Or the alcoholics," said Izzy, smiling. There were a lot of old cans.

Light perforated the gloomy space from horizontal slits in the top of a steel door embedded into the wall opposite. Leon stepped forward and tried to peek out through the gaps.

"It's the garage where we came in, I think," he confirmed.

"I wouldn't know," replied Izzy, rubbing her hands. "I was asleep."

"Sorry. Where I came in... Seems like whatever Quinn was going to do, he's done. The guard booth looks like it's smashed up and I can see smoke."

"What about the actual guards? Are they smashed up too?"

Leon shrugged. "I guess we'll have to find out."

He pulled on the handle and it turned reluctantly, stiff with age. The door, likewise, resisted as Leon tried to open it quietly. It got about halfway before the old metal caught in the frame and let out an unwanted squeal. He stopped pulling.

"Why don't you just stick your head out the door and scream hello," said Izzy.

"Be my guest," responded Leon, stepping to one side and literally showing her the door.

Instead of attempting to open it further, Izzy contorted herself to squeeze through the gap, then disappeared.

"Wait," called Leon after her in a harsh whisper.

Her head popped back into view. "Don't worry so much," she said, with a smile. "I'll be back in a minute."

Leon attempted to step through the gap himself but it was too much of a squeeze for him and, reluctant to draw any more attention with the door, he stepped back into the rocky vestibule. He was about to stick just his head through to get a better view of the garage when Izzy reappeared.

"I think we're good," she said.

"You think? We need to be sure."

"I had a look. There was definitely some kind of car accident. The booth is badly damaged and the car is on its side but no guards that I can tell."

"OK, let's get out of here," agreed Leon.

He pulled the door open another few inches to let himself

through and it honked like an animal. They waited theatrically to see if it would draw anyone out but when nothing happened, Leon stepped out and the pair scuttled away towards the exit, where light was bleeding in quite harshly through the broken shutters.

Stepping carefully through the wreckage of the security station, and past the still smoking carcass of the upturned car, they made a point of looking out for the cameras Quinn had warned them about. He assured them he'd be able to redirect them enough to provide a tight blind spot as long as they stayed close to the outside wall, but it would still be up to them to not just step out in front of one by mistake. Using a row of parked vehicles as cover, they were able to make their way across to the opposite side and, hugging the wall, made their way towards and through the fractured shutters.

The desert heat instantly hit them as they finally left the shelter of the complex and stepped out onto the roadway, despite being in the shade of the rocky outcrop towing above them.

"Wow," whispered Leon. "That heat is something else. And Quinn just wants us to wander around in this, waiting to be picked up? I didn't bring any sunblock."

"Dehydration is the biggest risk," replied Izzy. "We should move slowly and try not to talk until we get where we're going."

Leon nodded. "Agreed."

Staying close to the rocky escarpment, they moved carefully up the road and round to the left. A short way around the corner was an uneven fissure in the rock face big enough to walk in single file, just as Quinn had promised.

Leon suggested Izzy go first and then followed her into the gap, which smoothly zigzagged them away from the roadside until it was out of sight. They felt relieved to feel genuinely invisible for the first time since they arrived and paused to take stock. Up ahead they could see the path ran on unevenly for perhaps another twenty or thirty feet, where the crevice narrowed and ended, just as Quinn had described, with what looked a climbable rocky ladder of sorts. Leon looked up to see how far they'd have to climb. It was hard to be sure, but it looked easily as high as the path was long. And, as he could still feel the pain of the ascent they'd made from the hangar to the garage, the prospect of another thirty-foot climb didn't exactly fill him with glee.

"You think we might have made a mistake?" asked Izzy, not really meaning it.

"I think we didn't have much of a choice. And, since you're asking, I think there was something very wrong with that Frances Carson. That's what I think. And this place is probably filled with people like her, so it was either this"—Leon indicated the climb ahead of them—"or a bullet to the head."

"That did seem to be where she was going."

"Well, I know which one I prefer. Let's keep moving."

Frances Carson stumbled down the last set of steps in the emergency stairway. At the bottom were two doors. The main one, at the foot of the stairs, was clearly labelled, and would take her out to Hangar 17. But the second, set into the rear sidewall of the stairwell lobby, was not labelled and, in addition to the keycard reader, had a separate numbered keypad.

Carson entered the numbered code, flashed her card against the pad, and felt a wave of relief when it lit up green and the automated mechanical lock deactivated, releasing the door. It meant that Snark and the Ops team still hadn't managed to reverse the firewall protocol and lock her out of the system. She still had time.

The door led into a small dimly lit access corridor, made smaller still by a tangle of pipes and cabling that ran along the walls and ceiling. She half jogged down the long passageway, taking a couple of turns along the way until she reached another door at the far end. This one opened easily from the inside and brought her out directly into a large space that mirrored Hangar 17 in a lot of ways, except size.

Though still quite large, it was clearly a constructed space, much smaller than 17, and was kitted out more like a domestic aircraft hangar, with various workshop bays studded along the walls. In the centre section were two long, neat rows of small one or two-person-sized vehicles, about the size of an old-school family station wagon, parked in neat groups of four. The long, rounded, knobbly vehicles, however, were nothing like cars, and on their own always made Carson think they looked a bit like a giant pickle, except for the blended wing contours, the smooth glass cockpit bubble, and the perky tail fins that were straight out of 1950s Detroit. The Cardinals. Named for the eponymous bird, rather than St. Louis's home team, or the high-ranking clergyman, and painted an incredibly dark crimson to compliment the appellation. She never really understood why. Some boffin had a complex radar-related theory about the colour but to her it always felt a little prideful. Not really what you want for an ultra-secret piece of military hardware.

The hangar appeared to be empty, as Carson had expected, and she scuttled across the bay to the nearest group of Cardinals. Up close, it was clear they sat a couple of feet off the ground with no visible means of support. It still surprised her, even after years of working with the advanced technology. As was often her custom, she gave the craft a sharp push to satisfy her monkey brain that it was real. It wavered ever so slightly then immediately snapped back to its previous position.

She quickly activated the glass canopy, which slid neatly backwards, with a satisfying near-silent hiss. Stretching onto her toes, she was just able to reach into the top of the cabin and retrieve an unusually long-handled metal tool that looked like a slim silver wrench, with a curved socket on the end. She then began circling the exterior of the vehicle, running one hand along the shell as she went, as though to admire the smooth finish, and performed a set of preflight checks. This mainly consisted of inspecting a number of slatted vents along the lower part of the fuselage, before arriving at the rear where she opened a panel on each side, just below the fins, reached in with the extended tool, and adjusted something deep inside. She closed them carefully and completed her loop, returning to the left-hand side of the cockpit where she used the tool again, this time like a hook, to yank out a folded metal step from underneath the craft.

"Taking her out for a spin?" came a voice, some ways behind her.

She turned sharply, trying to cover her surprise, and saw Quinn coming towards her.

"Gregory Quinn," she said with a grin. "Come to give me a kiss goodbye, is that it?"

"If that's what you want to call it," he replied, casually closing the distance between them.

Carson regarded him for a moment, wondering why he'd come alone.

"Does Snark know you're here?"

"Snark knows everything, as always."

"Meaning what?"

"Meaning it's over, Carson. He knows it was you. And he's not going to permit you to leave."

Carson snorted. "He knows it was me? Ridiculous, and you know it. The old man only knows what I tell him."

"He'll be pleased to hear that, I'm sure. But here's what he does know, even though you somehow forgot to tell him."

Carson's right hand, still holding the silver tool, dropped casually to her side as she talked, while her other hand impulsively reached behind her searching for something she could hold on to.

"He knows you set up Mac, for starters."

"Mac..." she scoffed.

"Yes, Mac. You've always thought of Macintyre as just a useful tool, a blunt instrument—much like you think of me, I suspect— to be yanked out whenever you had a mess to clean up. But you forget that he's a real person. A man that Snark actually knows. They served together; did you know that? And not just down here in this old refrigerated basement of lost secrets but in battle. That does something to a man."

"Served together," hissed Carson. "There must be thirty years between them."

"Maybe so. But a terrified young recruit, coming into a live operational theater can respond strongly to a great leader. Imprints on them, you might even say. Especially when it can make the difference between living and dying. You think that doesn't mean anything? Maybe not to you: someone who's walked a golden path since your first drill at Annapolis. Maybe not to someone who's never seen active service."

"Don't be so sure about that."

"What—that little screw-up in Prague? Yeah, I know all about that. And well played, by the way. There's not many that could segue so sharply from a failed intelligence operation of that scale and fast-track out the other side into the heart of one of the most secret operations on Earth. I can't imagine what kind of dirt you must have locked away to have made that happen. But all's fair in love and war, right?"

"You're damn right it is. And who the hell are you to come in here and start lecturing me? You know all I have to do is call—"

"Me? I'm just the garbageman. Come to take out the trash."

Carson laughed cynically. "What—with a washed-up tactical officer who's been caught whining to his boss? Good luck with that."

Quinn took a step forward and Carson instinctively tried to retreat, feeling the cold surface of the craft pressing against her back.

"Oh, that's just to get us warmed up," countered Quinn. "You want me to dig into the bomb evidence? What about Manchego's team? I was there, dammit. I saw what happened to them and it wasn't blowback from the device: they were gunned down. Hunted down. And this is Manchego, for crying out loud. Can you imagine anyone getting the jump on him? Who knew he was even on site? One person. You. And how about that team sent to kill me at Benedict's? Just a lucky guess?"

"Bullshit!"

"Really."

"Bad comms. We'd just lost Helios. We had an international situation on our hands. We were scrambling."

"And yet these guys were all Obsidian. You think I wouldn't check? All off books. You said so yourself."

"I know I did," laughed Carson. "Jesus, Quinn, if this is all you've got, then—"

"That was a smart move, Frances. I'll give you that. Almost cast-iron.

"Almos—"

"But you forgot one thing. Your own investigative logs."

Carson tried to stay her reaction but the rage-fear cocktail brewing inside proved difficult to contain and she let out a contemptuous snort.

"Somehow," continued Quinn. "The team knew, before your fabricated investigation had even begun, just the right time frame to search for. Given that you could have been looking at an evidence chain going back, what, ten years? Twenty years? How could you know? And yet the analysts managed to start in just the right place. What was it you said to Mac? About how he might even have gotten away with it '...*if we weren't specifically looking for it* ?' It got me to thinking. How specifically were you looking for it? I asked around. Turns out it was you who told the team to conduct their search from one specific date onwards. Hellava lucky guess, Frances. Just think what you could do at Caesar's with that kind of luck."

"An informed hunch," responded Carson, weakly. "I'd had my eye on Mac for some time—since he returned from that botched capture in Antarctica and had begun to act out. Something was off, but as you say, he and Snark were tight so I gave him the benefit of the doubt. Then, when everything went up in flames last week, I figured that was a better starting point than groping around twenty-thirty years of records. If I was wrong, no harm, no foul. But I wasn't wrong. So if we're done here, I have business to attend to."

Carson made to turn back to the ship but was halted by Quinn's refusal to stop.

"But why that date in particular?"

"I just told you."

"Did you?"

Carson snapped back to face him.

"Look, I know you want to make this a thing. I get it. I've been hard on you. And I'm even a little bit sorry about that. But if I have to spell it out: Macintyre returned to duty on the eighteenth. He called in at 12:00. Shift change, of course. He's a creature of habit. And because he, at least, knows what duty and punctuality means.

"It was a straight six-month window so I told them to start there and we'd expand backwards if we needed to. Then we found his first communication at 17:00 the same day. We have the records. I thought it was clumsy of him, rushed, even, but—"

"Twelve-hundred. 17:00. On the eighteenth," repeated Quinn. "Amazing. And this communication, it can only be accessed from inside the base, yes?"

"Yes, Greg. You know this. Enough games. If you have something, spit it out. Otherwise, I'm done here. And so are you. I'll have MPs down here quicker than you can limp out of here," snapped Carson, disdainfully.

Quinn smiled but said nothing. And Carson felt the heat rise inside her as the unexpected silence continued.

"You get all that, sir?" said Quinn, finally.

Carson's eyes momentarily doubled in size as, mortified, she scanned the room for who he was talking to.

"I did, thank you, Captain," said Linden Snark, walking into view from the other side of the hangar.

The climb up and out of the fissure turned out to be easier than it had looked. Once Leon and Izzy reached the end wall, it became clear it was more like a series of uneven, rocky steps than a ladder.

And then, at the top, they found it opened out into a wider channel that meandered gently away through the high desert floor. Leon wondered if it was old riverbed, or the result of runoff from the rain and flash flooding that would occasionally hammer the region. It made him think of those satellite pictures of Mars he would sometimes pause over whenever NASA got overexcited at a new finding and published one of its ancient-water-on-Mars news stories.

In any case, it was deep enough to keep them in almost constant shade, which even at this late hour of the afternoon was a real lifesaver. And, as long as they kept their heads down, it had the double advantage of shielding them from view, should anyone be scouring the area in search of two pasty Brits on the run, with no water, sunblock, or any clear idea of how they planned to get out of the desert.

"You definitely sure he said south?" said Izzy, after they'd been jogging along the natural path for some time.

"That's what he said."

"And this is definitely south."

"Aren't you some kind of computer genius?" teased Leon. "You can figure out how to hack a UFO but not which way is south?"

"Computers I can do," confirmed Izzy. "But my sense of direction is shocking. Never ask me to read a map."

"Got it. OK, so it must be what—four, maybe five in the afternoon?"

Neither of them had a phone or even a watch to consult. Izzy shrugged. Leon pointed at the long shadow cast across the channel floor.

"Judging by the sun," he suggested.

"Ah," said Izzy, suddenly getting it. "Shadow's coming in from the right—west—so we must be going south, right?"

"You got it. Next up: shoe-tying."

"Hey," she protested. "I should have left you to get pounded up in that spaceship."

"Maybe you should have."

"Don't be dumb, Leon."

"Sorry," said Leon, now feeling dumb that he'd even said it.

"I mean, who would I have got to tie my shoes?"

They laughed. Partly at the conversation, but mainly at the growing sense of exhilaration they were feeling at being outside, being free. They knew their liberty might not last long, but neither of them wanted to talk about that and it wasn't long before their pace began to slow to a steady walk. Despite the soft breeze drifting down the slender gully and the welcome shade, it was really bloody hot.

"It's not for nothing that they call it the desert," said Leon after a while.

"No, they really cracked it with that name. I didn't even realise we were in the desert until we got outside. It came as kind of a surprise. I thought we must still be somewhere, I don't know... somewhere around New York."

"Of course," said Leon, feeling regretful that he hadn't really checked in with her about her journey here. "You were unconscious when they brought you in."

Izzy nodded but didn't say anything, so Leon's guilt filled the silence.

"Listen," he said. "About that—"

"Don't," said Izzy, firmly.

"But you don't know what I was going to say."

"I think I know exactly what you were going to say but don't. We both went into this with our eyes open."

"Maybe not that open," chuckled Leon.

Izzy smiled with him. "You're right. We both went into this with our eyes half-closed. But the point is, we did it together."

"But—"

"But nothing, Leon. Yes, sure I could've washed my hands of it, let you go it alone. But this insane thing we're in the middle of? It happened to me too. So why should you have all the fun?"

Leon smiled back. It seemed pointless to argue. Besides, not only was she right, he was realistic enough to know he could barely have got out of the plane on his own, never mind what they accomplished here.

"So, what about this Milk guy," said Izzy, changing tack. "Do you really trust him? I mean, you could have just said no."

"Sure I could," said Leon. "I mean, on the plus side, he's about the only person we've met in the past four days who hasn't tried to kill us. But the thing is..." he trailed off.

"The thing is...?"

"Well, the thing is...I would never have found you."

Izzy stopped walking and they turned to look at each other.

"You willingly jumped into a giant rabbit hole, with no idea how deep it went, and no guarantee of getting out, to find some artefact that may not even have been there...because of me?"

"That's the only reason I did it."

Izzy looked at him openly—this unlikely, clumsy, funny man, who she'd punched to the ground more than once but who still risked his life for hers—and realised, in that moment, that stumbling into a secret base full of UFOs might actually turn out to be the least amazing thing that had happened to her that day.

She reached up to touch his face, as the late afternoon sun shed its golden light behind him. He placed his hand on hers and they leaned in, breathing slowly, when suddenly an incredibly loud klaxon alarm tore through the earthy silence.

49

ROCK AND A HARD PLACE

F or a long moment the air in the hangar grew thick with unwelcome surprise and anticipation, as the sound of Snark's heavy footsteps on the rough concrete floor seemed to announce his intentions.

"Sir," began Carson, finally, suddenly desperate to regain her standing. "I can expl—"

"Enough!" shouted Snark. "I'm not interested in any more of your explanations."

Carson pulled herself to attention, more out of habit than any kind of protocol. They knew there was no protocol now that she had openly gone rogue, but nonetheless she watched Snark approach intently, and waited for him to speak.

"On the eighteenth of March, Steven Macintyre did indeed return to duty," began Snark. "And, as you rightly observed, being a man of habit and duty, he called in at shift change. Twelve o'clock your time."

"My time?" The blood drained from Carson's face as she began to realise what she'd done.

"Yes. Twelve o'clock, Nevada time. Eight a.m. New Zealand time. Eight o'clock in the morning of the *next day*. Mac had been on a layover there at my personal request, following that fiasco in

Western Australia. I had him review some business that our kiwi friends were eager to share. He was scheduled to fly out at 10:00 a.m. that morning but considered himself back on active duty even though he'd be in transit most of the day. He called in, like he should. But you never thought to check where he was. You assumed he was back on US soil and you set him up. You say he sent out a coded message to the Obsidian team at 17:00? I'd say he was just about over Tonga, drinking a scotch, neat. And sitting next to me."

"The only question," said Quinn, taking another step towards Carson as her face flushed with a combination of rage and panic. "Is why?"

Carson looked at Quinn, then back to Snark who was by now only a few feet away. She was fuming at the arrogance and audacity of these two men, who had somehow caught her out, using her own cover story as a trap. But she was mostly reeling at her own haste and failure to anticipate this outcome.

"Why?" she repeated.

"Yes, Frankie," said Snark, plaintively. "Why did you do it? You had everything here. You think I want to keep running the show? How much time do you think I have left? It could have been yours. All of it."

Carson gritted her teeth and tightened her grip on the long silver spanner in her right hand.

"I'll tell you why," she said, at last. Then suddenly brought up her hand and whacked the tool across the side of Quinn's head. He let out a yell of pain and staggered backwards, onto the ground, his hands clutching at his head.

Snark jumped forward quicker than Carson could have anticipated and, in a panic, she threw the wrench at his face. He fumbled to knock it aside, and she followed up with a hard kick to the stomach. He went down in a heap and, for just a second, she regretted her action, fearing she might actually have killed him.

She turned on her heel, climbed up into the ship, flipped a combination of switches and dials, and hit a large green button to the side of the dashboard. The craft hummed to life, lifting a couple of extra inches from the ground and wavering gently as Carson pulled a helmet over her head and clipped a harness into place.

At the far end of the hangar, a wide metal shutter was climbing up into the ceiling, revealing a large, angled shaft on the other side. A slice of sunlight cut sharply across the top part of the exposed rock channel and continued to grow as, presumably, another set of shutters rolled up on the outside of the underground structure.

Carson looked across to Snark, strangely relieved to see him struggle to lift himself into a seated position. While Quinn, looking much worse for wear with a bloody gash in his head, was just regaining his focus and looking back at her with a pained expression.

"I'm sorry, boys," she said, as the glass canopy slid closed past her head. "I really am. But I have to go."

She yanked an unseen lever, as Quinn made a sudden dash for the craft, and pulled back on a flattened wheel-like joystick in front of her. The craft lurched forward, pushing Quinn to one side with the invisible force of its UFO-enabled engine. It performed a dipped turn, like a speedboat in the water, then shot off towards the hangar exit.

Quinn scrambled to his feet as Carson disappeared through the open shutters, and ran for the next Cardinal in line. He hit the canopy switch and yanked out the metal step to climb into the cockpit. Then he paused to look at Snark, who was finally sitting up and nursing his rounded belly.

"Forget about me," he yelled. "She'll kill those two kids if she can, and then God only knows what. Get after her."

Quinn nodded and, foregoing any preflight, dropped into the craft and slid into the seat. He knew he should have checked the vents before he left, but there was no time. He'd just have to chance it. He snapped the switches with a stroke of one hand and released the holding lever next to his seat. The craft lurched to life and Quinn hit accelerate as the glass canopy rolled back over his head. The next second, he was gone.

Leon and Izzy heaved apart from their near embrace and instinctively ran to each side of the smooth, rocky furrow they'd been travelling down to see what was happening.

"Can you see anything?" yelled Leon, being careful not to raise his head above eye level as he scanned the horizon on his side and not seeing anything himself.

"Nothing," replied Izzy, who had done the same. "Wait, there's..."

"What? What is it?"

"I can see a dust cloud. But it's pretty far away."

"What kind of dust cloud?" replied Leon as he shuffled across to take look.

Izzy pointed. "See? I think it's moving. Do you think it's a car?"

"Could be. Hard to tell which way it's heading though. Maybe that's what the sirens are for."

"Or maybe the siren is for us," suggested Izzy, starkly.

"Whatever it is, we need to get to the fence and get out. Come on."

They turned quickly from the dusty slope and resumed their run south, heading along the length of the ancient water channel until they could finally see the perimeter chain-link fence up ahead. By now the gully had widened and become so shallow that any kind of concealment it provided was long since gone and they began to slow their pace, breathing hard from the effort and the heat, which remained thick in the air despite the slowly setting sun.

As they got nearer, Leon began to wonder if they'd even make it past the tall fence. If height alone wasn't a problem, they were close enough now to see the circles of razor wire curled around the top edge. There was no way they could just run at it. He gestured to Izzy to stop and they staggered to a halt perhaps twenty feet from the fence, then walked the last stretch, trying to catch their breath.

"I suppose it was too much to expect a nice little wooden gate," said Izzy, finally, struggling slightly to breathe and talk. "Now what?"

"Quinn seemed to think this was the way to go. But we can't climb over, and I forgot to pack my wire cutters."

"What did he say exactly?"

"Head for the fence."

"That's it? No actual exit plan?"

Leon held out his hands. "It was implied."

"Well, I guess we'll just have to imply our way through, then," said Izzy, doubtfully.

They split left and right to examine the bottom of the fence more closely, in case there was something they were missing, and continued walking in opposite directions. It didn't look very promising and after heading westward for a hundred feet or so Leon stopped searching. All he could see as he followed the fence with his eye was more of the same: a long, uneven boundary that ran on for perhaps another mile, until it slowly curved around a large rocky promontory and eventually out of sight. He looked back at Izzy who'd gone a similar distance in the other direction but prospects there seemed just as bleak. Worse even, as the uninterrupted view saw the fence snake on all the way to the far horizon.

He let out a sigh, wondering what they should do next, and started heading back when, in the distance, almost at the horizon line itself, he saw a dark object shoot up from what he assumed was the lower valley floor to the north. Although it was too far away to be sure, there was something odd about it he couldn't place. Too small to be a plane, and the wrong shape. And then there was the way it moved. He watched it take a long, high arc then stop, before pausing mid-air and then zipping south again. A moment later, another identical object shot up into the sky but in a clumsier path. It seemed to waver rather than pause, as though hitting a series of unseen obstacles, before evening out and heading straight after the first craft.

"Pretty bold," said Leon, to himself, wondering if these might be test flights. "I thought this stuff was supposed to be secret."

Then he glanced over to the south to see if he could track where they might be going, but his attention was caught by the dust cloud again, now much closer than before. Something was definitely coming in their direction, at speed, and he didn't like the idea of being caught out in the open. He called to Izzy.

"Something's coming," he shouted, waving his arm for her to walk towards him.

Izzy clocked the dust cloud and immediately started jogging in his direction.

"We need some cover," he shouted again, as they got closer to each other, and looked around at the lack of options. Then he pointed to the rocky ridge behind him, to the west.

"But isn't that back towards...?" began Izzy, now only a few feet away.

"It's that, or we just stand here and take our chances."

Izzy looked back at the cloud that, if anything, seemed to be speeding up.

"Someone's in too much of a hurry," she agreed.

They turned and started running up the slope.

Carson knew she should just focus on getting as far away as she could, ditch the Cardinal, and head off-grid. It wouldn't take long for them to send someone after her. But she also felt consumed by anger and intense frustration. Twenty years of work shot to hell in an afternoon. And all because of those two English clowns, she decided. Was she supposed to just let them get away with it?

By this time tomorrow, she was supposed to be sunning herself on Arik Runyon's second favourite yacht, heading west out of Acapulco with a new passport. But instead, it looked like she would be running for her life with only a giant bag of shit and a most-wanted listing to show for it. Then she thought about her dad. And everything that had happened to him. To them, as a family. And the promise she had made to herself when he died. When they killed him.

"I'm sorry, Dad," she muttered, clenching her fists as she cast her eye across the bleached desert basin below. It felt as empty and pointless as it did huge. Where would she even begin to look for them? "I ran out of time."

She accelerated south without really thinking about it. Maybe she could convince Runyon that her hands-on intel would be enough, even though she knew updates to operational protocols would already be underway. By the time she got to Mexico, it would be like a foreign country down there in that underground labyrinth. She needed hardware. Something she could trade. Practical technology that Runyon could use. The Cardinal would be a gift, certainly. But if she could get hold of the crystal...

Her tracking alarm went off; another Cardinal had entered the airspace. It was way too soon for the Tac team to have mounted up, and besides she knew Snark would never approve use of the Cardinals. Always so safe. Always reluctant to share his toys. It must be killing him that she'd gone public in one. It had to be Quinn. She'd be sure to hit him harder next time.

Then the rearview on her heads-up display picked him up making a wide arc in her direction, although his flying seemed erratic. Maybe that wrench to the head hadn't been wasted after all, she thought, as she adjusted her weapon sensors to zero in on him.

"Don't make it too easy, Greg," she murmured, before she pumped the air brakes, and flipped her Cardinal into a sharp U-turn, grateful for the inertial compensators they'd been able to replicate: otherwise she'd be paste with a move like that. She ratcheted back on the power and held her position.

Greg, however, was too preoccupied with stemming the blood seeping from the gash above his split ear to worry about whether he was making things easy or not. He was also trying to pilot a highly advanced experimental aircraft that, despite his seasoned aviator wings, he'd only ever sat simulations for. As ever, the real-life experience turned out to be something else, and he initially struggled to adjust to the sheer speed and hairpin manoeuvrability. It felt like he only had to breathe on the steering for the craft to lurch into a sharp ninety-degree turn. He needed to control his breathing somehow, take a pause, but his head injury and the adrenalin hammering his body had other ideas.

He thought of calling Carson, seeing if he could get her to slow somehow, or at least distract her, when he noticed she had come to a stop already. His display confirmed that Carson had pulled into a stationary position some four-point-eight klicks away. He couldn't be sure why she'd do that but kicked down on the air brakes anyway to slow his advance. Whatever her reasons, he could use the time. Then, as he came to a standstill, facing off in mid-air, still a couple of miles apart, like two old-world cowboys, she hissed in over the radio.

"I'm only going to say this one time, Greg," she said. "Do yourself a favor and stand down. While you still can. Unlike you, I have real flight hours on this bird."

"You know I can't do that, Frances," replied Quinn, after a moment.

He had used the pause to tear off a piece of his shirt and push it up into the gap between the helmet and his wound to help staunch the blood flow. He winced with the pain but now it was in place he could begin to focus on what he needed to do. He flipped a couple of switches and the weapons system came online, over-laying tactical information into his HUD.

"Think about it," she came back. "Just for a second. I know you think you have to do this, but you don't. It's over. I can't do any more damage down there, even if I wanted to do. And in less than an hour I can be over the border and in the wind. Before you've even figured out how to use those weapons you just brought online. You'll never see me again."

Quinn grimaced. Annoyed by her hubris but also that she found him so predictable.

"And you think—what—that I should just give you a free pass? For old time's sake?"

Carson laughed, tweaking the settings on her own tactical readouts.

"Something like that. The old man expects a lot. I, of all people, know that. But he's a pragmatist above all else. Say you lost me, say you had a malfunction, hell, say I shot you down—which I will do by the way—say whatever you like, but just remember that his number one priority in this world is his precious mission, five hundred feet below us. If I'm gone, if the threat is gone, he'll accept it. He won't like it, but he will accept it. Eventually."

"Nice speech," responded Quinn, as he scrolled through the onboard weapons complement; machine guns, micro air-to-air missiles—concussive, chaff, and sonic—and something he hadn't seen before called a primary field weapon that caused him to raise his eyebrows. He was impressed. "You been working on that all week?"

"I'm serious. You want to get yourself killed, fine. I just wanted to give you an out."

She hit the accelerator and started powering towards him at an unreasonable speed.

Leon and Izzy made it up the dusty slope to the natural henge-like grouping of rocks and small boulders near the crown. It gave them some notional cover in all directions except from the chain-link fence, which cut in close to the south side of the cluster. This was fortunate as, looking west, they could glimpse what they assumed was the main gate, way off in the distance. It was easily a couple of miles away, which on the flat would make it hard to spot, but the relative height of their position meant they could trace the snaking roadway where it intersected with the pencil-thin line of the fence. A couple of small structures seemed to mark the spot.

"We definitely won't be going there," confirmed Izzy, as they ducked down behind one of the larger boulders and lay on the ground.

They shuffled around to look back where they had come from, through a gap in the nest of rocks that surrounded them. They were warm to the touch from the desert sun.

"Check out what's happing up there," said Leon, pointing to a patch in the sky, where the two crafts he'd spotted earlier were now facing each other, completely stationary. "What do you think they are?"

"Hard to say," said Izzy. "Until today I would have assumed helicopters, but now I'm not so sure. Do you think they are something to do with us?"

"I don't think so. One seemed to be chasing the other a moment ago. Shame we forgot to pack binoculars."

"Isn't it? Look, they're moving!"

They watched as the one on the right instantly shot towards the one on the left. The left one then reacted sharply, curving up into a steep climb. The first craft swiftly adapted, and responded in kind. Then, together, they shifted into an enormously wide corkscrew ascent, as one object clearly tried to move away and the other pursued.

"Enjoying the show, folks?"

Leon and Izzy jumped at the unexpected voice, and scrambled to get off their stomachs and into a less prone position. Standing on the other side of the fence, with his hands clinging loosely to the chain links and wearing a big toothy grin, was Billy "Snakes" McGraw.

Quinn's collision alarm went off as Carson accelerated towards him, causing him to recoil, as much from the sheer volume as from the warning.

"Jesus," he blurted, lashing out at the audio controls. "Who turned everything up to eleven?"

He kicked the Cardinal into an evasive climb, and Carson followed suit. A moment later they were spiralling upwards in a graceful but deadly pursuit. Quinn ejected a handful of aerial mines into Carson's path, partly as a distraction. She avoided them with ease but, as she did so, Quinn was able to break out of his climb, then spun about to face her directly.

"Now we're cooking," screeched Carson across the radio, and shot off four air-to-air sonic missiles in an attempt to disable Quinn's craft but not kill him.

He was just able to avoid these with a rapid pivot roll and an ejection of chaff in an attempt to throw off their tracking. Then, in response, he leant hard on his controls and pushed his Cardinal into an acute rolling dive, heading straight for Carson, strafing her with all four guns as he approached. She skewed left, then down and away from him in a wide curve, which was what he wanted. He knew, whatever happened, he had to get her close to the ground. It was the only way there was a chance of either of them walking away.

"I'm sure we both have better places to be, Greg," said Carson, as she seriously considered simply bailing on this fight.

She might be more familiar with the vehicle, but in terms of brute tactical dogfighting, Quinn, as a veteran navy flyboy, would always have the edge. Her only hope was to get close enough that she could hit him with the electromagnetic weapon. It was a doozy, she had to admit, and it would take him out of the game completely. But only at point-blank range.

"You may have," replied Quinn. "But I'm good. I cleared my calendar for you."

"Sweet. But unnecessary."

She let rip another round of sonic missiles. Quinn wasn't snappy enough this time and two of them exploded thirty feet ahead of him. The shock waves rippled through the outer surface of his vehicle, literally peeling strips of it away and leaving visible scarring running front to back, including the polycarbonate canopy above his head, if that's what it was. It was plainly enhanced by some exotic material as, instead of fracturing, it rippled like a liquid, letting through enough subsonic waves to force him hard into his seat. Nice move, he thought, as he strained to regain his breath. He needed a better distraction.

"Tell me something, Frances," he began. "Before you rip the skin off this aircraft completely, and me along with it, why don't you clue me in on why we're even doing this?"

"Why?"

"Sure. Because an hour ago, you were the chief of staff for one of the most ambitious and clandestine technology programs this country's ever created. You had power at your disposal even the president doesn't know about. And now? Now you're just another failed domestic terrorist on the run."

"Don't be so crass." Carson resented his curiosity, and his tone. She accelerated away in a straight two-mile line, flipping back around for another hard run at him. It was time to finish this.

"What would you call it, then?"

"Payback."

"You did this for money?" responded Quinn, genuinely surprised by her answer. Whatever he had imagined her career-ending motives might have been, he didn't see that coming. "And you call me crass."

"You don't know what the hell you're talking about," she spat, enraged by his suggestion. "I didn't do this for money."

Then she floored the Cardinal in retaliation, covering the distance between them almost instantly. But Quinn was already ahead of her, easily clocking Carson's clumsy kill-run manoeuvre and dropped three hundred feet just as she arrived. Despite a last-second, forty-five-degree pivot, she clipped one of the three aerial mines Quinn had left behind. It exploded on impact and tore out a large chunk of her Cardinal's right rear flank. The craft lurched from the impact and loss of control, and its power levels started dropping. Carson swore at her miscalculation and tried reversing into a measured descent in an attempt to regain control, but the craft was too unstable. She saw Quinn below, as he smoothly carved out a wide circle, and knew she only had one good shot left. It was that or make a run for it, but she refused to give him the satisfaction.

She cranked up the controls and put the Cardinal into a semi-controlled dive, knowing that even though the engine was compromised, gravity would do half the work for her. Her plan was to pound him with the electromagnetic weapon and eject at the last moment. But, considering his relatively safe position, she hadn't counted on him turning directly into her path.

"Don't do it, Carson," yelled Quinn, as he carefully lined up his Cardinal with hers. "I won't yield. You still have a chance to walk away from this."

Carson sniggered at the suggestion. "You think I never played chicken before?"

She half swooped, half fell in a precipitously descending curve until she was maybe twenty feet from the ground. Quinn adjusted his heading to match, then accelerated directly towards her.

"Not with me," he said, pushing harder on the pedal.

It was two opposing speedway cars on a dead straight race to the finish. At the last possible instant, Carson punched the weapon, pulled a hard left, and reached for the eject lever beneath her seat. Quinn was immediately enveloped by an electromagnetic bubble. An invisible wave of power crashed over him, surging through every dial, screen, and control in the Cardinal and lighting up every hair and pore on his skin like a bulb, before sucking it all away like a greedy vampire.

Leon, Izzy, and McGraw looked up in unison as the sound of an immense explosion ripped across the darkening desert sky.

50

DUE SOUTH

McGraw let out a long whistle. Leon and Izzy turned to look at him.

"Sounds like somebody ain't coming home for supper tonight," he said.

"Snakes," responded Leon, ignoring his remark, "what are you doing here? How did you find us?"

"Snakes?" said Izzy, sceptically. "You actually know this guy?"

"He surely does," interjected McGraw, tipping his hat. "The name's McGraw. Billy "Snakes" McGraw. My friends all call me *Snakes*."

Leon and Izzy got up off the ground and dusted themselves off as they cautiously approached the fence.

"Why do they call you Snakes?" asked Izzy.

McGraw looked at her like she'd just asked the strangest question he'd ever heard.

"Because...it's my name?"

"Oh right," yielded Izzy, somewhat disappointed. "I thought there might be something else to it...like maybe you kept snakes."

"Ahh do keep snakes!" he yelped, with some glee.

Izzy shook her head.

"Snakes," said Leon, trying again. "What...why are you here?"

"For you, you dumbass. Quinn called me up. Told me to come git you. Din't leave much time for it neither. Damned near had to kill myself to do it."

"That was you?"

"Me what?"

"We saw a dust trail kicking up. Heading here. We thought someone…or something was coming for us."

"That was most likely me alright. Out here you don't get much road traffic on account of the military. Which reminds me. We better be getting you folks outta here lickety-split."

McGraw produced a heavy-duty pair of bolt cutters from inside his jacket and began to go to work on the base of the fence.

"Won't they have cameras?" asked Izzy.

"Normally, ma'am, you would be correct," answered McGraw, without looking up. "But Quinn took care of it. Tol' me I had about a fiff-teen-minute window to get in, and you out." He looked at his watch, clipped one last link to complete a small rectangular flap and pulled it up by way of an invitation for them to crawl through. "Of which we have about three minutes left. Better hurry."

Leon nudged Izzy through first then darted after her, letting the chain-link flap down with a tinny rattle against the metal frame. McGraw quickly applied a couple of cable ties to fasten it back into place, then led them down the slope running parallel to the fence. It quickly led into a wide gully before rising up again and over a steep ridge some forty feet away.

There was a punishing drop on the other side. It was much sharper than the one they had climbed up, but McGraw seemed to navigate it like an old mountain goat. Leon and Izzy did their best to keep up, narrowly avoiding several falls along the way and eventually reached the base of the near-vertical bluff. It led into a considerably deeper fissure than they had anticipated from the top but soon they saw why; it provided perfect cover for what looked like a historic mule track, not much wider than the old beat-up truck McGraw had parked there under an overhanging shelf. The last part of their descent involved dropping from that rocky shelf directly onto the truck bed.

"How did you know where we'd be?" asked Leon as he climbed into the cabin after Izzy.

"Some might say it was luck," replied McGraw, with a wink, as he started up the truck.

He yanked the gearstick into drive before Leon or Izzy could react and they lurched away, the gravel crunching loudly under the heavy tires.

Several miles away Captain Gregory Quinn lay on his back, cushioned by his aviation seat, staring up at the fading orange light of the setting sun, and watching it fight with the inky blue bleeding in from the east. The first cut of stars were beginning to show and he blinked hard, taking a moment to clear his head as he recalled those last seconds when his ejector seat wrenched him free of the Cardinal, just as Carson's weapon sucked all its power away. A controlled electromagnetic pulse, he realised too late, as he strained under the intense force pushing him up and out of danger. Clever. He should have used it himself. But then, as it turns out, he didn't need to, since the next moment there was a deafening blast as the now lifeless husk of his craft collided with Carson, who had not accounted for the damage to her own Cardinal before attempting to break away. He could feel the roiling heat of the fireball rip past him, even as he pulled away at twelve G's and wondered, in the second before he momentarily blacked out, if it would set fire to his parachute.

He smiled to himself at what might have been his very last thought. So poetic. It obviously hadn't, and he reached up to unclip himself from his harness, managing to roll sideways out of the seat, and clamber awkwardly into an upright position. He mentally checked his body for new injuries but found only muscle pain and stiffness in his back from the escape compression.

Behind him, the deflated parachute canopy was still attached to the seat, tugging at the end of its long cords, as the loose, silky nylon material flapped and rolled in the desert breeze.

To his right, perhaps three hundred feet away or more, he could see the crashed and burning remains of the two experimental aircrafts. He took a moment to look around for signs of another parachute, curious as to whether Carson had made it out, but he couldn't see anything.

Farther away, on the horizon, he spied a dust trail, illuminated against the low sun. Probably coming from a car, he thought, and hoped it was McGraw—complete with cargo—rather than a team from the base on its way to investigate the crash.

He checked over his flight chair and pulled out a small survival kit that contained a canister of water, a flare gun, and two clips of ammo for his standard issue sidearm. He drank the water down in one hit, then pulled out his M17 pistol. He popped the magazine from the handle, before shoving it back in and racking the slider to chamber a round.

"Expecting trouble, Captain?" came a voice from behind him. It was Carson. And he could tell just from her smugness that she was armed.

"Well, if it isn't good old Frances Carson," responded Quinn, dryly, as he slowly turned with his hands out, despite the handgun. "You know, I have to say, I'm kind of relieved. I thought you might be over there, turning into brisket with the old red birds."

Carson stood firmly, in a classic tactical stance, her own gun raised and supported by her left hand, aimed squarely at Quinn. Other than that, she looked terrible. Plainly she had been less fortunate when it came to her escape, and all the way down her left side she was variously cut and burned. The side of her face and head, in particular, was noticeably charred, cracked, and weeping, with some of her hair burnt away. Willpower alone seemed to be all that was keeping her standing.

"I'm touched. Really. But why don't we start with you handing over your weapon?"

Quinn acquiesced. Even without her obvious pain and frustration, he knew from experience that Carson wouldn't hesitate to shoot him. He had to imagine the only reason she hadn't done it already was because she needed something from him. He could use that.

He flipped his gun around and offered it to her handle-first. She snatched it with her free hand and threw it hard out across the dusty, rocky gloom that surrounded them. It hit a stratified band of rock sticking out of the ground and slid into a gully. Carson visibly relaxed a little but kept her gun firmly on Quinn.

"OK, so you left my gun for some poor kid to find one day. Can we talk now?" said Quinn, hoping to find a level with her.

"I can talk. You can do what I tell you. Let's go." Carson waved her gun to indicate a direction of travel.

Quinn sighed. Seemed she wanted to go the hard way.

"I gotta say, Frances, you look awful."

"I didn't ask."

"Maybe that's because you haven't seen yourself."

"Nice try. But unless you've got a dermal kit in your back pocket, I'll live with it." Quinn looked blankly at her. "I didn't think so," she continued, and waved her gun again. "Start walking."

"To where? Back to the base? I don't think you'll get much of a welcome."

"No, Greg. We're going to find your little British friends and take back what they stole."

"I'm not sure—"

"Don't even try," she snapped, gesturing towards the yellow-orange horizon where the dust trail was still just visible. "I saw that vehicle arrive when I was up there waiting to kick your ass outta the sky. I don't know how you did it but, whoever that was, it's the only way they could get out of here. On foot they'd be dead or captured in less than a day."

"Frances, I think you have the wrong idea."

She cocked the gun and aimed it at the top of his left thigh.

"You really want me to cripple the other one? I don't have to kill you. I can just put you in a chair for the rest of your life. Is that what you want?"

Quinn held up his hands. "OK. Alright."

They started walking in silence but after ten minutes or so Carson began to talk again. Quinn wondered if it was just to cover for her obvious pain.

"So, I figure you had a nice little arrangement going," she began. "I don't know why, or who for—Milk? Yeah, maybe Milk. I don't really give a shit at this point. I just want what they have and I know you wouldn't simply let them go off into the sunset. You must have a way of tracking them. Now gimme."

Quinn hesitated to respond. Of course he had slipped a tracker on them. How else would Snakes find them? But if he just gave it up, what then? He needed some way to stay close to her. He needed some leverage.

"Oh, you mean this?" he said, holding up his phone. Carson took a step forward to grab it from him. He jerked it out of her reach and her face darkened. "Not so fast."

"You're really going to make me shoot you."

"Up to you. But it's a company issue, and you know how these things work. Hell, you were the one who insisted on the protocol."

"Bio-locked," she muttered, aggravated by her own foresight and lack of it at the same time.

"That's right. Bio-locked. Anyone else tries to force access and it resets to zero. Then neither you, me, nor anyone else will find what you're looking for. Simples, as the kids like to say. I'm happy to just let them walk away, back to their lives. If I have to. Are you?"

"Goddammit. I don't need a passenger on this."

"And I don't want be one. So, I'll help you find them. But until we do—and you let those two kids go free—I'm your goddamn partner!"

.   .   .

Those two kids, meanwhile, sat in silence while McGraw carefully navigated the truck out of the long, snaking, and painfully uneven mule canyon. Or as close to silence as McGraw would allow. He insisted on whistling some chirpy little country tune that neither of them was familiar with (although, based on more than a few bum notes, Leon wasn't certain that McGraw was that familiar with it either). But they didn't mind so much, content to just be heading away from all the insanity. And the farther south they got, the better they began to feel.

Eventually the truck surfaced from the partially concealed and dangerously uneven track they'd been following, and the land levelled out into a more open and regular off-road course. This went on for another couple of miles before it met with and merged into a normal paved highway, complete with a bright yellow line down the centre.

"Feels good to be back in civil-i-zation, don't it?" said McGraw, breaking the peace.

"I really does," responded Izzy, smiling. "Where are you taking us?"

"He din't tell you?" he said, meaning Leon.

"No," said Leon. "We didn't exactly get a chance to talk it all through. Milk has a place nearby."

"Cobalt Flats."

"Sounds like a nice place," said Izzy, more to be friendly than anything else.

"Not much of a place, to be sure," said McGraw. "A one-horse town is kinda overstatin' it. Anyways, I dropped these folks off there this mornin'. That's 'bout all I know."

"Will Milk be there, waiting for us?" asked Izzy. She was keen to meet him. Not because he was Milk, or because she wanted to punch him in the face for putting Leon—and her—in such danger but because she figured billionaires probably have good security. That they'd finally be safe. She hoped.

"Cain't say I knows either way," replied McGraw. "I never met him. Your buddy Quinn says pick you up and take you there, that's what I do. That's what I'm paid to know. Which is fine by me."

"What do you do, Billy? Aside from picking up random English people in the middle of the desert."

"Snakes, ma'am. Please."

"Sorry—Snakes! Is this, like, your job?"

"No, ma'am, not normally it ain't. I got an auto repair shop up near Ely. Fix the cars myself too, when I can."

"How'd you get mixed up in all this?" asked Leon.

"How long've you got?" laughed McGraw.

"You tell me," chuckled Leon in return. "I have no idea where we're going."

"Well, let's just say, me and some of the boys in Milk's security team, we used to run together at one time. Not close. But we stayed connected. We was United States Marine Corps. Still am o' course."

"You're on active service?" asked Leon, doubtfully. McGraw didn't look it by at least fifteen years, and more than a friendly acquaintance with Jack Daniels if the empty bottles in the bottom of the cab were anything to go by.

"Nah. But you know what they say. Once a Marine... We have a code. I like to live by it and so I run a little off-books security on the side. Mostly jobs like this, that you cain't book an Uber for."

"Got it," said Leon.

"Do you have a family?" asked Izzy, curious about his motivations.

"I surely do, ma'am. Married eight years this December. Two little girls, seven and five. It's what I do this for. Gonna help pay for their college. Don't need them growin' up a grunt like their old man."

Izzy nodded, and they fell into silence once again. The truck slowly descended through a series of narrow gorges before the road finally spilled out of the low mountains they'd been travelling through and down into the wide-open valley of southeast Nevada. Despite the cover of night, it was still an impressive view across to the far side where the mountains rose up again to frame the star-speckled sky above. The valley floor itself was neatly punctuated by the straight seam of Route 93, cutting north to south, with a steady string of lights from all the cars and trucks.

"Looks purty, don't it?" said McGraw. "All the lights. The people comin' and goin'."

It was the last time he'd ever see it.

51

TINFOIL HAT

Carson and Quinn walked briskly southeast, heading for the nearest public road with the aim of sequestering a vehicle. Most of the area they'd been travelling through had been part of a large exclusion zone designed to protect Snark's installation, but fortunately for Carson their calamitous jaunt in the Cardinals had taken them right to the edge of it. They cautiously crunched their way down a meandering gravelly slope towards a narrow road curving its way around the hillside.

"You know, it really doesn't have to be like this," said Quinn as they got to the road.

"You want me to just give up the gun and turn myself in, is that it?"

"Well, I'm sure you think you have your reasons."

"Spare me your condescending bullshit. You think because we're shackled together, you're going to talk me down with a little discount Dr Phil? Please."

"Fine. But do you really think this will be the end of it? That I'll be the last person to come after you? You know better than that."

"I do."

"I'll certainly be the last person to come after you who gives a shit. I can tell you that."

Carson smiled bitterly. She still had a certain amount of grudging respect for Quinn, despite what he was trying to do. But she knew it wouldn't end well. Then she saw the glimmer of headlights cut into the bend up ahead and motioned for Quinn to stop.

"Something's coming. Stay here."

Carson scooted to the centre of the road, attempting to mask her pain, and raised her weapon. An old Wagoneer—a classic station wagon, complete with wooden panels—came gently round the corner. It was driven by an equally classic gentleman who'd probably had the car from new. He hit the brakes as soon as he saw Carson and came to a stop just a couple of feet in front of her.

Carson had been fully prepared to simply shoot the driver, whoever they turned out to be, but when she saw the old man's face, she paused. She knew it was probably a mistake but told herself that killing him would be too messy, even though she knew it was a lie.

"Out of the car, sir," shouted Carson. "Now."

The old man was clearly confused so Carson made it easier for him. She walked round to the driver's door, yanked it open, and pointed the gun at his head. His hands slowly went up.

"I said, out of the car."

The man climbed cautiously and awkwardly out of the car, while trying to keep his hands up.

"Are you OK, lady?" he said, noticing her injuries, and taking a step back. "Do you need—"

"What I need is for you to go sit over there on that rock."

Carson pointed with her gun to a group of rocks at the side of the road. He hesitated, looking back at his open car before shuffling slowly over to the rock as instructed. She looked back at the car to see what had made him vacillate and saw there was a large dog sitting patiently in the backseat. Probably as old as he was, she figured, and flipped open the rear door. The dog immediately jumped out and went to his master, sitting neatly by him. The man placed a hand on his head.

"I can see you're pretty beat up," said the man. "Did someone do that to you? You look like you could use some help."

"No, sir," replied Carson, wincing in pain as she reached into the passenger's seat and pulled out a half-empty gallon of water. She unscrewed the cap and took a couple of deep swigs using both hands to hold it up, before putting the lid back on and chucking at the man's feet. "What I could use is your car. This is federal business."

"This don't look like no federal business to me," said the old man. "Looks to me like stealing."

Carson looked at him. He looked small and pitiful. Why was she even bothering with him?

"You're stealing what don't belong to you," he continued. "For what—money? You hurting for something? Other than your beat-up face, I mean."

His words seemed to prick her. She felt enraged by his presumption. And a second later she was right up in his face, pressing the gun directly onto his head.

"Shut the fuck up, old man," she snarled. "Or I'll give you more than a goddamn story to tell your friends." Then raised the gun to clip him with it.

Quinn appeared behind her and touched her arm gently, to stay her hand.

"Leave it, Frances," he cautioned, quietly. "Leave the man be."

Carson snapped her arm away from him and skittered backwards to face both men, looking wildly from one to the other.

"Don't you touch me," she seethed, raising the gun again. "I'll do what the hell I like."

Quinn glanced at the old man, who raised his thick white eyebrows in return.

"She with you?" he ventured.

"You could say that," replied Quinn, ruefully.

The old man nodded sympathetically, as if he'd seen it all. "What is it, booze? Pills?"

"UFOs."

"You," shouted Carson at Quinn. By now she was back behind the car on the driver's side, using the roof to support her aim. "Get in the goddamn car!"

"Time to go," said Quinn, tapping the old man on his shoulder. "We'll leave your phone by the road some ways down. You should be able to get yourself a ride."

"Good luck," said the man, strangely at peace with this arrangement.

Quinn scooted over to the station wagon and dropped into the passenger seat as Carson started the car. She hit the gas and pulled away before he even had the door closed.

They rode on in silence and, after dropping off the old man's phone, followed the road south as it wove its way down the mountainside towards the wide-open valley below.

"What the hell was all that?" asked Quinn, finally.

"Would you have preferred it if I'd just shot him and left him for the birds?"

"No, I wouldn't have preferred it. But if you weren't going to kill him, did you really have to scare the crap out of him?"

"Sorry if it upset you."

"It didn't upset me, Frances... I just thought, maybe there was something else going on."

Carson laughed brashly.

"Like what?"

"Like why you're even doing all this? I thought maybe—"

"What do you want, Greg? A confession? I'm all good, thanks. This is just business. We're trading here: what you want, for what I want. Nothing more. Killing a random old man didn't seem very profitable."

"Nothing more," scoffed Quinn. "I know you, Frances. You may not think so, but we've worked together for—what—almost decade? And with you, it's never the trade we're making but always the one you're going to make. Hell, maybe even the one after that. I've never known you be anything less than three moves ahead. Except today. Today was something else. Something... personal. I think the old man had something to do with that."

Carson let out a frustrated sigh. He was never going to shut up.

"Do you know what it's like to grow up in a family of broken people, Greg?"

"Yeah, life's hard. Is that all you've got?"

"I'm not talking about divorce, or goddamn alcoholics and prescription painkillers here, Greg. I'm talking about people who have had their lives taken away, destroyed. Everything they were, everything they could have been. All they could have given—gone. Because they said the wrong thing to the wrong people. Because they wouldn't stay quiet."

"What the hell are you talking about?" Quinn was genuinely confused but, at the same time, didn't really care—only that she kept talking. That way, maybe Leon and Izzy had a chance.

"I'm talking about what happens when little people, real people, get caught up in the wheels of the military-industrial machine we call the US government."

Now it was Quinn's turn to laugh. "What is this—regret? You *are* the military-industrial machine."

Carson's jaw clenched tightly as stared down the road ahead, seething with a rage she could barely contain.

"1947, my grandfather owned a little farm in New Mexico. Nothing grand, not the biggest, but simple. Steady. Stood for quality. At least, it did once. Had been in the family for four generations. Then one day, literally outta the blue, something lands in one of his fields—"

"Oh Jesus," interrupted Quinn. "This? Roswell? You know better than anyone what really happened there. And now you want me to believe it was your granddaddy's farm? You wouldn't even be here if—"

"How fucking dare you!" screamed Carson. "You think you know? You don't know anything. My grandfather was old-school.

Patriotic. Fresh out of WWII. He cooperates all the way. They tell him to be quiet? Play along? He plays along. Hands over everything. Almost. He was a good soldier but not an idiot. He knew what he had. And he knew that it might really be worth something someday. So, he kept a little back for himself. Some photographs he never talked about. And some of the exotic material he found.

"He was going to let it all die down and, when the time was right, trade it up. For industry, or even back to the government. Hell, he didn't care, from what I heard. But best laid plans..."

"What happened?"

"Heart attack. 1958. By then the farm was on its knees. Something in the soil, goes the story. Something the government did to it after they cleared out the crash site in '47, they all said. Amazing the stories people will come up with, right?"

"Yeah, except some of them are true. But did we actually do anything like that back then?"

"Us. UFOs. Weather balloons. The commies. Does any of it really matter? Whatever, the crops began to fail and the cattle started dying. It was all pretty much gone by the time he died, his customers too. Some they'd known for over twenty years and my grandma never forgave them, or the government.

"He died leaving her, my dad, and his sister with nothing but a whole lot of debt. Bank called the loan a few months later then, next year rolls around and they were living out of a second-hand trailer in the ass end of the state."

"Wait, so you're telling me this is all just about money?"

"No, it's not about money," spat Carson.

"Then what!? Your dear old granddaddy must have been dead twenty years before you were even thought of. What does—"

"Actions have consequences, Greg. You know that better than most. See, my dad, he became a true believer. It's pretty much all he had growing up; my grandma's stories, and a whole lot of anger. She would never stop talking about it, even when I was a kid: about how a spaceship landed in their backyard, and the government took everything they had. Most folks in the town thought she was just a nut who enjoyed the juice a little too much. But my dad? He ate it all up like a good boy.

"By the time I showed up, he was all in. He may as well have gone around with a tinfoil hat. Him and my mom both. They met when they were too young to know any better, and drifted between a bunch of outsider communities—that's what they called them but hippies basically—because my dad had his mission. Always his mission. That's what he called it 'To Prove Dad Was Right, man.'" said Carson, putting on a deeper, well-practised hippy-ish voice. "...and that humanity were just mice in some big lab experiment and, I guess, to get some kind of compensation from the government. But good luck with that, right?"

Quinn nodded silently. He began to see where this was going but was curious how the hell Carson had hidden this from all the background checks. Surely Snark must have known.

"How are we doing?" asked Carson, meaning how close were they to Leon and Izzy.

"Not too far now, I think," Quinn replied, glancing at the tracker and wondering whether it was too soon to try to take Carson out. But talking seemed to be bringing her down to earth, and he reminded himself to be patient. "They're on an old service road, heading for the 93 south."

Carson gave Quinn a sideways glance.

"That means Vegas. We need to intercept before they get there."

"Looks like there's an old gas station just before the intersection. Maybe we'll all get lucky."

In a secure meeting room at the back of the main operations area, Linden Snark was conferring with Macintyre, Keynes, Milo, and a select number of operatives and tactical personnel. A medic was also in attendance, patiently trying to take Snark's blood pressure, but he was doing his best to ignore her ministrations.

"Listen up, beautiful people," he began, darkly. "As you know, our once good friend and colleague, Lieutenant Commander Carson, has gone rogue. Seems she has been leading us on a merry little dance all her own for God knows how long. And while we've spent the past four days climbing up our own ass, looking for a mole, seems she's been right here with us all along, holding the fricking ladder."

A general muttering of disapproval circled the room.

"So, let me start by being very clear: no one here is more regretful than I am. No one. But we are where we are, and there'll be plenty of time later for crying and finger-pointing. So, whatever you may be feeling, I want everybody to put a pin in it for now. We have a raging fire to put out. And if we don't do it quickly it's going to take all of us down with it.

"For right now, I need everyone to stay 100 percent focused. We need to find Frances Carson. And we need to find her now. We need to bring her in alive and see what else she has been doing to undermine decades of work. I don't care about why—that's for someone else. After I'm dead, which probably won't be very long. I care about what, and I care about who. In that order. Got it?"

Everyone nodded.

"Obviously, her security access has already been revoked. And we have at least one agent in the field tracking her as we speak. But as of right now we are initiating a full, global systems and intelligence sweep, from here to the Pentagon, from the White House to the goddamn Sixteenth Street Laundromat in NYC. Hell, if she went to the bathroom in a Starbucks in Singapore on a layover eight years ago, I want a team in there counting how many paper towels she used to dry her hands. I want to know everywhere Carson has been or touched in the past decade, and every person she has talked to. We have no idea who else may be involved or how dirty the rabbit hole will get, so I want it done qui-et-ly. Nothing goes outside of this room. Can everyone get their head around that?"

The group nodded once again and murmured their understanding.

"Good. Great. Then let's go to work."

The room broke up, and people began making calls or running to their workstations to begin their assignments. Keynes and Macintyre cornered Snark as he went to return to his office.

"What is it?"

"We think we might have something, sir," began Keynes, quietly.

"Already? I love you guys. Show me."

They stepped over to the nearest console where Keynes typed in a number of commands and brought up a live satellite feed, along with a row of heat maps.

"So, we tracked the Cardinals as you asked," said Keynes, pausing the satellite feed and jumping back to an earlier time-code. "Here's Carson exiting the complex and heading south, then a short time later you can see Quinn doing the same. If we track forward..." Keynes moved the timeline forward, then pulled up a number of different images. "It appears they engaged in hostilities here, resulting in the loss of both aircraft. We planned to send out a recovery team, but then we caught this—it's clear they not only both survived, but are now engaged in some overt action together. At first, we were optimistic that Quinn had merely taken Carson into custody. However, it quickly became evident they were not only heading away from us but, as you can see, must have requisitioned a vehicle of some kind."

"We have to assume Quinn has been co-opted into Carson's plan in some way," added Macintyre.

"Surely it would be easier to just kill him," suggested Snark.

"Exactly. Dragging him into it must be purely about leverage."

"That means he either has something she wants, or she's injured in some way and can't complete it on her own. Possibly both."

"That was our thought too, sir," said Keynes, bringing up another heat map. "Then we noticed this. Not long after Carson took off, we see another vehicle—a car most likely—skirting the very edge of our restricted area."

"Where did it come from? Is it one of ours?"

"It's not entirely clear, sir," said Macintyre. "But I'd say negative. I've already gone back through the logs with the vehicular systems team and everything seems to be accounted for. Minus the two Cardinals, of course."

Snark registered Mac's modest jibe but chose to ignore it. The man was way too attached to those little red flying cars. He'd have to do something about that, he decided.

"On closer inspection," continued Keynes. "We saw the vehicle emerge from one of the old mule gullies that crisscross the region. Unfortunately, we weren't able to track its arrival so it could have been there for several hours, for all we know, or even days."

"OK, fine. But what's the significance? It could just be a car full of nerds with tinfoil on their heads. We must get ten of those little truth-seekers a month cruising by," scoffed Snark.

"It's entirely possible, sir. But where it gets interesting is here." Keynes brought up another video feed, with some tracking data overlaid. "This one on the left—that's Carson. The other one coming in lower down from the right—that's the nerd car."

Snark cut Keynes a wry glance. *I like this one,* he thought.

"They keep going like that," realised Snark. "They're going to run into each other. And I don't believe in coincidence."

"Exactly. There are any number of back roads Carson could have taken if she just wanted to escape south. But it's clear from the data—and we've been over it several times—that Carson is purposefully adjusting her heading to match the other car."

"She's tracking it, somehow. Interesting. A planned rendezvous, do you think?"

"That's our working theory, sir," confirmed Macintyre. "She must have signalled for an exfiltration of some kind, before her hand was forced."

"Hmm," mumbled Snark, considering what he was seeing. "Or it could be those two Brits. Although it's difficult to see how the hell they could have organized it. Did we pick up anything at all on their departure?"

"Nothing so far, sir. We prioritized Carson, as you requested."

"Exactly right. They can wait. Goddamn tourists."

"Do you want me to prepare an intercept, sir?" offered Macintyre. "For Carson."

"Yes, Mac, I do. And no, before you ask, we won't be using the Cardinals. A helicopter will do just fine."

"Yes, sir," agreed Macintyre, with just a hint of disappointment.

"But I want to see how this plays out before we jump in. Got it? This could be our only chance to see who else is on the hook along with Carson. And if by some freaky-deaky chance it does turn out to be those two kids, then I'd prefer not to return them home in a box."

"Yes, sir," said Macintyre. "Understood."

"Keynes, excellent work."

"Thank you, sir."

"And I want you to stay on this exclusively while Mac and I head out. Have Milo assist you if you need it. But no one else."

"Sir?" interjected Macintyre, curious about Snark's comment.

"I'm coming with you, Mac. Problem?"

"No, sir. It's just—"

"Very good. Then we're all done."

52

HIT THE GAS

"So, help me out here," began Quinn, as Carson took a hard right and accelerated down an old dirt road that would bring them out close to the gas station. "Your dad was some kind of UFO nut job and somehow, against all the odds, you end up here, leading the operation that would prove he was right all along. And now you just want to trash the place so no one else can play—is that it? What the hell happened?"

"What happened is when Grandma died, and my dad cleared out her trailer, he found the box."

"The box?"

"He found Grandpa's little box of secrets. Pieces of strange metal, photographs of crashed vehicles and dead ETs. Yep, the whole schmear. And for my dad, this was the motherlode. But it was already too late for him. Even if it weren't all for the booze and the drugs and the alternative lifestyle issues, we—us, the government—were still operating a strict 'discredit, destroy, and recover' protocol. Dismiss the witness, destroy their reputation if they persisted and steal whatever evidence they had collected. You remember Project Blue Book."

"Sure, the public-facing Air Force study of UFOs. But that ended in, like, 1971 or something."

"1969. Officially, that is. 'Mass hysteria' is what they concluded. Misidentification, psychopathology, and mass hysteria. But you and I know that it never really went away. And in the meantime, the template was set. It was a perfect cover. Anyone who spoke up about it was simply dismissed as a nut job. You just said it yourself."

"Sorry, I was just—"

"It doesn't matter. You were right. And by the time my dad found that box, the drinking and the opiates pretty much did it for all of us. He was easy pickings. So, when he finally tried to play his hand, he couldn't even get a library card much less a meeting with his congressman. He tried going to the papers and you can imagine how that turned out. Eventually he tried forcing his way into an airbase and got arrested. And it was all downhill from there."

"So, you joining the Navy and finding your way here was, what, vindication? Control?"

"Payback."

"For what?"

"You know what they did with young kids back then when their parents are either in jail or wasted at the local flophouse? I ended up living with my aunt and her own string of bad choices. But not before she'd legally adopted me."

"Ah, so that's how you did it," mumbled Quinn.

"What?"

"That's how you got into the system without any of this shit coming up."

"That's right. Carson was my aunt's first husband. Fresh start as far as the Navy recruiting officer cared to look."

"And so all this," began Quinn, waving a hand. "This bullshit you've suckered me and Snark and the rest of us into, is just a revenge thing? For some—what—some bad luck?"

"What the hell would you know about it?" growled Carson, hitting the brakes and bringing them to a sharp halt. "I wanted payback for everything they took from me, my dad, my whole family. The life we could have had. I wanted to bring the whole thing down, and show the world the real cost of keeping all these secrets. And the people who have to pay it."

"Well, let me tell you what the hell I know about it," replied Quinn. "I know you're not the first kid to come up short on good parenting, and I know that therapy is probably a lot cheaper than giving up your whole life to a cause just so you can blow it all up. Did you even have a backup plan? Because from where I sit it seems to me you put your whole life on the line to end up with nothing."

"Fuck you," snapped Carson, and whacked him unconscious with the butt of her gun.

McGraw's truck rumbled into Quinn's gas station, just before Highway 93, as predicted. It was an antique two-pump affair, with a dusty old storefront that looked like it hadn't been touched since Project Blue Book was disbanded (officially). The proprietor was an equally worn-out gentleman in dirty overalls, and a thick, long beard, sitting out front on a grey wooden bench. He wore an oily baseball cap and was pulling on the last of a cigarette as McGraw stepped out of the truck.

"Well, well, if ain't old Dave McGraw's little man come to see me at last."

"How you doin', George?" replied Snakes with a grin. "You been saying that since I was fif-teen."

"That I have. So, what brings you out here to the boonies?"

"Little o' this, little o' that," said McGraw, as he pulled the nozzle out of the closest pump and hooked it up to his truck.

"I hear ya. And I see you got yerself some company," said George with a nod to Leon and Izzy in the cab. "Friends or trouble?"

"Friends, this time."

"Well, OK, then. Guess trouble must still be on its way. What can I do you for?"

"Just a little gas, and some water. Maybe somethin' to chew."

"Well, you know where everything is. Just leave your greens on the counter."

McGraw nodded, then stuck his head into the open truck window.

"You need anything?"

"A loo would be good," said Izzy. "If there is one."

"A what?"

"Restroom," translated Leon.

"Oh right," laughed McGraw, turning back to the old man. "George! Can these folks use your bathroom?"

George held out his arm in a sweeping gesture. *"Mi casa, su casa,"* he said, then spat ceremoniously onto the ground.

"Go through the store and head all the way in, to the right. You'll see a door marked Private. It ain't up to much but, believe me, you do *not* want to use the one out back."

Izzy nodded and jumped out of the cab, followed by Leon.

"I'll come with you," said Leon, and they walked in together, smiling at the old man as they passed. He tipped his oily hat at them in return. McGraw set the pump to fill and followed them in to gather some provisions and leave George his money.

When Leon and Izzy came back outside a short while later, there was another car parked up behind McGraw's truck, with its lights on full. It made it hard to see clearly. But there was no mistaking the voice that stepped out of it.

"Feeling better?" yelled Carson as she walked around the open driver's door.

Leon unconsciously stepped in front of Izzy and held up an arm in front of his eyes to try to block the light. He could see Carson walking slowly towards them, with her gun pointed directly at him. She looked awful, he thought. Half-cooked.

"Good boy," said Carson, cocking the handgun and adopting the shooter's position. "Both hands please. Up in the air. You too, Isabella."

"How did you find us?" said Izzy, raising her arms in the air.

"Just lucky, I guess." She waved them towards McGraw's truck with the pointed gun. "Both of you. Move."

They started walking, and as Carson crossed the headlight beams to follow, Leon noticed Quinn, unconscious or dead in the passenger seat. He wasn't sure whether he should feel relieved that he was there, or resigned that they would soon be joining him, when the sound of a shotgun being racked cut in.

"Not so fast, little miss," declared George, with a surprising power in his voice. He was standing now, with a shotgun aimed directly at Carson.

"Who the hell are you?" complained Carson, disdainfully.

"What does it say above the door?"

Carson glanced up, above the man's head. There was an old, weathered sign that read: Old George's Lucky 93. Gas & Oil.

"Old George, am I right?" quipped Carson.

"No, ma'am. Old George was my dad."

"What's lucky about it?"

"We're licensed for gamblin' inside."

"Not anymore," said Carson, bluntly, then shot George in the head. He fell where he stood and his shotgun went off as it hit the ground.

Leon and Izzy both screamed and backed up until they hit McGraw's truck. Their hands stayed up above their heads. And McGraw appeared in the doorway of George's not-so-lucky 93 store a moment later.

"What the hell!?" he shouted, as his unbelieving gaze fell upon the scene. He unconsciously began fumbling with his open belt buckle, as he'd literally run from the toilet when he heard the gunshots.

"Jesus," shouted Carson. "How many more of you back there?"

"Just me, ma'am," spluttered McGraw, trying to figure out what the hell had just happened. "Just me. What did you do to George?"

"His luck ran out."

"Well, I mean, that's just cruel," noted Leon to Izzy, quietly.

Carson shot him a look before turning back to McGraw.

"And who are you—George the fucking third?"

"McGraw, ma'am. Billy 'Snakes' McGr—"

"I don't really give a shit."

"Look, lady…" began McGraw, trying to defuse the situation. "If you want money, there's a register back there. And I'm sure—"

"I don't want the goddamn money, you idiot."

"Then what do you want?" asked Izzy. "Why have you followed us here?"

"You have something that doesn't belong to you. I've come to get it back."

Leon and Izzy looked at each other, then shrugged.

"Not really sure what you mean," said Leon, noticing that McGraw was reaching for something behind his back, and hoping it was more than his belt.

Carson made an exaggerated, frustrated sigh. "You really want to do this the hard way. How do you think that worked out for old George here? And he had a shotgun."

"I'm afraid I'm gonna' have to stop you there, ma'am," interrupted McGraw, holding a pistol of his own. He immediately began stepping sideways to avoid any retaliation from Carson. "I don't know what you want with these folks, but I cain't permit you to threaten them."

Carson laughed, despite the pain of her cracked and weeping skin.

"You can't permit me? What do you think is happening here?"

She fired her gun at McGraw and missed. He ducked and rolled on the ground to take up position behind a cluster of old water barrels filled with wizened desert plants and cigarette butts. Leon and Izzy used the distraction to scoot around McGraw's truck for protection. They only got as far as the engine hood before Carson fired a warning shot at them, halting them in their tracks.

"Stay put. I'm not done. Or the next one will really hurt."

She swung back to McGraw just as he fired his weapon. It

clipped her in her left shoulder, adding to her catalogue of pain. She staggered back with an enraged scream and responded with a volley of four shots in retaliation. They tore through the makeshift planters, shattering several of the shrubs and scattering dirt into the air. A moment later, McGraw fell into view from behind the barrels. He audibly groaned as he hit the ground and his gun tumbled from his open hand.

"No!" howled Izzy, impulsively coming back out from behind the truck to help him. Leon tried to hold her back, while Carson walked over to confirm that McGraw really was incapacitated.

"Stop, Izzy," Leon implored, quietly. "Or she'll shoot you too."

Izzy conceded reluctantly. She knew he was right, and fought to hold back the wave of emotion that threatened to overcome her. Yet another person dead...because of her.

"There was nothing we could do," said Leon, sensing her regret, and fending off some of his own. "But that doesn't mean there's nothing we can do."

Izzy glanced back at him. "What do you mean?"

"The old one-two," he replied, miming a rapid punch towards her stomach. "You've floored me with it twice, already."

Izzy smiled, remembering both times, and nodded.

"What are you two mumbling about?" Carson demanded to know, as she walked casually towards them, all threats neutralised.

"He had a family, you know," reproached Izzy.

"Everyone has a family," replied Carson, bitterly. "Doesn't mean you have to like it. Now, can we stop with all the bullshit? I'll make this as simple as I can: hand over the crystal now and I'll leave you to weep over your friend here. Or you can join him on the ground, with a bullet to the chest each. Take your pick."

"We'll go for the weeping," said Leon, agreeably.

"Good choice."

Carson held out her hand expectantly.

"It's in the truck," said Leon, and they walked around to the passenger door.

"Don't even think about trying anything," ordered Carson.

Izzy smiled passively while Leon groped about in the cab.

A moment later he handed Izzy an object wrapped in an old cloth. She took it from him and turned back to Carson. She stepped forward to take it when Izzy slammed her fist as hard as she could into Carson's stomach.

Carson doubled over and dropped her gun, howling in pain. A second later Leon heaved across the gap and jammed a pen into her already wounded shoulder, and she cried out again, twisting back in the other direction. Izzy grinned at Leon.

"Nice move," she said, then kicked Carson to the ground.

She and Leon scrambled back into the cab and slammed the door, where he started up the engine and hit the gas. The truck launched onto the road with a cloud of dust and gravel billowing out behind them.

Leon put his foot down hard and they both screamed in relief and triumph as the truck roared up towards the intersection and slid seamlessly into the loose stream of cars heading south.

53

THIN BLUE LINE

Quinn came to with a start just as Carson fired off her barrage at McGraw, wondering how long he'd been out. His head was pounding, and it took him a moment to realise where he was and what was going on. He looked up just in time to see McGraw fold over behind the water barrels and hear somebody shout out.

"Oh shit," he said to himself, putting everything together. "Poor bastard."

He surveyed the scene carefully to check how many shooters were involved but aside from another man he didn't recognise lying by a bench in front of the store, it was just Carson—who, if anything, looked worse than before—walking slowly towards McGraw's body. He took that as a sign that whatever action had just taken place was done.

Then he clocked Leon and Izzy hovering at the front of McGraw's truck, and realised the shout must have come from them. That they were still alive was really something, he thought. But also understood that, with no one to stop Carson, it wasn't much. He'd have to step in.

He observed Carson kick a gun away from McGraw's open hand, and then walk towards Leon and Izzy. It was clear they were talking to each other but he couldn't make out what they were saying. Better than shooting, he mused, reaching down for the door lever.

He quietly opened the passenger door and slipped out, making his way towards the rear of the vehicle and around the other side of the gas pumps. Remaining in a crouched position, he inched forward, using the pumps as a cover. He figured he could come up quietly from the rear of McGraw's truck, if he could just find something to use as a weapon.

Looking around, there wasn't much: a bucket of sand jammed with old cigarette butts and, bolted to the pump next him, a tall water container with a long squeegee handle sticking out. Perfect against fly-splat but against an angry, injured woman with a gun? He wasn't convinced. Then he reached up and grabbed the squeegee anyway. He was just about to move when he heard someone roar in pain. He half stood to see what was happening just in time to see Leon stretch past Izzy and jam something downward in a stabbing motion. Another wail of anguished pain rang out and, a second later, Leon and Izzy were climbing over each other to get back into the truck. The heavy V8 engine burst into life and almost before Quinn could scrabble backwards, McGraw's truck took off, leaving him covered in dust and grit.

In its place was an angry, cursing, spitting Frances Carson, scuttling about on her hands and knees like a cockroach, grabbing awkwardly at something embedded in her left shoulder. Quinn was impressed: they'd somehow managed to get away and literally left Carson in the dust. He wanted to laugh but realised this was his best moment to act.

He walked quietly over to the intensely distracted Carson.

"You want me to get that for you?" chuckled Quinn, meaning the pen jammed into her shoulder.

Carson immediately twisted around in surprise and, in spite of her punishing discomfort, tried to stand. Quinn reacted quickly, grabbing her left hand and bringing her arm up and behind, effectively immobilising her. She grunted resentfully, barely registering the new source of pain.

"Oh fuck you, partner," she seethed, boiling in her own anger and bitterness.

"Fuck me, is it?" he replied, leaning down and scooping her gun off the ground.

"Whatever. Just do what you have to do and spare me the gloating."

Quinn smiled. He felt good for the first time in days and was determined to enjoy it. Leon and Izzy were out of harm's way, for now at least. Carson was in custody and, he imagined, whatever other plays she had in motion would soon be taken care of. All her strangely warped motivations aside, Carson was, if nothing else, an expert pragmatist. She knew how the system worked better than anyone and would very likely trade whatever she could for a glimpse of daylight, which, as someone who had effectively committed treason, would be a rare commodity indeed.

Quinn paused by the dead old man with the shotgun as he dragged Carson back towards the stolen station wagon.

"Who was this?"

"Does it matter?"

"It mattered to him."

"Spare me the moral outrage, Gregory. How many ghosts have you got in your back pocket?"

Quinn balked at her question. She was right, of course, and he didn't really know why he was squeezing her on it. Maybe because the guy was clearly a civilian, which was always a line for him. Or maybe because it felt like the lifeless eyes—civilian or not—accused him, as they always did.

"Too many," he replied, ruefully.

Then he glanced at McGraw, as he steered the reluctant Carson away. Was it possible he was still breathing? He couldn't be certain, but if there was even a faint chance, he owed it to him to check. To get help. He just had to secure Carson first, then he could take a closer look. He pushed her again towards the passenger door and she fought him, so he yanked her arm up farther.

"I don't mind if it breaks," he said, plainly, as Carson yelped.

"OK! Alright! I'm moving," she fumed.

They reached the door, which he had left ajar, making it easier for him to tease it open with his foot. This was followed by an awkward moment as he holstered the gun into the back of his belt and attempted to manoeuvre Carson around the door and into the seat. All the while, his need to check on Snakes continued to play on his mind—after all, seconds could mean life or death for him —as he endeavoured to secure Carson when, suddenly, McGraw let out a soft groan. He was alive!

This was exactly the moment Carson had been hoping for. She felt Quinn's grip on her arms soften as his attention was pulled away by the superficially non-dead guy. In one impulsive movement, she pressed both feet onto the sill of the open door and pushed backwards with everything she had. Unprepared, and momentarily unfocused, Quinn was unable to react in time. He staggered backwards, letting go of Carson's arms, and tripped over the raised concrete dais at the base of the gas pumps in the process. He fell clumsily between them onto his back, while Carson was able to grab the open car door to prevent her fall.

She jumped into the car while Quinn floundered on the ground, and yanked the door shut behind her. She scooted over to the driver's seat, despite her agony, fired up the engine and hit the locks. Just as she pushed the stick into drive, the passenger window shattered. Quinn held a weapon into the empty space.

"Nice try," he yelled. "Where you gonna go?"

"You know where. So, either shoot or let me go."

He seriously thought about it but knew he had to bring her in alive.

"Without me? You have no idea where they're going."

"Oh, I'll find them," she said, hitting the gas. "It's Vegas, baby."

Quinn fumbled for the door but the car shot away, knocking

him to the side. He stepped back to see the car slide out onto the road. And then she was gone.

Carson clawed at her wounded shoulder as she hot-wheeled her way onto US Route 93 and finally yanked out the pen, tossing it out the open window. It hurt like hell, but then so did everything else. Not least her all-consuming rage from seeing the past twenty years go down the toilet, and all the sacrifices she'd made along the way. All because of two dumb tourists who'd wandered into her rearview mirror as she was backing out of the drive.

"Fucking tourists!" she screamed, slamming her hand down on top of the steering wheel, as she overtook a long, ultramodern RV that had finally dropped out of her lane. She blasted her horn at them as she passed.

Of course, she knew she was pushing her luck to the limit by going after them and that, if she had any real sense, she'd call it quits now and just get out while the getting was good. But she also knew this was her last chance to come away with something, and she'd be damned if she'd go through all this shit for a couple of country mice that didn't even know what they had.

Carson drove on in a fever dream, her hands clamped to the wheel and her gaze fixed, mile after mile, until she finally caught sight of McGraw's truck some ways ahead.

"There you are, my pretties," she muttered to herself, with some satisfaction.

The truck was doing a fair speed, she estimated. Perhaps as much as eighty, which she imagined was pushing it for the two Brits, no doubt feeling conscious that they might draw the wrong kind of attention if they drove any faster. Or, better yet, perhaps they felt they had simply outrun any danger. She could use that, and considered her options as she slowly drew closer.

One: run them off the road. This had a certain elegant utility and control but also presented danger to the vehicle she was driving, as well as to herself. Two: shoot out one of their tyres.

Less immediate danger to Carson herself but, depending on the skills of the driver, had the potential to introduce an unpredictable element to a volatile setting. Other vehicles could be affected, causing a pile-up, with any number of explosive elements. And it would almost certainly draw the authorities before she had time to retrieve the crystal. Scratch that. Three: shoot the driver. Hmm. She just liked that one best, and began to accelerate.

Despite the wicked thrill of their successful break for freedom, Leon and Izzy had soon come back down to earth as they tried to figure out what to do next. And it didn't take long to understand their options were limited. Quinn and Snakes had pretty much been their ticket out of this mess, but if they weren't dead already, they might as well be for all the help they could provide now. They could try to somehow find their way to Cobalt Flats but without a map or a working phone, it seemed like they may as well be trying to find their way to the moon. And what would they do if they even got there—ask someone at the local store if they knew where the tech billionaire Jordan Milk lived? And as for Milk himself, it was becoming clear he was their only hope. But how do you get hold of a billionaire when you need one?

They decided to just head straight for Las Vegas. If nothing else it would give them somewhere to lay over, get cleaned up, and plan their next move. Maybe they could even find a way to call or message Milk. But either way, it had the added advantage of being a very public and highly populated place, which made them feel safer. Unlike the sparsely populated highway they were currently driving down.

They'd tried to stay vigilant since their escape from the gas station. After all, it was hard not to feel intensely exposed to be driving a dead man's truck, in a foreign country, with no allies to call on, when every set of approach headlights could be Carson coming to kill them. But it was hard to keep it up. So, after the first thirty or forty miles, their initial exhilaration began to soften into exhaustion and, as it became apparent that no one seemed to be gunning for them, or pulling them over for grand theft auto, they finally began to relax a little. Izzy even took some time to close her eyes and try for a nap.

So it kind of freaked Leon out when an insane looking wide-eyed Frances Carson, with her charred face and blooded, matted hair levelled up next to them just as Route 93 began heading for the Interstate 15, and tried to shoot him in the face.

The glass of the driver's window shattered with the first bullet, which passed straight through the cab and out of the roof above Izzy's head. She screamed awake, while Leon did his best to avoid swerving into the next car, or off the road altogether. And when he looked back a second later, he could see Carson, her face squeezed by rage, teeing up for another shot. He briefly watched her car slip in and out of place with a kind of gruesome curiosity. He'd never experienced anything like it. She also seemed to be screaming something but neither he nor Izzy could make out what over the road noise, and the warm desert air blasting in through the open window frame.

"Leon," shouted Izzy. "Watch the road, not the crazy woman!"

"The crazy woman's trying to kill us!"

"I know she's trying to kill us—stop helping her! You drive, I'll watch!"

Leon abruptly put his foot down to try to force some distance between them and felt a metallic shunt at the rear as he started to pull ahead. Carson, in a bid to stop them, tried to push the truck off the road but only succeeded in clipping the back of it. Leon was just able to accelerate his way out of a likely disaster and pushed on hard towards the intersection ahead.

This action was made potentially more dangerous by the junction itself: effectively a long, slow, curved bend to the right where the two highways merged, and also where the approaching cars began reducing speed in advance to ensure their own safety.

This resulted in a gradual clustering of vehicles that meant

Leon had to somehow navigate a checkerboard of moving cars and trucks at high speed, on a bend, without either crashing the truck he was driving or killing anyone in the process. He fleetingly thought of his many hours spent playing *Gran Turismo* on his PS4 and how it was of absolutely zero help. But still wished he were back there now, with infinite lives, instead of weaving in and out of traffic at speed with just the one. Plus Izzy's, of course.

A tanker truck advertising All-Star Bio Propellant suddenly switched lanes right in front of them.

"Watch out!" barked Izzy.

"I see it, I see it."

Leon yanked the wheel hard to the right, narrowly clipping the tail of McGraw's truck against the rear of the truck. The truck thundered its horn, and the driver could be seen swearing through the window as they passed. Leon tried to make a friendly "sorry" wave of his hand, and got the middle finger in return.

Farther back, Carson seemed to be taking much less care to avoid death and injury, either for herself or others, as she almost gleefully smashed her way ahead, hitting one car after another, or forcing others off the road. A cacophony of horns began to unfold as she cleared the tailback and ploughed hard onto Interstate 15 in pursuit of Leon and Izzy who were, by now, four cars ahead of her, heading straight for the city.

This cat and mouse game continued, with Leon attempting to throw Carson off with jagged sweeps across the three lanes of busy traffic; from the central reservation, out to the low-rise gravelly escarpment that ran alongside the desert highway, which he used as a makeshift lane to try to get ahead before slipping back again. He knew he was courting trouble, both with other drivers and, likely sooner than later, the law, but when the alternative was death by an apparently psychotic madwoman, it came to feel like a really good choice.

Still Carson bore down on them, as though to prove Leon right, with a single-minded determination that had long since stopped making any real sense, even to her. The catching up and stopping them was all she could think about now. The why she needed to was lost, somewhere back on the US 93, and she no longer cared who knew it.

The options became increasingly narrow and difficult as the traffic and building density began to swell the closer they got to the city limits. By which time, inevitably, the authorities had not only been alerted but were in an active pursuit of their own, building up a growing tail of blue lights not far behind Carson's trailing vehicle.

Somewhere high above them, Leon began to hear the chopping melody of a helicopter. He assumed this must be yet more police and thought seriously about simply pulling over and giving up the chase. After all, it wasn't really clear to him exactly where or how this would end. He knew, at some level, he was relying on the presumed assistance of an eccentric billionaire who had told him a nice story. But, at this point, what else did he have? Then he looked across at Izzy and immediately knew the answer to that question. Surely, he had to put an end to this insanity.

Izzy looked back at him, as if she could read his thoughts. Maybe she could.

"Don't say it," she said.

"But you don't—"

"It doesn't matter. Whatever has to be said can wait."

He looked at all the red taillights building ahead of them and the luminous, multicoloured towering promise of Las Vegas beyond them.

"Well, look, I don't want to bring down the mood or anything," he said, holding a hand up, "but—"

She smiled and put her hand on his, holding it tightly.

"Then we don't make it. But right now, this is what we have. Keep driving until we get where we're going."

Leon nodded. He pulled his hand back to the wheel, yanked the truck back onto the paved road, and hit the gas.

· · ·

High above the interstate a Bell 429 helicopter was indeed tracking the growing hazard below. The sliding doors were open on one side, and the five passengers sitting inside were observing the thin blue line growing behind the two leading vehicles. But it wasn't the police.

"The line's dropped! Get me the goddamn White House again," bellowed Snark over his linked radio set. "This is getting out of hand. There must be forty cars following them."

"On it, sir," confirmed the comms officer.

"Mac, what have we got from the ground?"

As Tactical Ops leader, Macintyre had elected to stand at the open door so he could get an unobstructed view of events below. He held tightly on to the safety rail above the door and leaned back into the cabin to address Snark.

"We're already patched through to LVMPD. We've made our position clear, but it seems Captain Hernandez is determined to make this a terrorist response."

"Goddammit. Looking to make a little rep for himself, is he? We need to make that go away before somebody does something really stupid."

"Well, we've tried. But he feels he has the numbers on his side. Forcing him to act."

"What the hell does that mean?"

"It means 3.4 million visitors a month. And with two major conferences in town, and a championship fight, he can't afford have it turn into a ghost town because he failed to act. He says."

"Las Vegas is popular. Whoop-de-do. He must think he's the first person to notice."

"I did get that from him, sir. And there's something else."

"What is it?"

"Quinn called in."

"Finally! Why didn't anyone connect me?"

"You were on the line with the president, sir. We felt— "

"I'm not interested your feelings, Mac. This is big league time and you're up to bat. She would have waited."

"Who, the president?"

"Yes, the president. Are you feeling OK?"

"I'm fine, sir."

"Good, great. What did Quinn say?"

"That Carson had cooperated for a short time, which he was able to use for intel gathering before attempting to subdue her."

"Excellent!"

"But ultimately he was unsuccessful," added Macintyre, reluctantly. He braced for a Class A Snark invective, but was surprised when he merely waved the information away.

"What else?"

"He was able to confirm that Carson is in pursuit of the two foreign nationals and, at this point, is acting alone. He believes her original plan involved a third party, with a view to using the Cardinal as some kind of collateral. Obviously, events prevented that, but it seems she may now be in possession of what she believes is a strategic artifact she can leverage in its place."

"Then why not just get the hell out of here? What's with all the theatrics?"

"Quinn believes it's become personal for her."

"Personal? I think it's a bit late for all that, don't you?"

"That was our estimation also, sir."

"Where's Quinn now?"

"He was able to appropriate a vehicle of some kind from his prior location. I believe he's attempting to intercept."

"Good to know. He gets to come to the Christmas party this year."

"It's also worth noting, sir, that if Carson does indeed have the alleged artifact, she may try to detonate it when—"

"If, when, maybe. One thing at a time, Mac. For now, I need you to lay a trap and take Carson out of circulation quickly and precisely. But I still need her alive, Mac. Understood? Alive."

"Yes, sir. Then what about the PD?"

"I have the president for you now, sir," said the comms officer, cutting in.

"Very good. Connect me now," said Snark, winking at Macintyre. "I think we're about to give Captain Hernandez something else to think about."

54

WHAT HAPPENS IN VEGAS

Captain Hernandez replaced the handset on his desk in the mobile operations unit being set up north of the Strip, just below Fremont Street where the 159 cut across Las Vegas Boulevard. In case the circus came to town, Hernandez believed it would give them multiple access points, whether it stayed on I-15, or slipped onto a local route north or south.

"You OK, boss?" said Lieutenant Pitt, from the next desk down. He'd heard some of Hernandez's side of the conversation, but it had quickly become quite limited and formal. Evidently, whoever he was talking to was much further up the food chain. Maybe even the chief, he thought.

"Yeah, fine. We need to change our tactical response. Stand down the anti-terrorist rapid response unit. And get me SWAT Captain Finch on the horn."

"Stand dow... Sir, are you sure that's wise?"

"Wise or not, that's what we've been ordered to do."

"Ordered, Captain? By who—the chief?"

"You wouldn't believe me if I told you."

"The chief?" repeated Pitt, thinking Hernandez simply hadn't heard.

"Think bigger."

"Who's bigger than the chief?" It couldn't be the mayor, could it? he thought. What's he doing getting directly involved in operational affairs?

"How about president of the goddamn United States?" stated Hernandez with a mixture of pride and bewilderment.

"Get the fuck outta here," reacted Pitt, assuming Hernandez was just pulling his chain. "Sir," he added, as a respectful afterthought. However, the sassiness of his response seemed to snap the captain out of his reverie.

"I mean it, Lieutenant Pitt. I want you to stand down the ATRU and get me Captain Finch now. Then I want you to coordinate with state and city dispatch to bring back all those black-and-whites currently cruising the 15 downtown A-SAP, where they will be given new orders."

"Are you serious?"

"Do I not look serious to you, Lieutenant?"

"It's just...then who's going to—"

"Specialized federal unit. That's all I know. Details are being sent through as we speak. Our job will be to create and maintain an isolation zone between here and Tropicana Avenue, and ensure those two nut jobs we've been chasing find their way into it."

"Tropicana!? But that's almost the whole length of the Strip! Do you know how many people—"

"To Protect and To Serve, that's what I know, Lieutenant. We'll provide an armed cordon as required, and redirect the traffic on a rolling basis for minimum disruption. Nothing more. You have your orders."

Unfortunately for Captain Hernandez, and his nascent promise of congressional recognition, his intel was not quite as real-time as it should have been. Leon and Izzy had already breached the city limits way ahead of his contingency plan, which meant a lot of shouting down the phone for Lieutenant Pitt, and a huge scramble for squad cars and personnel across the city as they fought to redeploy ahead of the incoming wave of trouble.

The first raft of police cars only just managed to push ahead of McGraw's truck and force Leon towards the exit at Charleston Boulevard, barely a mile from where Hernandez was watching his dreams of a golden career slip from his greedy fingers.

The plan on paper had been to push the two cars past the mobile control centre and then straight down Las Vegas Boulevard where a number of roadblocks would be set up to slow—not stop—the speeding vehicles and, if possible, separate them. However, this idea immediately fell apart when Leon descended the off-ramp from the interstate and almost crashed into the waiting police cars at the main intersection, compelling him to make a hard left under the freeway.

With Carson only few car lengths behind him, Leon wanted to get off the main roads as quickly as he could, feeling the back-streets might provide better cover for an escape than a long straight road. Hitting the car horn hard, he forced his way through the other cars ahead, and with no real idea where he was going, took the first right he could see because the tower of the Stratosphere Hotel loomed into view, quickly followed by the incandescent cluster of more resort hotels from up and down the Strip.

He accelerated ahead, using the Stratosphere as a marker, but soon realised this was just another main road. Carson was narrowing the distance and Leon could almost feel the heat of her desperation on the back of his neck.

"You have to get off this road," shouted Izzy.

"I know, but where? They don't seem to have any little streets here."

Izzy could see the taillights of another car turning left up ahead.

"Take that one," she pointed.

But at this speed they would overshoot. He slammed the brakes and somehow managed to skid the truck into a left-hand turn across another lane of oncoming traffic. Behind them the sound of screeching tires and horns broke out as Carson tried the same manoeuvrer, busting the nose of an approaching car and jackknifing a poorly timed truck onto the sidewalk in her wake.

The incident gave them a small firebreak, but Leon didn't want to let up. He could see Carson in his rearview mirror and pushed on down Utah Avenue, keeping his speed as high as he dared. It felt to him like he might kill someone at any second but, fortunately, the street seemed to be mostly industrial units, and was quiet at this time on a Sunday night.

"The hotels," said Izzy. "They're moving off to the right. We're going the wrong way."

Then, at the far end of the road, Leon saw the strobe of a blue light. The police had reconfigured and were already coming at them. He yanked the truck through the next right turn and could see the Stratosphere heave into view, lit up like a carnival right at the end of the street.

"Yes!" said Leon, triumphantly, although without any real idea what he was so pleased about with a psycho-killer thirty feet behind him.

Then, as they got closer, he realised he had to make a choice in a hurry: the road bore round to the left, or there was a straight service road towards the hotel.

"Which way?"

"It looks like a dead end. We need to stay in the open. Follow the road."

He rolled the car around the bend and saw a flash of light glance off the hood. Carson had gone for a potshot as they turned ahead of her. And through the open window all they could hear was an orchestra of sirens and helicopters overhead. It sounded like they were coming from every direction.

"They're going to kill us, if we keep going, you know that," shouted Leon over the noise, as the short run of Oakey Boulevard veered right onto Main Street.

"She's going to kill us if we stop!" replied Izzy. "Take your pick."

Then, before they had time to understand where they were, they shot right past the Stratosphere's casino entrance, through a set of red traffic lights where a group of crossing tourists narrowly avoided death, and skidded straight out onto Las Vegas Boulevard: the Strip.

Between the sea of red taillights up ahead and the approaching wave of blue police lights farther behind them it seemed like they'd picked the busiest possible road in the whole city on which to make their escape.

"So much for the back roads," said Leon, as Carson took out another two cars behind them as she crashed her way across the intersection.

Leon and Izzy looked at each other.

"Just keep going," they both said at the same time, and laughed with the gallows humour of it all.

But then, as they wove their way farther down the Strip, zigzagging in and out of the traffic in a bid to stay ahead of Carson, an odd thing began to happen. The traffic started thinning out. At first, they didn't realise. So fixated were they on simply pushing forward, pushing on, getting away from the danger, that it wasn't until they reached the first of the luxury resort hotels, the Wynn, perhaps another mile farther down, that they began to notice all the police presence. It seems Hernandez and Pitt had finally caught up with events and had managed to start deploying teams ahead of Leon and Izzy's flight through the city. But only just.

Cordons were finally going up at every main intersection along the Strip, with traffic and pedestrians being redirected back towards the main hotels and casino buildings, which were all situated a significant distance from the road itself. So that by the time Leon and Izzy made it past Caesar's Palace and across Flamingo Road, it seemed as though they had the entire southbound road to themselves. They could see almost all the way to the edge of town.

"Wait, is this all for us?" said Izzy, turning her head around to try to take it all in.

Leon made a one-handed shrug.

"Who else?"

"Well, what does it mean? Is it an invitation to leave town or is it—"

Carson rammed the back of their truck, jolting Leon and Izzy forward despite the speed they were travelling at. Leon pulled to the left, to try to avoid another collision but Carson had anticipated his move and pushed hard into the side rear of their vehicle, forcing the truck off to the right, where a thick line of tourists and pedestrians were lining the street to watch. It was as though in a city as nuts as Las Vegas, this was merely street entertainment. The crowed screamed in fright as Leon and Izzy careened towards them, then cheered gleefully as Leon was able to regain control and jerk the truck back onto the roadway.

"These people are insane," shouted Izzy.

Carson was gaining now and it looked like she was lining up for another windowless head shot. Leon bumped the wheel left, crashing into the side of her station wagon before she could get in range. She tried to compensate and briefly mounted the central reservation before skidding back onto the road. Leon took that moment to accelerate hard and get back out in front her.

But now they could see that the apparently clear road ahead was not an invitation to leave but a net; as they crossed over Park Avenue and hurtled towards New York, New York and the MGM at the corner of Tropicana, they could see a double line of police cars stretch across the intersection.

"Oh shit," said Leon. "End of the line."

"She's right on top of us, Leon," yelled Izzy looking through the rear window where she could see a wide-eyed, frothing Carson, leaning over the steering wheel of her car. The windshield had already blown out from her last attempt to run them off the road, and her bloodied, dirty face was scrunched up against the rushing air. It looked like she was talking to herself. Like she was reciting a bitter incantation to bring Leon and Izzy down.

Leon's eyes darted between the row of police cars rushing towards them, and the rearview mirror to see the house of horrors bearing down on them. He had an idea.

"Izzy, brace yourself."

Her head snapped back to face him.

"What do you mean!?"

"There's no time. Just face forward and hold on. You have to trust me."

"But—"

Leon slammed on the bakes as hard as he could. The truck screamed to a halt, burning rubber and throwing them forward, hard enough against their seat belts that it felt like it would break them in two. Then, in almost the same second, another explosive push forwards, as Carson's car smashed head first into the back of them.

Carson was instantly ejected through the open windshield of her car. Her twisting body hammered painfully up against the back of McGraw's truck rear window, which shattered on impact. Her limp body fell back into the flat bed behind it as the now conjoined vehicles skidded forwards into the centre of the inter-section, before finally coming to a stop.

Silence descended on the crossroads like a blanket of snow.

And for a few moments, perhaps for the first time in the city's chequered history, nobody moved. None of the police officers lined up in front of their cars, nor any of the pedestrians looking on from the safety of the raised walkways that connected the hotels on all four corners.

The silence was abruptly broken by the sputtering roar of an approaching motorbike, as it tore down the Strip towards the crash site. This was swiftly followed by the hacking rhythm of a military helicopter that seemed almost to drop into view from nowhere as it flew over the faux skyline of New York, New York.

Inside the cab of McGraw's surprisingly resilient truck, Leon and Izzy sat perfectly still in their seats staring blankly out the front window. They listened, with intense relief, to the eerie silence that enveloped them. And then, as they heard the approaching vehicles, Leon reached across the seat to grab Izzy's hand.

"You OK?" he asked, giving it a gentle squeeze. She enfolded his hand in return.

"I am now," she said. Then, after a moment, "Thank you."

"For what?"

"For almost killing me to save my life."

Leon smiled.

"My pleasure."

"How long do you think this dreadful throbbing pain across my chest and down my back will last?"

Suddenly the approaching motorbike shot past the missing driver window and slid to a sharp halt six feet in front of the truck. It was Quinn. He jumped off the bike the second it came to a rest and let it fall to the ground as he approached the truck. Behind him the strobing shadow of the helicopter hove into view as it slowly descended onto the road ahead.

"Well, lookee here," said Quinn, smiling, and leaning casually on the sill of the hollow window frame. "A couple of goddamn heroes."

Leon and Izzy, unused to such brazen praise, both made bashful noises, but Quinn waved them away.

"That was a hellava thing you just did. How you feeling?"

"Everything hurts," said Izzy.

"It will. But only for a few days. We'll have the guys check you over before you leave," he replied, referring to a bunch of emergency vehicles—ambulances, EMTs, and a couple of fire trucks— that had all just pulled in behind and around the landing Bell 429. Various large and important-looking police SUVs also arrived, along with several others that had no livery to speak of. Just black and generally sinister-looking, with blackened glass.

Leon gestured at all the uniformed personnel getting out of their various cars and trucks.

"Do you think they'll actually let us leave?"

"Oh, I think we can probably work something out," replied Quinn, with a smile and wink, as if he'd seen it all before. Which, of course, he had.

"Probably?" said Leon, feeling like this really wasn't the time to sit on the fence.

Quinn's smile turned into a laugh.

"Don't worry so much. You only broke about thirty or forty state, federal, and international laws. I'll go talk to them."

And with that Quinn turned and walked towards the helicopter. The side door was already open, and a stocky, late middle-aged man with his shirt sleeves rolled up and a grumpy, determined look on his face was just clambering out. Leon and Izzy watched him as he was quickly surrounded by various people. Some were in suits, while others were in combat gear or uniform. Even from this distance, it was clear he was the man in charge.

"Who do you suppose that is?" said Izzy.

Leon went to respond, when a bloody, scorched arm snapped around his neck and began to squeeze.

"I'll tell you exactly who that is," hissed the febrile voice of Frances Carson, who had somehow dragged her tattered, bleeding body into the truck through the open back window without anyone noticing.

Izzy jumped back in surprise, while Leon's hands leapt up to Carson's arm around his neck and tried to pry it free. Her skin felt both crackly and moist, like badly barbecued meat.

"The man who's going to lock you up for the rest of your ridiculous lives, if you don't give me the crystal now."

"Are you fricking serious?" gasped Leon, as he struggled for air.

"As serious as a life sentence."

"What are you even going to do with it?"

"Give me the goddamn crystal!" she screeched, through clenched teeth, like a fairy-tale witch.

Despite the iron grip around his neck, Leon tried to signal Izzy with his rolling eyes to just do it, and she seemed to get it. She reached down into the foot well where she was sitting and brought up something about the size of an orange, wrapped in an oil cloth.

"You really want this?" said Izzy, regretfully.

Carson's eyes lit up at the prospect. She let go of Leon's neck, and her hands wavered in front of her, fingers twitching in anticipation.

"Gimme," she cackled.

Izzy hesitated for moment. Then smashed it into Carson's face. She instantly dropped into a heap in the backseat, more blood seeping from her mouth and nose. The crunching sound of Izzy's punch wasn't the crystal.

It took a couple of hours for all the paperwork and site clearance to get done, but Quinn was as good as his speculation. There'd been a bit of medical attention, and a friendly debrief with Quinn and the older man from the helicopter—Linden Snark—who only came over because, as he put it, he wanted to see the whites of their eyes. Otherwise, he didn't have much to say to either of them directly. Except for Izzy, who he quizzed briefly on her educational status and plans for when she was "done with playing at research."

"I'm still considering my options," said Izzy. "I had planned on going into advanced robotics, but all this, it's kind of rekindled my interest in cosmology."

"Ha," roared Snark. "I bet it has. Well, we have some damn fine affiliate programs over here. The best. I'll let Quinn hook you up. If you're interested."

"What about you, kid?" he said to Leon, blithely.

"I'm a planner," replied Leon, somewhat mournfully. And

when it looked like Snark had no idea what that meant, he added, "Or was. In an ad agency."

Snark's eyes glassed over for a moment, then he slapped Leon on the arm and yelled, "Great driving today, kiddo. One in a million." And walked off.

"Don't worry about him," said Quinn, when Snark was out of earshot. "He wouldn't normally talk to any civilians in a situation like this. He must really like you."

"Yeah, I felt that," replied Leon, doubtfully.

"What will happen to Carson?" asked Izzy.

"She's in pretty bad shape. But if she makes it through then... we'll see. Throw her into a deep, dark hole somewhere probably. She did a bad thing."

"Almost seems cruel to help her recover, only to lock her away," suggested Leon.

"Yeah, well, that can happen, I guess," replied Quinn, absently. His attention had been caught by Snark who was standing with Mac and a couple of police officials.

"Cut 'em loose," yelled Snark, spinning his hand.

Quinn acknowledged with a wave.

"You heard the man. Seems you're free to go. I'll walk you out."

The three of them walked over to the New York corner of the intersection, where a gate had been inserted into the barricade next to the one-third-size Statue of Liberty. A policeman standing there nodded and waved them through. Quinn stayed on the roadside.

"You want to get a drink with us, or something?" suggested Leon.

"Nah," said Quinn. "I mean, yeah. Sure. That would be great. But I got a ton of paperwork to take care of. And with Carson gone, there'll be some rebuilding to do."

"Understood."

The three of them exchanged looks. Quinn nodded.

"I'll see you around," he said.

Leon and Izzy turned to leave when, suddenly, Leon remembered.

"Hey, Greg. What about our, uhm, mutual friend?"

"Yes!" said Quinn, pantomiming a slap to the head. "I almost forgot."

He slipped a backpack off his shoulder and chucked it to Leon, who caught it in one hand.

"This what I think it is?"

But Quinn had already turned and walked away.

Leon and Izzy decided to walk back up the Strip. After all, this was Vegas. City of Lights. And it really lived up to its name. After all, they'd kind of missed the show on their way down.

Except for the intersection at Tropicana, the rest of Las Vegas Boulevard had been returned to all the businesses, conference-goers, tourists, gamblers, shoppers, and party people it had been built for. It was a busy place, filled with busy, preoccupied, and excited people running around like ants at a picnic.

They had got as far as the Bellagio, now one of the Strip's classic statements, with its grand Italian aesthetic, and the simulated romanticism of the Como-inspired lakefront, when an absurdly long stretch-Humvee pulled up next to them. They might not even have noticed except, as they turned from admiring the fountains to regard the audacious novelty of the Paris hotel opposite, the door popped open, and out stepped Annie, Milk's personal assistant.

"The boss would like to see you," she said, smiling warmly for a change, and holding open the rear door for them.

"Really?" said Leon. "I mean it's pretty late. And we've had a... busy day. Can't it wait until morning?"

Then, to their surprise, Jordan Milk himself leant forward, grinning from inside the open door.

"Come on, Leon. Don't be such drag. Come sit. Bring your friend."

He disappeared back into the cavernous interior and Annie, once again, held out her hand by way of an invitation. There was less of a smile this time.

"It's OK," said Izzy, squeezing Leon's hand. "I don't mind."

They climbed into the back of the car and Annie shut the door behind them as they took a seat on the wide leather sofa opposite Milk, who was spread out on one of his own. It was startlingly comfortable for a car seat.

"Jordan Milk," said Milk, offering his hand to Izzy. They shook. "And you must be Isabella."

"Izzy," said Izzy, smiling.

Annie climbed into the car farther down and took a seat facing the rear, as the car pulled away from the curb.

"Izzy it is!" said Milk, extravagantly. "I feel like I know you already. Champagne?"

Milk plucked two filled glasses from a small, recessed table next to him, and handed them to Leon and Izzy. There were two more glasses and a bottle resting in a bucket of ice.

"Annie?"

Annie tried to decline the offer, but Milk wouldn't have it.

"Come on," he insisted, infectiously. "We're celebrating. Drinks for everyone."

Annie relented and when they all had their drinks, Milk beamed broadly, opening his arms wide in a welcoming gesture.

"Guys, what can I tell you? You may have just changed the world."

"Oh, I don't know about that—" began Leon, but Milk cut him off.

"Nope. Not having it. You Brits are funny. Look, you did an incredible thing here today. And I just want to thank you and cele-brate that. And, hey, I know—believe me, I know—that it wasn't easy, and you probably feel you've paid a high price to help a rich man out. But I want you to know—"

"What about Billy McGraw?" said Izzy, sombrely. "I think it probably cost him the most."

Milk laughed unexpectedly. "Snakes? Is that what's bothering you? I'm surprised Quinn didn't tell you himself. He called it in. Right now he's in ICU at MountainView Hospital, about fifteen miles from here."

Leon and Izzy visibly relaxed, as though they'd been holding their breath for a long while.

"Thank God for that," said Leon.

"Is he going to be OK?" asked Izzy

"It was touch and go," said Annie. "But he's a tough nut, and the docs reckon he'll pull through."

"We can go see him if you like," added Milk. "Although I don't think we'll get much out of him for a while."

"No, it's fine," said Izzy. "I just felt, that for a guy who... Anyway, that's great news."

They all clinked glasses and toasted Snakes's recovery, and the mood inside the ridiculously large car lifted conspicuously. Then, after Milk took the opportunity to apologise to Izzy for her unexpected abduction, he took some time to tell her his personal UFO story. Leon couldn't help but notice the subtle ways he modified the details to appeal to her more directly, including her better grasp of physics and computing. He began to wonder if Milk reinvented the story every time and, if so, which parts of it were actually true. In the end, he decided it didn't matter. Whatever his motivations, Milk's sincerity and his desire to use technology for the benefit of everyone, rather than the few, shone through. And in the cool, safe, luxurious setting of the man's absurdly large limousine, he realised he really quite liked him.

Naturally Izzy had a bunch of technical questions about the craft he had in his possession, the crystal device, and what exactly he planned to do with the technology if he ever cracked it. But like a seasoned pro, he deflected it away with charm and a light touch for another time, along with a promise that he'd introduce her to Bryson Hawke, his "technical guru," sometime, to answer all her questions. Leon could see that Izzy knew something about who

Hawke was but clearly resisted the urge to jump on that, while Annie, at the back, seemed to be taking a lot of notes.

Then, finally, they got around to the crystal itself.

"So, do you have it!?" said Milk, like a twelve-year-old waiting for a birthday present.

"Good question," said Leon, who hadn't yet taken a look in Quinn's backpack.

He opened it up and had a good rummage around. The first thing he noticed, with some relief, was a bundle holding the two passports and the stack of cash that he and Izzy had brought into the country. There were also a couple of phones and, at the bottom, wrapped in an oil cloth, was the crystal that had turned Carson into an unhinged lunatic.

Leon pulled it out and tossed it to Milk, who snatched it up with one hand. He greedily unwrapped the cloth and his face literally lit up, as the ambient light emanating from the alien artefact gently pulsed, filling the cabin with a subtle power like the bubbles in the champagne they were drinking.

"I love you guys!" yelped Milk, gleefully.

Leon and Izzy laughed. His unbridled enthusiasm was infectiously endearing. Milk held it up and examined it closely, turning it slowly in his hand. Then they chatted for a little while about some of his plans, and what this could mean for the world. Then finally Milk wrapped the crystal back up and gave it to Annie, who placed it into a secure-looking box.

"Thank you. Both. You really don't know how much you have done here," said Milk. "I won't forget it. I promise you that."

"Thanks," said Leon.

"For now, let me drop you off. I've arranged a suite at Caesar's for you."

"I've arranged a suite for you," corrected Annie. Milk laughed.

"Yes, Annie's arranged everything. Just give your names at the desk. Granger and Bourne, wasn't it?" said Milk, mischievously.

They all chuckled.

"You know," said Leon. "I think we'd like to walk."

Izzy nodded in agreement and they said their farewells. The car pulled over and Milk let them out with his personal number, and a promise they could call him anytime. They were back where they started, in front of the Bellagio.

"You know what?" said Leon, as the Humvee slipped into traffic and drove away.

"What?"

"We haven't eaten all day. Do you fancy getting a pizza with me?"

Sinatra's "Fly Me to the Moon" was playing as the Bellagio's famous fountains came to life.

Izzy grinned.

AUTHORS NOTE

I really hope you've enjoyed this story. And if you did, please be sure to pop a review on Amazon. Even just a couple of lines or a rating can actually make a big difference. Plus, it will also help others to find and enjoy this book. Thank you -

Leon and Izzy will return...

For all of you who enjoyed meeting and spending time with Leon and Izzy, and would like to find out what happens to them after they get pizza—I'm working on it!

If you'd like to get updates on the next part of the story, please sign up to my list and I'll send you notes as things progress: head over to **www.oliverkenton.com** and drop your email address in the box. I promise not to spam you or share your details with anyone else!

ACKNOWLEDGMENTS

There's probably a long list of people that I need to acknowledge for the ways in which they've helped me finally get here, to this place, with a book in my hand. A book I ruminated on and toyed with writing for far too many years before actually doing it. I'm not sure I would be doing them—or you, frankly, if you've comes this far—a real favour by listing *everybody*, but there's certainly a few I must thank before anything else happens...

Mum and Dad, you're first up, even if you are doggedly and, sadly, MIA. Thanks for all the stories, the laughter, the love and, of course, Mum—for the best chicken soup that ever was.

The fabulous Victoria, Ava and Sophie: where would I be without you guys? Perhaps, more importantly, *who would I be*? Thank you for putting up with me, and for your cosmic levels of love, support, constant encouragement and actual excitement that I finally finished this book. And for not minding too much when I would inevitably disappear from time to time to write it. I am blessed.

To my brilliant life-long friend Paul C. for all the inspiration, and many years of debate and laughter about classic TV, great movies and interesting books that, I suspect, nourished much of what found its way here. Oh, and also to your buddy, James Carver, author of Gabe Devlin, avenging angel, priest *and* killer-on-a-mission, for all the patience, tips and sound advice. Thank you both.

Jason B, for kind of daring me to *just write a paragraph or two*, and not think about what it was, or where it was going. Seriously great advice, which I took, and almost immediately found Leon lying in that toilet. Who knew? Thanks, man.

Dr. Heather Stein. for being an early reader and honest appraiser of this book in its ungainly, antenatal form. Your constructive assessment was incredibly helpful and encouraging. Thank you.

Finally, huge thanks to my editorial crew: Anne-Marie Rutella, for all the heavy lifting, subtle corrections and suggestions (and brilliant sidenotes), and for showing such personal interest in the work. And Rina K, for bringing her exceptional eye and diamond polish to bear and literally proofing the hell out of it. Together, you somehow managed to both preserve *and* improve everything I had managed to pull together on my own, and this book is all the better for it.

And, of course, to everyone who went on the run with Leon and Izzy - and me – you're the best. I couldn't have done it with you.

A BIT ABOUT OLIVER K.

Before any of *this*, Oliver spent most of his professional life in design. Over the years, he's worked his way through a bunch of ad and design agencies you've probably never heard of until, eventually, he ended up as a Creative Director for a global digital consultancy. Then finally, after thinking about it for twenty-five years, and quite a few false starts, he wrote a book.

His casual if persistent addiction to great (and some not so great) movies and American TV, Marvel comics, and a lot of science fiction books, has kind of accidentally marinated Oliver in a whole bunch of *stuff* he can finally put to some use: from the Apollo moon landings to Star Trek, Columbo and The X-Files, to Stan Lee, Dr Who, Saul Bass, Carl Sagan, and all the Philips - Pullman, K. Dick and Roth - to Larry David, Christopher Nolan and The Matrix, to... well, it's a long list. But in any case, all these and more besides have helped warp him into the slightly geeky man he is today.

In the other bits of his life, Oliver rattles around north-west London trying to keep up with the (mostly) loving demands of his family and the other strange animals that live in his house. If there's any time left, he avoids dairy, goes for the odd run, and walks his dog Indiana (yes, yes, *that* Indiana). Occasionally he bakes sourdough bagels from scratch.

There's probably a bunch more stuff but, seriously, how much more of it could you really want?

Printed in Great Britain
by Amazon

45287256R00310